*Please turn the page
for more reviews . . .*

W9-BKN-534

"Reading *The Wild Road* is rather like slipping into another culture, almost as if it has been very well translated from a feline language. The view is uncompromisingly catlike: These are felines that respect themselves. In addition, the use of language in the writing is a pleasure in itself. A very exciting read: I loved it!"

—ROBIN HOBB
Author of *Assassin's Apprentice*

"*The Wild Road* is a charming book—the ultimate animal adventure—and every cat owner knows it's probably true!"

—TERRY PRATCHETT
Author of the *Discworld* novels

"Insightful, sharply observant, and filled with four-footed characters to steal the heart, *The Wild Road* offers a mystical odyssey to haunt mind and spirit long after the last page is turned."

—JANNY WURTS
Author of *Fugitive Prince*

"*The Wild Road* took me places that even I had never been! And I must say, I enjoyed the ride."
—NORTON, the cat who went to Paris

"A debut with tingling ideas, respectable characters, rousing adventures, and well-versed cat lore."
—*Kirkus Reviews*

"A quest and a coming-of-age story . . . A prrrty nice book."
—*The San Diego Union-Tribune*

"Enchanting."
—*Publishers Weekly*

By Gabriel King
Published by The Ballantine Publishing Group:

THE WILD ROAD
THE GOLDEN CAT*

*Forthcoming

THE
WILD
ROAD

Gabriel King

A Del Rey® Book
THE BALLANTINE PUBLISHING GROUP • NEW YORK

This book contains an excerpt from *The Golden Cat* by Gabriel King. This excerpt has been set for this edition only and may not reflect the final content of the forthcoming edition.

A Del Rey® Book
Published by The Ballantine Publishing Group
Copyright © 1997 by Gabriel King
Excerpt from from *The Golden Cat* by Gabriel King copyright © 1999 by Gabriel King.

www.randomhouse.com/delrey/

Library of Congress Catalog Card Number: 98-93741

ISBN 0-345-42303-8

Manufactured in the United States of America

First American Hardcover Edition: March 1998
First American Mass Market Edition: March 1999

10 9 8 7 6 5 4 3 2 1

For Iggy and Finn

The smallest feline is a masterpiece.
—LEONARDO DA VINCI

CONTENTS

xii   *Contents*

ACKNOWLEDGMENTS

With grateful thanks to Russ Galen and Veronica Chapman for their enthusiasm and support; to Jamie Dyer for his patience and to Joseph James for his eagle eye; to Ginny Black and Joyce Newman for breeding such beautiful cats; to friends and family; and to all cat-lovers everywhere, especially those, like Rita, who feed and care for the feral cats of America.

The cat is called in Hebrew, *Catul*; in Greek, *ailouros*; and in Latin, *Catus, felis*. The Egyptians named it *mau*, for the sound of its voice, and gave it worship. To the Northern peoples, it is a Creature of fertility and fortune; but the Romany call it *majicou*, and abhor its presence.

All Cats are of a single nature and agree much in one Shape, though they be of different Magnitude; each being a Beast of Prey, the Wild and the Tame, it being in the opinion of many a diminutive Tyger.

The most miraculous of Beasts, it walks invisibly and silently the highways of the Earth, and many believe it invested with the Magick of the World.

The Ancients have prophesied that in every eighty-first generation of the most ancient of the Felidae there shall come a Cat of Power, which shall not be greatest of Magnitude, but possessed of the most exquisite Soul. And the greatest of these shall be the Golden Cat, which shall come only when the ancient north joins with the Eye of Horus, and it shall have the Power to harness the Sunne and the Moon and the Wild Roads, and may render to any so lucky as to possess it the very Key to knowledge of the Natural World.

—WILLIAM HERRINGE
The Diminutive Tyger, 1562

Part One

Love the World and Follow Your Nose

PROLOGUE

The one-eyed black cat called Majicou sat between a rusting cage and two sacks of stale grain on a shelf in a shop on Cutting Lane.

He had positioned himself with care; of the shop's inhabitants, only the spiders he had dispossessed were sure he was there. He seemed to be asleep among the shadows and soft gray cobwebs. But his one eye was half open, and from it he had a hunter's line of sight through the shop to the street door, where small rippled-glass windows admitted just enough weak afternoon light to illuminate a stock of leather collars, tartan-lined wicker baskets, and gaudy paper sacks of dried animal feed. Among this poor stuff, a human being moved clumsily about its business in a cloud of disturbed dust. It seemed to Majicou as tired and greedy as most of its kind. It seemed as ill as they all were from the bad air and bad food they had made for themselves. Majicou watched it idly for a moment as it pushed a rat's nest of straw, torn paper, and spilled fish food around the old wooden floor with a broom.

Unless their affairs touched his, the black cat had no interest in human beings. He sat on his shelf as still as a stone, and half his mind was somewhere else. There, fires broke out; there were cries of terror both human and feline; he was responsible and not responsible. It was long ago but not so far away. The other half was on the shop—where, despite the gloom, nothing escaped him. If his cold eye could not penetrate, his whiskers mapped the air currents instead. His nose was full of the thick, complex smell of imprisoned animals—"pets," reeking of their own pent-up energy and tired resignation. Fish swam around their tanks in circles. Mice and rabbits crouched listlessly in heaps of straw. A cage of finches filled the shop with sad electrical peeps and chirps.

There was a single kitten in a wire cage.

At sixteen weeks, he was already a little old to sell easily. He was too big. He had lost the awkward delight of the very young, the appearance of a charmed life, the mixture of fragility and iron, timidity and courage. Nevertheless, he was still striking, with lambent, shockingly green eyes set in a sharp, intelligent, Oriental face. He had enough energy for every other animal in the shop. His fur, creamy white beneath, shaded above to an almost metallic gray. When he paced his cage this thick-piled coat seemed to shift and ripple restlessly in the gloom, emphasizing each muscle and movement; polished by passing gleams of light, it leapt out silver to the watching eye. There were faint gray tiger stripes high up on his forelegs, and a darker stripe ran the length of his spine. Did this reflect a darker stripe to his character? Majicou hoped so; but before he let things go further he had to find out. He would not call the kitten by its true name until he knew.

Let someone else name it until then.

Oblivious of this decision, the kitten climbed to the top of his cage and, clinging to the wire with powerful little claws, fixed a determined eye on the finches across the aisle. The finches scolded. The kitten glittered at them in a predatory fashion and made strange clicking noises under his breath.

The black cat watched.

Suddenly, the shop bell rang. Two humans, a male and a female, came in from Cutting Lane. The shopkeeper glanced up into the shadows for a moment, then rested its broom against the counter and approached them.

Human beings were as shadowy to Majicou as he was to them. But in his lifetime—which was long—he had watched them come and go, come and go, and he knew their qualities. This pair were young and nervous—he could smell it on them— and a little disoriented by the darkness of the shop. They were cheerful, harmless, well provided for, and keen to share their luck. They were eager to adopt. The moment they saw the kitten, they forgot everything else. This suited perfectly his design: they would fulfill the kitten's needs until Majicou was ready for him. Nevertheless, the black cat watched exasperatedly as, through body languages of need and self-deception, all the age-old misunderstandings and betrayals enacted themselves again.

The male poked its fingers into the cage to attract the kitten's attention. It made a noise at the back of its soft palate, *"Cs cs cs."* The female laughed. At first, obsessed by the finches, the kitten ignored them both. Then, jumping down as if he had grown bored with what he couldn't have, he strutted over, stiff legged, tail up, cocky and curious and full of himself, to have a look. Ambushed by the beauty of his wild barred face and huge green eyes, the female gaped in delight.

Seeing this, the shopkeeper smiled a complex smile, deftly opened the cage, and scooped the kitten out into the female's waiting arms.

For his part, the kitten sat still and stared intently at the two huge faces that loomed above him. His nose was full of the thick, pleasantly odd smell of them. His mind was full of possibilities. He sensed great positive change. He began to purr. His purr was like a great soft engine that trembled through his warm white pelt into the woman's arms, from his bones to her bones. "Take me with you," said the purr. "Take me with you. A fine home and room to roam! Take me there and feed me sardines. Game casserole. Beef and kidney. *Tuna in brine!*" The kitten rolled over to display his pure white belly. "Look! Take me home!"

Majicou viewed this performance emptily. Charm them now, he thought. Charm them well. But how will you help yourself when they have charmed you in return?

The silver kitten wriggled and purred.

Fifteen minutes later, he was leaving his prison forever, riding in a large wicker basket.

The shopkeeper stood like a wound-down toy for a moment, watching them go off along the empty street. Then, the smile fading suddenly from its face, it backed into the shop, shut the door, and peered out between advertisements—dog food shaped like a bone, cat food shaped like a bird. It reached up with its free hand, changed the sign from OPEN to CLOSED.

Then, without warning, every animal in the shop seemed to go mad.

Finches hopped from perch to perch, filling the air with shrieks and whistles of alarm. Noses twitching, the fat hamsters and guinea pigs stared panically through their bars, then buried themselves as fast as they could in their straw. The Belgian rabbits turned their backs, as if this gesture could render them invisible. Even the fish seemed agitated, flickering through the bubbles in their water worlds.

The shopkeeper turned to see what was the matter. Its broom clattered to the floor. It stared wildly around and seemed to be about to say something, deny something, apologize for something. Instead, for no apparent reason, it opened the street door again. The one-eyed black cat slipped out into Cutting Lane.

Chapter One
THE GREAT OUTDOORS

Among human beings a cat is merely a cat;
among cats a cat is a prowling shadow in a jungle.
—KAREL ČAPEK

*T*hey called the kitten Tag. They fed him, and he grew. They put a collar around his neck. They entertained him, and the world began to take on shape.

It was *his* world, full of novelty yet always reliable, exciting yet secure. He was a small king; and by the time a week was out, he had explored every inch of his new kingdom. He liked the kitchen best. It was warm in there on a cold day, and from the windowsill he could see out into the garden. In the kitchen they made food, which was easy to get off them. He had bowls of his own to eat it from. He had a box of clean dirt to scrat in. The kitchen wasn't entirely comfortable—especially in the morning, when things went off or went around very loudly without warning—but elsewhere they had given him a large sofa, covered in dark red velvet, among the scattered cushions of which he scrabbled and burrowed and slept. He had brass tubs with plants and some very interesting fireplaces full of dried flowers, out of which flowed odors damp and sooty.

Up a flight of stairs and into every room, every cupboard and corner! It was big up there, and full of unattended human things. At first he wouldn't go on his own but always made one of them accompany him while he inspected the shelves stuffed with clean linen and dusty books.

"Come on, come on!" he urged them. "Here now! Look, here!" They never answered.

They were too dull.

A further flight up, and it was as if nobody had ever lived there—echoes on the uncarpeted stairs, gray floorboards and open doors, pale bright light pouring in through uncurtained windows. Up there, each bare floor had a smell of its own; each ball of fluff had a personality. If he listened, he could hear dead spiders contracting behind the woodwork. Left to himself up there he danced, for reasons he barely understood. It was a territorial dance, grave yet full of energy. Simply to occupy the space, perhaps, he leapt and pounced and hurled himself about, then slept in a pool of sunshine as if someone had switched him off. When he woke, the sun had moved away, and they were calling him to come and eat more new things.

They called him Tag. He called them dull.

"Come on, dulls!" he urged them. "Come on!"

They had a room where they poured water on themselves. Every morning he hid outside it and jumped out on the big dull bare feet that passed. Nice but dull, they were never quick enough or nimble enough to avoid him. They never learned. They remained shadowy to him—a large smell, cheerful if meaningless goings-on, a caring face suspended over him like the moon through the window if he woke afraid. They remained patient, amiable, easily convinced, less focused than a tin of meat-and-liver dinner. The dulls were for food or comfort or play. Especially for play. One of his earliest memories was of chasing soap bubbles. The light of an autumn evening shifted gently from blue to a deep orange. Up and down the room rushed Tag, clapping his front paws in the air. He loved the movement. He loved the heavy warmth of the air. Everything was exciting. Everything was golden. The iridescence of each bubble was a brand-new world, a brand-new opportunity. It was like waking up in the morning.

Bubble! Tag thought. Another bubble!

He thought, Chase the bubbles!

As leggy and unsteady, as easily surprised, as easy to tease, as full of daft energy as every kitten, Tag pursued the bubbles, and the bubbles—each with its tiny reflected picture of the room in strange, slippery colors—evaded him smoothly and neatly and then hid among a sheaf of dried flowers or floated slowly up the chimney, or blundered without a care into a piece of furniture and burst. He *heard* them burst, in a way a human being never could, with a sound like tapped porcelain.

Evanescence and infinite renewal!

Any cat who wants to live forever should watch bubbles. Only kittens should chase them.

Tag would chase anything. But the toy he enjoyed most was a small cloth mouse with a very energetic odor. It had been bright red to start with. Now it was rather dirty, and to its original smell had been added that of floor polish. Tag whacked it around the shiny living room floor. Off it skidded. Tag skidded after it, scrabbling to keep upright on the tighter turns.

One day he found a real mouse hiding under the Welsh dresser.

A real mouse was a different thing.

Tag could see it, a little pointed black shape against the gray dimness. He could smell it too, sharp and terrified against the customary smell of fluff balls and seasoned pine. It knew he was there! It kept very still, but there was a lick of light off one beady eye, and he could feel the thoughts racing and racing through its tiny head. All the mouse's fear was trapped there under the dresser, stretched taut between the two of them like a wire. Tag vibrated with it. He wanted to chase and pounce. He wanted to eat the mouse; he didn't want to eat it. He felt powerful and predatory; he felt bigger than himself. At the same time he was anxious and frightened—for himself and the mouse. Eating someone was such a big step. He rather regretted his bravado with the pet shop finches.

He watched the mouse for some time. It watched him. Suddenly, Tag decided not to change either of their lives. His old cloth mouse had a nicer smell anyway. He reached in expertly, hooked it out, and walked away with it in his jaws. "Got you!" he told it. He flung it in the air and caught it. After a few minutes he had forgotten the real mouse, though it probably never forgot him—and his dreams were never the same.

That afternoon he took the cloth mouse with him up to the third floor where he could pat it about in a drench of cool light.

When he got bored with this he jumped up on the windowsill. From up there he had a view of the gardens stretching away right and left between the houses. However much he cajoled or bullied them, the dulls never seemed to understand that he wanted to go out there. It fascinated him. His own garden had a lawn full of moss and clover that sloped down toward the house, where a steep rockery gave way to the lichen-stained tiles of the checkerboard patio. Lime trees overhung the back fence, along which—almost obscured by colonies of coton-easter, monbretia, and fuchsia—ran a dark, narrow path of crazy paving. Cool smells came up from the garden after rain. Wood pigeons shifted furtively in the branches all endless sunny afternoon, then burst into loud, aimless cooing. At twilight, the sleepy liquid call of blackbird and thrush seemed to come from another world; and the greens of the lawn looked mysterious and unreal. Dawn filled the trees with squirrels, who chased one another from branch to branch, looting as they went, while birds quartered the lawn or hopped in circles around the mossy stone birdbath.

Transfixed with excitement, Tag watched them pull up worms.

That afternoon, a magpie was in blatant possession of the lawn, strutting around the birdbath and every so often emitting loud and raucous cries. It was a big, glossy bird, proud of its elegant black-and-white livery and metallic blue flashes. Tag had seen it before. He hated its bobbing head and powerful, ugly beak. He hated its flat, ironic eyes. Most of all he hated the way it seemed to look directly up at him, as if to say, My lawn!

Tag narrowed his eyes. Angry chattering sounds he couldn't control came from his throat. He jumped off the windowsill, then back up again. "Wrong!" he said. "Wrong!"

But the bird pretended not to hear him—though he was certain it could—and unable to bear its smug proprietorial air, Tag sat down, curled his tail around himself, and closed his eyes. After a while, he fell asleep, thinking confusedly, My mouse. This seemed to lead him into a dream.

He dreamed that he was under the Welsh dresser, eating something. Somehow, the dark gap beneath the dresser was big enough for him to enter; he had followed something in there, and was eating it. The soft parts had a warm, acrid, salty taste, and he could hardly get them down fast enough. Before he was able to swallow the tougher bits he had to shear them with the carnassial teeth at the side of his jaw, breathing heavily through his mouth as he did so. That was enjoyable too. Just as he was finishing off—licking his lips, snuffing the dusty floor where it had been in case he had missed anything—he heard a voice in the dark whisper quite close to him, "Tag is not your true name."

He whirled around. Nothing. Yet someone was there under the dresser with him. He could almost feel the heat of its body, the smell of its breath, the unsettling companionable feel of it. It had quietly watched him eat and said nothing. Now he felt guilty, angry, afraid. His fur bristled. He tried to back out from under the dresser, but now everything was the right size again and he was stuck, squeezed down tight in a dark space that smelled of wood and dust and blood with a creature he couldn't see. "Tag," it whispered. "Listen. Tag is not your true name." He felt that if he stayed there any longer, it would push its face right into his, touch him in the dark, tell him something he didn't want to hear . . .

"Tag *is* my name!" he cried, and woke up—to a loud, rapid hammering noise near his ear. While he slept, the magpie had flown up from the garden. It was strutting to and fro on the ledge directly outside the window, screeching and cawing, flapping its wings against the glass, filling the whole world with its clamor. Now its face was right next to his, and its chipped, wicked beak was drumming against the glass and it was shouting at him.

"Call yourself a cat? Call yourself a cat?"

And he fell off the windowsill and hit his head hard on the floor.

Everything went a soft dark brown color, like comforting fur. When he woke up again, the bird was gone and he could hear the dulls preparing their food downstairs, and he thought it had all been the same dream.

Tag had lived in the house for two months. It seemed much longer, a great stretch of time in which he was never unhappy.

He never wanted for anything. He doubled in size. His sleep was sound, his dreams infrequent and full of kitten things. All that seemed to be changing. Now, as he curled up on the velvet sofa, he wondered what would happen when he closed his eyes. Each time he slept, he lived another life—or fragments of it, a life of which he had no understanding.

In one dream he was walking beneath a sliver of yellow moon, with ragged clouds high up; he heard the loud roar of some distant animal. In another, he saw the vague shape of two cats huddled together with heads bowed, waiting in the pouring rain; they were so hungry and in such trouble that when he saw them, a grief he could not understand welled up inside him like a pain. In a third dream, he was standing on a windswept cliff high above the sea. There were dark gorse bushes under a strange, unreal light. There was a sense of vast space, the sound of water crashing rhythmically on rocks below. In the teeth of the wind, Tag heard a voice at his side say quietly, "I am one who becomes two; I am two who become four; I am four who become eight; I am one more after that." It was the voice of a cat. Or was it?

"Tintagel," it said. "Tag! Tag! Listen! Listen to the waves!"

All the dreams were different, but that voice was always the same—quiet, persuasive, companionable, frightening. It wanted to tell him things. It wanted him to do things.

All the dreams were strange; but perhaps this was the strangest dream of all.

He dreamed it was evening, and he was sitting on a windowsill while behind him in the room, the dulls ate their food, talking and waving their big arms about. Tag stared out. It was dark. There were clouds high up, obscuring the waning moon, but the moonlight broke fitfully through. Something was happening at the very end of the garden. He couldn't quite see what it was. Every night, he sensed, animals went along the path down there, entering the garden at one side and leaving at the other. They were on business of their own, business to enthrall a young cat. It was a highway, with constantly exciting traffic.

In the dream there was an animal out there, but he couldn't see it clearly or hear it. For a moment the moonlight seemed to resolve it into the shape of a large black cat—a cat with only one eye. Then it was nothing but a shadow again. He shifted his feet uneasily. He wanted to be out there; he didn't want to be out there. Clouds obscured the moon again. He put his face close to the glass. "Be quiet!" he tried to tell the dulls. "Watch! Watch now!"

As he spoke, the animal out there seemed to see him. He felt its eye on him. He felt its will begin to engage his own. He thought he heard it whisper, "I have a task for you, Tag. A great task!"

Behind him in the room, the dulls laughed at something one of them had said. Tag shook himself, expecting to wake up. But when he looked around, he was still in that room, and he had never been asleep. As if sensing his confusion, the female got up and, putting her face close to his as if it wanted to see exactly what he was seeing, stared out into the darkness. It shivered. "You don't want to go out there," it said softly. "Cold and dangerous for a little cat like you. *Brrr!*" It stroked his head. The purr rose in Tag's throat. When he turned back to the garden, the one-eyed cat had gone.

Early one morning, before the household was awake, Tag saw the sun coming up, carmine colored, flat and pale with promise. A few shreds of mist hung about the branches of the lime trees. Soon, three or four sparrows and a robin had alighted on the lawn and begun hopping about among the fallen leaves. This was all as it should be. Tag hunched forward to get a better look. My birds! he thought. But then they flew up suddenly, to be replaced by his enemy the magpie, who strode on long legs in a rough circle around the birdbath, shining with health and self-importance. It stopped, stretched its neck, opened its beak to reveal a short, thick purple-gray tongue, and let forth its abrasive cry.

"*Raaark. Raaark.*"

Oh yes? thought Tag. We'll see about that!

But what could he do? Only jump on and off the windowsill in a fever of frustration. At last he heard the dulls getting up, and there was something else to think about. He raced down the stairs and stood by his bowl in the kitchen.

"Breakfast," he demanded. Chicken and game casserole! "In here. Put it in this bowl. Breakfast!"

Chicken and game!

That was a smell he would remember later on.

Two minutes after he had got his face into the bowl, one of the dulls opened the back door without thinking. Tag felt the cool morning air on his nose. It was full of smells. It was full of opportunity. And the magpie was still out there, strutting around the lawn as if he owned it.

My lawn! thought Tag. Breakfast later!

And he was out in a flash, straight between a pair of legs, across the lawn—scattering leaves and hurling himself at the bird, who turned its sly black head at the last moment, said clearly, "Not this time, sonny," and flew like an arrow through a hole in the fence, leaving one small white body feather floating in the air behind it. Tag, enraged, went sprinting after, his hind feet digging up lawn and flower bed. He heard the dulls shouting after him. Then he was through the fence and into the garden next door. The magpie was sitting on a fence, regarding him amusedly from one beady eye. *"Raaark."* Off they went again. Every time he thought he had caught it, the bird only led him farther afield, until, when Tag looked back at his house, he couldn't see it anymore.

He hesitated a moment.

"Call yourself a cat?" sneered the magpie, almost in his ear. "This is where you belong, out here in the wild world—not a toy cat on a windowsill!" But when Tag whirled around, ready to renew the chase, it had vanished into thin air.

Tag sat down and washed himself. He looked around.

New gardens! New gardens that went on forever. Through one and into the next, forever.

Out! he thought. I got out!

He forgot the magpie. He forgot his home. For the rest of that day he was as happy as he'd ever been. He explored the new gardens one by one, moving farther and farther away from the dulls and their house. There were gardens overgrown with weeds and elder, in which the sun barely struck through to the earth and the dusty, powerfully smelling roots. There were gardens so neat they were just like front rooms. There were gardens full of rusty household objects. Tag had a look at all of them. They were all interesting. But by late afternoon he had found the garden of his dreams. It was wilder than his own, a narrow shady cleft between old brick walls, sagging wooden trellis, and overgrown buddleia bushes, into which reached long bright fingers of sun. It was full of ancient flowerpots and white metal garden furniture green with moss. At one side was a bent old damson tree, its sagging boughs held up by wooden supports; at the other a well-grown holly. Tag sat in the sun between them, cleaning his fur. A family of bullfinches piped from the branches of the damson. A bee hummed past! After it he went, whacking out with his front paws until he could clutch the stunned insect inside one of them. He put the bee carefully into his mouth and let it buzz about a bit in there. What a feeling! Then he swallowed it. "Not bad," he told himself. "Good bee." For a while he patrolled an old flower bed now overgrown with mint, in case he got another. After that, he went to sleep. When he woke up, he was hungry. It was late afternoon, and he had no idea where he was.

Two hours later, he was huddled—hungry, cold, and disoriented—on someone's back doorstep. Afternoon had given way to evening as he made his way from garden to garden, recognizing nothing. At first it had seemed like a great game. Then the fences had got higher and harder to jump, the tangled rose briars harder to push through, the smells of other cats more threatening. Human beings had shouted at him through a window—he had run off thoughtlessly and got turned back on himself, ending up in the garden he had started from. Now he was so tired he couldn't think. He knew it wasn't his own house. But he was grateful to sit on the doorstep anyway. He was grateful for the old damson tree, spreading its branches over the white garden furniture glowing in the dusk. These things were familiar, at least. He gave a little yowl now and then, in case someone came home and let him in.

As he sat there, the light went slowly out of the sky. The sun was a great cool red ball behind the garden trees. Rooks began to settle their evening quarrels—"My branch, I think." "No, *my* branch!"—the whole ragged ignoble colony of them whirling up into the sky to wheel and caw before settling again, one by one, into silence. Suddenly the air was colder. Shadows crept out of the box hedges. The garden seemed to change shape, becoming shorter and broader. The lawn, the shrubs in their borders, the lighted windows of the houses yellow with warmth and company—everything seemed closer and yet farther away. The apple trees faded to a uniform gray.

Night had come. Tag had never been out in it before.

He knew the night only from warm rooms behind double-glazed windows. Then it had seemed exciting. Now it was only menacing and strange. As human activity decreased, the real sounds and smells of the world came through: the sudden low twitter of a bird disturbed, the slow tarry reek of leaf mold from under the hedges, the bitter smell of a rusting iron bucket, a dog barking somewhere down at the end of the road, thickly woven odors of snails eating their way through the soft fleshy leaves of the hostas. And then, suddenly, from the gloom at the very end of the garden, came a smell that made Tag's heart race with fear and excitement! His head went up. Almost despite himself, he sniffed the air. Something moving down there! It was a highway, like the one that ran along the bottom of his own garden! Something was trotting down there, fast and purposeful, its paws moving silently across the broken, lichenous old flagstones as it made its way from left to right along the tunnelly overgrown path between the flower bed and the sagging board fence. Tag could barely keep still. He wanted to make himself known. He wanted to hide. Every part of him wanted to say something. Every part of him wanted to stay silent.

In the end, though, he must have moved, or made some sound, because the animal on the highway stopped. It sniffed the air for him. He *heard* it. Terribly afraid, he huddled into the doorway. Too late. It was aware of him. He could see a dark silhouette, a thick black shadow with four legs and a blunt muzzle, its head turning this way and that. A single bright, pale, reflective eye that seemed to switch itself on suddenly, like a lamp. It was looking at him. There was a long pause. Then a wave of scent, a sharp, live, musky reek in the garden air.

"Little cat," it said in a soft voice. "Your true name is not Tag. Do you want to discover your true name? If so, you must undertake the task which lies before you."

He shrank back in the doorway until his head was pressed so tightly into the corner his face hurt. To no avail. The thing that inhabited that shadow could see him whatever he did. There was a low, grunting laugh.

"Don't be afraid," said the voice. "Come with me now."

Its owner took a pace toward him.

He cowered into his doorway.

There was a sudden impatient sigh, as if the creature had been interrupted. It paused to listen, then, purposeful and urgent, it loped off into the night without another word.

Tag huddled on the doorstep until it was light again. Exhaustion made him shake; anxiety kept him awake. Every sound, familiar or not, seemed to threaten him, from the abrupt shriek of an owl to the patient snuffling and rootling of a hedgehog in the next garden. He was afraid to make any noise of his own.

Toward dawn he fell into a restless sleep, only to dream of the animals on their highway. Tag could never be sure what he saw—what he sensed—moving along it. They were cats, certainly, although in the dream they seemed much larger than a cat should be, and they had deeply disturbing, shadowy shapes. They moved in their own powerful stink—vague, slippery, indistinct, always angry or excited. Their voices came toward him from a long distance, in the echoing yet glutinous speech of dreams.

"A task," they told him, "a great task."

The next morning he was stiff and tired, but the sunshine made him feel optimistic. Breakfast! he thought. He sat up, stretched himself, and gave a huge yawn. "Chicken and game!" He jumped on top of a fence and looked across the gardens. They lay before him: a lawn as precise as a living-room carpet, bordered with regiments of red flowers; then rusty objects propped against a shed; then bedsheets flapping on a line. He jumped down, nosed around. There, on the concrete path as it warmed up in the sunshine, was his own smell from yesterday, faint but distinct!

Follow myself home, he thought. No problem.

But it was a problem.

Chasing the magpie, he had taken an alarmingly random course, zigzagging, turning back on himself, often going in circles. In the night, other animals had passed; other scents had overlaid his own. While it was a good idea, the attempt to follow himself was doomed from the start. High old brick walls, espaliered with fruit trees, blocked his path. Abundant crops of nettles forced him to divert. He blundered into another cat—or rather the insane face of another cat was thrust unexpectedly into his own, screaming at him so loudly that he jumped in fear and ran off under some bushes and came out disoriented twenty minutes later to find himself trapped in a place that didn't even seem to be a garden. The spines of dying foxgloves mopped and mowed against a tottering wooden fence. What had once been an open space was now a jungle: fireweed seeding down to ashes, a choke of brambles and old rose suckers bound together in the dusty heat by convolvulus and grape ivy. The air was thick, still, and oppressive, full of the sleepy drone of insects. Eventually he pushed his way out. He was hot and tired and out of temper. The house in front of him had blue shutters, peeling to show the gray wood beneath, and a blue door. Not much else could be seen through the skeins of honeysuckle and wiry climbing roses colonizing its pebbledashed walls. Its windows were of rippled glass, dim with dirt. Compressed between the wilderness and the house, the remains of its garden—the patch of yellowed lawn on which he stood, the beds overgrown with rubbery hostas, the tottering wooden shed that had also at some time been painted blue—would soon be engulfed.

Tag sighed and sat down suddenly in the shade of some terracotta pots full of dead geraniums. It was already noon, and he still hadn't eaten. He crouched down, tucked his front paws neatly under him, and let his nose rest on the ground. Not knowing what else to do, he slept. When he woke, the magpie was perched on a broken pot in front of him.

"Raaark," it said. "On your own then, Kit-e-Kat?"

"Don't call me that!" said Tag.

The magpie laughed. "Call yourself a cat?" it asked. It added mysteriously, "I don't know why he bothers with you. If he could find them on his own, he wouldn't." Then it put its head on one side, regarded him with one beady eye, and said with measured nastiness, "Oh yes, you're on your own now, Kit-e-Kat!"

Tag was enraged. He jumped up and rushed the magpie. "My name's Tag!" he cried. "I *am* a cat, and they call me Tag, not Kit-e-Kat!"

The magpie only bobbed its head wickedly and took flight. It flapped with a dreamy slowness up from the lawn and into the rowan tree. As it flew it looked less like a bird than a series of brilliant sketches of one. For an instant—while it was still rising but almost into the tree—it seemed to wear its own wings like a black, shiny cloak. Then it perched, quickly ruffled its feathers, and looked down at Tag, its head tilted on one side to show a bright cruel eye.

"They call *me* One for Sorrow," it said. "And you won't forget me in a hurry."

Alone, thought Tag.

He tested this idea until sudden panic swept through him. He ran around and around the lawn until he was tired again. He licked his fur in the sunshine for ten minutes. He couldn't think what to do. He jumped up onto a windowsill and rubbed both sides of his face on the window pane. "Breakfast!" he demanded. But clearly it would not be feeding him today. So he jumped down and tried the same with the back door. No luck. Clearly no one would be feeding him today.

He had a new idea. He would feed himself.

Eat a bee, he thought. Eat more than one.

And he tore off excitedly across the lawn, the little bell on his collar jingling.

An hour later he had chased four houseflies, a blackbird, two sparrows, and a leaf. He had caught one of the houseflies and the leaf. The leaf proved to be unpalatable. No bees were about. All this effort made him hungrier than before. He went back to the house and jumped up on the windowsill again.

"Yow!" he said.

Nothing. It was silent and empty in there.

He stalked a wren, which scolded him from a safe place inside a hedge. He tried it on with two squirrels, who bobbed their tails at him and sped off along the top of a board fence at a breakneck pace, vying with each other for the lead and calling "Stuff you!" and "Stuff your nuts, mate!" as they ran. Then he tried a thrush, which kept a lazy eye on him while it shelled its breakfast—a yellow snail—against a stone, then rose up neatly as he pounced, and with no fuss or fluster cleared his optimistic jaws by four inches and left him clapping his front paws silently on empty air.

"Nice technique," said an interested voice behind him.

"Pretty stupid cat, though," answered another. "Anyone could have caught that."

Tag thought he recognized one of the voices, but he was too ashamed to turn around and look. For the rest of that day, he ate flies. They were easy to catch and, depending on what they had eaten recently, even tasted good. In the middle of the afternoon he bullied some sparrows off half a slice of buttered white bread two gardens along the row. Finally, he went back to the place where he had argued with the thrush. There he caught some snails. They didn't taste in the slightest bit good, but at least, he thought, he was denying them to the thrush.

Toward evening it began to rain.

The rain came stealthily at first, a drop here and a drop there. It tapped and popped on the leaves of the hostas, where it gathered as shiny beads—each containing a tiny curved image of the world—that soon collapsed into little short-lived rivulets. The snails, sensing the rain, opened themselves up gratefully.

Then, sensing Tag, they shut themselves away again. There was a kind of hush around the sound of each raindrop.

Tag watched the snails and waited. A cat with a thick coat doesn't feel the rain until too late. Suddenly it was pouring down on him, straight as a stair rod, cold and penetrating as a needle. He was surprised and disgusted to find himself soaked. His skin twitched. He stretched and stood up. He shook out first one front paw, then the other. He retreated to the back doorstep.

No good.

A gust of wind shook the shrubbery and blew the rain across the garden in swirls, right into his shelter. He sat there grimly for a bit, trying to lick the damp off his fur, fluffing up, blinking, shaking himself, licking again. But in the end he had to admit that he was just as wet there as he would have been in the middle of the lawn.

I hate rain, he thought.

He dashed out into the downpour to try the windowsill.

Wet.

He found a dry patch in the lee of the terra-cotta pots. The wind changed and blew the rain into his face.

He tried sitting under the trees.

Wet.

Soon it was coming dark. "Stop raining now," said Tag. Every time he changed position he got wetter. He was hungry again, and cold. But if he scampered about to keep warm he felt tired very suddenly. He ordered the rain, "Leave me alone, now." The rain didn't listen. The garden didn't listen. The wind was like a live thing. It was always blowing from behind him, ruffling his fur up the wrong way to find and chill any part of him that still had any warmth left. He turned around and tried to bite the harder gusts. He ran blindly about or simply sat, becoming more and more bedraggled. Suddenly he realized that he was sitting by the door of the garden shed.

Inside, he thought.

He hooked his paw around the bottom of the door and pulled hard. It wouldn't move. Open! he heard himself think. Open, now! He hooked again and pulled harder. This made him so

weary he needed to sit down; but after a moment he was cold
again and had to force himself to get up.

Hook. Pull. No good.

"Come on, Tag," he encouraged himself. "Come on!"

Hook. Pull. The door scraped open an inch. Then two.

That's enough! thought Tag.

For some minutes he was too worn out to do anything but
sit in front of the door with his head down, looking at nothing.
Then he pushed his face cautiously into the gap, and the rest
of him, bedraggled and shivering, seemed to follow of its own
accord.

It rained. Days and nights came and went, and still no one summoned him for "the task." The house remained empty and the
lawn filled with puddles. Then the last leaves fell from the trees,
and the nights drew in tight, like a collar around a young cat's
neck. Smoke hung low over the gardens in the late afternoon;
the days began with thick mists. Winter ushered itself in, quietly
and without fuss, in the voice of the roosting crows, the raw
chill in the evening air. Tag lived in the shed, and soon became
familiar with its pungent smells of ancient sacks and insecti-
cides, spiderwebs and mice. He never caught a mouse there, but
it was reassuring to think that one day he might. If it was not
warm, the shed was at least dry. The shed saved him.

When he felt strong, he ranged up and down the gardens,
three or four houses in every direction. He ate flies. He ate
earthworms. He ate anything that could be caught without a
great expenditure of energy. He got up in the dawn to beat the
squirrels to the scraps of bread and lard and meat that other cats'
dulls put out for the birds. He became thin and quick but easier
and easier to tire. He avoided confrontations. Seen in the distance in the gardens at sunrise on a cold morning, he was like a
white ghost, a twist of breath in the frost. Close to, his silver
coat was tangled and muddy and out of condition.

Some days it was all he could do to find the energy to crouch
at a puddle and lap up rainwater, then make his way back to the
shed. Eat something tomorrow, he would think; and then after a

confused doze get up again in the belief that tomorrow had already come. Which in a way it had.

He never left the gardens. If he thought about his life, he thought that this was the way he would live it now. Tiredness, and the comforting sound of the rain on the roof of the shed.

Then one night everything changed again.

Chapter Two

THE HIGHWAY

Let none who might belong to himself
belong to another.
— AGRIPPA

*I*t was a night without rain after a day of frost. Everything in the gardens was very still. A sliver of moon hung high up behind the lacy fretwork of lime and sycamore branches. The gardens seemed to stretch away forever under it, silvered less with moonlight than with cold.

There was a highway cutting across a corner of the lawn not ten yards from the house with blue shutters. Every night, cats came and went on it, big with errands Tag didn't understand. Traffic had increased with the colder weather, each traveler transfigured and urgent in the moonlight—more serious, more animal. Full of aggression and pride, posing and pausing, they whipped their tails, bubbling with outrage. His encounter with the one-eyed creature in the shadows had left him deeply attracted, deeply repelled. He wanted to know about them. He desperately wanted to be one of them. He desperately wanted to stay as he was.

He lay on his heap of sacks, listening to them pass, and lapsed into an unrestful dream in which all the food and warmth he remembered from his vanished kittenhood had somehow become wound up with images of the highway. He was sitting on a windowsill looking out, and somehow at the same time standing on the highway looking in. Around him on the highway a kind of wild energy seemed to flow. The animals he saw were only discrete packets of that energy. Without them it would still flow. It would always flow, as if for every live thing that made a journey, a million ghosts made it too, rushing in both directions forever. In the dream, that energy brushed Tag, touched him like stroking fingers, filled him with grimness and determination.

24

Along that road, the one-eyed shadow awaited him. It sat roaring up at the moon, the biggest cat he had ever seen. It turned to face him and he thought it said, "Tag, I am the Majicou."

At this, a great terror entered Tag's body, and he ran away. But the Majicou was always in front of him. It said, "Tag, wherever you run I will be there first. It is in my nature, and yours. Listen. You must help me—"

"No!" said Tag.

He had to get away. He struggled to wake up. The dream wrapped itself into a parcel, shrank suddenly in front of him, and rushed away down the long black emptiness. As it diminished, the black cat was calling urgently, "Tag . . . the spring equinox . . . time is running out!" Its voice seemed to fade into the distance. Then, so far away it was barely audible, *"Tintagel . . ."*

Tag woke to a series of shrieks echoing through the cruel air, as some animal caught and killed another in the jungle at the end of the lawn. In the deep silence that followed, he could hear spiders scuttling about in the shed—survivors who had learned to stay high up in the roof where he couldn't reach them. He shuddered. He turned around and tucked his nose under his tail. He drifted off again.

Perhaps ten minutes later, half awake, half asleep, moving like an automaton, he got up and left the shed.

The highway, he thought.

He thought, It's just a garden path.

It was just an overgrown garden path at the corner of a lawn. At the same time it was a strange, dark, shifting blur only an animal could understand, rich with motion, stuffed with meaning. Everything has two natures, Tag thought confusedly, the wild and the tame. He stood, neither a pet cat nor a wild one, swaying at its edge. He was ready to take his place in the flow. But when he pushed forward, something resisted him. He felt as if he were pushing against a taut plastic membrane that fitted so closely around his face that his nostrils were stopped up. There was a faint stretched noise, like the surface of a bubble before it bursts. Nothing happened. Tag stood there. He was fully awake now, or thought he was, and paralyzed with fear. Why had he done this? He didn't dare move. The animals went to and fro in front of him.

Suddenly Tag shuddered convulsively. He summoned up all his energy and stepped into the flux.

His first time on the wild road, everything was like the worst dream he had ever had—darkness, objects rushing past, shapes unrecognizable and haunted. There was a cold continual wind blowing from whichever direction he faced. Tag turned around and around on his haunches, trying to see where it was coming from. It was icy and dusty at once. The noise was unbearable: a million animal voices, slurred and strung out, so deep they seemed to move in Tag's bowels, so high-pitched they shattered something in his head. And shattered it again, and again and again. Smells so simple they made him gag. Smells so complex they could never be decoded. Things brushed him. He heard laughter at his expense, echoing and re-echoing into a space that was rigidly linear—the highway—and yet seemed to extend *in all directions at once.* The garden had vanished. The house with blue shutters had vanished. He wasn't in the world he knew. He wasn't anywhere, he knew. He felt himself panic. He ran a few steps at random, at a loss. Something huge appeared, traveling very fast. He flinched, crouched.

"Little cat!" he heard a voice say in a long, stretched, gluey growl. "Little cat, don't stand your ground!"

Suddenly something hit him very hard in the side and he was bowled over and over through the darkness, as if one of the dulls had picked him up and thrown him through the air and walked away and let him fall . . .

When he woke, he was sprawled on the lawn, and a large fox was standing over him.

"I can see you like to live dangerously," it said. "What on earth possessed you to try that one?"

"What one?" said Tag. He felt bruised all over. His throat was dry and hot. His stomach ached from a bad earthworm he had eaten earlier in the day. "I was asleep," he said resentfully.

"Then you're a tough dreamer," said the fox. "That's all I can say." It considered this. "No one gains entry headfirst and full tilt like that," it remarked. It added, "Not at your age anyway."

It was a handsome animal: long-backed, reddish, brindling toward its hindquarters and long tail, exuding a fine strong reek of fox. It regarded him for a moment, head on one side, bright eyes full of a mixture of greed and humor, cunning and good-will, all those oppositions that make up the character of the fox. It grinned, and hung its long tongue out of the corner of its mouth.

"I'm not sure I could do that myself," it said. "And I'm good."

"What at?" said Tag.

"Anyway, look, if you're all right now, I'll be off."

"Thanks," said Tag.

He felt dizzy and lonely. He felt like someone who lived on a pile of sacks in a shed. He liked the fox despite himself. He wanted to say, Stay for a bit until I feel better, but his voice wasn't working well enough.

So off went the fox at a relaxed lope, in circles with its nose to the lawn. It found a puddle of water, stopped, and drank at length, looking up every so often. Then it pushed its way out of the garden, its white-tipped tail vanishing among some elders, leafless laburnum bushes, and apple trees. Tag dragged himself to his feet. He could hear the fox blundering about noisily in the leaf mold.

"Come back," he called. "Come back now.

"Please."

There was a silence. Then the fox's nose appeared out of the undergrowth some distance from where it had left the garden.

"Was it you who ran me over?" demanded Tag.

"No," said the fox, coming a little way into Tag's garden again and sitting down. "If you'd been run over nothing could have helped you. I got you out of its way in time."

"What was it?"

The fox said, "You don't want to know, little cat." It added, "Believe me."

"Why did it hate me?"

The fox looked puzzled. "It didn't have any feelings about you one way or another."

"Can you help me?" said Tag.

The fox grinned. "No one can help you with the wild road. It's a knack."

"No," said Tag. "Not that. I never want to do that again. I only want to have a quiet life. Have you ever lived in a house and eaten chicken and game casserole? That's what I want. A quiet life."

The fox looked at him. "Mm," it said. "Can you walk now?"

"Yes."

"Then I'll take you to someone who can help you with your life," offered the fox. "He doesn't live too far from here. Follow me." And it set off at a fast clip.

Tag was delighted, but he soon found it hard to keep up. "Don't hang about," advised the fox, as it leapt one fence, then squeezed itself between two loose boards of another. "Come on, come on."

It circled a kidney-shaped pond, pushed through some bushes into a passageway down the side of a house. Under a gate they went. There was a reek of something chemical and burnt. There were lights high up over a great expanse of tarmac. "Wait here," ordered the fox. Tag blinked in the buzzing orange light. Something huge and reeking roared past, twenty inches from his nose! He winced away. "Don't bother about that," ordered the fox. "It's just a car. They can't kill you if you're quick. Come on, come on!" And then it was gardens again, at a cracking pace.

Eventually they came to an arbor or summerhouse built of old gray wooden trellis, twined inside and out with fifty or sixty summers and winters of clematis and climbing rose. Tag stood with the fox at the entrance. Inside was a rough wooden bench. The back wall seemed too solid to be made of trellis. It had a strange shine. It seemed to be full of moonlight.

"Does he live here?"

"Among other places."

"What must I do?"

"Just go in," advised the fox.

"What?"

"Just go in and see what happens."

Tag approached the threshold.

Another cat had come into the summerhouse while he was talking to the fox. It was staring suspiciously out at him from the gloom. Another cat! Before he could stop himself, he had run away across the lawn. Half turning back, hindquarters low to the ground, he sniffed the air. Another cat—and one a lot more powerful, dirty, and tattered than he was. A cat of his own age, but with much more experience. A real outdoor cat with lean muscles and a desperate look about him. Just the sort of cat Tag avoided when he could. Just the sort of cat whose help he needed. He sniffed again. He couldn't smell anything.

He crept back to the fox's side.

"I dare not speak to the wild cat," he said. "I'm afraid to look at him."

The fox chuckled. "Go in. You can touch him."

"No."

The fox loomed up.

"Touch him," it said menacingly.

Tag shrank away from the fox. He crept up to the threshold of the summerhouse. Inside, he approached the other cat. It approached him. He kept low; it kept low. When he flattened his ears, it flattened its ears. When he stretched out a paw and tapped, a paw was outstretched to tap his paw. Glass! It was glass! With a flood of relief and disappointment he understood who he was looking at.

"But that's only me," said Tag.

The fox laughed wryly. "You had it right the first time," it said. It came and sat beside Tag so that its own reflection appeared in the glass next to his. "There's a real tearaway in there," it said, studying Tag's image with some interest. "A genuine desperado. Still, I rest my case. *Only me,* eh? Is that how you see yourself? *Only you* is worth a good deal more than you think."

It stared almost puzzledly back and forth, from Tag's reflection to Tag himself. "Is there," it asked itself, in such a low voice that Tag was never to be certain what he had heard it say, "a Great Cat in there somewhere?" It cocked its head. "Majicou must have his reasons." And then, louder, "A good deal more than you think. But I suppose you'll have to find that out for yourself."

Tag felt weary and depressed. He had eaten a bad worm, and he was bruised all over, and he wasn't going to have any help after all.

"I'm sick of this Majicou," he said, "and the nightmares he sends me. I had a nice life in a house, and I want to go back to it. I had somewhere to sleep and dulls who fed me."

Suddenly the fox yawned. "The fact is," it said, "I'm not very interested in human beings. Who cares about them? If you want to make something of yourself in this world—forget it, if you only want to *eat* in this world—you've got to make it as yourself. Not as someone else's property."

"I—" Tag began.

But the fox was already trotting off.

"Do you understand me, little cat?" it called back. "Yourself!"

"My name is Tag," Tag said, "not Little Cat."

The fox, which had got as far as the edge of the lawn, paused and looked back.

"That's a start," it admitted.

Then it was gone.

"Tag," said Tag.

Then he realized he was alone again.

Unsure what to do with himself now, Tag curled up on the threshold of the summerhouse and looked out across the lawn. It was a good garden. Down one side of it ran a high stone wall. Along this grew the gnarled golden-brown trunk of an old wisteria. Some light mist lay on the lawn, so that it looked like a lake.

Genuine desperado, he thought. He remembered how his mirror image had looked out at him, tough and self-possessed. "A real tearaway, me."

And he fell asleep.

He dreamed of a highway.

Though he was looking into it from outside, it seemed to stretch away in all directions at once. A cold wind blew, lonely and comfortless, down the elongated perspectives.

After some time, a single black cat came into view, distant at first, then closer, bounding along on some urgent errand. Soon it was so close Tag could smell the musk and sweat of it. Its energy seemed ferocious in that unfeeling emptiness. Long muscles stretched and flexed, stretched and flexed. Huge paws thudded soft and rhythmic on the cold dusty ground. Light spilled off shiny black fur. Heat poured into the withering air, effort shed with a kind of profligate contempt for distance, weariness, hunger. Days passed like this. The great cat's stride never varied. It was steady. It was like slow motion. Then suddenly it stopped. Tag watched with a sense of dread as its huge head turned, and it stared out of the highway at him.

One eye! One eye!

"TAG!" it roared, and its voice seemed to echo toward him from a million miles away. *"TAG!"*

Then it was off again, and Tag was inside the dream with it, bounding along on oiled limbs, burning the magic fuels that young animals are given to burn so that nothing seems an effort to them and the one long day of their lives goes on and on forever.

"Tag!" commanded the one-eyed cat, in that huge and hollow voice. "Jump and eat! Jump and eat forever!"

They ran on.

In slow motion—in the slowest of motion, so that fluid movement failed and was broken into a chain of distinct instants—a bird flew up in front of them. Tag had never seen such a bird. It had a crest like a scarlet crown and a tail like a train of sparks. Its feathers were the colors of turquoise and brass. Its beak strained wide with a long and liquid song, the unrepeating song of the bird's life. The notes of this song were gold. They issued visibly from its mouth.

"Tag!" said the black cat. "I am Majicou. The highway is yours. Embrace your life!"

And he leapt into the air and caught the bird in his mouth.

Turquoise feathers scattered and dulled. The golden song arched and died. The bird lay still across Majicou's mouth like a strip of blue and yellow cloth. One pale, stern eye observed Tag from above it.

"Even this," said Majicou.

"I won't!" said Tag. "I won't!"

"Tag, you must. The wild road is your heritage. Comfort is behind you. Duty lies before. Time to understand the truth about yourself. You are no longer a kitten."

Perhaps not, but he felt like one. No matter how he struggled or tried to bite, he was stuck in the dream, pinned down as securely as if a huge black paw lay across his neck.

"It's time you learned your true name," Majicou told him. "It's time you understood the real nature of the world! Do you want to live in a house all your life and be pampered and meaningless?"

"Yes," said Tag. "I do."

"You do not!" growled Majicou.

"I will never eat something so beautiful as that bird," Tag burst out angrily. "I can tell you that. I would rather die."

Majicou laughed. "And yet," he said, with infinite contempt, "you eat insects. When you aren't fighting squirrels for a lump of damp bread, you eat snails." He paused. "You ate the mouse under the cupboard," he pointed out, more gently.

Outraged, Tag cried, "That was only a dream!"

A great hollow laugh rolled away to the edges of everything. *"This* is only a dream."

Tag could hardly deny that. Instead he writhed abruptly, caught the black cat a lucky bang on the nose, and wrenched himself awake. For a moment he was nowhere at all. He was barely himself. He was a toppling atom of perception in a dark, oppressive, accordion-pleated void. The thoughts that passed through his mind were unpleasant. Panic enfolded him. Then he woke, limbs flailing, in the summerhouse. He was free! But even as his eyes opened, he thought he saw the shadow of a bird, beak gaping in misery and despair, flutter across the wall. Somewhere the dream was still unrolling. It lay in wait behind his eyes; and he knew he must not go back to sleep. To keep himself awake he sat thinking about the dulls, and remembering all the different things they had given him to eat.

Tuna fish in oil.
Tuna fish in brine.
Tuna fish mayonnaise.
Tuna fish salad with crispy bacon.
Tins of things:
chicken and game casserole,
fish and liver dinner.

It was a long list. Every time he drifted toward sleep, Tag repeated it to himself. More often than not he thought of a new item. *"Mackerel pâté!"* he remembered toward dawn, "always very good." But his eyes were closing; the dream was ready to capture him again; and his own feet were carrying him onward whatever he did, toward the inevitable.

"No!"

"Yes, Tag. Yes!"

Somehow, the mackerel pâté of memory had escaped its wrapper, skipped its kitchen dish, and turned into a flickering silver shoal, darting and twisting in terror against an empty darkness. Through the shoal danced Majicou, lunging and pouncing, jumping and cuffing. Living silver fishes! Yet each one the black cat touched was transformed—into a bird, a butterfly, a scuttering mouse! "Life, Tag!" invited the great cat. "Your life!" And suddenly, despite himself, Tag was compelled to rush and dance and hunt, too, until they were both tired and sated and Majicou sat down as suddenly as a kitten, licked his huge jaws, and stared at Tag from one shining eye.

"You see?" he said.

"I see," said Tag.

They sat companionably for a while. Then Tag asked, "Why have you shown me this?"

"For many reasons. It is your birthright, for one. For another, you were named, you were marked out long ago. But mainly, I admit, because at the moment I need your help. There is something only you can do." He considered this. "How can I explain? Tag, these highways are the most important thing in the world."

"For cats?" said Tag. He leaned forward excitedly. "I see cats on them every night!"

"Not just for cats. For everyone. The highways—" Majicou began, then stopped. Sometimes, he did look like a very old cat, gray around the muzzle, curved in the spine. "This is important and there is so little time to explain— The wild roads, Tag, carry the natural energies of the world. If they are not cared for, all is chaos and disaster. A long time ago I came to be their caretaker. I have kept them well, and in return they have given me long life and power." He shook his head regretfully to and fro. "That was a two-edged blessing," he said. "Now I am so old, I can't live away from them. Here, I hunt and jump like you— Better! I am the Majicou, after all!—but in the world, just at the moment of the world's gravest danger, I find myself as feeble as a kitten. I must use proxies, like the fox and the magpie. The world needs me, Tag, and I have let it down. I have lost the King and Queen, and only another cat can bring them back to me."

"Can't your fox do it?"

"Tag, they won't go with a fox. Cats hate foxes—"

"I don't," said Tag.

"And they *eat* birds. Why was I sent such a dull apprentice?"

Tag, rather stung by this, found himself saying, "All right. I'll find them for you."

"Good," said Majicou. "Go, go now."

Tag shivered suddenly. He had the feeling that he had committed his whole life to someone else's cause. He would need a new kind of life now. He would need to be a new kind of cat.

He walked all night through the gardens, and in the morning decided that the first act of his new life would be to get rid of his collar. If he was to take on the great task before him it would not be as someone else's property.

The collar—a six-inch strip of felted material half an inch

wide with an elastic insert, a tinny little bell, and a dusting of blue, red, and green sequins, an object of which he had once been rather proud—had been fastened around his neck by the dulls the day they bought him from the pet shop. It had spread a reek of chemicals to his fur. Weeks of wear in the gardens, weeks of the outdoor life, had dulled its smell, rubbed off the sequins, and reduced it to a blackened thong, greasy with impregnated dirt. It was always getting caught on things. Worse, the bell warned off his lunch.

Tag trotted along in the sunshine until he found the tools he needed. A fence of lapped boards green with lichen, the top of which fell in pretty curves like suspended chain. At the end of that, a square wooden gatepost with a wrought-iron spike on top. Tag leapt onto the fence, teetered a little, then turned carefully and ran along the top of it. He had learned how to do this by chasing squirrels. When he reached the gatepost he rubbed his face against the spike, as if he were saying hello to it. After a moment the spike slipped neatly under his collar. Now all he had to do was back away along the fence, and the spike would drag the collar over his head. It was a good plan. The collar would be left empty on the spike. People would wonder how it came to be there.

More than clever, thought Tag.

He backed away. The collar slid forward, reached his ears, and stuck. He pulled harder. No good. He tried lowering his head and pulling. He tried raising it. Nothing. The problem was that his paws had to stay all in a line on the fence. He couldn't spread them to pull.

"Waugh."

In the end, he steadied himself as best he could and gave a vast tug. His feet slipped straight off the fence. Before he knew it he was hanging by the neck. He couldn't breathe. He couldn't move his head. All he could see was the top corner of a house and a bit of blue sky. He was so shocked he couldn't think what to do. His back legs tucked themselves up of their own accord and scraped wildly at the collar. He tried to get one front paw under it. Somehow, that became trapped too. Up came his back legs again and scraped until he was exhausted. He hung there with black patches coming and going in front of his eyes. Every few seconds he felt himself struggle and thrash, then go limp.

Damn, he thought. He felt a fool.

After a short time the black patches were replaced by lapses of concentration. During these he seemed to see or hear things from his kittenhood. Sometimes he even did them. He raced about after the soap bubbles. He *heard* them burst. He had been very happy that day. He tried to think, Chase the bubbles! But then he was looking at the corner of the house again. There was the same belvedere window in its dressing of ivy. There was the same patch of blue sky. Then, after a particularly long lapse—during which he lived a whole day from breakfast to supper—he heard a derisive squawking noise.

"*Raaargh!* Call yourself a cat?"

Into his limited field of view, at a strange angle and full of vitriolic amusement, had been inserted a black, streamlined, beady-eyed face tapering to a monolithic black beak. It belonged to the magpie One for Sorrow.

"Hello," the magpie said. "What's this?"

"Please go away," said Tag. "I'm trying to look at that house."

"*Raaargh,*" said One for Sorrow.

It chuckled.

It winked, and its head was slowly withdrawn. After that, there was a silence, broken only by the furtive dry rattling sound of scaly feet somewhere on the fence behind him as the magpie assessed the situation. "Mm," it muttered quietly. "*Raa.*" More rattling. Suddenly, Tag felt it take off and flap energetically about just above him, fanning him with stale air from beneath its wings. Then, with a triumphant shout, it had fastened its claws savagely into the loose skin behind his head, and its beak was driving down toward him.

"*Raargh! Haraargh!*"

Hey! Tag tried to shout.

The pressure of the collar on his neck increased until the black spots danced madly in front of his eyes and covered everything, and suddenly he wasn't there anymore. A long falling sensation followed. Black accordion pleats. A cold wind. A distant voice, *"Tintagel . . . the equinox—"*

When he woke, he *was* falling.

"Waugh!"

He took in a huge breath, only to have it knocked out of him again by the ground. There he lay, in the shadow of the fence, his throat bruised, his ribs battered, the air going in and out of him in one continuous desperate wheeze, while he slowly became aware of the magpie dancing about in front of him, rendered almost as helpless as he was by a sense of its own importance, fluttering its wings and squawking, "Yes! *Yes!*"

"You bit me!" accused Tag.

The bird strode to and fro. It preened.

"I bit your *collar*, you ridiculous cat! I set you free. But don't thank me. Just remember that Majicou might be impressed with you *but I'm not*."

Without thinking, Tag dragged himself up and sprang. He was slow; but this time the magpie, stuffed up with its own ego like a chicken full of sage and onion, was slower. Trying to take off, it lost its balance and fell down. Its feet scrabbled for purchase. It was a ball of undignified feathers, its wings clutching panically at the air. Too late. To his astonishment, Tag had caught it. Feathers filled his mouth with a dry, musty, not very pleasant taste. The bird struggled furiously, beating its wings in his face and making outraged noises into his ear. Tag hung on grimly, thinking, I got you, I got you! He was elated. Then he remembered that the bird was One for Sorrow. Aghast, he dropped it. The magpie, still squawking and struggling as if it were in his mouth, rolled violently a little way away, then got up in surprise.

"I can't eat you!" Tag said in horror.

The magpie settled its feathers.

"More fool you," it said, and flew off.

Tag laughed.

"You can't eat your friends!" he called after it.

He looked around. He felt better. The day was going to be a

good one. The sun had spilled itself in a kind of golden, rosy-orange shimmer across the blue of the sky. He thought, I'm *Tag*. After all that—I'm Tag. Suddenly he was happier than he had been since he chased the soap bubbles.

He set out upon his task.

The First Life of Cats

*B*efore the first life of the Felidae there was nothing but darkness and silence. The darkness was complete, and nothing stirred within it. But the silence was the silence of stillness before turmoil. Inside the silence there waited a sound, but nothing stirred in the darkness, for that which was the darkness and the silence had not yet woken. Nothing felt the vast breath of the void.

Air moved in darkness.

Eons came and went.

At last, the first sound broke the silence. Rhythmic and insistent, charged and vital. Every corner was filled with awe and comfort, comfort and awe.

But there were no cats yet to know the glory that was the first purr.

Breath braided now like rivers; warmer, faster, warmer and faster. Something stirred, as from a deep sleep. Two vast shafts of light illuminated the void. One shaft was of silver, the other of gold. At the center of each lay a vast circle of dark. This is how light spilled into the world—with darkness at its heart—and the world was light; and a great sigh hung in the air of the world.

The Cat of the World, the Great Cat, had woken to Herself.

Now She blinks her eyes—darkness and void for an instant!—and when they open again, motes dance in the gold and silver beams, motes whirl and leap and grow and differentiate themselves. They come together, they break apart, they dance the dance of life. Motes spiral and swim and spin to the rumble and spark of the endless purr—a bright tapestry of movement—a retinal measure, a tapetum lucidum of created things.

Birds soared in the Great Cat's eyes; fish swam, and insects swarmed. Mice and rabbits bolted and scurried toward the light. Out they leapt! Out leapt the frog with its slick and virid skin. Out leapt the magpie, cawing and croaking. Out leapt the bank vole and stopped to groom its whiskers. Out leapt fleas and fledglings, hedge mice and velvet moles. Out leapt tufted duck and corncrake, shrike and shrew and stoat! Down they tumbled, into the fur of the Great Cat. And behind them came the Felidae, already hunting.

In the pupil of the gold eye burned two sudden green, determined specks. A blunt, proud head and a shaggy ruff pushed out, then in a rush the paws and talons of a brand-new trade, and at last the plumed tail. Down it jumped with a flicker of feet and a back arched like a question mark, its striped coat gleaming in the golden light. The First Male!

Partridge and rabbits scattered before him, but he hunted them among the fur of the Great Cat, and his pursuit was unrelenting.

Now the First Female glints in the Great Cat's silver eye! Fluid as water, strong as the tide, a rosy sorrel coat and pointed ears to lengthen the fine lines of her head, she leaps down. Head on this side, head on that, face as sharp as iron, delicate as a shell, she looks around. Morning! Things are good!

Fish cascade out in front of her as bright as the brand-new light. Off she dances to fish her way down the Great Cat's fur, down the shoulder, over the flanks, and far away.

The First Female!

She catches a salmon to take to him.

He catches a hare to take to her.

What those two did when they met is another story!

So the torrent of life flooded down the coat of the Great Cat, and She approved of what She saw. She was as content with Her predators—Felidae without parallel or peril—as with their prey. Each kept to its own sphere; all would breed and thrive and take their proper place.

At last, the tapetum lucidum was quiet, and light poured forth once more—warm and refulgent, cool and healing—and as the light in the world intensified, so the Great Cat's pupils

contracted and shrank. Just as it seemed they would close for-
ever, new shapes appeared from the darkness.

They walked on two legs; they were pale and furless. They
shrank from the world outside, but they were too dissatisfied to
stay where they belonged. Out they squeezed, into the light. To
them, the Great Cat's body was hill and mountain, jungle and
forest, strand and ocean, while Her gold and silver eyes shone
irretrievably as sun and moon. There was no dance for them.
They fled down Her foreleg in terror, to shelter from the gaze
that made them. At last Her paws reared above them, and there
at the base they took up lodging in the deepest of caves.

That was how human beings made their way into the World
of the Cat: unbidden and out of darkness, the last things that
God made. And that is how they live today, dissatisfied with one
world and frightened of the other, wary and watchful of the life
that surrounds them.

Chapter Three
THE WILD AND THE TAME

A cat may look at a queen.
— PROVERB

*F*inding the King and Queen, Tag realized, was going to be easier said than done.

They were cats, he supposed; but he had no idea who they were, what they looked like, or where the search should begin. He had frightened the magpie off, so there was no help there. The fox was long gone, pursuing its own foxy business. There was no clue in his recent dreams of the Majicou; and all that remained of the earlier ones was a dim cobwebby voice whispering, "Tintagel."

Well then, he thought, perhaps Tintagel is a place, and I'll find them there.

It would do to be going on with.

He had a last good look at the discarded collar, to remind himself what a genuine desperado he was. Then he turned his face to the world.

The world turned out to be a maze.

Chestnut trees and dappled wintry sunshine gave way to busy streets and rank air. He stood uncertainly at an intersection, a little light-headed from hunger, used to the stillness of the gardens; and everywhere he looked, something was going on. Lights flashed red and green, dust rose, discarded rubbish bowled along, and the huge objects the fox had called "cars" went grinding to and fro, filthy with smoke. There was no rest for the eyes. The smells ran together into one thick, pulpy reek, like wet cardboard forced over his nose. The noise was extraordinary: shouts, shrieks, roars, clangs, peeps, and warbles—a cacophony of information that made his head hurt. "I'm not sure I like this," he told himself. He scampered across the pavement and into a front garden gateway; he stared out. How could any animal learn to manage this? Every time he poked his nose out, another lot of human beings clumped past inches from it, great dull heavily wrapped animals jostling and coughing angrily along on enormous feet, barely aware of one another, let alone anything that might be going on below their eye level. His heart raced and fluttered. He was afraid for his paws. He was afraid for his tail. They would tread on anything and grind it to pulp. They would *never know*.

Eventually, he gave up on the street. The front gardens here were often no more than bare concrete squares rank with fumes, piled with fat black dustbin sacks, but they were safe. Tag jumped walls, ran along under windows, crouched beneath littered laurel hedges. At the end of each row of houses, the gardens ran out and he was forced to cross a side road. *Cars!* he remembered the fox claiming dismissively. *They can't kill you if you're quick.* But Tag always waited until things seemed quiet before he put his ears back and made a dash for it.

It was the most tiring way to travel. By noon, he had managed perhaps a mile. The sun went in, and it began to rain. He hadn't eaten since the night before. Huddled between some dustbins in a side passage, he fell into a light doze. When he woke, it was dark. He waited until the gabble of voices and the roar of machinery had died down, then began to walk again.

Over the next few days he made his way across the city, in a series of random curves and excursions. He tried to dream of Majicou, but his sleep was untroubled. He kept an eye open for fox and magpie; he never saw them. Every time he came across another cat, he inquired, "Tintagel? Do you know Tintagel—?"

Few replied. They had lives to live. Like the cats he had known—or, rather, avoided—when he lived in the gardens, most of them were shy and furtive. The rest were toms: hard-favored and spectacularly muscled, scarred about the face from their Olympian turf wars and sexual encounters, they were proud, high-profiled, and short-lived. All he could expect as he navigated their richly scented territorial map was a steady glare, a snarl, and a contemptuous, "Get out of here, mate."

"Or the King and the Queen?"

"I'm the king, mate. Get out of it while you can still walk."

So he took the hint and walked. Days and nights went past. It rained, and then rain changed to soft wet flakes of snow that melted as soon as they touched the ground. The partly familiar terrain—houses and gardens, neutral zones, and tribal turfs—gave way to bleak hinterlands of concrete, lighted at night by glaring greenish lamps that seemed to hang in the air without visible support. Buildings towered up; roads grew wider and wider. The danger here came not from patrolling toms, but from the great articulated machines that roared and rumbled all night long behind tall chain-link fences. He stopped and watched. He saw how human beings climbed up into them and forced them to go. He wondered if the fox knew that. They jerked and hissed impatiently as they were maneuvered to and fro; then, once out on the roads, thundered past, dwarfing cars and cats alike, spraying up filthy water as if to mark their territories.

His feet were sore. He was always hungry. If the main roads were untenable, even the lesser streets made him feel exposed. His shadow, thrown against a billboard, grew huge; but he felt smaller than ever. He learned to creep along the top of a wall; remain still for a long time in the shadow of a hedge.

Animal highways ran everywhere—down an empty alley here, around a secret sunny corner there, across wasteland choked with elder and bramble—everywhere that was private or hidden. But Tag remembered his last attempt to use one and how only the fox's kind heart had saved him. He couldn't count on the same help twice. So though he sometimes stood on the edge of one and watched for ten minutes or so—rocking back and forth between his desire to join the flow and his fear of the consequences—he never used them. He stuck to gardens whenever he could. This rule meant he could dine off scraps thrown out for the birds, half a saucer of food someone had left on the doorstep for a pet, and the inevitable snails. On the other hand, he found the toms there aggressive and hard to avoid. And the going tended to be slow—the houses were often small and crammed together, which meant more garden fences to climb. The gardens themselves were nothing much. Bleak turf and broken bicycles. One wet night, pausing between two metal bollards at the mouth of a rain-polished alley, Tag watched a dozen feral cats rip open a bin bag. They pulled its contents savagely about in the raw orange light.

Bacon rinds! thought Tag.

Then, seeing how they fought in the long black shadows, "Never." He promised himself, "Never that."

By now, he looked like a cat who had been on the run for days. His eyes, huge in his dirty face, were needy and no longer quite so optimistic. His fur was unkempt, always damp. He was emaciated. He slept in holes and under piles of things, and he never got warm. He felt strange without the collar. He would forget for an hour or two that he had got rid of it, then shiver delightedly, feeling elated and free. Or with a sense of utter terror realize he had lost everything worth having in life. Care. Comfort. Above all a home.

It was a big city. Tag made his way through one district after another. He learned all about cars—or thought he did. He grew used to the noise, the constant change, the constant fear. Finally he fetched up at the Caribbean Road—which he crossed by means of a seeping, tiled underpass—and Mayflower Docks. And that was where, toward the end of one dismal, soaking-wet day, he found himself on a busy street, crouched out of the way of human shoes, gazing across at a cardboard box someone had thrown carelessly into a doorway. He knew there was another cat living in it. For that reason alone he would find it hard to approach. In addition, he was afraid to cross the road, which was packed tight with cars and other vehicles. But it had been a bad afternoon. There had been snow in the rain again. Two children had first cooed at him, then tried to cram him into a plastic bag. Now he was sick with hunger and so wet he was frightened of what might happen to him if he didn't find shelter.

So he waited another minute, then, before he could argue with himself any further, dodged out into the greasy road. Around the back of one machine, between the wheels of another.

Straight in front of the next. *They can't kill you if you're quick!*—But this one was bearing down on him with incredible speed and violence! Tag dithered. Could he go back? Too late! He was already inside its envelope of hot reeking air. He couldn't think what to do—

The car shrieked and stopped.

Tag stopped.

Cat and driver stared helplessly at one another. Then horns blared, lights flickered, and Tag was off again. White faces, blurred screens, wipers bang-banging, engines racing. Tag's heart raced too. His back legs skidded and pumped like a hare's in the half dark. Fumes choked him. He streaked across the glassy pavement. He was so stuffed with panic and madness he had sprung into the cardboard box before he knew it.

"Look," he panted. "I won't hurt you if you won't hurt me."

The occupant of the box stared at him. It blinked. Its eyes were so milky with age it could barely tell he was another cat. "Doubt if I could harm a kitten at present," it admitted thoughtfully. "So you might as well come in."

"Oh," said Tag.

The old cat had once been a fine tabby male, with neat little white paws and a broad black central stripe that whirled down his sides into complex, glossy patterns. Now great patches of his fur were missing. The bare skin revealed was creased, dirty, and patched with eczema. Two marks like the tracks of tears ran down the side of his nose. He shivered and sneezed, and huddled away from Tag in the driest corner of the box. He smelled, quite strongly. Every so often he said something like, "Wet old day, then."

To which Tag could reply only, "It certainly is."

"Wet old day."

They sat like that for twenty minutes or so. Then—smell or no smell—Tag found himself edging closer. The cardboard box wasn't quite as dry as it seemed, especially toward the front where rain had been splashing in all afternoon. He was freezing cold, and he felt as if he would never be dry again. The winter had worked its way through to his skin and settled in there to leech all the warmth and joy out of him. He missed his collar now. He missed the dulls, about whom his memory was confused. He missed their food, which he remembered with a distinctness bordering on the hallucinatory.

"Ever eaten crumpets?" he asked the old cat. "You have them with butter." Then he suggested, "We'd be warmer if we curled up together."

"It's all the same to me. You're soaked and I'm bald. Bugger all warmth to be had out of that." After delivering himself of this wisdom, the old tabby was silent for a long time. Then he said, "Trumpets I know nothing about. But butter. Well that's another thing."

"What?"

"Butter's another thing altogether."

Tag spent the night in the cardboard box. A hundred yards up the road there was an enormous rectangular hole with an illuminated sign above it and railed steps leading down into some echoing, brightly lit subterranean interior. Human beings trudged endlessly up and down the steps, bumping into one another, looking weary and annoyed. Every so often, something massive shifted in the hole and made the ground rumble. A faint, eerie vibration filled the cardboard box, traveling up through Tag's bones and into his skull, where it displaced every thought he had. He tried to take his cue from the old cat. He watched him anxiously—should they abandon the box?—but he seemed unperturbed. Things were easier once night had fallen, and human activity subsided. He licked himself for an hour until he felt cleaner, if not dry. He tried to keep up a conversation with the old cat. He was asleep or drowsing most of the time, farting uncomfortably to himself, his paws tucked up in the sticky fur of his chest. Tag talked anyway. He told the old cat about the cloth mouse he had once owned. He gave him a broad picture of his dulls and their house. He described at length the meals they had served him. At this the old cat showed some interest, and would often repeat in a ruminative way the things Tag said.

"Mashed sardines, eh?" Or, "Pilchards, now. Seen a few of those in my time. Be lying if I said I hadn't. Pilchards, eh? Oh yes."

"Well, my dulls were always pretty generous with stuff like

that," Tag boasted. Then, "I'm looking for the King and Queen of Cats. Do you know them?"

A variety of indecipherable expressions passed across the old vagrant's face. Then he sat upright, cocked one leg in the air, and began to lick quite energetically at his scabby bottom. "Oh yes," he wheezed at last.

Tag waited expectantly.

"Know 'em well. Lovely they are, gold collars and all. Fat as butter. The *meals* I've had with that pair! Pilchards? Nothing to the food I've et round their place. King and Queen of Cats? Oh yes. You name it, they'll have it warmed up and served to you. Lovely." And he licked his cracked old lips in reminiscence.

Tag was delighted. "Where can I find them?" he asked. "It's so important—!"

"Be round shortly, I'd say. Often hang out with Manky Jack here." The old cat gave a raffish wink. "Manky Jack: that's what *she* calls me. And where'll you find the King and Queen of Cats?" he asked him. "Why, up your own arse, most like." He snorted. "You must be on one, laddie. Do I look as if I'd know any Royals?" He paused for a moment, seeking the perfect phrase. "Laddie," he condemned him finally, "you're still wet behind the ears." He nodded with satisfaction, closed his eyes, and crouched down on bony haunches. "King and Queen of Cats?" he added gently. "Be sensible."

"Oh," said Tag.

He allowed a few minutes for this information to seep into his brain like cold sleet through a fur coat. "How about Tintagel?" he said, examining the scarred old face and watery eyes for a further outbreak of irony.

None was forthcoming. Instead, at the word *Tintagel*, the old cat's ears pricked up, and a great alertness came over him. "That's Tintagel *Court*, laddie," he said, in his faded, papery voice. He thought for a moment. "Tintagel Court?" he asked himself. "Oh, I know Tintagel Court all right!" He gave a cheerful laugh. "Had many a good time there until I got too old. Oh yes. That's a fine place for a young cat that can turn over a dustbin, Tintagel Court."

Dustbin? thought Tag.

In his dreams *Tintagel* was clearly associated with waves breaking at the foot of steep cliffs, a blustery wind, a headland above the sea. There had been no dustbins.

"I don't think that can be right."

"Which of us has been there, laddie?" the old cat demanded angrily. "Tell me that!"

Tag couldn't argue with him.

"Is it close? And can you tell me how to get there?"

The old cat could. "You'll find some dustbins around there!" he promised. He laughed again. "Oh yes."

"Why don't you come with me!" suggested Tag.

But the old cat only stared at him emptily. "I don't think so, laddie," he said.

After that, Tag slept a little. Soon, it was dawn. The rain had eased. Tag woke from a light as whispery as the old cat's voice, revealing the walls of the cardboard box heavy and soft with water. The streets and buildings eased out of darkness, a yellowish-gray color, slicked with freezing rain. Even the air was a yellowish gray. Tag saw that if he had walked a little way farther, he would have been able to sleep in the dry, under the arches of a bridge. He turned to tell the old cat this. But he had slipped away while Tag was asleep, and the box was empty.

The old cat's directions had amounted in the end to little more than "You follow your nose, laddie."

"Pardon?"

"Follow your nose. That's what cats do."

And when Tag had asked, "You couldn't be more specific?" he had only sneezed, turned his head away, and accused, "Which of us has been there, laddie? Eh? Tell me that!"

Tintagel Court—an extensive low-rise development that had once enclosed half an acre of lawns—lay stunned between the Caribbean Road and the river. Built out of dull brown brick, it was no more than fifteen years old and already abandoned. Confused and directionless, a human family or two still huddled behind the intact windows. The rest of the flats were boarded

up. Mornings, the courtyard seemed to echo faintly the groan
and thud of distant traffic. The rest of the day it kept a strange
rainy silence. It was entered by a wide single arch from Tintagel
Street. The lawns had long been trodden to hard black earth.
Three tall Norway maples remained, and around their scarred
trunks the real life of the court now went on.

Cats were everywhere. The dark, empty flats were alive
with them.

They crouched skinny and hot-eyed, hungry and full of rage,
all facing in different directions as if they couldn't bear to look
at one another. By day they scavenged the nearby streets. After
dark they patrolled the ramps and walkways. From a community of mislaid souls—nonjudgmental, loosely knit, maintained
without visible consensus—a handful of rag-eared toms commanded what was at best a nominal fealty. Tooley, the Big Gib,
Septum, and the rest cared less about society than sex; their disputes were as princely as their coats, and fights only broke out
between them when one of the less scabrous females came into
heat. Midnight on some concrete walkway in the sky: snarls
and wails echoed out over the courtyard, followed by a prolonged hiss and hasty scuffle as tonight's loser made another
dignified exit. Maculate toms and their glamorous queens! The
outfall of their liaisons fizzed and tumbled everywhere, such
quaint scrawny little kittens, nipping at one another with
predatory milk teeth, pouncing silently—leaping back in mock
fear—collapsing in heaps of multicolored fur to wheeze and
dream until hunger, itchy ears, and runny noses woke them up
again.

Despite the old cat's memories, life wasn't good in the bar-
rens of Tintagel Court. None of those cats had enough to eat.

They were used to it. Few of them were strays, in any mean-
ingful sense of that word; they were feral. To those who had
ever had a home, home was long ago and far away; by now they
had given up on that whole idea. The rest had never had an idea
to give up on. But among them at that time you could find two
cats who *had* strayed, and knew it. Their eyes were huge with
shock. They jumped at every sound. They had the air of being
marooned among tribes. They lived in an unlit corner far from

the fights and noise, kept themselves to themselves, and stayed as close to one another as they could, especially at night.

At night, something very strange indeed was going on in Tintagel Court.

When he poked his head around the corner of the arch and looked in, Tag knew none of this.

Clearly, though, he was in the wrong place.

He scanned the concrete walkways looming above him. He sniffed disgustedly the thin, subtle smell of feline misery, the rank ashes and human rubbish in the corners, the soft dead leaves of the Norway maples like gray fingers rotting down in heaps. By the time he got there, the sky had a strange dull pewter sheen above the river, and the wind had moved into the north. Cold air sat like a sheet of dirty glass over it all, and through it fell a few dry flakes of snow. The court was empty of any worthwhile kind of life. No King and Queen would ever live here. Better not stay. Better try and find the Tintagel of his dreams.

Yet as he turned to leave he heard a noise from above.

Something was moving up there.

"Hello?" called Tag. He thought, Now that was stupid.

Before he could check himself, he had said it again. "Hello?"

A faint echo. No answer. Then a kind of muffled dragging sound.

"I'm coming up," called Tag. He thought, What do you mean? No you're not.

Too late.

His feet had found a staircase. Enclosed and smelly, littered with plastic bags full of hardened glue, it was under an inch of dirty old rainwater. On every landing Tag had to pick his way gingerly between piles of sodden newspaper. As he neared the top, he heard movement again, less furtive this time. Then an outbreak of yowling and spitting. Half a dozen cats were up there, maybe more. Run away, Tag thought. Run away now. Instead, flattening himself carefully so as to remain unseen, he stuck his head over the final step. This action put his eyes at the level of a walkway that stretched away from him in bleak, puddled perspective, lined with boarded-up doors and windows. About halfway along it, a very large black cat had got itself surrounded by some other cats and was now spitting and bubbling defiantly if rather helplessly at a closing circle of enemies. They were led by a stocky, one-eared marmalade tom. Every so often, this animal would inch forward stiffly, head down, fur abristle, and unsheath a pawful of razors honed to a gleam. At this, the rest would close in too. The black cat didn't seem to know what to do. It had eyes the brightest green Tag had ever seen. It had a tangled leonine ruff of immensely long fur.

It appeared to be sitting on a purple velvet cushion.

"Waugh," said Tag quietly to himself.

Not quietly enough. Every eye turned his way. Everyone's concentration broke. The black cat made a dash for it, then changed his mind and went back for the cushion. It was instantly set upon by the tom and two others. The rest of them came down on Tag with a sound like a cold wind in December.

Tag, who had planned to retreat if this happened, found his legs urging him forward instead. His fur stood on end all down his back. His lips peeled back from his teeth. Strident sounds came out his mouth. He looked spiny, twice his actual size, and completely mad. In that moment he was so angry he had no idea who he was. At the same time, he knew he was Tag. He was *TAG*! He leapt the top step with a foot to spare and met the first of them while he was still in flight. It was like running into a brick wall. The breath went out of him with a gasp. He was bowled over. He clutched his assailant tight in both arms, buried his teeth in its neck, and slashed rapidly with his back claws at what he hoped was its belly.

"Tag," he told it. "I'm Tag, I'm Tag, I'm *Tag*!"

"So what?" it said.

Something dragged down his cheek like hot wire. Teeth met in the muscles of his upper shoulder. Foul breath was in his face. For an instant he was looking straight into the flecked amber eyes and scarred features of some flat-faced fighter half his size. Then he had bitten its underlip apart just behind the chin, and with a howl it was gone, only to be replaced by another.

How long did this go on? Seconds. It felt like forever, but it lasted seconds.

Suddenly, everything had slowed down again. Tag found himself crouched in the center of the ring with the black cat. He was out of breath. There was fur all over the serviceway. In front of Tag stood the marmalade tom. It didn't even look angry. And it wasn't breathing hard at all.

"Oh dear me," it said. "Beginners."

It raised a front paw and studied its own claws, which seemed to have become clogged with black fur. Behind it, from the staircases at each end, more and more cats were slipping down the serviceway. They hadn't come to watch.

"I think we've had it," Tag told the black cat.

"I think you have," agreed the marmalade tom.

Tag launched himself at its face. It welcomed him with a powerful embrace.

What could Tag do? Despite his poor condition, he was a well-grown young cat: long and lithe, muscular. He was brave enough. But he lacked experience. And perhaps more important, he was just too good-natured. As a result the marmalade tom soon had him by the throat. However much he writhed and squawled, he couldn't escape. Neither could he reach anything worth biting. Scrabbling with his back legs, he got a good one into the tom's eye, but he only clamped his teeth tighter and said in a muffled but amused voice, "Tell me about it."

Strangled twice in a week, thought Tag, as things started to turn black. Not so clever. At this point something strange happened.

A large black-and-white object, traveling fast, crashed into the ribs of the marmalade tom. Winded, the tom let go of Tag's neck. Tag fell back, trying to focus. Whatever had arrived was angry and covered in feathers. He was anxious not to be in its way. Thrashing and squawking as if in its fury it had lost command of its own nervous system, it set about the tomcat's companions, beating black wings in their astonished faces, stabbing at them with its big black beak.

Unnerved, they turned and ran.

"And don't come back!" called the enraged bird. Then it spoke to Tag. "Well?" it demanded.

It was the magpie known as One for Sorrow.

Tag stared up and down the serviceway. Empty, but for the big black cat. Without stopping to thank anyone, this animal had straddled the purple velvet cushion like a leopard its kill and was now dragging it awkwardly away. Feathers, mixed up with bloodied fur, floated about its head in the cold wind. It vanished around a corner. Tag blinked. He shook his head. His vision was still poor. His face was stiff with a dozen cuts.

"Well?" repeated One for Sorrow. "What are you waiting for, little cat?"

"I—"

"Go on, before they come back!"

"Thank you."

"Thank you?" said One for Sorrow. He cocked his head in disgust. *"Thank you!"* he said savagely. "Oh, they all say that." He hopped up on the guardrail and began to preen. His disarrayed feathers glimmered like metal in the bitter light. "They all say *that*."

"Look," apologized Tag, "I'm sorry. But I've got to go and talk to that cat." He ran a few groggy steps, turned back. "Will you wait here for me?" he said. "How are the gardens? I'm glad I didn't eat you."

"Charmed, I'm sure."

"Stop!" called Tag to the black cat. "Stop! I won't hurt you!"

A few minutes later, still encumbered by the purple velvet cushion, the black cat halted outside a boarded-up flat somewhere in the maze of Tintagel Court. It looked carefully up and down the walkway, then backed into a hole in the front door, hauling the cushion in after it. The cushion wedged briefly. There was a ragging sound, and after a moment it popped through. The black cat's head appeared, and it checked the walkway once more before withdrawing.

Tag watched. When nothing else had happened for some time, he approached the hole.

It was dim inside. He couldn't see much, and what he could see was intensely squalid: ripped linoleum and broken furniture, wallpaper smeared with filth and graffiti, all decaying in a light that wouldn't change much from night to day. The corners were littered. The whole place reeked. The front door, in the days when it still worked, had opened directly onto the kitchen, from which a short passage led via a glass door into the front room. There, sprawled across two or three sheets of yellowing newspaper in a single ray of wan light, was the most beautiful cat Tag had ever seen. She was perhaps a year old, and the fur lay on her long curved bones like softly flecked rose-gray velvet. When he looked closer he could see the faintest of brown stripes, like a watermark. Her ears, tall and elegant, extended in a medium as translucent as porcelain the sharp, triangular lines of her tiny head. Her feet were the most delicate feet he had ever seen on a cat. And her eyes! Had they been properly open, those eyes would have transfixed him forever. But something was wrong with her, and they were filmed, lidded, unaware. Her breath came too fast and noisy in the silent room. Tag could see every rib. And her face—as accurate as the head of an axe, the face of an ancient feline carved in stone—had the blind, weary expression of a week-old kitten.

Standing over her, looking lost and puzzled in that filthy place, was the black cat. It had dragged the purple cushion as far as the edge of the newspaper, then given up the struggle. When it saw Tag, its great ruff bristled. It drew itself up in readiness. Then it recognized him and sat down tiredly.

"So. You see," it admitted, in a soft, foreign voice. "We need help."

"That's clear," said Tag.

"I watched you fight. You are of very strong character, I believe."

"I don't know about that," said Tag. "A fox once called me a tearaway, but I think now that he was joking."

"Even so."

Carefully, so as not to frighten her—so slowly and carefully he might have been stalking a mouse—Tag approached the cat on the newspaper. Some fever dream caused her to shift rest-lessly, and he was prompted to lick her worn face. He had no idea why. Only that his heart would break to see her like that and not do anything at all. She was hot. Her dreams were burning her from inside. He heard from her a faint trembling purr. But her eyes registered nothing. Milky and opaque, they lent that face such an air of intelligence and pain! It was as if she knew something about life Tag couldn't know, and she could protect him from that knowledge only as long as he could pro-tect her from the world.

"What do you call her?"

"Her name is Pertelot Fitzwilliam," said the black cat. "I have been trying to get her to sit on this cushion. It would be nicer for her."

Tag was horrified. "Nicer? Are you an idiot? She's ill!"

"I know this," said the black cat.

"She's ill," Tag repeated. "Is this the best you can do? If it is, I should have left you to that lot out there!" After a moment he inquired, "And what do they call you? Prince Stupid?"

The black cat drew himself up. "I am Ragnar Gustaffson Coeur de Lion."

Tag thought about biting him.

"She's ill," he tried to explain. "And you bring her a cushion to sit on."

"She would be more comfortable."

"When did she last *eat*?"

"I am sorry," said Ragnar. "We aren't good at these things, she and I." He stared around, puzzled, disgusted, defeated. "How do you live out here in the world? Who brings you your food? We ran away from a cat show to be together. We had no idea it would be like this."

Hearing him, Pertelot Fitzwilliam shivered suddenly in her ray of light.

"Raggy," she whispered, "they mustn't find us," and was silent again.

"We can't have this," said Tag.

"Just so. You can help?"

"I don't know. I'll do what I can." Ragnar made Tag feel

competent. But he knew he wasn't. He had no idea what a *cat show* was; and when he stared around that dismal room with its sweetish smells of illness and rubbish, a kind of exhaustion overcame him. "Some days," he was forced to admit, "I can barely take care of myself, let alone anyone else. Still." He gave Ragnar a look he hoped was determined. "Who *are* you, the pair of you?" he said. And before the black cat could answer, "Never mind. Whoever you are, you can't go on living here."

"Look for yourself, my friend. It isn't so easy for her to move."

"Both of you need to eat," said Tag decisively.

He had intended to ask the magpie for help. By the time he found his way back to the right walkway, however, One for Sorrow had flown. Tag jumped up on the guardrail and teetered there, craning his neck. A single speck hung in the air, high up; but it could have been any bird. So he decided to go and look for food on his own.

"You'll find some dustbins around there!" he remembered the old cat saying. And indeed the streets of occupied houses surrounding the court were full of them. Unfortunately, though, they had all been visited already. Some expert had surgically entered each black plastic bag, then pulled out its contents for investigation. All that was left was the smell. Working his way out in a widening spiral from the court, Tag wasted the afternoon sniffing things that would make a cat gag. Then, finding himself at the river, he averted his face from the biting wind and turned to follow the setting sun.

That was how he ended up three or four hours later in a narrow cobbled passage. It was dark. The wind was cruel. Tag was completely lost. From one end of the passage, he could see a wide wet street, shop windows, the wavery reflections of lights changing from green to orange and red. At the other end, the night. And—running purposefully up from the slaty chill of the river toward the tree-lined graveyard of All Saints Church—a highway. He could see it rather like a plastic tube of movement, a discomfiting smoky blur of life. He had been sitting by it for fifteen or twenty minutes, trying to make himself step in. Perhaps it would be warm in there. It might lead him back to Tintagel Court. On it, he might find something he could take back to Pertelot and Ragnar.

On the other hand, he thought, nothing like that happened last time. Last time, all I got was hurt.

He was still weighing these things up when, out of the corner of his eye, he saw a fox trot past the other end of the alley. It was a young, well-set-up animal, long-backed, reddish, brindling toward its hindquarters and long tail, exuding a fine strong reek of fox. Tag thought he recognized it. He rushed to the end of the alley.

"Hey!"

The fox stopped halfway across the street. It looked back. Its mouth was stuffed with half a cooked chicken coated lovingly with charred orange spices and issuing to the windy night a powerful smell of tandoori. This it dropped, so as to be able to speak.

"Go away, Tag," it said.

"You remembered my name."

"I'm a fox."

"But you never told me yours."

"What use would a cat have for a fox's name? Go away now. This is an open place. It isn't wise to talk in an open place."

"I took your advice," said Tag.

"Good. Now take it again."

"What *is* your name?"

The fox looked proud and embarrassed at the same time.

"Loves a Dustbin."

Tag laughed. "Everyone loves a dustbin," he said.

Then he said, "Is that a chicken?"

"Nearly."

The smell of the chicken had made Tag drool a little. He swallowed. "Where did you get it?"

"This is my chicken," said Loves a Dustbin.

"But you got it somewhere."

Loves a Dustbin grinned. "Down the road," he said. "Bengali takeaway on Arbor Street. Nipped in there, made my choice, had it away on my feet. Simple."

"Clever technique," said Tag. "I want that chicken."

"This is my chicken."

"A fox like you can find a chicken anywhere."

The fox looked pleased. "True," he admitted.

"Then give me that one."

The fox put his head on one side. "No," he said. Then, "Why?"

"I need it for someone else," said Tag. "I've just rescued two cats. One of them isn't well. The other's an idiot."

"So am I," said Loves a Dustbin.

He scanned the empty street warily, as if to make sure no other fox was watching, then picked up the chicken and dropped it at Tag's feet. "Cats!" he said. "Cats are always out of it. Right out of it." He said, "I don't know why I like you. I must be out of it too." He trotted off in the direction he had come from. "Never tell anyone I gave you that," he said over his shoulder.

"Wait!" called Tag.

"What now?"

"I don't know how to get back to Tintagel Court."

The fox sighed. "I'll come with you as far as Tintagel Street. You're not fit to be allowed out."

Tag was delighted.

He picked up the chicken. It was heavy. It was still warm from the oven.

After a few minutes of companionable walking, he looked up at his friend and said around the chicken, "It's hard for me not to eat this. Was it hard for you?"

The fox would not go into Tintagel Court.

"I'm off," he said quietly, and slipped into the shadows. "I hate this place. There's something wrong here."

"Will I see you again?" called Tag.

"Not if I see you first."

"Good-bye."

"Be careful, Tag."

"I will," said Tag.

Only then did he realize that they had not spoken a word about Majicou.

"Wait! The black cat! I—"

But the fox had vanished. Tag, whose jaws had gotten quite tired, picked up the chicken for the last time and fled around the edge of the court. His shadow was thrown briefly onto the walls, but no one noticed it. Up the stairs he went, careful not to drop his prize. He crept along the walkways, freezing at the slightest sound. When he arrived, both the other cats were asleep in the moonlight that seeped between the window boards. Ragnar had dragged the purple cushion onto the newspaper, and now lay curved so that Pertelot was safe between him and it. Tag, who had expected them to be waiting for him, was disappointed.

"Wake up!" he said.

Two bright green eyes snapped open, there was a quick hiss, and suddenly Ragnar was in Tag's face, teeth bared. At that distance, he looked less of an idiot.

"It's me!" said Tag. "Food!"

"You should be more careful," Ragnar said. "That is my advice to you."

"I'll remember."

"To shout is not always good. You see?"

"I see that, yes."

"So that is my advice to you, to be careful not to shout—"

"Shut up, Ragnar."

Pertelot could eat nothing at first, though they shredded the chicken very fine. But they managed to get her to take some of the juices. She licked feebly at what they offered and fell asleep again immediately. Sleeping in snatches, turn and turn about, they watched her until near dawn, when she woke up without warning and began to eat ravenously.

Shortly afterward she was as sick as a kitten. But she had kept some of it down; and by the time the dim gray daylight had filtered in, she was awake and able to speak. Properly open, her eyes were revealed to be almond-shaped and green. A pale and elusive green one moment, Nile-green the next—the green of water pouring into some sacred vessel, lit from within by its own life-giving power. On her forehead she carried a strange mark. She stared from Ragnar to Tag in a kind of delighted wonder.

"Who is he, Raggy?"

"As you see, he is a cat," said Ragnar.

"Did he bring this food?"

"He did."

"You're so beautiful!" she said to Tag. "What do they call you?"

Tag drew himself up.

"I shall call you Mercury," she said, before he could speak, "because of your color. I shall call you Mercury."

"I'd rather you called me Tag."

Chapter Four

FERAL LIFE

*There is some truth to the assertion that the cat,
with the exception of a few luxury breeds . . . is
no domestic animal but a completely wild being.*
—KONRAD LORENZ

$\mathcal{P}$ertelot Fitzwilliam was asleep again.

Tag and Ragnar measured each other silently in the growing daylight. Tag saw a large, squarish cat as big as a fox, robust and muscular, with sturdy legs almost hidden by a long black winter coat. Ragnar's nose was long and wide, and in profile resembled the nose guard of a Norman helmet. Electric eyes, upright bearing, flowing tail, and prominent whiskers. An impressive animal.

"So. You rescue us," he said at last. "Now I might ask, What kind of cat are you?"

"Just a cat," said Tag.

Ragnar tilted his head to one side. "Not just any cat," he said, "I think."

There was a friendly pause while Tag absorbed this compliment. "Thank you," he said at last. Politeness made him add, "What kind of cat are you?"

Ragnar nodded formally, as if he had been waiting for just this question. "Pleased to meet you. Norwegian Forest cat. Grand Champion Ragnar Gustaffson Coeur de Lion. This breed—do you see? It is a Viking cat, the *Norsk Skogkatt!*—must be big. I am very big. Seventeen pounds show weight. And the profuse neck ruff? Oh yes, this is important for a career on the show bench. And to be very straight up. Very square." He demonstrated. "Large paws with heavy pads. And we have the double coat for warmth and waterproofing. Very oily guard hairs. Very rugged and hardy, dries out in fifteen minutes. Although," he was forced to admit, "we spend most of our time in houses."

Tag thought for a moment. "I'm afraid I don't know what a cat show is."

Astonished by this ignorance, and shouldering it as a burden of his own, Ragnar Gustaffson Coeur de Lion was unsure how to proceed. "Well then," he kept repeating puzzledly. "Well then." He busied himself with Pertelot's cushion and news-papers. After a good deal of tugging and scraping, sure that she remained comfortable and there was nothing more to be done, he announced, "I suppose I must be explaining even now."

"I suppose you must," said Tag.

It took some time, and much of Ragnar's explanation had itself to be explained, but in the end Tag was able to visualize the huge hall where a cat show was held, the batteries of fluo-rescent lamps above, the smell of human food, the dense air overheated to keep drafts off the hundreds of fragile animals in their display cages beneath. Cages! Well, he could easily imagine those, row upon row of them under the pitiless lights, separated by narrow concrete aisles packed with the human beings who moved to and fro with a kind of reverent bustle—that, at least, was how Ragnar put it—to take care of the cats inside. Like the pet shop cages, they were perfectly good—airy, clean, even comfortable—but, as he said to Rag-nar, "A cage is a cage is a cage, and you're better off outside one than in."

Harder to understand were the cats themselves.

Oh, he could imagine them, as beautiful and different and myriad as their names—Korat and Birman, Ragdoll and Snow-shoe and Russian Blue. Pewters and lilacs, longhaired and short, cobby or long boned, with eyes the color of glass or grass, eyes of colors to which he couldn't give a name. Striped cats, spangled cats, self-colors; cats, like the naked Sphinx, radical or bizarre. Cats enriched rather than bowed down by the weight of their own beauty and strangeness. He could see Ragnar and Pertelot there among their peers, standing tall on the show bench. What he couldn't understand was how they came to be there or why.

"It is to see who is the best," Ragnar tried to explain. "To understand this, we need go no further than ask ourselves, Who has the purest bloodline? Who has the perfect shape, the perfect conformation?"

"But *why*?"

"We are bred to do this. By our owners. By human beings."

Tag shook his head. "Bred by human beings?" he repeated incredulously.

Ragnar sighed. "I must assert, 'Human beings own cats, and that is the way of it.' "

"No one owns me," Tag told him.

And they left the subject there. Casting about for something else to say, Tag went on, "And Pertelot Fitzwilliam? What kind of cat is she?"

"Mau," said Ragnar.

"Pardon?"

"Champion Pertelot Fitzwilliam of Hi-Fashion," he recited, "first in class at many shows: *Egyptian Mau*. Excuse me. She is a very old kind of cat." It was a fact that didn't seem to cheer him. "Perhaps the oldest kind of all," he proposed. Then he sighed and added, "Also, she is now the most dangerous cat in the world."

That was hard to make anything of, so Tag ignored it politely. Instead he asked, "And the mark. The mark on her forehead?"

Ragnar was silent. A Scandinavian gloom descended on him, full of fog, ice, and long dark nights above the Arctic Circle. From out of it he explained at last, "It is the scarab. This is the image of—I can only ask, how to say this?—the *sacred beetle*, drawn by the Egyptian gods on the forehead of the first Mau. A pretty good story! you say. I say, This is the sign of the Mau."

"She's very beautiful, isn't she? That's the first thing you notice."

"I love her," said Ragnar.

After a time he went on, "But the human who bred her didn't want this. It had other plans for her. She and I, we have very pure, very ancient blood. The lines are not supposed to mix." He dipped his head shyly. "But we saw each other and we did not care about anyone else's plans. We wanted to be together." He looked down at the Mau. "I love her," he repeated simply.

At that, Pertelot Fitzwilliam awoke. She lifted her perfect

rose-gray head, blessed—and cursed too—by its sacred mark. "Or perhaps we were," she corrected him. "Perhaps we *were* meant to be together and that's what frightens them so. It frightens me sometimes." She sneezed. Then she said, "Oh, Rags, do you really?"

Rags! thought Tag. *Cat show!*

"Eat more chicken," he ordered.

Tag was a practical cat, a cat with a simple heart. Puzzled—if rather charmed—to find his life webbed so suddenly into the lives of others, he shelved his curiosity and followed his nose. He had promised to feed them, and now he had done that. He had promised to find them a better place to live, and now he would do that, too. Quick and clever, filled with energy, unafraid of the ferals, he ranged the cold acres of Tintagel Court seeking new accommodation.

He found it on the third afternoon.

The upper north side of the court, with its airy situation and extensive views across the river, had been the last to be abandoned. As a result, the flats along that side, especially those served by the very top walkway, were still intact. Doors lay unforced behind brand-new straw-colored chipboard. Windows remained unbroken. The whole floor seemed uninhabited and quiet. Even the air seemed fresher. The problem was how to gain entry. Tag marched up and down with his tail in the air, demanding, "Me in now!" Surprisingly, the doors held. He sat at the top of the stairs. He wrapped his tail around him. He looked down the walkway and pondered.

After a moment or two, he heard an irregular tapping sound. This he traced to a broken ventilator cover, opening and closing in the wind high up on a kitchen wall two or three flats along. It was a hinged metal grille not much bigger than his own head. An athletic cat, a cat of agility and power—a cat like himself—might reach it by a diagonal leap from the front room windowsill. Tag settled himself there at once and, at the first opportunity, jumped. The wind banged the ventilator shut, midleap. Down he fell, all the way to the concrete. No good! he thought. He had given his head a knock. He picked himself up.

Had anyone been watching? Too bad. He twisted around to lick briefly and energetically at a patch of fur on his back, then climbed onto the windowsill again. The pads of his front paws hurt.

He waited. He watched. He judged his moment and his jump. He thrust his head into the gap behind the grille and got his front paws over the edge. For thirty seconds he struggled on the lip like that. Then he fell off again.

Third time pays for all. The wind opened and closed the ventilator. Would it be blocked on the inside? Find out soon, thought Tag. He leapt, scrabbled, hung. He tucked up his back legs, scraped the brickwork until his claws caught on mortar, and began to haul himself through. His shoulders jammed. Half a cat was hanging out of the wall. The other half was stuffed inside a dusty hole, its head gargoyling over a deserted kitchen.

How undignified.

"Go forward," he instructed himself.

A wriggle, some desperate squirming, and he was in.

"*Yes!*" he congratulated himself.

He found the layout familiar. Kitchen, passage, front room. After that, nothing was the same. The kitchen was clean and cheerful, the glass connecting door unbroken. Best of all, perhaps, it was dry. Tag sat in the middle of the front room and purred. He had a wash. He viewed the rest of his acquisition. River light poured over him as he nudged open the bedroom door. Since not even a monkey could climb the featureless outer face of Tintagel Court, they had left the windows unboarded on that side. Tag blinked slowly. From the window he could see everything. The tide was in. Gulls banked and planed, white and graceful on a brisk wind, about the towers of a fantastic bridge—he called it that to himself the moment he saw it, the Fantastic Bridge. A big white machine chugged and bumbled along the river toward the heart of the city. You could stay here and watch all day. For a moment, Tag was as happy as he had been with his dulls. He imagined Pertelot Fitzwilliam, asleep in the water light. She was well again. Her delicate feet trembled in some perilous dream of "Egypt." Later she would wake and say, surprised all over again, "Tag, you're so beautiful!" And from his perch on the windowsill, Ragnar Gustaffson Coeur de Lion, who was keeping an eye on the gulls as they dipped and dived beneath the arches of the Fantastic Bridge, would have to agree.

We could live here until she's better, Tag thought. I could get food for all of us.

Fifteen minutes later a faulty ventilator grille popped open onto an empty concrete skyway somewhere in Tintagel Court. A minute after that, two paws and a small silver muzzle with faint gray tabby markings and a brick-pink nose squeezed themselves out into the windy afternoon. Tag jumped down with satisfying thuds, first to the windowsill and then to the ground. He looked one way and then the other.

The situation seemed ideal.

"But I'll be back," he promised.

At a different time of day, it might be another story.

A curious thing happened to him on the return journey. It was snowing again. Small hard flakes blew about the courtyard like sparks on a strong wind. The snow drifted stealthily into corners. It settled in the open stairwell landings, where it was received without enthusiasm or rancor. Passing quickly across one of these square bleak spaces in the growing dark, Tag noticed a disturbance of the air or, more properly, of the light. He stopped, puzzled. It was as if a wild road ran through the building itself and, exiting through the very brickwork, cut briefly and obliquely across the back of the landing. Flakes of snow drifted into the stairwell, trapped on slowly moving currents of cold air. As Tag watched, they were first attracted to, then repulsed by the strange smoky twist of light in the corner. The corner was breathing. Tag could hear it. Snowflakes went in and out. Then after a moment or two a small convulsion like a sneeze took place, a current of *warm* air passed across the landing, and everything returned to normal. Tag put his nose carefully into the corner and sniffed. Cat pee. Human pee. Well, that was normal. He sat for a bit, but nothing else happened, so he went home.

* * *

Pertelot Fitzwilliam ate. Ragnar ate. Tag ate. The chicken lasted
for three days. Then they were hungry again. A smell of tandoori issued faintly from the very walls. Bones were scattered
about the floor, brown with cooking, highly polished, of per-
plexing shape. Tag woke up, looked at Pertelot, saw how in the
dawn her fur turned from rose to taupe along a complex and re-
warding spectrum. He saw how she tapped the chicken bones
lazily about with one long paw. He saw how beautiful she was.

"This *Egypt*," he said. "What's it like?"

She turned her head slowly. The beam of light from the
boarded-up window sprayed about her profile, coronal and
savage, so that she seemed for a moment to be carved in stone.

Mau! thought Tag. Egyptian Mau!

"Mercury," she said gently, "how could I know? I was never
there."

Tag purred. He was Mercury!

"I think I'll go hunting today," he said.

He had already chosen the site.

It was about half a mile along the Caribbean Road in the direction of the Fantastic Bridge. Once, it had been a newsagent
and tobacconist's shop. Now the sign on the front read, if you
could read: BURGESS SUPERMART & DELI.

Tag had made his way through the morning foot traffic,
creeping along between a pavement and a wall, crouching and
veering to avoid pram wheels here, the grasping hands of a tod-
dler there. He had been chased by a bull terrier so fat it could
barely waddle. Worse, he had been splashed with freezing brown
water by passing cars. Now he stood in the doorway, looking
down the long narrow aisle of shelves, piled high with bags of
chips, plastic tubs of butter, bread cut and wrapped, breakfast
cereals in huge cheery boxes. He loved the bright colors under
the flickering fluorescent lights. He loved the smells that poured
out over him in the warm shop air. Dried pulses and spices,
diced cold meat. Sliced fruit in sauces. Strange orange sausages, shriveled and dry. Sweet rolls, powerful cheeses, and
faint flowery yogurts that reminded him of Pertelot's perfect
breath. It was all in there, ready to be freed.

Tag was nervous. His pads were cold and dirty. "Don't dither here!" he told himself. "Don't dither. Go in now!"

Now he was here, he had no plan.

There was a tangle of wire baskets on the warped old wooden floor by the door. Tag stood beside them, kneading the doormat with his front paws and looking up at the bulging legs of a human customer. Its big maroon coat smelled wet. Its shoes smelled of dog. "Everyone stocks them but you," it was complaining in a voice both mournful and accusatory. "Everyone."

"Hi," said Tag. He rubbed against its legs. Dull, he thought.

"Will you look at that?" it told the shopkeeper. "I never knew you had a cat."

Tag withdrew shyly and slipped behind the wire baskets. *Dull, dull, dull.*

"What cat? There's no cat here. I hate cats."

The customer was puzzled. It put its head out of the door and had a look up and down the street. Then it shrugged. "Well anyway," it said, "they stock them everywhere else but here."

When it had gone, Tag came out again. "Got any tandoori chicken?" he asked. "It's orange."

No answer. The shopkeeper was dull, too. Tag rubbed against the counter. He hoisted his tail like a flag. He had to crane his neck to see past the till. The dull behind the counter was reading a newspaper, so it couldn't see Tag at all.

"I'm down here."

No reply.

Oh well, thought Tag, and he trotted along to the freezer cabinet at the back of the shop. It was bright in there, and all the food was wrapped. Strips of yellowing plastic hung down in front, to keep the cold air in. Tag stood on his hind legs and butted between them. Then he jumped in. He sniffed the white tubs and shiny packages. He could make out—as if from a long way off—the smells of cream and butter. He could smell bacon. Leaving the cabinet proved harder than entering it. The bacon kept tangling itself in the plastic strips. He dropped the first packet inside and had to get back in to fetch it. Then he dropped it again, when he landed on the floor outside. This gave him an idea. Soon he had quite a large pile of bacon. He wasn't sure how he would transport it. But the shop was empty, so clearly there would be time to think about that.

He was taking the last pack out of the cabinet when three more customers, women bundled up against the weather, came into the shop and began to browse along the shelves, wire baskets over their arms. One of them, murmuring and hooting quietly to itself, headed slowly for the freezer, where it bent over and, looming above Tag like a sodden tree, began rummaging through the processed cheese, the wrapped sausages, the pepperoni in foil. Then it rummaged through the butter-free spread, the fat-free cream, and the Greek mountain yogurt. It touched Tag's foot.

Tag pressed himself back into a corner. Should he run?

Too late.

The woman looked straight down at Tag.

Tag looked up at it.

It opened its mouth. Its broad, stubby hands reached in to grab him.

Tag fled.

On the way out he snatched up one of his packets of bacon and, half carrying, half dragging it, pelted down the aisle. Out the door he went, onto the pavement, skidding in the slush. Then he put his mind to it and *ran*. Behind him ran the shopkeeper, shouting. Behind the shopkeeper—although they soon gave up—ran the three customers, waving their great thick arms. The bacon kept shifting in Tag's mouth. He would get a good grip in the middle of it, only to find that it had slipped to one side and begun to lever itself out. Or he would knock it on something as he raced around a corner, and it would be snatched straight out of his jaws.

"Waugh!"

He looked back. The shopkeeper was still there.

Run, Tag! thought Tag. Run now!

In and out of passing legs. Dive into the gutter. Swerve into the roadway, head down, ears down, down toward the river! A wild white cat, caught stealing rashers from the Caribbean Road! When he next looked up, Tintagel Court lay in front of him, and the pursuit was no longer to be seen. Tag wheezed up the seeping stairs. When at last he dropped the package on the floor in front of Pertelot Fitzwilliam, his lungs were burning and his jaws ached. He had clung so grimly to his catch that his teeth had punctured the plastic. The Mau stretched and purred languidly. She was half asleep.

"Mercury!" she whispered.

Pertelot Fitzwilliam ate. Ragnar ate. Tag ate.

Ragnar sighed. "I can say, This was good! Though I am not sure about the tough bit on the outside."

"I didn't eat any of that," said Tag.

So it went—for two or three days, perhaps a week. Pertelot and Ragnar hid from the world; and though their supper came more often from a garbage bag than a freezer cabinet, Tag looked after them. Sometimes, waking up cold in the drifting gray dawn or shivering to and fro across Tintagel Court to the dust-bins, Tag thought guiltily of Majicou and the search for the King and Queen. But no one had ever depended on him before, and he knew that he couldn't abandon his new friends now, however exasperated they made him.

Every day, he visited his new dwelling. No one ever came there now, human or cat. One or two silent pigeons eyed him from the gutters, ruffling their feathers in an uncomfortable way, as if he made them embarrassed.

The problem that took up his attention as he hurried home each day was this: the new flat was safe, but how would he get Pertelot Fitzwilliam inside? He had already quarreled with Ragnar over this. Clearly, the Mau was too weak to jump through the ventilator. Though food had improved her condi-tion, she still slept for twenty hours out of twenty-four. When you woke her she sneezed until she was exhausted. Her nose ran. Her eyes ran.

"This place doesn't help," Tag said grimly. "Look at it!"

Damp hung in the air. The wallpaper sagged with it. There were mushrooms growing, yellow and tough and shaped like human ears, in every corner. "We ought to move her to the new den now. I'll think of a way in."

Ragnar disagreed. "She can barely stand," he pointed out. She would be vulnerable. She would be slow on her feet. It would be a disaster. "I think we would be discovered and ambushed so easily."

Tag was disgusted. "Ambushed by who?" he said.

"Who knows?"

"I'm not afraid of the feral cats."

"So."

"Are you afraid of them?"

"No."

"Then you're afraid of leaving," accused Tag. "You hate it here, but you're afraid to leave."

Turning away, Ragnar said quietly, "I am afraid of nothing. But if we leave here, Pertelot's owner will find us, and that would be a disaster for everyone."

"I don't believe in owners," said Tag. "If you want to make something of yourself in this world—forget it, if you only want to *eat* in this world—you've got to make it as yourself. Not as someone else's property. That's what I think."

He appealed to the Mau. "Don't you?"

But the Mau only said suddenly, eyes wide, as if she hadn't heard a word of it, "The owner! He mustn't find me!"

This was too much for Tag. "Let's get something to eat," he suggested.

In the end the decision was taken away from them anyway. Tag woke one night to find Pertelot Fitzwilliam in a high fever. She was lying on her side, writhing to and fro like a garden worm that has been cut in half. She had torn her newspapers to shreds and pulled the stuffing out of the purple cushion. Her lips were drawn back over her teeth, and her coat was streaked black and damp. As he woke, Tag had the impression that *someone had been in the room.* Bad light flickered across the walls. The ghosts of words hung in the dark damp air, as if they had been spoken over Pertelot Fitzwilliam while she slept—as if they were being spoken still. But only Ragnar was there, licking the Mau's head to reassure her, his green eyes huge and desperate in the gloom.

"Ragnar! I thought—"

"I too. But nothing is here."

"Ragnar, lights! Lights on the walls!"

"I think only the moonlight."

Tag heaved himself to his feet. He felt slow and heavy. He felt like some other cat. He couldn't get his head to work. Dreams chased themselves away from him, gray and feathery, very menacing. At length, he made himself say, "What's the matter with her?"

"Tag, I think we have had it here."

"She's still alive," said Tag. "You haven't had it while you're still alive."

He thought. "Water!" he said. "Get water!"

"How?"

"Do I have to do everything? Ragnar, I don't *know* how!"

Just then, Pertelot Fitzwilliam woke, yowling mournfully. She jumped to her feet and, before either of the other cats could move, fled from the room. Tag and Ragnar stared at one another. Regular thudding sounds issued from the kitchen. They found Pertelot there, throwing herself repeatedly at the outside door. She stopped suddenly and sat down. "Raggy," she said, in a clear, reasonable voice, "please show me how to get out of here. I don't seem to know." Her front legs buckled. She tumbled onto the dirty linoleum, a startled expression on her face. "Do help," she implored. "I'm stuck in myself. You mustn't let him find me." And she seemed to pass out again where she had fallen. Her mouth gaped in wonder at what she was seeing. Her breath came fast and shallow. She said something that sounded like "Golden cat."

"Tag!" said Ragnar. "We must—"

But even as they moved toward her the Mau got lightly to her feet and pushed her head through the hole in the door.

"Not out there!" called Ragnar. "Pertelot, come back!"

She ignored him. Only her tail was left in the kitchen. Ragnar sprang on it, all seventeen pounds of him. He held it tight between his teeth. There was a shriek of rage from the other side of the door, and the tail became violently agitated. Then abruptly it relaxed, and a calm voice said, "Ragnar Gustaffson, how dare you?"

Ragnar looked guilty and defeated. He held on a moment more, then opened his mouth. Instantly, the rose-gray tail withdrew.

"Thank you," said Pertelot.

"I'm sure," said Ragnar.

"Idiot," said Tag.

He raced across the kitchen and got his head through the door in time to see her ascend the nearest staircase, then scamper along the walkway and descend the next. The night was cold with moonlight. It was clear air and clouds high up. Pertelot cut across the courtyard, then back again. Did she know where she was going? Tag wasn't sure. She would slow to a trot, tail raised and tip curled, look around, dash off again. She seemed relaxed, rational yet vague, as if the fever had less receded than somehow clarified itself within her. Soon she had visited every part of the building but one.

It was a strange chase.

The Mau fled silently through the moonlight, her shadow long and oblique. Tag followed her. Ragnar followed Tag. No one spoke.

They were running, the three of them, down a flight of stairs on the river side of the building, when somehow the entire staircase twisted out of shape, elongating itself and angling upward, so that it seemed like a horizontal tunnel. Tag stopped, confused. If he looked forward, the tunnel went on forever. A strange noise echoed back toward him. If he looked back, he found that all he had done was descend half a quite ordinary flight of stairs. There was Ragnar behind him, head on one side! Ragnar was equally confused.

"I'm not seeing this," he said.

Tag said, "There's a landing down here somewhere."

Then he remembered which landing it was.

"Quick!" he said.

But they were too late to catch her. By the time they arrived, she was approaching the "highway" in reluctant little runs and pauses. Since Tag had last seen it, it had pivoted upright and, reaching from floor to ceiling, occupied most of the landing. It was six or seven feet in diameter, a filmy tube full of bluish-brown gases moving upward in random pulses. Sometimes these dissipated before they reached the ceiling. Sometimes they seemed to solidify, like chemicals fused and welded into a vibrating colored mass, streaked and marbled with the most beautiful deep blues and reds.

It was a highway. It wasn't a highway.

It was alive.

When it saw the Mau, a shudder passed through it. Lights flickered deep inside. Suddenly it bellied toward her like a fire in the wind, breaking up into grayish sparks and wet-looking cinders. There she stood, dwarfed, a lean silhouette of a cat looking up. There was a deep groan. Then chanting began. Something was chanting in there. At this, Pertelot went rigid. All along her spine the fur was up on end. Stiff legged, a pace at a time, she moved toward it. In response it pulsed and roared and shot up in a towering fountain of strange colors and lights.

"Come on, Ragnar!" urged Tag.

But Ragnar Gustaffson was staring back up the stairs.

"Look!" he called.

Cats were pouring along toward them! Cats in waves, cats like a sea: every cat in Tintagel Court that night had crowded onto the walkway above. There must have been a hundred of them—black cats, white cats, black-and-white cats; cats gray, brown, and marmalade; tabbies, tortoiseshells, and smokes; cats male and female and somewhere in between; one-eyed ginger toms and their three-legged skewbald queens; unwise cats with the moon in their eyes; cats large and small, old and young, sick and healthy . . . Now they stood at the top of the stairs and slowly, like milk just beginning to boil over the edge of a saucepan, began to descend.

"We can't go back!" cried Ragnar.

Pertelot Fitzwilliam had no intention of it. Pace by pace, shaking with delirium, her eyes lit up from within like lamps, she approached the thing on the landing. Suddenly, the colors died away, leaving only a column of milky, translucent light veined with startling Nilotic green. There was some kind of music from within—bells, a reed flute, small drums arrhythmic and perverse. There were movements, as of a dance. A human voice said, "Come to me. Come to me now."

At this, two things happened. Tag threw himself between Pertelot and the ruseating column. And Pertelot, clearly recognizing the voice, bolted.

Tag stared at the thing looming above him and lost the use of his legs.

"Waugh!"

Huge hard hands went around his ribs and, when he clawed and bit, around his neck. Pliable with fear, his dignity gone, shock creeping through his blood, Tag hung from those hands like a kitten in its mother's mouth. Before he was snatched away, he had time to see the Mau and her consort fighting their way back up the staircase side by side, like two small gallant ships at sea. "Pertelot! Ragnar!" he cried. Wave after wave of cats engulfed them. Yet they breasted each one with ease, and met little resistance. The ferals weren't interested in them. They were intent only on the column of misty light around the feet of the figure. Into this, as soon as they reached it, they threw themselves a dozen at a time like cats onto a medieval bonfire, their voices mingling in a thready yowl of delight and despair.

Tag shuddered. Around him was white. There were smells he hated. Sounds came to him from a long way off, muffled and mangled. Something brown and rubbery was clamped over his face. The grip on his neck shifted. Fingers pinched up the loose skin there. He felt a sharp pain. He writhed once, then hung down again, two feet of creamy-white pelt, like a dead ermine. Before he lost consciousness he heard the words, "Wrong one! Wrong cat!"

When he woke, it was to find himself stretched out on cold, dirty concrete, staring into a scorched-looking corner that smelled of ammonia. His head hurt, and though his heart was calm, his soul still seemed to be hammering in panic. When he got up, he hurt. "Yow!" he said. He was alone. The landing was empty. Everything was quiet. A few strange sparks blowing about on the concrete soon turned out to be flakes of snow in the wind. It was late, and Tintagel Court was as silent as death. Limping and stiff in the moonlight, Tag made his way back to the apartment, to see if Ragnar and Pertelot were there. But the feral cats were in possession. The door had been ripped open. A smell of fire came out. Up and down outside, like a wild animal at the entrance to some blackened desert cave, paraded the marmalade tom Tag had fought with on his first day at the court. Tag watched for a few minutes, then left quietly.

Daylight found him tired and desperate. He had been over every inch of Tintagel Court, but there was no sign of his friends. He had peered into blackened waste chutes. He had teetered on the edges of the huge unused dustbins under the great archway. He had scoured the surrounding streets, paying special attention to coal bunkers and garden sheds, wrecked cars with broken windows—any bolt-hole into which their panic might have sent them. He had roamed up and down the river, upstream to the Fantastic Bridge and downstream as far as Mayflower Docks and Observatory Quay.

Nothing. It was as if they had vanished into the air.

Eventually, he was so tired he fell down in a foul-smelling corner as far away from a stairwell as he could manage, and slept. But his sleep was full of bad dreams. Dark shapes fluttered and whispered. The one-eyed cat stalked him as if he were a bird. "Why are you doing this?" Tag begged. "Because you have failed me," answered the familiar stern and hollow voice. Somehow the Majicou had become mixed up with the thing Tag had seen in the pillar of light. In the dream, Tag was walking past a highway behind the Caribbean Road. Morning, full daylight. Something that was the Majicou from the waist up and Pertelot's owner from the waist down reached out without warning and pulled him in. "Wrong cat!" it screamed. It was like drowning. After that he didn't dare sleep again. Instead, he settled himself as best he could, his paws tucked up under him and his nose almost resting on the cold floor, and tried to think about what to do next. All that happened was that he fell into a reverie of his vanished friends. They were lapped in a clear hallucinatory light, a little more real than real.

The Mau, her fur turning from rose to taupe in the light of

dawn, her ancient profile carved in stone. Ragnar, boxy and determined, facing off the ferals to protect a purple cushion. "I shall call you Mercury," he remembered Pertelot whispering. How proud he had been then, and how he had tried to disguise it! He remembered Ragnar complimenting him, "Not just any cat, I think." He remembered the story they had told him one quiet afternoon soon after he arrived, of how they had escaped the cat show together.

"You have to imagine this," began the Mau. "Row upon row of cages under the lights . . ."

Bustle and chatter. Human beings trudging down the narrow aisles, to view Siamese kittens with legs like little curved bone ornaments; big Maine Coon veterans noisily demanding food, mates, freedom; the exotic Spangles with their shy jungly eyes.

"We sat, Rags and I, in our cages on opposite sides of the aisle, trying to talk without saying anything as we waited our separate turns at the show bench. But that call never came, because, in the thick of it, with the show at its height and two thousand human beings packed into the hall, our cage doors were opened!" Down they jumped, those two—as the Mau put it, "like the First Cats from the Mother's eye—" and scampered between the milling human feet, through overpowering smells of sweat and dried food, past the concession stalls, past the *show bench itself*, to the doors—to find themselves in the huge and inhospitable streets of the city.

"A *human* let you out?" Tag asked.

"No!" said the Mau. "No! It was a cat who let us out."

"He knew how to open cages," Ragnar added, "perhaps simply by looking at them. I do not know. He was a very clever cat."

An uncomfortable story, which was trying to tell him something else. From a haunted half sleep, Tag struggled to comprehend. Then suddenly he was wide awake, and it was morning in Tintagel Court, and the extent of his error was made clear to him.

Bloodlines of great antiquity.

Two cats of impeccable pedigree abroad in an uncaring world.

An animal who "seemed to be able to open cages just by looking at them"!

It was the Majicou who had released Ragnar and the Mau. They *were* the King and the Queen. Tag had come to the wrong Tintagel only to find—against all the odds—the right cats.

But now he had lost them again.

Afternoon at Tintagel Court. The ferals lay about, stunned with hunger, boredom, self-disgust. Bins had been inspected, territory mapped. Disputes had been settled—flattened ears, a quick pounce, a flash of razors in the morning light! What was there left to do until dark? Into the afternoon the smell of the river spoke like a voice. "Low tide—mud and stones. High tide— water and mud. Leave here now," it whispered. "Upriver—fields and trees. Downriver—the sea. Leave here now."

All day there had been a bird high in the sky above the court; but if it was a magpie, it never came down. No message from Majicou there. The fox, as good as its word, had never returned.

There was still some daylight left. Tag had a last look around the silent courtyard.

Then he set off to remedy his mistake.

Chapter Five

CY FOR CYPHER

The rat stops when the eyes of the cat shine.
— MADAGASCAN PROVERB

*G*uilt urged him on.

Four o'clock: sleet driving across the gray, wind-scalloped river, dull gray light falling matter-of-factly on the tidal mud to reveal nests of blackened twigs, rusty cans, broken umbrellas. Bits of sodden newspaper blew across the little dull strip of grass in front of All Hallows Church. All Hallows was Tag's last bet for the day. Two royal cats, lost and running blind, might easily choose it as a place to hide.

It was colder inside than out; the air in there was still and old. Tag sniffed up and down the rows of wooden pews. Polish and dust. A chilly staircase spiraled up inside the tower. Cobwebs obscured the little slit windows in thick torn layers, like silk left to rot. He searched the empty belfry, with its sagging wooden louvers.

Nothing.

All Hallows had two smells he recognized—mice, stale and lively at the same time; pigeons merely stale—and a third he didn't.

It wasn't in the pews. It wasn't in the belfry. It came and went, rank and vigorous, a river smell. Mud and musk and something else, Tag couldn't tell what. He forgot the King and Queen again the moment he smelled it. It made his nose itch. It made things itch deep inside him. He was excited. Down from the tower he came, back into the body of the church. Glimmers of warm brass. Red berries like drops of blood in the calm light. Human voices, quietly echoing: two or three women, arranging holly and yew for the Christmas services. Coming and going beneath the tall east window—

its lozengy colors muted by the wet light passing through it—they seemed less dull than tranquil, less self-obsessed than simply happy to be where they were. He had never thought of human beings that way before. It soon passed.

Toward the front of the church was a tall, hollow boxlike structure capped with a carved wooden bird—all hooked beak and varnished talons—the spread wings of which supported a book. His dulls had owned books. "Don't climb on the books, Tag. Don't sit on that *book*!" Tag jumped up and stood on the bird's back. Light poured down on him so that his fur was like ice. And as he gazed out along the rows of shiny brass plaques and leaded side windows, he heard one of the women say in a quiet voice, "Look! There in the pulpit! On the lectern! Isn't he beautiful?"

At the precise moment the women caught sight of Tag, Tag caught sight of the owner of the smell. It was scuttling busily down the aisle away from him toward the back of the church. If you counted its naked scaly tail—which he did—it was nearly half Tag's length. Its coat, rank and brown, seemed to have been slicked down in spikes with engine oil or worse. Its eyes, set wide on a sleek pointed head, glittered like black beads. As it ran it kept close to the edge of the aisle to gain cover from the shadow of the pews. Once or twice it stopped and rose boldly on its hind legs to have a look back at the women. It was full of cheery malice and intelligence. Its feet were hands.

It was a rat.

"*Waugh!*" said Tag loudly to the women. "See that?" he warned them. "*My* rat!"

And he threw himself off the pulpit and into the air.

It was a twelve-ounce brown rat, full grown and not afraid of much. It lacked agility, as adult brown rats do, but it had plenty of gall, and what it lacked in speed it could make up for in cunning. It watched Tag hit the floor, calmly took a second or so to assess him—*big but young, never caught a rat before*—and, at the last moment, leapt onto the back of the nearest pew. Tag shot past, braking heavily. By the time he had changed direction, the rat was scampering away along the back of the pew. Suddenly, it jumped for the back of the next pew forward and then, with great aplomb, to the one forward of that. It was making straight for the front of the church and the flower women, who, their mouths already open in surprise, began to shriek. Tag climbed gingerly up onto the back of the first pew to give chase. The wood was shiny and rounded. He slipped off again immediately.

"Come on, shipmate!" urged the rat. It halted two or three pews ahead of him and deftly smoothed its whiskers. "Call yourself a cat?" it asked him.

"Yes," said Tag.

"A cat *lies in ambush*. It's your *dog* that chases. Where's your skills? Where's your training?

"Shipmate, where's your *trade*?"

Tag was furious. Too late, he understood that if he had simply crept down the aisle to the front pew and waited . . .

By the time he got there, the rat had made another cool leap, landing this time on the coat collar of one of the women. She cried out in disgust and battered at it with her hands. The rat was amused. "Pardon me, ma'am, I'm sure!" it said. "But we're none of us here for long, are we?" and jumped for the lectern Tag had so recently vacated. The woman staggered backward. As a result, the rat misjudged its spring and fell with a despairing squeak headfirst into the side of the pulpit. From there it cartwheeled, short arms and legs outstretched, to the cold church floor, where it lay on its back for a second, unable to think. The women began to stamp up and down on it. Tag arrived half a second later and snatched it up from under their feet.

"Mine!"

"Don't kill me!" gasped the rat. "I come with news, passed on to me, rat by rat along the river. Now tell me: Is it sensible to eat the messenger before you get the message?"

Tag sneered.

"But it's true!" the rat insisted, its harsh voice full of desperation. "I was to look for a silver cat. I was to tell it this: the King and Queen! You wasn't to *meet* them at Tintagel. You was to find them and *take* them to Tintagel. That's how it was passed on to me! That's what the black cat said!"

Too late, thought Tag. "Eat you," he promised indistinctly around the rat, and shook it as hard as he could.

"Ignore me then, shipmate," groaned the rat, "but I ain't done yet."

It twisted in Tag's jaws, bared its great curved yellow teeth, and bit off some of his left ear.

"Waugh!" said Tag.

He hissed at the women in case any of them tried to take the rat. *"Mngau,"* he added. "You see? Now I've been bitten! That was *your fault.*" They stared at him, then anxiously at one another. A rat is bad enough, they seemed to be thinking in their slow human way, but now this! *"Nguaraa,"* said Tag, in an attempt to reassure them. He turned and left All Hallows.

Outside it was blowing rain, dark skies over the river. When Tag looked back at the big east window of the church, it was black and unwelcoming. There was a thread of peachy-green light to the west, with the Fantastic Bridge hung across it like a safety net. Tag ran round the graveyard, the rat moving more and more feebly in his jaws. He was full of excitement but unsure how to proceed. No one had ever taught him how to eat a rat. Eventually he laid it down in the shadow of a gravestone across which some long-ago sculptor had fashioned a skein of ivy.

"Don't eat me, shipmate," said the rat. "Just let me rest awhile, here on the land." Its voice grew fainter. A foul breath of the river came up from it. "I've had a full life," it said, "but I was never at the Ivory Coast."

It bared its teeth a last time.

"You'll get no luck from eating me," it promised. And even as it died, "Set your tiller west by sou'west, shipmate. The clouds is gathering. Tintagel, straight as the black-backed gull above the waves! Tintagel, in time for the equinox!"

Tag stood up tall and straight, facing the north wind. He planted his front legs firmly and extended his haunches. His ear hurt. The side of his face was stiff with blood. But he was his own cat, and he had caught a rat, and the wind rippled the pewter fur along his powerful body so that in the dying light he looked like a real cat at last, not someone who had once passed up the chance of a live house mouse because he preferred a toy made of felt.

In the shadow of All Hallows, he ate the rat.

Mine! he thought.

Everything went wrong after that.

Almost immediately, he began to feel unwell.

It wasn't so much the ear—though as the day's excitement wore off, that became an ache, a throb, a bag of pain balanced on the left side of his face. It was the dizziness. Winter, and he was too hot in his fur! His head ached. His left eye blinked of its own accord. To make things worse, the Caribbean Road was all confusion at that time of day. It was too dark. It was too brightly lit. It was all traffic. It was all legs. Tag wove his way at random between them, thirsty and light-headed, looking up now and then to ask, "Have you seen two cats?" And to add, "I mean, at least *listen!*"

In this condition, he came to a place where the road broadened. Red and green lights ushered side roads in. Everything stank of rubber and chemicals, and the tarmac was filmed with black grease. They had been forced to separate the cars from one another, like wild animals, with metal barriers. Nobody with any sense would try to walk across that road. Even human beings used the reeking underpass. Down there you were safe; up here it was inimical to life. Tag stood swaying at the curb for a moment, sucked gently sideways by the airstream of a passing cab.

He looked out across the road.

A kitten was playing there among the traffic.

She was tabby and longhaired, and she had found a desiccated brown leaf. As the traffic roared past, displaced air propelled the leaf gaily up into the air. Exhilarated as much by the life in herself as by the dance of the leaf, she dashed and darted. The leaf fluttered shyly. Too late! She reared up on her short, comically trousered back legs and sprang at it with velvet paws. Whack! Whack! What now? She would catch it gracefully, like this, above her own head. But it evaded her suddenly and fluttered off. The cars flashed past her. She had no fear in that place. Tag was astonished. She had no fear at all.

He looked around. "Isn't somebody going to do something?"

Human legs, rushing along in the rain without a generous thought.

"Oh no," said Tag.

His own legs had walked him out into the traffic. The noise was unbearable. Rainbow plumes of dirt and spray engulfed him. Tires roared and hissed in his face. No one wanted to acknowledge him. No one was going to admit that a cat had walked out in front of them in the dark at half past five on a winter evening. No one tried to stop, though once or twice Tag saw a face pale with guilt behind a streaming windshield, and a car missed him by an inch. Horns blared, but not at Tag. They were only warning one another, "Don't slow down! Don't change direction! Don't slow down in front of me!"

Tag closed his eyes. Kill me, then, he thought.

The kitten looked up. "Hello!" she said delightedly.

She rushed upon the leaf, batted it gently toward him, then backed away and sat down suddenly in the same movement. He saw with some surprise that it wasn't a leaf at all, but a small brown butterfly with bright blue tips to its black-speckled wings! Where could she have found that in winter! Even as Tag considered this, the butterfly—so fragile as to be invincible— was swept up by the thundering slipstreams, and the last he saw of it was a strange, random, delicate flutter high in the air above the road.

"Want to play?" said the tabby. "Let's play now!"

Tag picked her up the way her mother had, and, turning himself painfully around, set out on the long slow journey back. This time the cars did pull to a halt, their open-mouthed occupants watching as a large silver cat—bedraggled, determined, hauling its kitten by the scruff of the neck—calmly negotiated the mayhem all around them. The tabby gave Tag no help. It hung down passively, bright-eyed and uncontrite, its bulk compelling him to adopt an awkward outswinging stride. Almost at the other side, he stopped to regard with satisfaction the confusion he had caused. Then, shifting his grip on the back of the kitten's neck, he marched the last few steps to the curb.

There he dropped his burden thankfully, crouched down, stretched out his neck, and in two or three convulsive heaves threw up the contents of his stomach.

A lot of the rat had come back up. Not all of it by any means, but quite a lot. Tag thought that perhaps he shouldn't have eaten the fur. That was the mistake, he thought, to eat the fur. He thought, I didn't like the eyes much, either. The rat's image was before him. A memory of its beady intelligent eyes caused him to heave dryly a couple of times. "You certainly got your own back," he congratulated it. When he was able to look up again, he saw the tabby making her way back into the road to be killed.

"Were you born yesterday?" demanded Tag, dragging her onto the pavement again.

She surveyed him with delight. "Maybe!" she said. "Why do you say that?" She said, "You're beautiful!"

She turned around suddenly, dropped her front end to the ground, presented her bottom to him, and peered at him upside down.

Tag stared at her blankly.

When she faced him again he realized she wasn't a kitten at all, only a very small, sturdy, short-coupled tabby cat with white socks on each stubby front foot. Symmetrical black marks curled like flames all down her ribby sides. Her face was square. A white patch under the chin gave her a pink nose and made her head look as if it was always tilted a little to one side, listening for a voice no one else could hear. Her eyes were a tawny yellow. She was all eyes. They were direct; they were full of laughter. But there was something strange in them too. To begin with, Tag thought it was something missing. Then he wondered if it might in fact be something extra— another color, one he couldn't quite see, some fleck in the bright tapestry of the iris.

"My name's Cy," she said. "What's yours?"

"I'm Tag."

She looked disappointed. "You're not," she said.

"I'm not?"

She said, "You're not! I won't have you called that!"

A piece of silver foil bowled past them along the pavement. Without a thought, the tabby went racing after it. "No," she decided, returning to drop it at his feet. "You're this. You're fast, you're flash, you're Quicksilver! Quick, Silver, *you're* no gray old Tag! You're an air cat, Ace, all Hearts on Fire, all quick-step soldier and blue-sky bound!" She was out of breath. "See?" she added.

Tag gave up. Being sick had made him feel better, but not for long. He crouched dully on the curb. His head hurt again, and he was very thirsty. Stationary objects approached and withdrew disconcertingly as he tried to focus on them. One moment he felt as if he were baking in his own skin, the next he was shivering helplessly. He thought, I've got to get something to drink.

"Plenty of water in the river," said the tabby.

Tag glared at her.

"Did I speak?" he said. "Look, I haven't got time for you. I'm poisoned. I've lost the King and the Queen. And I can't think why the Majicou has to send me a message in my food." He stared at the tabby. "Who is Majicou anyway? Whose side is he on?"

"Kings and queens, jumping beans: nothing's ever what it seems," said the tabby, cryptically, and began to chase her tail. After a while she stopped, dizzy, and sat down.

"I don't know what you're talking about," she declared.

"Good. I'm off."

"I'll come too."

"Do what you like," Tag said. "But next time you go in the road, stay there."

After that things grew blurred. He drank from any puddle he could find. For a while, he sat vaguely on a renovated brick wall, looking down at the moonlight on the river while he tried to wash crusty blood off the side of his face. But when he got his paw near the ripped ear the pain was quite sharp, and he soon gave up. Behind him lay a little cobbled arena—steps, a graceful leafless birch tree, two benches, and a waste bin. The cobbles had been laid in clever fans and circles. He was trying to describe the King and—especially—the Queen, as much to himself as the tabby.

"She's beautiful—"

"I'm beautiful too! See?"

"But it's not so much that. It's something in the way she needs help, and you want to give it. Of course, they're both a bit vague. In fact he's an idiot." He thought for a minute, then added, "She's Egyptian. They can't have gone far. They must be around here somewhere."

"I'll find them," said the tabby. "I'm everywhere. Look!"

She started running in tight circles around the waste bin, apparently trapped by the pattern of cobbles surrounding it. To Tag, her shadow seemed a little slow, a little far behind, though it was clearly as attached to her as she was to Tag. She had followed him everywhere. He didn't want her, and he kept forgetting her name. "I'm Cy," she reminded him. "Cy for Cypher, get it? I'm Cy. The one with the open mind." Her behavior had first puzzled, then upset him. She talked nonsense. She talked all the time. There was something wrong with her. She was full of energy but often quite uncertain on her feet. At the first opportunity she would try to eat unsuitable things. She had an attention span of perhaps thirty seconds. He felt too ill to be in charge of her.

"I'll find them for you!"

"I don't want you with me," said Tag.

Standing up and stretching, he swayed toward the water twenty feet below. Moon reflections welcomed him down. He kept his head and didn't fall.

You're not a kitten, he tried to tell Cy, so just go away.

He tried to tell her, I don't have to look after you.

She seemed less hurt than puzzled.

"But I'm looking after you," she said, as if he should have known that all along.

Later, in a steep narrow lane somewhere above Coldheath, where Tag had allowed himself a moment's rest, she fell down and became engaged in an ungainly struggle with her own legs, at which she hissed and scolded as if they belonged to some other cat. The moon was down. The tarmac was romantic with rain. The gutters glimmered with it. From two distinguished gateposts at the side of the lane, a gravel drive curved away between well-grown trees to a house with creeper-covered white walls and faded blue louvered shutters either side of warmly lit windows.

Regaining control just as suddenly as she had lost it, the tabby got upright and headed off with a kind of groggy cheerfulness into the laurel hedge on the other side of the road. There she rooted noisily about until she had unearthed a large square of disintegrating linoleum. This she dragged out and began to gnaw at it with great energy, pausing every so often to look around and lick her lips.

"Want some?" she invited Tag.

"No," he said. "Leave it alone; it's lino."

"If you don't want my food, don't insult it," Cy said.

"Go away," said Tag.

Cy dragged the linoleum back into the hedge and set about burying it.

"I'm ill and you're mad," he told her.

Turning himself around thoughtfully—if he moved too fast the world tended to spin—he caught sight of the white house with its blue shutters. "You know," he informed the hedge vaguely, "this place reminds me of somewhere I used to know." And off he staggered, downhill into the rain and the dark. All his joints felt stiff and hot.

"Good-bye!" he called.

For a moment or two after he had gone, the lane was silent. Then a gust of wind spattered raindrops across it. The little tabby cat burst out of the hedge, gave a fierce and filthy look around, and rushed silently after him.

In the end, Tag had to rest. He wasn't going to find Ragnar and Pertelot that night, if ever. In fact, as the rat's curse filled him up with fever like a glass with muddy water, he began to wonder *if he had ever met them at all*. The whole adventure had seemed headlong and unreal from the moment he came upon Ragnar

Gustaffson Coeur de Lion hauling the faded purple cushion along that walkway in the sky. Nothing could be less likely than a King and a Queen in Tintagel Court.

"They won't go back there," Tag told himself. "Not now."

He told himself, "I must go on too."

He fell asleep, only to jerk awake—perhaps a minute later—to the sound of his own voice, which whispered hoarsely, "The Half-and-Half! No! The Half-and-Half!" He had a fading impression of terror, mistaken assumptions, pursuit. The Half-and-Half! Since he ate the rat, this image had dominated his fevers. It jumped out at him from every corner. Sometimes it was Majicou, sometimes Pertelot's owner. Sometimes it was both.

Sometimes, it was a cat's head impaled on a stick, ribbons blowing out beneath it in the wind.

He shivered.

Had Majicou betrayed them all?

"Pertelot!" he called, his voice echoing across Coldheath. "Ragnar!"

At this the tabby woke up and made a loud grating noise—much like someone using a food processor—in his bad ear. It was her idea of purring.

"Lick me," she demanded sleepily.

It was nearly dawn. He had only the most confused memories of leaving the river. His ear hurt less, but everything else felt worse. He and Cy were curled up together in the back of a bus shelter to get out of the weather. He hadn't the energy to discourage her anymore. It was comforting to have someone near anyway. She did most of the sleeping. For his part, Tag stared rather dully in front of him, watching the rain turn to sleet and then back again into rain. The odd car shushed past.

"Wash me. I'm nice."

"You're not nice," he grumbled.

But he did his best.

Her ears were smelly. When he tried to clean them she shook them in his face, so he gave up and moved on to the crown of her head. There he found a hard object that tasted metallic on his tongue. He was fascinated. He licked the fur away from it to get a better look, and there it was: a short stud made of something shiny, embedded in the skull. Her skin had grown up tight to the base of it. He cleaned around it, then without thinking took it between his teeth and pulled. Cy shot to her feet, banging him in the mouth. *"Arouw!"* she said. She began to whirl around and around in a very tight circle among the discarded candy wrappers, bits of chewing gum, and cigarette butts on the bus shelter floor. After a second or two she scuttled out into the falling sleet and stared expectantly upward.

"Sparks!" she said. "Sparks falling from the forge of God! Sparks, get your headphones on! Message from the dead: Stay home wet days! Over and out."

She fell down.

Tag wearily pulled her into the bus shelter again. There she blinked and gazed at him happily.

"I've got a spark plug in my head!"

"Go to sleep now."

The next morning, they fell in with some cats who lived rough under the arches of a disused rail bridge somewhere on the western edge of Coldheath.

Coldheath wasn't much of a place. Tag didn't know how long he stayed. It was more than a week, less than two. Whatever disease he had caught from the rat took a firm hold as soon as he got there, and time started slipping about in his head, and for much of it he was barely conscious. Of the dozen or two dozen cats gathered on the bleak apron of grass in front of the bridge, he would in the end remember little but the names that leaked in and out of his brain like groundwater after rain.

Names are free. Owning nothing else, the Coldheath cats awarded each other names capricious, baroque, and indulgent. There was Iggy the Fish. There was Tumbledown Tom. There were Bedroll, Razor, and Clint the Mint. There was a slow cat from the provinces called Stilton. Then there was the cat who insisted on being called Also Known as Fitz, as if he had once had some other name he wanted to keep to himself. It was AKA Fitz who greeted them the day they wandered in from Coldheath. His coat was an off-white color, except for his tail, which was black, and one black patch partway down his left side. His head and shoulders were as big as a bull terrier's. His large round face was covered with scabs. He liked to fight.

He looked Tag up and down. "Who's the tart?" he said.

"Pardon?"

"You deaf? I can see you're sick. We're all sick here. Nothing new about that. I said, *Who's the tart?* But never mind—" pushing his face into Tag's "—because all the tarts here are mine."

Tag stared at him.

"Not that I can fancy the little ones much," said AKA Fitz, glancing at Cy. And he stalked off.

Tag watched him go. He thought, *We're all sick here.*

They were. They had stiff joints, swollen lymph nodes, and mange. They had anemia, toxemia, septicemia, hematoma ear, eczema, runny eyes, and constant low-grade fevers. Their teeth were loose or broken. They were wormy. External parasites made them irritable. Not far beneath their misery they had that explosive glandular energy common to outcasts, and nothing to do all day but bicker. Thus a typical encounter between Iggy the Fish and Bedroll would go like this:

"Stuff you, mate."

"No, mate. Stuff you."

"I know you, mate. Stuff that."

"Mate? You don't know a mate from stuff."

Then, to the other cats, who had assembled to watch, "You heard this stuffer?"

"Stuff you, mate!"

And so on, until, sitting back on his haunches suddenly, one or the other would give a bubbling cry and, slipping his front claws, hit out so suddenly and so quickly that Tag could barely follow what had happened. An ear would rip, an eyelid would bleed. Fur, as they say, would fly, until the loser backed away, muttering as if he still had fight left in him, "Slip one on me, would you? Stuff you."

And it would all begin again.

Often, though, they were too lethargic to do much at all, and like ferals everywhere simply sat hunched up, staring into the rain. They looked as if they were waiting for something. They were. Various human beings fed them, old men and women for the most part, barely better off than the cats themselves. Most days, by the time he got there, there wasn't much food left. It was disgusting, mostly fishmeal dyed a kind of neon pink, coming apart in the teeming rain. He ate it anyway. His ear had healed, but he felt depleted. He sat alone in the rain, staring ahead of himself at nothing. He gathered with the others to lick the lukewarm fat off fish-and-chip papers people threw away under the rail arches. At night, the Half-and-Half ruled his dreams; by day it stalked his delirium. Refusing to give in to it, he huddled up and thought about Ragnar and Pertelot. What were they doing now? Would he ever see them again? How would the Mau get anything to eat without his help?

Cy the tabby stayed close by, though much of the time he wouldn't acknowledge her. Her stream of nonsense soothed him. She cared for him according to her whim and as best she could. She would wash him inexpertly for a moment or two, then forget what she was doing and wander off. She would sometimes cuddle up to him at night. And she fetched him nourishing items from the railway bank beyond the bridge—one bicycle spoke, the lid of a shoe box, part of a long-dead pigeon.

"Get that down you, Jack," she advised. "It'll make a man of you."

The Coldheath cats slipped in and out of Tag's awareness, looming or distant according to his level of fever. They had, underneath it all, a strange durability. They saw themselves less as castoffs than as independent agents. Life under the arches was just the price they paid for freedom. The tortoise-shell with the collapsed cheek and glaucoma eye, the little black dying from feline influenza—if they had a motto, it was "Never Go Home." They knew Tag was a transient. They suspected he was a toff. But he was bigger than most of them and generally they left him alone. On the other hand, Cy—ungainly in her movements, forever giving the wrong response—brought out the worst in them. They drove her away when the food arrived. They set upon her when she was asleep.

They backed her into corners. If she resisted, they ganged up. AKA Fitz took the lead. He called her Smelly Nellie, which drove her into impressive rages, for she was not a clean little cat and knew it. He bit her in the back of the neck until she submitted, then walked away without doing anything.

AKA Fitz took the lead in everything. Whenever Tag turned his head—however ill he felt—there was AKA Fitz, stalking across his field of view. AKA Fitz was always looking out of the corner of his eye, to make sure the other cats respected him. AKA Fitz let them eat. AKA Fitz filled the arches with his personality the way he marked the sodden brickwork with his stink.

It was a cloud of violence. As Tag recovered, he resented it increasingly. *Also Known As!* he thought with contempt.

Late one afternoon he woke to the sound of pigeons cooing in their roosts high up in the bridgework, from whence they peered doubtfully at the cats gathered around the banquet spread on the bleak ground below. Tag sat up. His vision seemed clearer. Over the next two days, his strength returned. Soon, he couldn't get enough to eat; and one morning, he was Tag again. The rat, perhaps, had forgiven him at last. The Half-and-Half had vacated his dreams—though his doubts remained. He shook himself suddenly and had a thorough wash. Then, seeing AKA Fitz leave the arches, and curious to know where that animal might be going, he followed him.

AKA Fitz made his way against the grain of the back gardens north of the bridge, running nimbly along the board fences and skirting any open place. He stopped frequently to make certain he wasn't being followed. This strategy brought him to a quiet street lined with parked cars in various stages of disintegration. AKA Fitz marched openly down the middle of the road, through a gateway about eight doors down, and jumped onto the low sill of an old bay window.

There, his whole demeanor changed. He looked around once, as if to make sure he wasn't observed, then sat up straight, wrapped his tail neatly around his feet, and stared intently into the parlor the other side of the window. After a moment, a noise came out of him. *"Ow?"* he begged. And again, *"Ow? Ma-*

rauow?" And then, *"Ow? Marauow? Marauow?"* And he
went on like that for three or four minutes, until the front door
was opened with a sigh and a sweet old voice said, "Pimpie!
Pimpeeee? Is it a little Pimpie, then? It *is*! It's a little Pimpie!
Does he want his *milk*? Pimpie? Yes? *Yes!* Yes, Pimpie, little
Pimpee! Well, I suppose you must come in then, mustn't you!
You must come in, little Pimpie!"

Tag, who had hidden in a privet hedge to watch, was beside
himself.

So much for AKA Fitz.

AKA Pimpie, he thought with delight. AKA My Little
Milkie-Wilkie then.

And he slipped back along the gardens to the bridge to see if
he could get anything to eat. The tabby was off on business of
her own. She had left a small coin, two cigarette butts, and an
empty chocolate wrapper in the place where he usually sat. He
wondered where she was. He thought he would look for her on
the railway bank and perhaps try his paw at a vole or two in the
tangled couch grass and bramble colonies. An hour later, perhaps more, he found that though illness had given him all the
patience in the world, any speed he had once had was quite
gone. Even quite old voles were walking away from him. He
yawned and got up stiffly. "I'll be back," he promised them.

Cy was nowhere up on the bank; and when he looked out
across the miserable grass strip, he couldn't see her there, either. There wasn't a cat in view. It seemed like a quiet afternoon for the Coldheath ferals. But as he came down the bank,
he heard some voices raised; and eventually he found her.

They had penned her up on the charred, pigeon-dunged
slope of earth in the back of one of the arches—Bedroll, Razor,
Iggy the Fish, Bunco Rap, Spiky George the Sailor, Fortune
Smiles, and half a dozen more—and now sat in a half circle
egging one another on and waiting to see what she would do.
There was a vapor of testosterone in the air. There was bad
will. There was rape.

Cy stared at them resentfully, as if they had interrupted an
important message from outer space. She looked small. Blood
had caked around the base of her spark plug and down the side

of her nose. Water dripped onto her back from somewhere up in the curve of the arch, catching the light as it fell. Each time she shuffled uncomfortably and moved back, they moved forward. Soon she would be against the wall, and there would be nowhere else to go. At some other time, she might have reveled in their interest, rolling and purring like any feral queen. Now, her signals fatally mixed, she only said, "I don't want you."

"You do," said Spiky George.

"Let her go now," said Tag.

A dozen heads turned to him as one, then away again.

"Stuff off," said Iggy the Fish.

"No, wait," said another voice.

Out of the circle stepped AKA Fitz. His head was down, and his fur was up. With slow and stiff-legged gait, he made his approach. With slow and measured insolence he thrust that huge round face of his into Tag's.

"This toff wants a word with us," he said. His pale blue eyes were an inch away. "Do you?" he asked. "*Do* you want a word with us? Because—" suddenly thrusting himself even closer "—*we* want a word with *you*." He sat down suddenly, as if exhausted by this display, held one of his front paws up to his face, and inspected it clinically.

"Slip him the old razors, Fitz," said Bedroll.

Spiky George suggested, "Slip him a pawful, Fitzy."

While this was going on, Tag had crouched back further and further on his haunches, filled with fear and anger until his whole body felt wound up like a spring. Now, suddenly, all tension seemed to rush out of him. It was replaced, now that he knew what he was going to do, by a calmness hardly less unpleasant. He made himself look coldly at each of the ferals who had assembled in a half circle to watch their leader destroy him. He yawned, as if he were on his own and had just woken up.

Then he said quietly, "Who's this *Fitz*? I thought I was talking to Little Pimpie."

He considered this. "Little Pimpie Wimpie," he said. "Mm."

He stared straight into AKA Fitz's astonished eyes.

Fitz lunged, forelegs open.

All his fight was in his front end, in the thick neck and barrel chest of the mature tomcat. If he could, he would hold, bite, and maul. But Tag had been in embraces like that before. He knew he hadn't the weight for them. Rather than submit to Fitz's clutch the way he'd submitted to the marmalade tom's at Tintagel Court, he sprang as high as he could into the air. As Fitz passed beneath him, beginning to be puzzled, Tag turned and landed with his teeth buried in the back of that surprised cat's neck. Fitz, an uncontrollable pack of bone and muscle, had writhed out from under in an instant. He was so fast! The damage, though, was already done. Twisting about like that under Tag's clamped teeth, Fitz had torn out a triangular lump of himself, which now flapped at the back of his neck like a little red and white bandanna. Worse, he had lost his orientation. Even worse, perhaps, he had lost his dignity.

Tag slapped him in the face.

Tag rocked to one side to evade the counterblow.

Tag blinked and spat.

"Come on, Pimpie!" he said.

But AKA Fitz had backed away.

Astonished, Tag watched him lower his hindquarters and hurry off.

"And don't come back!"

At that, the rest of the cats turned on Tag. He wasn't sure what he had expected. That they would be cowed, perhaps. Or grateful. Wrong. With AKA Fitz two streets away and begging to be let in by the nice milk lady, all bets were off. The ferals set about Tag. They set about one another. Filthy Mike sprang on Hairy Mary, whom he had never liked. Microchip, quite a small cat who nevertheless believed he should replace Fitz, fixed his teeth in the left rear leg of Razor, quite a large one who was determined that he shouldn't. Soon the strip of grass in front of the arches was nothing but a wheeling, screeching whirligig of Felidae, deep in the midst of which the cat who had started it all was desperately trying to keep his skin.

Yow! thought Tag.

It was his last thought for some time. His very personality had vanished into the need to fight. Tag was gone. All that remained was an increment of rage in the common pool. He was saved by an unlooked-for turn of events. Into the melee stepped an extraordinary figure. It was the female feral the Coldheath cats called Sealink.

Chapter Six

SEALINK

If man could be crossed with the cat, it would
improve man but deteriorate the cat.
—MARK TWAIN

*F*eral wasn't quite the right word, Tag would find out later, for a cat of Sealink's quality. She lived outside; she lived off her wits. But any resemblance to AKA Fitz's tribe ended right there. Sealink didn't have time to get mange. They never saw her under the arches more than once or twice a year. Some years they saw her not at all. No one asked where she spent the rest of her life, so she never told them. She was her own cat.

If Sealink's pedigree was uncertain, her country of origin was not. Ancestors in Maine had bequeathed her their stature and heavy bones. Her color was Cape Cod calico, bracing orange and black on white. To balance this Puritan heritage she had the charm, manners, and warm golden eyes of the honey-dripping South. Her feet were big. What you're born with you can add to, was one of Sealink's beliefs. She had added to herself. She had eaten oysters in Detroit, lasagne in Los Angeles, and alligator sausage in New Orleans. Dishes like that had made her proud in her flesh.

For size she was the equal of Ragnar Gustaffson. Her temper was less certain than his. She looked about her now with the devastating calm of a mother amid warring kittens, who identifies all parties to the quarrel, and who wades in, laying out right and left about her. As thick as kapok wadding, her Maine Coon coat confounded tooth and claw. Her eye was quick. Her arm was quicker. If anyone looked like getting the better of the cat called Sealink, she simply fell on him. With a kind of grandeur, rolling hips and furry haunches, she made her way through Spiky George the Sailor, Iggy the Fish, and

Fortune Smiles, bowling Bedroll over on the way. Hairy Mary she spared.

Then she looked around. "Hey!" she said. In her voice competed Kentucky mountain vowels, the Creole sugar of the French Quarter, the edgy bark of Manhattan. "Don't none of you guys want to *play*?"

None but Tag had stayed to answer. "Hi," he said. "I'm Tag." He was ravished.

"I ain't concerned with you," said Sealink. She looked him over. "Though you're cute, and tough enough. I seen you dust that AKA Fitz. Not bad." She swept past him and into the echo chamber of the arch. Her voice rang like a ship's bell in a fog in San Francisco Bay. "Now, honey," she said to little Cy, "you come to me and be comforted. Because, honey, all males are brutes."

She looked down her nose at Tag.

"You *know* it to be true."

Early afternoon. A pale but warming sun broke through the clouds. It gilded the grass arena and picked out the fur that lay scattered there in tufts and swatches. All colors and textures were represented, along with several varieties of tipping. Three cats sat before the railway arches enjoying the warmth. The largest was grooming the smallest with long sweeps of a rough pink tongue the size of a small vole, while the third, a cat of surprising color, told his story. In this tale the soap bubbles of kittenhood led inevitably to garden life and thence to the dreary fevers of Coldheath. Tag described how the cunning magpie had lured him from his home. How he had blundered onto the highway and been rescued by a fox. He gave account of the long cold nights and unfamiliar staircase arrangements of Tintagel Court. How he had met the King and Queen, lost them, and only then discovered that he should have *taken* them to Tintagel, not *found* them there. He dwelt on shopping expeditions, the way to eat a rat, and his discovery that not everyone is always what they seem. If he spoke of the Majicou, it was glancingly; and his darker fears he did not name.

"So here I am," he finished. And he blinked up into the benign sun. "On my way to Tintagel, I suppose. As soon as I find them again."

Having ensured that Cy—now sleeping peacefully, even through the clatter of her own purr—was for once in her life quite a clean cat, Sealink too looked up. She nodded. "I said you was tough enough," she remarked, only to add— "but you left out the toughest thing you did."

"I did?" said Tag.

Sealink looked down at the sleeping tabby, then back at Tag. There was a silence, then after a moment she purred. "You gonna tell me your name, kitten?"

"Tag!" said Tag, surprised out of the reverie into which her voice had thrown him. "I'm Tag."

Sealink deliberated on this. "Yeah," she said. "I guess you are."

A little shyly, Tag asked, "What's your name?" Then, "Do you live here?"

"I've lived about everywhere, hon," she said complacently. "You don't mind if I proceed to groom myself?"

"No, no. Of course not!"

"As to names, why I've had 'em all—

"In New Orleans, the town where I was born, they called me the Delta Queen. I was known as Rocket for a while in Houston, Texas—never could think why. Spent a summer in Missoura, picked up the name Amibelle. And in Alaska, one-forty below, I lived with a pipeliner name of Pete called me Trouble—but, hon, he weren't no more than a fighting tomcat himself. Loved women.

"Abroad—" Sealink shifted her weight a little so that she could extend one mighty back foot. She spread its sinewy toes to clean between them. "Abroad, they'll call you anything: Cleo, Minouche, Justine, Isadora, Brunhilde—can you believe that? I was in Sweden for a week, they called me Volvo. Or was it Vulva?" She laughed.

Her feet dealt with, she now passed to her great brushy tail. This, as she said, was an animal all its own, and a damn nuisance, though it had had its admirers.

"Under these arches they call me Sealink, you know why?

'Cause I once crossed the Channel on a ferry of the same name. *Ferry?* That's a boat to you, kitten. How'd I *get* on it? Well, I *stowed away*! Countries, cities, I seen most of 'em. Cairo, Constantinople, Prague"—this she pronounced to rhyme with *vague*—"Amsterdam, I been there. Budapest, you know? Liked the food well enough though." She licked her lips. "Liked them Magyar tomcats, too. Enjoyed them droopy whiskers."

She thought for a bit. She gave her tail a final lick.

"Ain't never been to that Mother Russia," she admitted, "or flown the Atlantic Ocean both directions. But I aim to change that soon."

Tag was entranced.

Most of what she said was meaningless to him. But her fur shone in the sun, and her voice was gold dissolved in honey. She made things feel brand-new again. Her life seemed huge to him. It flickered hypnotically before his eyes. It was a world in itself. He sought for something to say—something that would impress a traveler of the world. He sighed. "I suppose Tintagel seems nothing to a cat like you." He paused. "You don't happen to know where it is, do you?"

Sealink gave him a sharp look. "You got a lot to learn, hon," she said. "A journey's a journey to a cat like me. Hey! I might just come along! Ain't got nothing better to do right now. Sounds like fun. Might even help you *find* these Royals!" She gave him a sharp look. "Maybe meet this one-eyed creature you don't talk too much about." She said, "You just wait here a minute, hon. I got someone here I want you to meet." And she sailed off across the grass, up to the disused tracks where they inclined north, and out of sight.

Five minutes later, she was back. With her she had a cat the color of an old-fashioned shellac comb. His coat was so heavily mottled and patterned, so dark in places, as to be almost black. The fur itself was very short and coarse, with a suspicion of a curl. One of his eyes was a frank and open speedwell blue, the eye of an honest country cat. The other seemed to belong to a more urban kind of animal altogether. It was the color of a sodium lamp. The effect was rakish and undependable.

"This here's my friend," said Sealink, "when I'm under the

arches." She stared at the tortoiseshell with her head to one side. "Ain't no use for anything but the two F's. But we travel together."

The tortoiseshell introduced himself.

"My name's Marsebref."

"Marsebref?" said Tag.

"Marsebref. *Marse*bref."

"Oh, *Mouse*breath!"

"Yeah. My name's Marsebref."

He seemed to think for a moment. When Mousebreath was thinking, his thoughts passed from one eye to the other like slowly swimming fish. You wondered which eye they would finish up in. Blue or orange? Town or country?

"I seen you about the arches," he acknowledged eventually. "I seen you about."

"I think he likes you, hon," Sealink told Tag.

"I never been to Tintagel," said Mousebreath. "But I had an uncle come from there, and he told me the way. He called himself Tinner. Said he did, anyway. Said he come from there."

So it was arranged.

"We'll leave as soon as it's dark," said Sealink. Then she caught Tag's eye. "Okay, hon," she said. "You told me something. Now I'm gonna tell you something. Fair exchange. It's this. You want to get to Tintagel before the end of the century, you got to do better than you been doing."

"I have?"

"You have. Now, I don't say I understand all the Kings 'n' Queensy stuff you told me. Nor yet this problem you been having with the highway. But the rest of your trouble's simple."

"It is?"

"It is. Why, kitten, you got no plan! Until you met my old mate, you didn't even know where Tintagel *was*! This whole trip so far, you just got pushed from pillar to post. Every way the wind blowed, you went! A traveler's at the will of the journey, hon. No one accepts that more than me. But you got to *learn* that will, then use your skills!" She rose to her feet and stretched magnificently. "Speaking of which, I'm going stir-crazy," she said. She looked fondly upon her consort, who had sat down next to Cy and closed his eyes. "Mousebreath can look after the little one an hour or two; he's just got brains enough for that." At this Mousebreath opened his eyes again and winked the speedwell blue one heavily at Tag. "So you and me can take a turn around. Get to understand each other's journeys, keep an eye open for your friends. You like that? As an idea?"

Tag loved it. "I do," he said.

It had turned out to be one of those sunny winter afternoons that appear tantalizingly between the sleet and frost. Sharp, still air and a cloudless sky made distances look magical and gray. Birds, surprised into activity by the sudden sunshine, were competing by opera for the available space— "My little territory!" "Oh no, I don't think so!" —as Sealink led Tag up onto the derelict railway track that stretched in both directions like a country lane. Sunlight fell across the old gravel roadbed through dense growths of hawthorn, young birch, and elder. The sounds of the city seemed to recede. As she walked, Sealink talked. "I ain't been everywhere, kitten, and I ain't seen everything. But I sure seen a lot. Human beings, now—"

"The fact is," Tag announced, "I'm not very interested in human beings." He added proudly, "Who cares about them?"

Sealink stopped and stared at him. "That ain't your own opinion, hon," she said, as if she could look into his heart. "And it shows how much you know."

Tag was surprised. "If you want to make it in this world," he persisted, "you have to make it on your own, not as someone else's property."

"No one owns me, kitten," said Sealink, her voice dangerously calm. "Nor ever will. But we share this world with human folks for good or ill, and we got to work around them. I heard some cats call humans *it* as if humans got no feelings. Wrong. Course, that's only my view. But follow me now and I'll show you why." She thought for a moment. "One other thing," she said.

"What's that?"

"You journey in a foreign land, you better learn the language."

And so as they walked, she tried to explain the human world.

She explained the things you saw in the sky— "Them's *airplanes*, hon, and I stowed away on more than one!" She explained the things you saw on the ground. Many of the latter items Tag had already encountered, some close to, some as mere objects in the distance, menacing and strange. But Sealink had opened up the world for him in a stream of light and now, for instance, he was able to boast, "Cars! I've run in front of one or two."

"Have you indeed," said Sealink with a grin.

Looking down from the railbed at some men ripping up the pavement in the street below, she was engaged in explaining *roadworks*. "See that, hon? Well, that's a *traffic cone*."

"What does it do?"

"I ain't got the slightest idea."

Later she would tell him about railway tracks, and where this one began. Where did it end? Tag wanted to know.

"Ain't no ending but it's a new beginning, hon."

Sealink quizzed Tag about his life. She was interested by the most ordinary things he'd done. Everything interested Sealink: a sudden smell of fresh earth, flickers of light off a car window in the street below as they passed over a bridge; the rush and hiss of a flock of pigeons going by—less a sound than a brief change in the nature of the air. Everything drew from her a response of delight tempered by her knowledge of the world. When you were with her, sights, sounds, colors, smells, seemed new. They seemed refreshed. Things were more themselves. Tag, too, had a feeling of being more himself; even, somehow, more *than* himself. It was as if Sealink's experience was a kind of light she shone on the simplest and dullest objects.

"You got your own light, Tag," she advised him gently when he suggested this. "People already admire you for the light you cast on things." Later, in the darkness and despair of another journey, he was to remember that.

After perhaps half an hour of walking, he asked, "Where are we going, then?"

Sealink laughed. "Don't tell me you missed the point already, hon. The journey is the life! But if you're looking for an actual *destination*, why I think we want to leave this track . . . around about here!"

She hurried down the railway bank, her long fur streaming back as if she were running in the wind. Below was a short street of shops and restaurants. The shopfronts were painted in muted reds and blues and greens. Little trees grew in tubs on the pavement. The windows were splendid with clothes and shoes, furniture and picture frames, trinkets, and boxes to put them in. Sealink stopped outside a café. Tag stood beside her and stared in. Checkered floor, mirrored walls, big menus. Shiny black bentwood chairs arranged 'round marble-topped tables.

PIZZA, signaled the bright green neon sign above the window. PIZZA. PIZZA. PIZZA.

"Some friends of mine run this place," said Sealink. "They got a kid since we was last close. Nice, huh? These guys like me a lot, and I like them. Let's go in." She stopped suddenly and gave Tag a look. "You ever eat pizza topping before?" she asked. "Oh, not pizza!" she said dismissively. "Pizza, that's just bread." She half closed her eyes. "But now, pizza *topping* . . ." Her voice lowered and was filled suddenly with a contralto heat, a languid noon dreaminess. Then she laughed and shook herself. "Well!" she said. "Oh my! Let's go right in."

"Door's closed," observed Tag.

"Hon, it won't be closed for long."

Whereupon the traveler stood upon her hind legs, drew back her right front paw, spread the toes, and—bang!—dealt the plate-glass window such a blow it reverberated like distant thunder. Quite soon after, the door was opened by a short broad man in a white apron. His eyes seemed a little tired but sharp and full of humor. Beside him stood a dark-haired woman, with long legs and a dreamy sensuous grin.

The man knelt down and cuffed Sealink briskly about the head and neck.

"You want to come in, Isadora?" he invited.

"Or," the woman added, "did you just come by to break our windows?"

Sealink seemed to enjoy this. She purred loudly. "Stand aside," she ordered them. "Don't be between me an' them there anch-*oh*vies." To Tag she explained, "I met these guys four years back in San Francisco. When they come over here last summer, they said, 'Hey! Cool! Here's a calico cat, just like the one we knew back home!' So they give me the same name and everything, say how like I am this other cat. They say, 'Must be real good luck!' " She laughed. "*Isadora,* huh? I drop in once a week, play with the baby."

"Do you think they'll ever guess?"

"Tag, human beings can be awful cute. But they ain't known for their brains."

"I used to call mine *dulls.*"

"They're dull, but they ain't all bad. Look at her! You going to call her *it*? She feels as much as you or me. Oh now, look at *this* . . ."

Soon Tag and Sealink had a bowl each of pizza topping. "Heavy on the anchovies, heavy on the capers, heavy on the tomato." It was heavy, in fact, on everything. Sealink growled as she ate. Any moment, you were afraid, she would simply get down in the food and roll about. Though Tag approached more cautiously, he had to admit it was good. She made him switch bowls. " 'Cause I already remarked," she said, "that you ain't keen on them hot chili peppers. Well, step aside, boy. Momma loves 'em. Also, I left you a piece of that—you see that? —pepperoni. Honey, *you're gonna like that.*"

"Well?" the man asked them later. "Can I cook? Or can I cook? Which is it?" He examined the empty bowls. "I can cook," he concluded.

"You could always cook," said the woman. She smiled quizzically down at Tag. "Was it good for you too?"

"Not the green bits," said Tag, offering his head to be stroked. He said, "You can call me Tag."

"Look at the way he does that!"

"Cute boyfriend, Isadora," said the woman. "Pity about the chewed ear. I'd fancy him myself." She grinned.

Sealink said, "Roll the baby out, you two. I ain't seen it in a week. After that, we got to run." To Tag, she whispered, "I love these guys, but they'll keep you talking."

* * *

By the time they got back to Coldheath, it was chilly again.
Sunset was a pale rose and terra-cotta wash behind the houses.
Above it, two stars and a bright new moon had already appeared in a sky shading from green to ultramarine. Out in the
middle of the grass, in the pervasive, eerie light of the afterglow, Mousebreath and the tabby were playing a game of Cy's
devising.

Tag began to descend. But Sealink, now a dark still figure
watching alertly from the summit of the embankment, cau-
tioned him, "Wait!"

In front of Mousebreath, Cy had arranged a collection of objects. Some of them Tag recognized: strips of silver foil with
light clinging to them in the dusk, the bicycle spoke she had
brought him to eat when he was ill. Others, he did not. There
were some quite large things—part of a broken picture frame
about a foot long, glimmering with gold and cinnabar paint; a
deflated tennis ball, sulfurous yellow; and a shiny can without a
label, which would later prove to contain one inch of clear
water—and some peculiar ones. She had included a bunch of
plastic anemones, the detached head of a doll complete with
platinum-colored nylon hair, a white piano key.

Mousebreath looked on uncomprehending. The tabby chattered excitedly. She dragged her bric-a-brac about in front of
him, as if to settle it into a pattern he would recognize. Nothing.
Irritably, she gave up. Then, after further thought, she began to
run between the objects, slowly at first, then faster and faster—
always taking the same course—faster still and faster, until she
stopped being a cat at all and became a blur and seemed to be
everywhere at once along her own path; and that path became a
design, a symbol, or a knot that hung just above the ground in
the now-darkened air.

☿

Suddenly, she fell down and didn't get up again.
"Come on!" cried Sealink.
Tag just sat there. He felt agitated but unable to move.

Sealink's voice seemed to come from far off. Far off and some other day. It had been important then, but it wasn't now. The symbol Cy had drawn in the dusk fluoresced as an afterimage on his field of view. But instead of fading it brightened to electric blue and at the same time grew until he could see nothing else. There! Had someone in the distance called his name? Someone he wasn't sure he liked? Then, "Wake up, you fool!" he heard, and Sealink batted him quite hard—"upside the head," as she would put it later—with one of those huge paws of hers. He shook himself awake and went bounding down the embankment beside her.

They found the tabby unconscious. Curled up so motionless and tight into herself, she could have been a cat carved from an oval stone. Mousebreath was distressed.

"Couldn't see what she were about," he repeated several times. "Thought it were a gyme."

"*Gyme?*" said Tag.

Mousebreath shook his head angrily. "*Gyme!*" he said. "Gyme a kitten plays."

"It wasn't a game," said Tag, remembering the shape that had hung inside his eyes. He sniffed among the gathered things. They seemed warm. A breeze dispersed the silver foil, ruffled the platinum hair of the doll's head. Mousebreath watched him miserably.

"Couldn't make it out," he apologized in his faded, cobwebby voice. "She slept most of the afternoon."

"Hey!" Sealink chided him. "Lover, you done what you could. No one's blaming you." Then she gave the tabby's head a lick, and said to Tag, "This thing in her skull. It ain't natural, that's for sure."

There was a silence.

Sealink gazed across the darkening field to the black bulk of the embankment. She shivered. "Mousebreath, honey, come and sit beside me. I got a bad feeling about this place."

Tag said, "I think we should leave."

"We're gone from here," agreed Sealink. "Soon as she can walk."

* * *

It was still dark when the tabby regained consciousness. She opened her eyes, made a sound like a badly tuned mowing machine, which the other cats took to be a purr, and said, "Jack's here, and back flip! Look out!" She wobbled cheerfully off into the dark and had to be fetched back so they could get up on the railway bank and start their journey. There was a small contretemps with her legs, which wanted to walk in different directions. Thereafter she gamboled on ahead, chasing the shadows of bats and branches down the charred perspective of the old roadbed, and calling out, "We're off to see the wazzock!"

Or to Sealink, in a curiously apt approximation of that cat's deep queenly honeyed boom, "When does the voodoo start, podna?"

Sealink shook her head indulgently. "See?" she told her consort. "She ain't taken no harm." And when Mousebreath still looked abashed, "Honey, you done well with her."

Cy cocked her head at Tag. "Hi," she said. "I'm Cy. Cy for Sign Here. I'm the one with her head in a bag." She brought him two black feathers and one small stone. She danced with his shadow. Dawn found her walking by his side in a jerky, short-legged imitation of his prowling stride, lowered head swinging left and right. She looked ridiculous. It put Tag on his dignity.

"You aren't a kitten," he reminded her.

"Who cares?" she said. "It's nice out, and you've got shiny eyes." She said, "I love you like tigers do. You're my kind sky pilot." She laughed and looked down coyly. "I'm shier than I seem, you know."

It was a dawn of wide cold beauty. White sky above a peach horizon. As the day advanced, black branches rattled in a chilly wind. From his new perspective, Tag watched the human beings settling to their employment in the streets below. They were hammering and banging. They were scraping a spade through wet cement or a trowel through wet mortar. There was a rattle of diesel engines like dice in the palm of a hand. Shops and offices were opening. Bakery smells, fishmonger smells, greetings and laughter, flakes of ash: all of these sensations drifted up over the arches of the old railway and into the abandoned stations, where Tag's nose and ears and eyes greeted them with trepidation. The human world was noisy and smelly and often frightening—and he wasn't going to accept it all at once, whatever Sealink said—but at least now it had all come alive for him.

Sealink, meanwhile, strolled benignly along as if she owned the day, naming things to right and left. "See that yellow hat, hon? *Site helmet!* Means he's a *builder*—makes houses and all. See them toecap boots?" That day, she said, it seemed as if the whole city were being rebuilt around them as they looked. She jumped onto the guardrail of a rusty bridge to look down at two roofers dragging steel poles off the bed of a truck while a third tended the tar seething in its iron barrel.

The *scaffolding* tolled and rang. Sealink lifted her head and sniffed deeply. A great slow shudder of pleasure passed along her spine.

"Just smell that tar down there!" she said to Tag. And when he looked puzzled, "Honey, we got the morning. We got the weather. We got the roadbed. This here's travel! New tastes, new smells. A new thing to see. Mornings like this you can feel so much *yourself* it outright frightens you. That much fun can be a scary way to live!" She laughed. "But what way ain't? Huh? That's why we love it!"

"I'm not so sure about that," said Tag.

"Come *on*. I'm hearing this from an animal who walked out into two lanes of rush-hour traffic *with another animal in his mouth*? Give me a break!"

Tag said, "Oh, that's different."

"You ain't done learning, kitten."

"Is that the toughest thing I did?"

"Say what?"

"Back at Coldheath you said I'd left out the toughest thing I did. Was that it, to carry Cy over the road?"

Sealink studied him. "No, honey," she said. "The toughest thing you did was to take that little cat on at all." There was something unfathomable in her eyes when she added, "That's one of the toughest things you ever gonna do."

But I haven't taken her on, thought Tag. Have I?

Shortly after that, Mousebreath and Sealink conferred briefly, and Mousebreath disappeared into a thicket of leafless elders.

Sealink sat down to wait. "Nice!" she said.

Tag looked around.

Strips of plastic fluttered from the elder branches in the pale sunshine. Winter had bleached the couch grass to white. Rose briars were taking to themselves a washing machine, a discarded bicycle, a heap of mossy wooden balks. Tag watched Cy approach the bicycle cautiously from different angles and finally touch it with a paw. She leapt back. "Wow!" she said. "I thought that tree was a dead horse!" She wandered erratically off to lap rainwater from a chipped enamel bowl. Tag could smell the river again.

A few minutes later, Mousebreath returned.

"It's here all right," he told Sealink. "We go down here."

Down here turned out to be waste lots piled with broken bricks. After that it was brand-new buildings—clean, windy piazzas called *Pageant Stairs* or *Carib Dock*. Then very old ones, weed-grown and commercial, with the names of vanished warehousing companies fading away high up on their graying brickwork. Then back to waste lots again. Wherever you went, it was silent, untenanted even by animals. There were deep wells of shadow, shafts of sun, sudden openings out where Tag could sense the great wide sweep of the river. Just after noon, this strange, apparently unused region gave way once more to life and habitation. Sealink led the way around a corner, and suddenly the whole rush of things was on them again. There was a broadway bustling with lunchtime shoppers. There was traffic, marshaled by the changing colored lights of a five-way intersection.

Men were digging the pavement up.

An irregular hole perhaps ten feet by three and two feet deep had filled overnight with pale brown water. *Traffic cones* lay tumbled about. There were piles of sand, jackhammer lines snaking everywhere, something Sealink called a *pump* with a fat hose and its own engine. The pump didn't work. A man was bent over the hole, bailing it out with a plastic container.

He had on a gray suit, green rubber boots, and a yellow site helmet.

Cy was enchanted. Before Tag could stop her, she had rushed over to him, purring, and started sniffing shyly around the cones near his feet.

At that moment, one of the other men got the pump going. Its motor clattered and chugged into life. Its fat hose bulged and pulsed like a live thing. A small spurt of water was ejected into the gutter. Cy took one terrified look at the hose's behavior and jumped into the hole. Tag jumped in after her. Once in, he couldn't seem to do anything but pedal about, trying to keep his head dry. The icy water took his breath away. It took away his ability to think. It had thrown Cy straight into a fit. When he found her at last, she clung to him and pulled him under. Her eyes were so full of fear he barely recognized her. As they sank she was trying to tell him something. Underneath, it was mad and dark, and you couldn't tell which way up you were. The tabby slipped away. Tag thrashed about, full of anger. How could he help her when he could barely help himself? It was a nightmare. When he surfaced again he had lost sight of her. Sealink and Mousebreath were in the water now, swimming powerfully if rather aimlessly around, fur plastered to their bodies so that even the calico looked tiny and ratlike.

Suddenly, Cy's head popped to the surface. "As above, so below!" she called. "Mercury, quick! I— Yes—yes, it's that. It's blackened walls in the sky. It's in the can. Smoke signals? It's in all those broken cymbals!"

Before she could sink again, Tag grabbed her by the scruff. "Be still!" he said.

She wailed. She scratched. "I've seen all of it," she warned him. "I'm a queen too! Blue-gold beans from Lima! The red and white, and all those neat advertisements. Mercury, quick! Telegram from God's store: Don't buy now!—Cheap— Bye-bye now."

Bubbles came out of her nose.

The man in the yellow helmet watched all this with a kind of detached astonishment. He bent down kindly and fished out Tag and Cy, one in each fist. Tag, heart thundering, looked

squarely up into the big red face and bit the hand that held him.
"Ow!" cried the man, and dropped them both on a pile of sand,
where the tabby flopped about, squalling. Tag grabbed her by
the scruff and dragged her off down a side street. Behind him
Mousebreath and Sealink were hauling themselves disgustedly
out of the water.

The man in the yellow hat watched them until they were out
of sight, nursing his bitten hand.

They holed up for the afternoon under tumbled bricks on some
waste lot. Things looked bad. Cy was covered in a paste of sand.
Her seizure had burned out into unconsciousness and delirium.
The other cats licked and licked at her to dry her fur. From out of
her dreams she babbled of imprisonment, cages emptied once a
day under a cruel white light. She flinched and mewed.

"I don't want the wires!" she cried.

She cried, "The Alchemist!"

Sealink looked meaningfully at Tag.

"I heard that name again and again from cats," she said, "cats
all over the world."

That afternoon the tabby was being drawn away from them,
away from life. They huddled close. They tried to remind her
how warm life could be. It was hard to feel that. They were wet
too. Shivering fits passed through the little group in waves.

"We're in bad shape," said Sealink. "Come dark we got to
move."

"This cat's ill," said Mousebreath.

"Honey, we got to keep warm. We got to find stuff to eat."

"She's ill," said Mousebreath stubbornly.

But in the end Cy woke again. This time, she seemed feeble
and disoriented, but they were able to move on.

Now that it was evening the river hinterland was coming
back to life. Car doors slammed. Echoes rang across cobbled
piazzas that had been deserted since the morning rush. Music
eddied from windows whose warm light seemed to make
ripples on the waters of the darkened canals. A man in a white
apron looked out of a brand-new fish and chip shop. Nervous

with hunger, the cats raised their noses but kept away. They felt safer on the cracked and hollowed ground of deserted yards or in the shadows at the base of some unused building. They were a sorry bunch, Felidae under a yellow moon, slinking between cold waste lots and the river. Even Sealink was unnerved. They were not ready for what happened next. From a condemned warehouse somewhere between Carib Dock and Pageant Stair, they heard a plaintive *miaou*.

Tag looked up dully. The warehouse towered over him, a bowed and blackened wall of brick straining against its ancient rusty iron ties. Once it had been filled with bale on bale of exotic rugs figured in red, black, and cream. Before that, it had been consecrated to porcelain, paint, and tea—China blue, China white, gunpowder green, Lapsang suchong. And before that, cocoa beans, dark new gold from the Caribbean! Its past was three vast sprawling floors of commerce and energy, loaded from the river. Its future was a waste lot. For now, it was dark and silent all the way to the top.

Yet up there, behind the last blind row of windows, flickering lights came and went, green one moment, blue the next. And up there was the cat they had heard. Somehow it had slipped between reinforcing bars and broken glass and now patrolled a sagging window ledge fifty feet above the road. Moonlight glazed its eyes and raked its shadow across the crumbling bricks beneath, every angle sharp with fear. Seeing Tag and his little band, it stiffened suddenly and was still. It vanished for a second. They heard it speak excitedly to someone in the building. Then its head reappeared over the ledge, and it called down in a clear voice, vague but polite, "Excuse me! Excuse me! I wonder if you could help us?"

It was a Mau.

It was rose-gray.

It was Pertelot Fitzwilliam.

"Pertelot! Pertelot!" cried Tag.

She didn't seem to hear.

"We have to go in!" he told Sealink. "We have to help! It's the Queen!"

"We'd have to help anyway, hon. It's a cat."

Tag barely heard. He was trying to think his way through the warehouse double doors that reared up before him huge and forbidding, grimy and gouged, ancient with red paint and flecks of fossilized white lettering.

They were firmly shut.

"She shouldn't be up there!" he said. "How did she get up there?"

"Calm down, hon," advised Sealink.

"Little cat's bad again," said Mousebreath quietly from behind them.

Cy had looked upward, caught sight of the Mau, and promptly toppled head down in the road. As they watched, her eyes widened and bulged. She rolled slowly onto her side to curl up like a dead wasp, while her mouth gaped open on a painful, unvoiced snarl. Her breath was fast and shallow. From deep inside her there issued a long, meaningless whine. Tag had time to think, That's a sound no cat should ever make. Then awareness snapped back into the tabby's eyes, and she began to writhe to and fro with the effort to speak.

"*Khi!* The light formed by light!" she wailed. "Golden cats!

"Don't go!" she said to Tag. "The Alchemist! He's up there! He wants his Queen!" She pulled herself toward him. "Quicksilver, please don't go. It's—I— It's this: I feel cold. I'm not so good."

"What can I do?" said Tag. "I have to help Pertelot!"

"You go," said Mousebreath, in a voice without expression. "You go to your friend now," he said. "I'll look after this one." He nodded at Sealink. "You go, too," he said. "Look!"

He had spotted a broken pane in a lower window. It could be reached by a good jump. Tag knew how to do that.

"Thanks!" he said.

Mousebreath said, "Pay me later."

He pronounced it *pie*.

Pie me lyter.

Tag found himself staring into a high narrow corridor, painted long ago a shiny green. It was cold and full of echoes. A sour smell drifted past him on faint currents of air. Sealink leapt up beside him.

"Staircases at each end," she said. "Hurry, hon!"

The corridor ran the whole length of the building, past a cavernous black elevator shaft and doors painted the same color as the walls. Tag and Sealink ran down it, then dashed up stairs, the metal treads of which had first been polished by human feet, then left to tarnish twenty years in silence. As they went from story to story, skidding around corners, running out into vast empty spaces full of dust and dripping water—"Wrong floor! Wrong floor!"—light filtered down the stairwell toward them, now tremulous and rose-colored, now a baleful orange. They began to hear human shouts, angry and faint at first, and the distressed wail of cats. None of this prepared them for the sight that met their eyes on the top floor.

The loft stretched away, one vast undivided space, with support pillars like old-fashioned lampposts. The air smelled of friar's balsam and tasted like brass. Shadows jigged and flickered across the walls and between the pillars.

In the farthest corner, a column of light issued from the floor, roaring like an inverted waterfall, thrashing and twisting to exit now through the ceiling, now through the nearest wall. The shifting glare cast by this object fell on an indistinct human figure, dressed in a pale robe. Over its head was pulled a black rubber mask or helmet with yellow-tinted glass eyepieces. Its movements—mimed and excessive, as if it wasn't quite human after all but some other species testing out a new body—made Tag remember Tintagel Court, where its hands had pinched up his flesh to insert the needle and its voice had exclaimed "Wrong cat! Wrong cat!"

It was Pertelot's breeder.

It was the Alchemist.

In one hand, the Alchemist held a closed brass vessel streaming smoke, in the other, a short thick staff devised from the mummified foreleg and paw of some large black animal. Weird light flared off the eyepieces of his mask. Around him broke a tide of cats.

They seemed confused.

Tintagel Court was the last good place they had known. Many of them now had shallow unhealed wounds where patches of skin had been removed, especially about the head. Others looked sleek and well fed, a little larger than they had been, full of a rather bemused, undirected health. Some seemed to have been changed out of all recognition. Their movements were odd, uncatlike—though that was probably an effect of the light. They pooled and eddied about the feet of the Alchemist. They were completely silent, yet the air was full of their purring speech. He raised his staff: that gesture launched them like a wave. They moved as one.

Sealink watched, appalled. Then she said, "Tag, I ain't never seen anything like this. Which of these cats do we *want*?"

"Those!" said Tag. "Pertelot! Rags! Over here! Ragnar Gustaffson! It's me!"

Pertelot had come back through the window and now crouched on its dusty inner ledge. Five feet beneath her on the floor, Raggy confronted the Alchemist as if this were one last, awful championship. His great mane bristled. Ragnar Gustaffson—Coeur de Lion!—held himself as he had on the show bench: brave, square, and upright, but only with a terrible effort. His coat was full of broken sticks and knots. It was matted with oil. But he would not let the Mau be taken. As for her: fever-eyes, hollow ribs. You could follow every curve of her bones. All she had left was a rose-gray heart. All she had left was the will to live. She was burning and sullen with it.

"Ragnar! Pertelot!"

They turned their heads, eyes streaming from the strange balsamic smoke.

"Mercury!" cried Pertelot. "Oh, help!"

The Alchemist flung up his arm. His cats rolled toward Tag and Sealink like a silent surf.

"Hon," said Sealink, "I wonder what you got us into here?"

"A fight," said Tag. "Sorry."

It was a strange business. The eyes of the ferals were bright and empty. Their choking, musty smell was full of contradictory signals. "Where are we?" it said. "What's happened to us?" None of them could answer. But they could fight well enough. Tag chopped his way grimly toward the window ledge, the calico beside him. You had to be careful near her. She sent things flying wherever she went. She was like a terrier with rats. They fought well together, cutting and ducking, leaping and bashing in the weird light. But soon the ferals closed around them, separated them, and by sheer weight of numbers began to press them toward the Alchemist. He stood and waited in the middle of the floor, his arms hanging down by his sides, a trail of vapor rising from the vessel in his hand.

"Frankly," Sealink admitted to Tag, "things look bad for us."

The Alchemist knelt. He whistled. He held out his arms. The great hooded head reared over them. You could smell the human sweat on him, the black rubber boots on his feet. A whiff of the canister—friar's balsam and the taste of metal in Tag's mouth—made things whirl dizzily. Tag caught a sudden glimpse of Sealink, her lips drawn back off her teeth in a puzzled snarl, her face a mask of bleeding cuts. Then he seemed to be on his back, looking up at the huge hands coming down toward him for the second time in his life.

As the fight moved away from her, Pertelot Fitzwilliam had abandoned the window ledge. Seeing Tag in such trouble, she and Ragnar now crept bellydown as close to the edge of things as they dared. Suddenly, Pertelot stood up tall and showed herself to her tormentor.

"Now me!" she sang out. "I'm here!"

Abandoning Tag and Sealink immediately, he whirled upon her. She dashed away across the loft. Soon he was darting here and there trying to squirt her with alchemical smoke while, spent and without further ideas, she trotted in exhausted zigzags about the open space looking for places to hide. Ragnar ran to and fro between them, yowling fiercely. The Alchemist laughed. He raised his staff. His sea of cats began to move. Pertelot shrank back. The thing in the corner roared and spat, flared up heraldic red and gold. In that light everything was changed, and you could barely say what you saw. Tag wobbled to his feet. But he was still full of the Alchemist's smoke, and when he ordered his body forward it only swayed unhappily about. And Sealink, who had gotten a bigger dose, was asleep on the floor.

Things would have gone hard with everybody, but at that moment one of the warehouse windows burst in. Broken glass spurted through the air like a cloud of colored steam. Inside it appeared a mysterious violent shape: a bird of fire trailing fantails of sparks, which plunged haphazardly across the room banging from pillar to pillar and finally slammed into the back of the Alchemist's head—after which, spent, it skidded two or three yards across the floor like a loose Catherine wheel and seemed to burn itself out. This extraordinary attack knocked the Alchemist onto his face and dislodged his mask. He balanced for a moment, bent forward, his weight shared between his forehead and his knees. Then he fell onto his side and curled up like a dead insect. Vapors wreathed around his head from the alchemical vessel, which had fallen from his right hand.

In his left hand, though, he still clutched his staff. As Tag watched, he began to make slow, powerful clenching motions, the muscles of his forearm flexing and relaxing, its thick raised veins pulsing with blood. After a little of this, the preserved foreleg out of which the staff was made began to flex too. It was alive. It was as if the Alchemist was pumping life into it. From its mummified paw slipped five hooked claws . . .

"Out!" said a harsh voice in Tag's ear. "Get up and get out!"

Tag looked up dizzily.

Standing over him was the fox Loves a Dustbin. His coat was muddy, his teeth were bared, his eyes were wild, and he smelled angry. He sank his white teeth into Tag's scruff, dragged him upright, and set him untidily on his feet.

"Can you hear me," he barked, "little cat?"

"Don't call me that," Tag began to say.

But the fox only interrupted, "Out! There isn't time! *Do you want to be here when he changes?*"

"Is he a black cat? A huge black cat?"

"Get these animals out of here!"

Tag stared. "All right," he said.

"Tag, honey, have I been asleep?" said Sealink blearily from behind him.

Then she said, "Oh my. Is that a dog?"

Sealink grumbled sleepily, but she helped Tag shepherd Pertelot and Ragnar down the stairs and into the street. Unwholesome light seeped down after them. Even in the street the air felt hot and charged with electricity. They turned as one animal to stare up warily at the top floor windows. Up there, light pulsed faster and faster, flickering the whole width of the spectrum from a deep bloody red to a dazzling white glare. There was a prolonged grinding noise. And rising to challenge it was a long roar of rage from some unimaginable throat. Then—pop!—darkness and silence. After a second or so, a quiet explosion blew all the windows out of their frames. Flames leapt upward. Glass and hot cinders rained down among the cats, who scuttled backward; and the fox burst out of the building at a dead run, staring behind him with fear-whitened eyes.

It was a shabby-looking team that reassembled in the street. Loves a Dustbin sat silently in the shadows with his back to the warehouse, as if he didn't want to be associated with it. Ragnar and Pertelot stood quietly shoulder to shoulder, a little shy and separate. Suddenly the Mau lay down tiredly; and Ragnar began to lick her thin, worn face. In the fierce orange and gold light, they stood out sharp and pictorial. Sealink sat and groomed determinedly, as if all she wanted now was some quiet, practical time to herself. Mousebreath—who had greeted no one, not even his calico queen—was standing stiffly and awkwardly over the tabby, who still seemed to be unconscious.

The fox made the cats nervous. The cats made the fox irritable. Everyone was dirty and exhausted and no one knew what to say.

Tag blinked up at the flames. He felt the heat on his face. Some part of him, gassed and confused, felt as if it were still in the warehouse. The things that had happened up there—the things that had happened at Tintagel Court, the voices he had heard in his dreams—tangled about themselves like threads of alchemical smoke. He shook his head to try and clear it. Then he went over to have a look at the tabby.

"How is she?" he asked Mousebreath.

Mousebreath looked at the fire. Then at Tag. And at last back down at the little cat.

"She's dead," he said.

The Second Life of Cats

*I*n the beginning, the world was a very different place from the one we know now, for the Felidae roamed freely through daylight and dark.

There were the Big Cats, made in the image of the Creator, tawny and black and orange, who ranged over savannahs and mountains—which had been Her shoulders; and the striped Forest Cats who loved the dark jungle—which had been Her fur. There were the Desert Cats, sorrel and roan, or yellow as the sands, padding in the shadow of the dunes or along the bright seashores; and the White Cats who stalked tundra and snowy waste. There was prey for all and to spare; they were the lords of all they surveyed.

In those days the Felidae were afraid of nothing, and all other creatures walked in fear of them, especially the human beings.

What tale can be told about them?

They had squeezed themselves into life uninvited from out of the Great Creator's silver eye—the eye, it is said, that looks inward upon the place of the dead and the spirits while Her golden eye looks outward upon the world—and straight away had taken themselves off into the caves. They weren't so good at living! They could only stare out in awe and envy when the Felidae came by—so strong and quick and deadly, so proud by day, such lamp-eyed hunters by night!

How could human beings take on such qualities?

They could paint cats upon the walls of the caves, as talismans for their own hunt, but it was hard to capture the nature of creatures that moved so silently and swiftly through the *darkness, and so the painted cats had eyes like bowls of silver, teeth like scythes, and claws like knives. They drew cats bringing down first antelope, then buffalo, then even elephants, as if the skill of the cats knew no bounds.*

Humans!

They would imitate the movements of the cats: they danced and danced about the fires, chasing one another and feigning the death of prey. Their backbones were stiff and awkward, their two feet clumped on the clay of the beaten earth, and the springs and pounces they made were feebler than the springs and pounces of any month-old kitten! The Felidae looked on in amusement.

And then one day, one of the humans said to its fellows, "If I was to wear the skin of a cat upon my back, with his head upon my head, and his mouth above my mouth, with his claws upon my fingers and his tail waving behind me, would I not then be able to hunt like a cat?"

And so the next day they went out searching for the hide of a dead cat to bind upon their finest hunter. Eventually, they came upon old Pardus, curled at the foot of a tree, waiting peacefully for his spirit to walk the wild road to the other land, through the Great Cat's silver eye. The humans watched old Pardus warily, for of all the Felidae the spotted cats were most feared for their speed and the power of their great paws and jaws.

They debated as to whether they should try to hasten him upon his journey; but good sense, which is rare among humankind, prevailed and back home they went, empty-handed.

The following day, off they went to the tree again, and this time luck was with them, for in the night Pardus's spirit had traveled down the wild road. But maybe he was just sleeping! Three times the hunters approached, and three times they lost their nerve and ran away into the bushes; until at last the bravest took its long spear and prodded Pardus's chest. The spotted cat's head lolled; again they leapt away! But when he made no other movement they felt more courageous and, binding his feet to the long spear, slung him upon their shoulders and carried him back to the caves.

It was dark when the hunters returned. Flaming torches lit the air as the females and the small ones and the old ones came out of their caves. They gathered around and stared at the big cat's carcass with great awe. To be so close to such a killer!

They stroked Pardus's fine pelt and pressed the huge paws until his gleaming claws protruded; they opened his jaws and peered into his terrifying mouth. They lifted his tail and felt with reverence the weight of his balls.

And when they had done all this they found that their fear of him had somewhat diminished. Then they skinned him with their sharp flint knives and bound his hide upon their greatest hunter, so that his back was on its back, and his head was on its head, and his mouth was above its mouth, and his claws were upon its fingers, and his tail was waving behind it. Then it started to dance around the fire and as they watched its whirling and leaping it seemed to them that the human moved just like a great cat. It prowled and roared and cut the air with its new claws; and all the humans fell back in awe from the one they thought they knew. And after that night the aura of the great cat seemed still to be with that human even when it did not wear his skin upon its back. And so it became their chief and the humans walked in fear of it.

In this way, then, humans started to learn to draw our power and our magic down into themselves. They tamed the weak-willed dogs of the plain—the craven Canidae—and during the day hunted us down and killed us where we slept or nursed our young. They took our skins and bound them on their backs.

But at night, they kept to the caves, built the fires high, and watched for the flash of our eyes in the dark . . .

Chapter Seven

THE ONE-EYED CAT

It is bad luck to see a black cat before breakfast.
—MIDWEST SAYING

*M*ousebreath said loudly, so that everyone else could hear, "That's how she is, mate. She's dead."

Tag looked down at Cy. She had uncurled in her last moments and now lay stretched out on the cracked pavement in the pose of a cat walking lightheartedly across a road on a sunny morning—legs striding out, head held high. Walking too lightheartedly, perhaps. Her mouth was still open, but her eyes were closed. Her face looked small and pained, as if to say, My life was sad but I didn't want to leave it.

Tag put his face in her fur. It was still warm and smelly. He heard her say, "Hi! I'm Cy. Cy for Sign Here!" He saw her playing with a butterfly in two lanes of rush-hour traffic. He saw her scampering awkwardly toward him, dragging a piece of deteriorating linoleum.

The other cats had gathered around to look down at her. Puzzled and disoriented, as animals often are by death, they purred and rubbed their faces against her, against Tag. "She never *washed*!" he told them, as if that explained anything. "I don't want her to be dead," he said. He could hardly make the words come. He looked from Mousebreath to Sealink, Ragnar to the Mau. He appealed, "What can we do?"

They looked away from him.

"Tell me!" he demanded.

At this the fox stepped out of the shadows. "Let me look," he said gently.

But Mousebreath stood in his way.

"You're a dog, mate," he said. "What can dogs do—raise the dead?"

126

"You know I'm not a dog," said Loves a Dustbin, "but I've got something a dog has."

"Have you? How convenient."

The fox brushed past him with a kind of angry patience, approached the dead tabby, and lowered his head until he seemed almost to touch his nose to hers. Then he was very still and quiet. When at last he raised his sharp triangular mask, the flames from the burning warehouse laid red light across his eyes, so that he looked a very equivocal creature indeed.

"I've got a good nose," he told Mousebreath, "which is more than any cat ever had." He turned to Tag. "She's not dead yet," he said. "I can smell the life in her."

Mousebreath laughed bitterly. "What's that mean?" he demanded.

The fox ignored him and said to Tag, "She may recover, she may not. In any case you should move her. There's no shelter here. I can hear fire sirens in the distance, and the Alchemist may come back." Minute by minute, the heat was forcing them farther away from the building. Puddles were drying on the pavement. Up on the top floor, things sagged and broke and fell farther into the fire. The fox looked around. "You can't stay here much longer."

In his misery, Mousebreath wouldn't give up. "What's that mean, then, *smell it in her*?" he said. Something dangerous and unpredictable swam slowly from the blue eye to the orange. "What's that mean, mate?"

All this time, Sealink had been nipping cinders and tangles of burned hair out of her coat, eyeing covertly the King, the Queen, and—especially—the fox. Now she stood up, stretched, rearranged herself with a kind of gargantuan grace, and sat down again. "You come over here with me, honey," she advised her consort, "and leave kind Mr. Fox alone." When Mousebreath went, he went reluctantly.

Loves a Dustbin stared at them. "Cats!" he said.

The calico returned him stare for stare. "Honey," she told him, "I ain't never had truck with a *fox* before, though I been downwind of them in fourteen countries." She resumed her toilette. "Can we-all not quarrel, and give some thought to what to do?"

They locked eyes one moment more, then Loves a Dustbin turned away and walked slowly over the road toward the warehouse. There, he sat as close to the double doors as the fire allowed. His head hung down. The heat made him pant. Once or twice he looked up at the top story, as if he were thinking of going back in. Tag went over to join him.

"I'm sorry they don't like you," he said.

"Who?" said the fox. "Oh, them. They don't have to like me." Then he asked, "You didn't see the magpie get out, did you? I waited as long as I could, but he was slow to wake up and it was already an inferno." He shivered. "And who could face that thing in there?" he asked himself. "Not me."

"I don't understand," said Tag. "The bird of fire was a magpie? In that light it hardly looked like a bird at all. What a brave creature!"

He said, "*I* know a magpie. He's called One for Sorrow."

The fox stared blankly at him. "I wonder about you, Tag," he said. "The bird up there—that *was* One for Sorrow. Who did you think it was?" He chuckled suddenly. " 'Bird of fire!' He'd have loved that." He got to his feet, bent himself around so that his long whippy spine made a complete circle, and began to root pensively about with his teeth in the fur of one haunch. "I told him he'd break his neck."

"I don't understand," said Tag miserably.

"It was him," said the fox. "Take it from me."

"No," said Tag. "I mean I don't understand how you knew each other."

The fox's sad laugh came back. "We know each other very well, all we creatures of Majicou," he said. "One for Sorrow and I, we knew each other very well."

And he would add no more.

They took the fox's advice and left the warehouse burning like a beacon. It was a slow, dreary retreat. Rain fell in every gust of wind, always against the lie of their fur. Every street was a blind alley that brought them up against the river.

Mousebreath would allow no one else to carry Cy. The fox observed his struggles with unconcealed irony. Sealink picked arguments with the fox: "Oh, excuse *me*, sir. Ain't no need to sniff like that. I'm sure I didn't see you there!" And Ragnar and Pertelot dawdled shyly along, always a hundred yards behind, living in their own world, a world composed of memory and pain.

"They're none too friendly, hon," complained Sealink to Tag.

"Can you blame them?" jeered the fox. "You saw what waits for them."

"Pardon me for speaking, I declare."

"They want to be friendly," said Tag, "but you frighten them. Both of you."

Seven animals spent the rest of an uncomfortable night in a partly finished development about a half mile upriver. It was to be called, a builder's board informed the reading world, Piper's Quay. There at Piper's Quay, the moon shone down through unglazed windows. Pale dust blew across the floor on drafts that smelled of cement, mastic, cheap raw new wood. The fox sat down watchfully in one corner, Sealink and Mousebreath in another, the King and the Queen in a third. Cy lay motionless wherever she was put; if life stayed somewhere in her heart, if her breath continued to go in and out, only the fox could detect it. Mousebreath huddled close to her. No one wanted to say anything. No one slept. Tag was angry with them all. They were supposed to be his friends. It was Ragnar who broke the silence. After about a half hour, he stood up and announced in his show-bench voice, "Pleased to meet you all. From the South of England, grand champion three times Ragnar Gustaffson Coeur de Lion here. *Norsk Skogkatt,* if you know what that is! Also I might introduce you to Champion Pertelot Fitzwilliam of Hi-Fashion, first in class at many shows: Egyptian Mau. Very old breed. Excuse me, we are quite tired. After this battle."

There was a silence.

"Well, well," said Mousebreath eventually, "it's the Queen of Sheba. And look here! As if that's not enough, he's brought his missus with him."

Ragnar, who had understood not a single word of this, looked at him uncertainly. It was Pertelot Fitzwilliam who answered. "It isn't our fault your little friend is ill," she told Mousebreath. "We want to help her as much as you do. You feel contempt for us, but by what right? I cannot help being who I am, any more than you can. I did not choose to be born with this blood."

She stood up, drew muscle and fur about her as if her soul were cold, and laughed sadly. "Look what it has brought me to," she whispered. "He pursues me without let!" She shuddered. "I would like to be an ordinary cat. I would like to sit close to Cy in the night. I would like to comfort her. I want to do the things every cat does, before he catches me and it is all over. Mousebreath, won't you help me? Your eyes see two worlds," she told him. "One orange, one blue. Can't you see that I love her too? No one has a monopoly on compassion."

The room was quiet. Mousebreath looked away. "When you put it like that," he said gruffly.

She stepped forward and rubbed her face against his to thank him.

"They're beautiful eyes," she said.

A loud, rough purr filled the air.

The Queen now went on. "Ragnar Gustaffson wanted to say thank you for helping us. We must leave soon. My breeder, whom you call the Alchemist, will not give up. He will not let me go. He calls me the Mother. He will kill anyone, human or animal, who gets in his way. Centuries ago, he came upon a prophecy as old as the Nile—a prophecy that foretold the breeding of a Golden Cat, a cat he believes will bring him enormous power and knowledge."

The Queen shuddered.

" *'The blood is a book,'* " she said. She laughed dully. "Raggy, come and stand by me. I don't feel well. *'The blood is a book,'* that is what he says." She looked up and continued. "I understand little more of this than you. He believes he will breed the Golden Cat from me. If the blood is a book, mine is old, and it is a text he has read over and again. All his experiments point this way: one more birth is necessary if he is to get what he wants. Three hundred years' work—so many generations of my forebears lived and died in his laboratories! I am the last of them. He believes he is close to the end, and he won't give up until he has taken me back. Even as I speak, I feel him near. If he finds you with me, he will kill you all! You are in terrible danger while we stay with you. We'll be gone from here by morning."

Loves a Dustbin, who had been pretending to ignore the entire exchange, sprang to his feet. "No!" he cried. "You must not leave!"

He looked angry, defeated, and anxious all at once.

"Who are you to tell her what to do?" inquired Mousebreath. "You're just a dog."

The fox snarled. "If you had an ounce of intelligence . . ."

Amusement swam gently out of Mousebreath's blue eye and into the orange one. There it settled and after a moment hardened like cement. His big broad head went down, his ears furled back. "Ain't no use for anything but the two F's," Sealink had once said of him.

"Tell me about it," he said quietly.

"I think I will," the fox said. "I think it's time I—"

"Stop!" cried Pertelot Fitzwilliam.

The fox, who, with his hackles rising and his black lips pulled back off his teeth in a cunning bony rictus, had been slipping across a puddle of moonlight to flank Mousebreath on his blue-eyed side, swung to face her.

"Be careful!" he warned.

She backed away, then stood her ground. She was half his height, and his smell was stronger than she was. Her long curved limbs and exotic profile glowed in the angular moonlight. The signature of the sacred beetle stood out on her forehead, a letter in a forgotten alphabet. Her eyes shone like reflections off satin. When he realized who he was looking at—how afraid she was, and how brave—the fox seemed to return to himself.

"That wasn't very well done," he admitted.

To Mousebreath he said, "This will keep."

"Only if I say so."

"Then I'll persuade you," the fox said. "What happens here

is as important for the tabby as it is for anyone else. Her fate is tied up with theirs."

"You say that."

"I say that."

Mousebreath stared at him for some time. "Fair enough," he said. "Later, then."

"Oh yes," the fox promised him quietly. "You can depend on it." And he turned his attention to the Mau. "Pertelot Fitzwilliam," he said, "so much is at stake here! You will have to forgive me . . ." He didn't seem to know how to continue. When he spoke again it was to try and persuade her. "We are your friends here. If we frighten you, I'm sorry. We're a rough lot, but we do have your interests at heart. The Alchemist frightens us, but we are not without resources. We won't let him take you, I promise."

And then, without warning and rather awkwardly, he knelt down in front of her.

Sealink had been watching these events with a certain relish. "I've seen it all now," she said. She heaved herself to her feet. "Honey," she told the Queen, "you just rest yourself where you are and let me give you a real wash." While to the fox, with a grudging respect, she said, "I never knew an animal stand up to Mousebreath before. Plus, it ain't often you hear a fox promise to look after a cat. So you're okay right now. But come morning someone'd better be able to explain this-all to me."

They made such a tableau in the moonlight. In the center sat Pertelot Fitzwilliam, as close as she could get to the unconscious Cy. The fox knelt in front of her, in his gaze a strange mixture of calculation and reverence. Sealink, left of center, washed the Mau's tired eyes like the mother of all cats while Ragnar Gustaffson and Mousebreath stood still as bookends at either side. Without thinking, Mousebreath had taken on Ragnar's characteristic square tall stance. It looked odd but rather fine, Sealink said, on a street tom with mismatched eyes. "Some show cat, huh?"

Tag stared at his friends.

At least they were talking to one another.

* * *

One by one they all slept.

Tag dreamed that a black cat came to him and said, "Tag, listen to me."

It said, "I am Majicou."

It was the cat it had always been in his dreams, although now it was his own size. A proper cat, not quite the monster he remembered, one-eyed and perhaps a little old but still filled with life. Its coat was good. Its movements were graceful and economic. Its eye was— He couldn't place the color of its eye. But it was an eye dancing with wisdom one moment, thoughtful and strange the next, with the personality in it barely present—or at least seeming to arrive from a great distance.

"Are you the Alchemist?" asked Tag fearlessly.

Everything went dark. Tag had the impression of something enormous looming above him, ablaze with malice and intelligence, so that even its breath was like hot smoke. "Never doubt me!" it warned him. "Never doubt me!" Then everything came back again, and Majicou sat before him, blinking amusedly.

"Do you think you would be alive if I was?"

"I don't know," said Tag.

When he looked around him in his dream he saw that he and the black cat were standing just outside Piper's Quay, on a wall above the river. The moon plated the water with silver, picked out the warehouses on the opposite bank, and made the pink halogen lamps seem dim.

"What do you see?" the old cat asked Tag.

"I don't know."

"You see a highway. If you could travel it, you would. Tag, wake up."

Tag woke up and found that he had walked in his sleep and now stood just outside Piper's Quay on a wall above the river, under a white moon like an arc of tinfoil. A damp breeze blew up from the eastern reach, ruffled his fur the wrong way. Beside him was a one-eyed black cat. He was old but still filled with life. "Waking or dreaming I am always with you," he promised. "Do you see?" He wasn't a big cat, but his soul seemed huge and it overflowed, so that he filled up more space than any cat should.

"Come with me, Tag," he suggested. "Come for a walk with me."

"I won't come."

But his feet came despite him.

A walk with Majicou was not like a walk with any other cat. Majicou walked in a measured way, giving every step its full weight. Nevertheless, he covered considerable ground. Majicou took note of everything that passed, and his one eye saw more clearly than another cat's two. Majicou talked as he went. Talking with Majicou was not like talking to any other cat.

"What is a highway?" he asked. Then before Tag could respond, "If I heard the answer, *A convenient line between two points,* I would be talking to a human being. Are you a human being?"

"No!" said Tag, rather shocked.

One eye caught the moonlight. It was no color, all colors. A ghost of laughter hung in the air. "How does an animal answer, then?"

"I don't know," Tag said truthfully.

"Good," said Majicou.

He walked in a contented silence for a while. "Very well," he continued, almost as if talking to himself. "How does a *cat* answer?"

"I don't know that, either."

"Good!" said Majicou. "Do you know anything at all?"

Tag stared at him. "Eat when you're hungry, sleep where it's dry. No one is ever what they seem."

"Hm," the old cat said, not altogether approvingly; and when he began again, it was on a different note. "So," he said, "what am I to tell you, Tag?

"That if, as the pretty myth has it, cats are allotted nine lives, I have lived out eight of mine? It would be true to say that. That I am as old as the highways I care for and that sustain me in return? That cats once got up on their hind legs at night and held not just a parliament but a just parliament with human beings? Ridiculous. No cat has ever wanted to walk like a man. Yet it's a pity we can't talk to them, Tag."

"I thought you hated human beings," Tag said.

Majicou stopped walking. "Ah!" he said. "Here we are."

He had led Tag back to the warehouse.

It was a very different sight now. The fire was out. The roof was blackened rafters. The walls leaned in on one another for support. Smoke rose thinly from a gutted shell. Two or three huge red machines were still gathered in a shudder of flashing blue light in the street outside. Men shuttled to and fro between them, dirty and smelling of charred wood. Inside they were busy damping the embers down with hoses. Water swilled from the double doors of the building and into the gutters. The hoses wove patterns like writing in the road. The pump engines vibrated.

Majicou looked up. His eye gleamed. "As a young cat," he said, "I loved a fire." Then he added, "You did well in there."

"How do you know?"

"Ah."

"We did do well," said Tag proudly.

Majicou was walking about unconcernedly among the firemen. Somehow they didn't see him. He wove, like the hoses, in and out of their feet. But they were always looking in another direction. Tag followed him. "How are we doing this?" he said, delighted. "Are we invisible . . . ?"

Instead of answering, Majicou stared quietly up at the gutted and blackened shell. "Hardraw Wharf!" he mused. "I knew this place many years ago as Hardraw Wharf! The fastest three-masters in the world tied up here, and Norway rats—black rats, with eyes like opals—poured ashore from the straw-packed porcelain in their holds. The sweetest cat I ever knew caught Norway rats to order here, for fish heads in a bowl!" He laughed. "The warehousemen had named her Blue—"

"I caught a rat once," said Tag. "It was brown."

He thought.

"Why did you send me a message by rat?"

"What else was I to do? I tried to speak to you through dreams, but *he* had touched you, and you were too frightened and miserable to listen. Quick, Tag. In we go!"

Majicou had gained the far pavement, jumped neatly across a shallow puddle, and was now measuring the distance to the very window Tag had used to gain entrance earlier that evening.

"I'm not going in there again!"

But Majicou had already disappeared.

"You must, Tag," came his muffled but urgent reply. "You must!"

Inside it was still warm.

A small stream swirled along the middle of the corridor, submerging the firemen's hoses. These ran in a sheaf for a few yards from the main entrance, then branched off, one to each burned-down door. There were distant-sounding thuds and shouts. From the lamps of the working firemen a fitful yellow glow leaked back into the corridor, augmented every so often by flames as the fire flared up again. By this light, Tag saw that the stairs at each end of the corridor were choked with seared brick and shattered roof tile, supported on rafts of broken wooden beams. Nevertheless Majicou stood waiting at the bottom of the right-hand stairwell.

"What do we do now?"

"We go up."

"But the stairs are blocked!"

"Not to us, Tag." A tiny twist of firelight winked in Majicou's eye. "We're too determined. Look!"

At one side of the stairwell the rubble was less densely packed than it seemed. Various items—part of a bed frame, an enormous wooden pulley block tangled in hemp rope, a broken desk from an upper office—were wedged at odd angles. About a foot off the ground, Majicou had found an irregular hole big enough to admit a cat. Water trickled from it down the bricks, then made off, floury with suspended ash, to join the main stream in the corridor.

"Come on, Tag!"

Heat throbbed in the rubble. There was a sour, dusty smell. Tag never put a foot to the stairs. Instead he found himself squeezing his way through something that was less a tunnel than a thousand separate cramped spaces linked by his own progress. His head and shoulders squirmed in one direction around half a brick; his body above the pelvis was facing in another to negotiate a length of ten-inch earthenware pipe; meanwhile, his rear legs scrabbled for traction on a loose surface he had already passed and forgotten. Every time the rubble shifted or creaked he felt an intense rush of fear and anger. His coat was filthy again. His eyes were full of dust. The heat and effort had made him thirsty, and the only clue to his next move was the scent of the old cat on the rubble just ahead.

"Why are you making me do this?" he called.

No answer.

Ten or fifteen minutes later he pulled himself out of the rubble and looked around.

It had once been a first-floor corridor. Most of it had fallen away, along with all the inner walls and the remaining two floors. He was marooned on a short, buckled gallery listing over a pit of smoking rubble. Above, through skeletal rafters, he could see the moon.

"Very clever," he said. "Now what?"

Majicou looked down into the pit. "Time is on no one's side," he remarked to himself. Then he said, "Tag, how did you find your way here?"

"I followed you."

"So, what *is* a highway?"

"How would I know?" said Tag.

"Then let me show you."

Without so much as a second glance over the edge, Majicou jumped off.

Tag looked down.

Nothing.

"Majicou?"

Smoke. Dark. Heat.

"Old cat?"

No answer.

Then something—a sound perhaps, or a smell or a movement in the corner of his eye—made Tag look outward into the space above the pit. The moonlit air trembled with heat. There was Majicou. Behind him Tag could see the distorted image of the far wall with its lampblacked brick, aimless cracks, and empty windows. He stood with his bushy tail curled back over his body in a flat *S*, like a cat on an Oriental vase. At first, he seemed to be floating perhaps five or six feet out from the shattered edge of the gallery. But when Tag looked more carefully, he saw under the old cat's feet a faint, smoky surface like tinted glass.

"Well?"

"Well what?" said Tag.

"Will you come?"

Tag looked down into the pit. He looked across at Majicou.

"It's a long way," admitted Majicou.

Tag remembered his lost home. A kitten on a windowsill in the rain.

"I've come a long way already."

He gathered his powerful gray back legs under him and leapt out into whatever would happen.

"I brought you here," said Majicou, "because this highway is already fading. It isn't old enough to have any real memory of itself. Situated like this it is unlikely to be found again. We will probably be the last animals to use it." He sighed. "It was a pleasant route, less a highway than a path, used by the Hardraw Wharf cats to get to and from a flat roof overlooking the river. The roof vanished when the original wooden building was rebuilt with brick. Until then, the sun had warmed it daily for a hundred years, a little while after dawn and before sunset. There the cats would lie bathed in light, watching the ships pass up and down the river. Later wharf cats used it for other day-to-day journeys. For the most part they were gentle animals. Oh, they were merciless with a rat—"

"Me too," said Tag.

"—and they would fight their eyes out over a queen. And they often died here, of one disease or another. But they were tranquil animals, and this is their tranquil little highway. Do you see?"

"No," said Tag.

He had taken the precaution of closing his eyes when he

jumped. Now, calmed by Majicou's voice, he opened them. He found himself neither falling, as he had half expected, into a cinder pit nor hanging unsupported in the middle of the air.

Instead, he was standing in a narrow passage with oaken walls and floors age-bleached and knocked about by use. Sometimes the light within it shifted and changed so quickly that it couldn't properly be described as one corridor at all. Perhaps it was the same place seen at different times, the same place flickering through its rapidly fading memories of itself. It was spring and summer all at once. It was winter sun. It was rose-gray with dawn—he heard pigeons flap up suddenly outside—then flecked with the light of an early autumn evening. A great bar of noon sun entered it at a steep angle through a single unglazed window, to plunge down through drifting motes of dust. Its air was full of strong fascinating smells, among which Tag could name tea, straw, mice, salty tidal mud—and cats . . .

A hundred cats, a thousand of them!

As he stood there, captivated, he had a sense of all those cats moving past him. Old cats sleepily ambling, young cats rushing and stalking, kittens tumbling and gawping, all hurrying toward something they wanted or needed, something not very far away, something delightful or healing or exciting—

"The cats!" whispered Tag. "Oh, the wonderful cats!"

He thought of his travels with Sealink. He thought of the railway bank, of Mousebreath and Cy and their walk through the drifting dawn and how the day had opened up around them all like a flower.

He stared at Majicou. He heard himself say, "A cat would answer you this: A highway is the cats that have traveled it."

"Even so," said Majicou. He laughed gently. "Even so, little cat."

"I want to see the roof and the old ships passing up and down!"

"Then walk."

So that was how Tag, a cat embarking on his very first life, was enabled by Majicou, a cat at the end of his last, to sun himself for a little while above quite another river, in quite another city to the one he knew. This river was fishy mud, masted ships creaking, the reek of fresh tar and sewage, gangplanks teetering on black stilts awry across the shingle. This city was barely more than a country town—meadows and creeks, a horizontal scatter of buildings stretching away to the peach and gold sky behind the dome of a distant cathedral. It was church bells. It was a quiet ripple on the water at sunset. There! Two men in tricorn hats, rowing a boat to catch the rising tide.

They sculled slowly east and north across the golden water. Their oars stirred its surface into gentle concentric circles, soft, sucking whirlpools, eddies that broke into eddies and then into eddies of eddies.

As he watched, the late sunshine fell mercifully on Tag's fur, hypnotizing him, warming his aching muscles and tired limbs, penetrating deeper and deeper until it found an answering glow somewhere so deep inside him that it might have been his soul, entangled with the soul of the day and the bells and the endless water-eddies and the quiet spires of the city. He sat up with his chin high and his eyes barely open, relaxed but straight, purring as loud as he could; and he felt as though he were radiating a light of his own. The sun had touched him, and for a moment he felt as if he had become a beacon of silver that announced to passing sailors "Tag. Tag. Tag."

Suddenly, there was a cry from the water. The oars were shipped, the rowing boat slowed. The man in its stern twisted around sharply to scan the wharves, his black eyes piercing and cold. For a moment they seemed to meet Tag's eyes. They narrowed against the light, narrowed further as he struggled to understand something. Then his gaze went blank and he turned away again, as if he had seen nothing after all.

Slowly, Tag came back to himself.

"Twenty years or a hundred," Majicou was explaining, "they rarely last long. The little paths like this shift and fade, happy or sad, useful or not. While they remain, though, they are tributaries. They serve the wild roads, which have lasted not a hundred, not a hundred thousand, but millions of years. They are the oldest things in the world, Tag, and the most dangerous. They channel the earth's own power, and cats have used that power to travel since time began. We were here long before the earliest men. When they stumbled across our roads, they retained just enough sense of themselves as wild things in the world to recognize what they saw, but not enough to use it. They built great markers at each locus—Stonehenge, Avebury, Glastonbury, and the ancient fort at Tintagel. They could never travel the wild roads as we do; but their oldest track follows the wildest of them all, the Great Highway that cuts across the northern chalk, the track the first cats made.

"The Alchemist has spent three hundred years looking for the key to the highway. He is close, Tag—so close! As soon as he is able to transform himself—" Suddenly, he stopped. "Tag," he said, "do you hear that?"

"What?"

"That voice! That cat—!"

"I hear nothing."

Majicou turned, his haunches down, one forepaw raised. He sniffed the air. "Something I smell," he said to himself. "What does this mean? I don't understand this." He cocked his head to listen. His one eye glittered angrily; he turned and turned again until he had faced all the cardinal points but one.

"Quick, Tag!" he cried. "Quick! Or we're damned!"

In a hundred yards, the highway faded around them. It had led them like a kind old ghost out of Hardraw Wharf, along a dreamy sunlit cobbled alley, and back into the moonlit streets Tag knew—a last gift of cats to cats. Tag looked back.

"Good-bye," he whispered.

"No time for that!" the old cat said. "Somewhere here— Yes!"

He darted underneath a parked car.

Without thinking, Tag followed.

Somewhere between the curb and the car, between the wheels and the road, in the reek of oil and rubber, the ordinary world was whirled away. He was on the highway again. It was neither day nor night. It was uniformly gray. There was no horizon. The wind howled at him from all directions at once, flinging powdered ice in his eyes. He screwed them tight shut. "No!" he cried. "I won't do this!" He was a kitten again. He was before the pet shop, he was before "Tag," he was three weeks old, blind and lost, a whole carpet away from his mother. How had this happened? He flattened himself on the cold ground in panic. "Majicou!" he cried, "Majicou!" His voice echoed back to him as unfeeling as the wind.

"Be still," said the old cat. "Be still and let me listen!"

Nothing for a long time. Tag tried not to be there. He tried to think of kittenhood, sunshine, his time in the gardens, game casserole. But all that came to him was the memory of the wind buffeting him, and the rain beating down while he ran everywhere to avoid it. At last, Majicou said, "Good. Very good.

"We're safe here. He knew I was somewhere near, but the line of the old highway confused him. He could not associate me with such a powerless little road." Then he added, in a different voice, "Tag, this is a real highway, and it is yours."

"I don't want it," said Tag.

But the panic was leaving him even as he spoke. He relaxed. He ceased to tremble. Calmed by the old cat's presence and authority, his honest heart—the heart of a cat, full of curiosity and life—had taken command. His own fear had exhausted him, though, and his eyes remained tight shut.

"The wind!" he cried. "Old cat, the wind!"

Majicou laughed. "Isn't it fine? It's a million-year wind, Tag, blowing east to west, dawn to dusk around the compass rose. It blows all cats on their journeys, and at one and the same time it *is* those cats, it is those journeys—the lives and destinies and fears and hopes of all the cats that ever walked."

"I can't bear it."

"You can. You can. Tag, *the souls of cats* are rushing past us! This is the line of power they laid down, generation by generation! Their heritage, your birthright!"

And again, quietly, "Your birthright. Tag, open your eyes now. Claim it."

So Tag opened his eyes and claimed it.

He saw three things.

The first was Majicou, sitting beside him straight and tall, his one eye gleaming with power and mystery and pleasure. The spirit wind barely ruffled his fur.

The second thing Tag saw was the wild road.

He shuddered. "What kinds of cats made this?" he asked.

"Tag," answered Majicou, "this is a dangerous place to be. The magic of the First Cats still moves within it. They lived in ice and snow, Tag. They were as big as cars, and their teeth were as long as your body. They were wild animals, and they made a savage road. When we travel it now, we partake of that. We are a little of them as well as ourselves. This is the oldest magic there is!"

"I preferred the little highway," said Tag. "I preferred the sun."

What stretched away from him was bare, yet formed and purposeful. Lit by the same moon that shone down on the wharves—though here its light was a little harsher, perhaps, a little more direct—the great road came in from the east and immediately swung south, away from the river. Tag and Majicou stood in the crook of that wide powerful curve, in a landscape hard to interpret. There were buildings, certainly; there were trees. The river was there, though its banks were hard to place. There were gentle landforms toward the south, rising to tree-tangled chalk downs beyond. None of these things were vague; indeed the problem, perhaps, was that they were somehow *too dense*—as if a hundred houses occupied the space of one house, a thousand trees the space of one tree—but they were difficult to see. The wind hissed around him, full of distant, murmuring voices. At any moment Tag felt, if he wasn't careful, he might hear the cat-souls as they passed. If he wasn't careful he might see them, a strange, brownish fog flooding across the landscape as cat blurred into cat into cat into cat into cat without end— eddying and whirling, flowing and fuming like smoke in a retort, fixing itself suddenly and terrifyingly into a single instantly passing image: a tiger of the ice, huge head raised to display its saber teeth to the emptiness and send out a roar that would be heard ten thousand years! And then a more lasting private terror, which was to feel that giant stir in his own soul . . .

"Where does this highway go?" he whispered.

"To Tintagel, Tag. To the sea!"

The third thing Tag saw was a dead cat. It was a small tabby with dusty fur. It lay like any animal that has been knocked down by a passing car on some more ordinary road: somehow sprawled and huddled at the same time, as if it had curled into it-self at the last, to eke out the spark of its passing life. At first, it looked like a cat curled up in front of a fire, then you saw how its head was thrown back and its throat exposed.

It was Cy.

"How did she get here!" cried Tag.

He ran to her and looked down. He weaved about, despite himself, in a desolate, mourning figure eight.

"Oh, Majicou, how I hate this place!"

The old cat said gently, "Tag, watch."

Exactly as the fox had done, he touched his nose to the tabby's. He drew in a long, silent breath, so gentle he seemed motionless. Then he exhaled powerfully into her nostrils, and with a delighted sneeze she sat up, full of laughter, to stare at him. "Oh, you're *very* nice," she said. "Look after this cat you've found!" she advised Tag. "He's beautiful, but he's a fool. He'll get in every kind of trouble, waking people up like that!" She jumped up. Her feet tried to run off on their own, but she held them back long enough to call, "Good-bye! I had a good dream, Quicksilver! Good-bye!" And off she went. She seemed to diminish too rapidly, as if the highway itself were moving her along. Two or three huge moths appeared, their eyes like cheap red jewels in the bluish moonlight, and fluttered around her head. She batted at them with velvet paws.

Tag watched her go. He was astonished. "How did you do that?" he asked Majicou.

No answer.

"Majicou?"

Still no answer.

As he turned to the old cat to ask again, Tag saw that he was with another animal altogether. It was shrinking even as he caught sight of it. But it still sat four or five feet tall, with shoulder blades as sharp as knives. Its fur was of a savage, shiny black, dappled like woodland shade with faint tobacco-brown rosettes. It gave off a rank and untamed smell. Its square muzzle and stony yellow eye were absolutely still. It knew he was there. He looked quickly away. He felt less afraid than shy. But he didn't want the slightest glimpse of what happened next, even out of the edge of his eye. He didn't want to watch the big cat shrivel back down to the Majicou he knew . . .

"You brought her back to life," he said.

There was the faintest of rustles, a kind of settling noise. A sigh.

Then Majicou answered wearily, "Much is illusion in these places. I have traveled the wild roads for longer than I can remember, Tag, and I still don't understand everything they can do. I'm not sure she was here at all. If she was, the Alchemist had a hand in it."

"I don't understand."

"He knew where we were, after all. He watched us leave the warehouse along the old highway. He sent me a message—a challenge, if you like. I have signaled my reply. He will hate that," said Majicou with satisfaction. Staring after the departing tabby, he said, "That little animal is not entirely what she seems. Have a care with her, as well as for her. The Alchemist has a special fate in store for her." Then, as if that reminded him of something, he asked himself, "I wonder. He had to get into the warehouse somehow. Has he poisoned this road too?" He considered this. "It's a pity we can't talk to human beings, Tag. From them has always come our greatest danger; and the Alchemist is the most dangerous of them all. No cat has ever wanted to walk like a man. But he is a man who wants to walk like a cat. Down the years I have wondered if there is anything wrong with that ambition in itself." Majicou shivered. "But he will destroy everything in pursuit of it. Everything I have ever worked for."

"You speak as if you know him."

The old cat was silent. Then he said, "I was his cat for many years, Tag. He called me Hobbe, and I sat by his fire."

Chapter Eight
THE CAT THIEVES

What can you have of a cat but her skin?
— PROVERB

"*I* must go now," said Majicou.

They had returned to Piper's Quay.

The moon was not yet down, though it hung close to the ir-regular line of rooftops on the far bank. A chilly northeast wind made the surface of the river resemble a cobbled street after rain. Perhaps an hour had passed since they'd left.

An hour hardly seemed long enough to contain the things that had happened. Tag knew he would never forget his glimpse of that other river, closed and secured by history, as fixed as the image on a cameo: the calm light playing from every ripple, the cats playing calmly in the light. And the highway! His legs were still trembling from the journey back, with the spirit wind blowing firmly from behind and the one-eyed cat loping en-couragingly in front. What had seemed effortless at the time now seemed eerie. He had run with a growing sense that he had no idea of his own size. A sense that to travel this way was simply to become as large as the distance between the start and the finish of the journey!

He was tired and puzzled. He was elated. He didn't want the old cat to leave. There was such a lot more to know. But now that Majicou had brought Tag safely back, he seemed preoccupied. If a breeze fluffed the water, he lifted his nose to interrogate it. If he heard a car pass on the Caribbean Road, his head came up and he stopped speaking until the sound had faded.

"There are things you must learn," he said, "and this is a way to learn them. Do you understand?"

"No."

"Good."

"Why do you always congratulate me when I don't know something?"

"The first thing an apprentice must learn is that you can't learn by knowing."

"Am I your apprentice?"

Majicou regarded him with exasperated affection. "Unfortunately," he said.

"Why?"

"Because I need a young cat like you who can walk the world in my place."

"How will I learn if you aren't here to teach?"

"A good question, to which you may find your own answer. But I will come when I can. Meanwhile, if you need help, there is the fox."

"Oh, the fox."

"He has looked after you well, little cat."

"Must you go?"

Majicou sighed.

"I must, Tag. Something important—something magnificent—is going on in the world. This part of it, I believe, has been entrusted to you. You are strong enough to bear the weight of it; though when I first saw you I wasn't so sure of that! You must take the King and Queen to Tintagel, where the wild roads meet. It is a place of great power. There is not much time—a few weeks only. When the hours of light and dark fall equal on the vernal equinox a new age will dawn . . ." He became thoughtful. "I have other tasks. If the Alchemist is everywhere, I must be everywhere too. His artificial highways are undependable and short-lived. Except by proxy, he has no access to the real ones; but as his reason gives way to something else, they will cease to resist him, and already his experiments have begun to warp and tangle them. Old forces have woken, to travel the wild roads again, out of control. I must go!"

"Don't leave me," said Tag.

"I must. I am too old and too weary for the world. Go to Tintagel. Go as fast as you can. Take them with you, and keep them safe from the Alchemist. Tag, keep her safe especially! Take her as fast as you can; she is your responsibility now."

"But—"

"Tell no one but the fox that I was here!"

And Majicou bounded off across the unfinished piazza of Piper's Quay, a dark soft-edged shadow against the newly laid setts. He was fifty yards away, then a hundred. Was he growing larger as he went? It was impossible to decide. He paused for an instant on the bank of the ornamental canal, then, extending himself contemptuously, seemed to fly over it. On the other side he halted. He was larger. His eye gleamed fiercely in the moonlight.

"Good-bye, Tag! Look for me as you go!" And he was off again.

"Where shall I see you?" called Tag.

"Follow your nose, Tag!" he heard the distant voice reply.

The moon sank behind the houses, and Majicou had gone.

Tag looked around dispiritedly. A cold wind came up off the river. He closed his eyes and let himself remember for a minute or two the other wind, the spirit wind that blows a million years. He had claimed his heritage. He remembered the other cats—big or small, angry or hungry, untamed, unassuaged, determined to live—who had seemed to run alongside him as he followed Majicou down the ghostly road. He lived in the heat of them, the breath going in and out of them, the sharp white teeth of them. He felt their joy and he felt their pain. He wanted to be one of them. He wanted to be a baby cat again, safe at home with no one to look after. He had claimed his heritage, and found it more a burden than a blessing. He shivered. "This won't get anything done," he said. He sighed, drew himself up as tall as he could, and went inside to find his friends.

Morning arrived gusty and raw. The wind dashed a few dry flakes of snow across the piazza outside. Inside, the cats looked up, then put their heads down, huddled together for warmth, and went back to sleep.

An hour or two later, Tag woke to find snow billowing in quietly through the unglazed window to sift down among the plastic wrap, discarded nails, and offcuts scattered across the partly finished floor. He shivered. He was hungry. Today they would have to get food. A glance around the room revealed Loves a Dustbin and Mousebreath to be missing. The Mau slept peacefully between Sealink and Ragnar, all but the tip of her elegant nose buried in their thick fur. Cy lay on her own in a corner, her condition unchanged.

That part of it was a dream, then, thought Tag.

Just in case, he went over and tried to wake her by touching the side of her face gently with his paw. Nothing. Before he knew what he was doing, he had shut his eyes, put his mouth close to her nose, and exhaled sharply into her nostrils. How would Majicou have brought the magic down for her? How would he have commanded it, or let it command him? Tag had no idea, so he just thought very hard, Wake up now. Wake up!

Nothing happened.

He thought, No one can really breathe someone back to life. So that part was a dream too. He thought disappointedly, Perhaps it was all a dream.

That morning everyone was slow, cold, and hard to love. Nobody wanted to talk. The comradeship of the night before had evaporated, leaving behind an uneasy truce. It felt as if they were waiting for something. The fox returned. He paced the edges of the room. Mousebreath returned separately and gave him an absurdly wide berth. Sealink fluffed up her fur and stared forward with slitted eyes at nothing; she barely said a word. Only Ragnar seemed happy. He went outside and spent some time with the weather. Through the window they could see him galloping energetically if aimlessly to and fro. "The *Norsk Skogkatt* is most viable in snow terrain, I should say," he announced on his return. "Very good grip from these claws, and—" he showed them the underside of his front left paw "—note the tufts of fur insulating the paws of this specimen." He beamed. "Very survivable. And, yes, now breakfast!"

"Don't hold your breath, hon," Sealink counseled him. "There ain't any."

As for the Mau, who knew what she thought? Her eyes were

clouded with Africa, mist rising over green water in the morning, ibis like newly washed white handkerchiefs flapping in the air. Her eyes were just this side of some long, sacred panic, history that sees itself passing. They rested for a moment on the motionless tabby. Then she trembled, got to her feet, and—her back legs staggering a little as if they were still asleep—went over to begin licking and licking Cy's face.

"Can't we help her? We must help her," she said distractedly. "*Can't* we help somehow?" When no one answered, she licked and licked. "Someone must help me with her." Lick, lick, lick. "Please!"

The fox stopped pacing, stared at her for a long time, and then said quietly to Tag, "We should talk, you and I."

They went out into the cold and watched the snow fall into the ornamental canal. There was a fraction of a second in which each snowflake, still distinct but softening and growing transparent, lay on the water. Then it *was* water and could no longer be snow, and that was that.

"She sees her own plight in the tabby's," said the fox. "She sees her own fears."

Tag said angrily, "What do you think I can do?"

His tone surprised the fox. "But Majicou—"

"Oh, Majicou!" said Tag dismissively.

He hadn't intended to speak like that. He stared hard at the snowflakes. Because he liked the fox so much, he wasn't sure where anger left off and hurt began. "I thought you were my friend," he accused, "but you only helped me because the black cat had set you to watch over me."

"Ah," said the fox gently. "I see. I'm sorry." He began carefully, "I am your friend—"

"Are you?"

"—for my sins. But life is complex, little cat, and things are rarely what they seem. Don't take it so hard."

"My name's Tag," said Tag. "I want to be liked for who I am, not what use I can be."

The fox looked exasperated. "Don't you understand that Majicou has made you one of us?" he said. "Since you took up the cause of the King and the Queen you have been no less an agent of Majicou than I am, or the magpie was. Yet why do you take care of them? Only because you love them! Oh dear," he said, "part of you is still such a young cat." He thought this over. Then he said, "To be honest, I like that part a lot."

"Good," said Tag coldly.

"So are we friends again?"

Tag would not answer. The fox looked upset. "What do you know about me?" he asked bitterly. "What I might like, how I might feel? Nothing! You never even asked. You just took what I offered."

That's true, Tag thought. But I don't know how to apologize. Instead he heard himself suggest, "Everyone is hungry. We should get some food first, then find a way to help Cy and the Mau."

The fox tried to make his voice businesslike. "At least this snow won't last," he said. "That's one good thing."

After a moment Tag said, "I'm sorry. I do want to be friends."

"I can't make more sense of you than any other cat," said Loves a Dustbin.

"I'm sorry," said Tag.

Then he went quickly back inside.

There, he found Pertelot restlessly quartering the floor around the inert tabby's body.

Her pain and confusion were clear to see. She would take three or four urgent steps, as if she had had an idea, stop abruptly, as if she had thought of something else, then take three or four steps in a fresh direction. She faltered at every draft, every change of light in the room. Her eyes shone blankly. She was in a fever of motherhood, kittenhood, fear, and need. Her signals were crossed. Up and down she roamed, purring in distress, carrying her tail high, stopping only to rub her head against Cy's or to lick, lick, lick at the dull fur. She paused with one elegant forepaw raised as Tag came in. Then she turned away and began to knead the tabby's ribs, as if that ancient plea of the kitten to the mother—Feed me!—might gain Cy's attention.

Ragnar, Mousebreath, and Sealink sat as far away from her

as they could get, arranged along the base of the wall like a row of china cats.

"Can't you do anything?" Tag asked them.

"We tried, hon. She just ain't at home."

"She's got a bite on her," said Mousebreath with a certain admiration. "If you get too near, she'll have you. She's had His Highness there once or twice."

Ragnar sat puzzled and hurt, too unhappy to speak.

Tag thought, Well I must do something! He approached the Mau with care. "Pertelot Fitzwilliam," he said quietly.

She eyed him like a speck in the distance, like something on the horizon in the noon haze, something she was not sure she had seen.

"Pertelot Fitzwilliam, what do you want from this cat?"

"I want her to waken."

"We all want that."

"Then help me!"

"Pertelot Fitzwilliam, that isn't the way to wake a cat like her."

She stopped and regarded him. "In Egypt they mourned Her three days," she began in a febrile, singsong voice. "If She would not wake, they took Her to the canopic room—" She looked around her suddenly. "I was never in Egypt," she said puzzledly. "What can I do for her, then?" she asked.

Tag went close to the tabby's face. "Watch," he said.

He took in a long, quiet breath. He exhaled sharply into her nostrils. The tabby remained motionless. Tag felt Pertelot's eyes upon him. There was puzzlement in them but less fever. "See?" he said.

As he turned away, he felt her staring after him distrustfully. But he had made her think, and she was already calmer. When he looked next, she had settled herself down so close to the tabby that their heads were almost touching. Her eyes were closed. Her tail lashed once or twice, as if she were gathering herself. Then she slept.

Silence filled the room.

"Boy's a diplomat," acknowledged Sealink.

Two or three minutes later there was an outbreak of deranged barking from the piazza.

Tag ran to look out.

The snow had already melted. The cloud base was softening and breaking up. Patches of blue sky were appearing. A wintry sun warmed the piazza—dimmed briefly, so that things seemed to shrink—then struck through the cloud again, this time as a ray of pale golden light.

In that ray, framed by the doorway so that it looked like a picture rather than a real event, a curious scene was being enacted. All along the axis of the piazza ran a string of reproduction Victorian lampposts, painted a dignified dark gray-blue, their cast-iron moldings picked out in gold and their glass lamps faceted like the seed cases of poppies. The fox Loves a Dustbin was running full tilt around and around the base of one of these, barking and yelping, jumping up, standing on his hind legs and scratching at the paint. Above him, sometimes perched on the lamp or the crossbars beneath it, sometimes fluttering precariously in the air a foot above his snapping jaws, was a large bird. Its black-and-white livery was sadly charred, and some of its tail feathers were missing, so that it seemed scruffier and less agile than it had once been. But there was nothing wrong with its voice or its self-esteem. The empty piazza rang and echoed. Between the bird's harsh croak and the fox's ringing yelp, it was bedlam at Piper's Quay. They were mad with their own delight. Around and around they went, like a windup toy. Wings cracked and flapped. Claws scraped on the setts. The morning pigeons fled and scattered across the sky like shot.

"One for Sorrow!" cried Tag. "It's One for Sorrow!"

He sprinted out across the setts to join them, then slithered shyly to a halt. It was their reunion after all. They were Majicou's longtime helpers, and he was only an apprentice. But as soon as the magpie saw him it fluttered down and flapped noisily around his ears, calling him all the same names as it had done when he'd nearly eaten it. The fox danced around both of them, barking. Tag felt as if he would burst with pride to be part of it all.

"One for Sorrow!" he cried.

"They'd better believe it," the magpie said. "That's who I am! Fire and flood, I made it out with my feathers on!" He perched on the ground between Tag and the fox. He cocked his wicked head and looked from one to the other. "One for Sorrow's who I am!"

But today he was one for joy.

A little later, the fox and the cat sat at the bottom of the lamp-post listening to the magpie, an inventive but fidgety narrator who, as he told his story, strutted about in front of them squawking with amusement or rage, slyly eyeing his audience for signs of approval. Every so often he stopped to shake out his charred feathers with a noise like dry reeds rustling in the wind. Sometimes he drove his beak into them like a bird who has at last located a live-in adversary of considerable age, evasiveness, and durability.

He began by reminding Tag and Loves a Dustbin how he had burst into the warehouse. "That was some window!" he bragged. "Oh, that was a window all right. You needed a skull on you for a window like that!"

Already disoriented and half stunned by this grand entrance, he had finished himself off with his dramatic assault on the Alchemist. All he remembered of that was the aftermath—pinwheeling across the room at floor level with, as he put it, all the lights going out.

"By then," he said, "I was well out of it. Well out of it!"

He had woken half blinded by concussion. The place was full of dancing shadows. "Could I make any of it out? Not for the life of me! I was as weak as a chick off the nest." He had no idea who had won the fight. He had no idea if the Alchemist was still there. "Had he gone? Had he *changed*? I didn't want to find out!" He had reeled about a bit with the underside of his beak on the floor and his wings rotating uselessly until his vision cleared. "Well, then I saw! All that was left was the Alchemist's highway!

"Terror?" the magpie asked his audience. "I was gripped!" He looked dramatically from Tag to the fox. "So, then," he invited them, "put yourselves in my place! What was I going to do? Leave, of course! Get out! Exit!" He hopped away across the piazza in his excitement, then back again. "Too late!" he said.

The false highway had collapsed in on itself as he watched. A plane of fire ripped across the floor half an inch above his head. "Before I knew it, my tail was in flames!" All he could do was hold his breath and wait for the fire to pass. It was an instant, no more—but it was the instant of a magpie's life, passed in an agony of suspense. "I was running out of breath. I was running out of time!" He thought for a moment. "I was running out of *tail feathers*!" In the end he had taken his hope in his wings, launched himself into the burning air, and lunged blindly toward the window he had entered by. His chances of finding it, he knew, were low. "But I'm a magpie. So what do I think?" He paused, bobbed his head, regarded his friends with a beady eye. When they weren't quick enough to respond, he said triumphantly, "I think: You haven't had it till you're dead!"

"Very philosophic," said the fox. "I'm impressed." He winked at Tag. But Tag didn't notice. He was too awed by the magpie's simple determination.

"What did you do?" he whispered.

"Little cat, *I flew*!"

Out through the window he had gone. Clipped the edge of it. Cartwheeled into the night half conscious and half on fire, until he lost height suddenly and, fainting, fell into a puddle of water somewhere on a trading estate downstream. "It put the flames out, anyway!" He had lain like Lucifer in this puddle until morning woke him. "Two *cats* were moving in on me!" he exclaimed disgustedly. He eyed Tag. "Grubby pair. Thought I was dead!" He chuckled. "Damn near was," he said. "But I still gave them a seeing-to!" He took off and perched on top of the lamppost, so they had to crane their necks to look up at him. "Damn near *was* dead!" He cawed loudly enough for the whole world to hear. "But now I'm alive again!" He raised his head, opened his beak, and flapped his wings.

Infected by this blatant display of joie de vivre, Loves a Dustbin went back to leaping around the base of the lamppost.

The bird crowed. The fox danced. Tag egged them on.

There was a polite noise behind him.

When he turned around, he found five cats standing in a row watching him curiously.

A little ponderous, a little puzzled this morning, Sealink had led them out onto the piazza, planting her feet as if the ground could be a steadying influence. Now she and Mousebreath stood on one side, Ragnar and Pertelot on the other, and between them, blinking in the daylight but as bright eyed and ready to live as any kitten, was the tabby. She looked like a cat who had had enough sleep to last a lifetime. Thanks to the attentions of Sealink and the Mau her ears were presentable, her coat glossy and dense, its black stripes like polished glass. Her socks had a detergent whiteness. Even the plug in her head glittered brassily in the sun. When she moved, it shed sparks of light. She stood square on her stubby legs, bottom up, tail carried high with the tip waving to and fro. Her yellow eyes danced. As Tag and the fox guttered into an astonished silence, she looked interestedly around and gave a huge yawn.

"Shiny out," she remarked. "Where's the wedding?"

The first thing she saw was One for Sorrow, who, on the arrival of so many hungry-looking Felidae, had prudently resumed his perch below the lamp. Slitting her eyes against the light, she got down on her stomach and began to stalk him with care, flattening herself as if the edges of the setts would provide cover. She gave Tag a hard look.

"My bird," she warned him. "My bird!"

The magpie choked with laughter, lost its balance, and had to fly in a wide circle above the piazza to recover its dignity.

Cy watched it go. "You spoiled that," she accused Tag. "We could have taken it home and planted it." She looked up at the fox.

"Wow!" she said. "You smell!"

The fox could scarcely contain his amusement. "So do you," he said.

She told him shyly, "When you took my breath from me it was all sparks. All sparks where I was"—this she almost sang—

"all dust drifting in rays of light." She stretched luxuriously, planting her forepaws, pulling back and up from them. She said, "I feel brand-new!"

And that was how she looked.

Tag was stunned. Accepting on faith his secondhand magic, Pertelot Fitzwilliam had worked into it from out of her need, from out of her deep dream of Egypt. She had brought the tabby back. All bets, as the Coldheath ferals would have said, were off. Majicou's world of magic now seemed rather more tangled with the world Tag knew—the magic of home and friends and sunshine, delight in right things happening—than he had thought. That morning, he had wondered how much of it had been a dream.

Now he would have to think again.

What the other cats made of these events was difficult to say. After all, the dead are so rarely brought back to life. They had taken refuge in cat nature . . .

Only the quick flicker of thoughts from blue eye to orange and back again, from delight to irony to acceptance, betrayed Mousebreath's surprise.

The Mau stared voracious and unassuaged at the object of her care. For her, the tabby's return had resolved a superficial issue. She remained haunted . . .

Ragnar Gustaffson could strike only the simplest of attitudes, but his was the most difficult reaction to gauge. He seemed awed but at the same time full of a bubbling, secret excitement. Back and forth went his gaze, like Mousebreath's thoughts, from Mau to tabby, tabby to Mau, as if he were trying to add something up.

As for Sealink . . . "Hon," she asked Tag, almost plaintively, "can you and me have a *word*?"

And she led him away from the celebrations, along the bank of the ornamental canal. A few yards down they found a steeply arched bridge so new it still smelled of cut wood and timber preservative. But it had warmed up quickly in the sun, and Sealink sat down comfortably in the middle of it. From there she could maintain a good view of the little group around the lamppost. The magpie had returned to his perch and seemed to be orchestrating the party. The fox chased the tabby around in a circle. The tabby chased him back the other way. The Mau watched like a cat carved on a pyramid. Every so often, she closed her eyes in a long, slow blink. Ragnar was demonstrating for Mousebreath some move he believed to be specific to the *Norsk Skogkatt*. It required a turn and a rather elephantine pounce. You could almost hear him trying to explain. These events seemed odd but full of joy. It was a summer image come to winter.

"Don't they look wonderful?" Tag said.

"Real wonderful, hon," said Sealink. "Considering one of them's been dead for a day. Would you mind if I asked you to *explain* all this?"

Tag was at a loss. What could he tell her? *Mention me to no one but the fox!* the one-eyed cat had warned him. He was uncertain what had happened, anyway.

"I didn't think it would work," he said. "I didn't think she would be able to do it."

Sealink sighed. "Oh, it worked all right, hon," she said. "But it wasn't her that done it."

She studied the cats in the piazza. Ragnar had given up his attempt to impress Mousebreath and was watching Cy again. Even at a distance his expression could be recognized as one of wonder, possessiveness, and—Tag now saw—pride.

"It was him," he said. "I don't believe it." He laughed with delight. "It was the King! But how?"

"Oh, he's a fool, hon; but no King's half the fool he looks. I watched him watching every move you showed her. Soon as she's asleep and you're out the door, he's over there, blowing in that little cat's nostrils—" She stopped suddenly. "You been keeping things from us," she said. "You and that fox. I don't like that. For one thing, you learned that stuff somewhere. For another, you been on the highway." She laughed at Tag's change of expression. "How do I know that? Why, I see it in your eyes! You lost your cherry."

Tag looked away. "I can't tell you," he said miserably. "The

King, the Queen— It's—" He shook himself angrily. "Oh, I don't know what it is—! All I know is that everything that's happened to us is only a small part of something else." Struggling to convince her, he heard Majicou's calm voice telling him, *This part of it, I believe, has been entrusted to you,* and saw suddenly how wonderful a thing it might be.

"Sealink, something amazing is going on. And we're up to our necks in it!"

It was the right thing to say. For the calico cat, the world was only worthwhile if an adventure was revealed every time she lifted a corner of it. "An ordinary cat," she would often claim, "avoids intense experience. Calico cat, she *seeks out* intense experience. That's the difference, hon." Sensing the presence of adventure now, she was ready—at least for the moment—to give him the benefit of the doubt. Nevertheless, she regarded him with her head on one side, and warned him, "Lot of goodness inside you, kitten. Just make sure you spread it about." She indicated the party in the piazza. "Some of these folks depend on you. Then there's this: folks help you, they deserve the truth." She laughed. "What the hell! I figure you'll tell me in your own time." She thought for a moment. "But that Mousebreath's a different kind of guy. You know? He commits, he wants to know what he's into—"

"I hardly know what's going on myself!"

"Hey! Come on, lover, it's a sunny day! If we're in something amazing, don't be so downcast. Let's walk awhile."

The piazza lay on the northern limit of Piper's Quay, which was developing itself as a maze of waterways and cobbled lanes that served everything from windy apartment blocks—each boasting the cantilevered porch, Chinese roof, or Japanese windows that almost saved it from looking like a brand-new warehouse—to terraced houses with gardens the size of futons. Strolling south, away from the piles of bricks and raw new setts, Tag and Sealink soon found themselves at the heart of the original site, a modest enclave broken up with tiny woods and shallow bowls of grassy open ground supporting a hawthorn tree, a pond, a heron on a stump. The old

docks had long been filled in to make a park. Only their great
worn granite edges remained to show that this had been a sea-
faring place at all.

"So, hon," said Sealink, as she sailed in her stately way down
the chilly perspectives provided by one of these, "the highway.
Tell me!"

Tag was delighted by the invitation. But when he thought
about it, he could hardly gather his thoughts to begin. "I liked
the little highways. The places where ordinary cats lived their
lives. But the wild roads! Oh, now those! Do you know that
thing where the light seems to go into itself like brown smoke?
You can see, but you can't *see*? And the places where the air
echoes and echoes, as if there were a roof somewhere unimag-
inably high above your head? And—" Suddenly he couldn't
stop talking. He told her about the cats great and small who had
flowed out ahead of him down their road like fierce living
water. About the sense he had had of being so much larger than
himself. About his glimpse of the ice tiger whose voice had
called across ten thousand years.

Sealink was a good listener. But he soon found out that her
attitude to the highways was quite different from Majicou's.

"Tried them, honey. Didn't get much from them. Didn't get
that shiver up the spine. You know? Doesn't seem real in there
to me. Oh, I use them when I need to. What else would I do? I'm
a cat! But when you tell me, 'Highways! That's the way to
travel!' why kitten, I got to disagree." She laughed at Tag's
crestfallen expression. "Nah," she said. "For me, the highways
are *a* way to travel. Honey, *the* way to travel—the only way to
travel—is in the wheel bay of a Boeing 707 jet airplane. You
ever try that?"

"No," said Tag, who had no idea what she meant.

The calico expanded her chest. A rich, sonorous purr broke
forth. "Well then," she said, "walk right up alongside me here
for a minute or two, kitten, and let me tell you all about the real
thing . . ."

And from a filled-in dock, a quay that would send no one
sailing again, she took him on a journey. She described the

boats she had stowed away on, large and small, from ports as different as Galveston and Marseilles. How she had once ridden halfway across Texas in the engine compartment of a metallic blue Ford Galaxy. "Was it noisy?" "Noisy? I don't know, hon. It sure stank. I was sick for days after!" How she had spent a season as a railway cat at a station in Nepal. "Developed a taste for onion bhaji there. Ate some real exotic rodents." How in Saigon she had met a lilac Oriental called Tom Yang, the love of her life—who, she said, "led me nothing but a dance. But, honey, he was just such a male. You know?"—only to lose him again to cat flu in South Korea. She told him her theory that cats in Thailand could still talk to human beings. "They been doing things a different way to us for centuries." And how Tokyo housecats wore neckerchiefs instead of flea collars. She took Tag around the world on ships and trains and airplanes, only to end up in Alaska again—forty below—with Pete the pipeliner. "Strange days!" as she said. Strange days indeed, each with a moment of something at the end of it—happiness, perhaps. Sometimes not even that. Sometimes sadness, sometimes real tears.

"Travel's hard. You got to take the knocks. You got to walk your feet off. Oh, them highways are interesting all right—don't get me wrong. You'll have a time or two on those before you're through. But to me they don't seem a real part of the world. I'm a modern girl, I guess. Takes a different kind of determination to smuggle yourself on board a Boeing, hon. Tell me about it! But it's sure a lot of fun." She thought for a moment. "I don't find many folks agree on that," she said.

A moment later she was drawing Tag's attention to an irregular patch of bright blue sky visible between two steadily closing gray clouds. She had spotted a fine white trail curving across it, just like a whisker. Like a whisker it seemed sharp, delineated, intensely itself. Like a whisker it thickened toward one end, where if you squinted you could make out the silver jet itself, forging its way north and west through the unimaginable cold, the icy sunshine of the upper air. Sealink sighed. Her big, comfortable body seemed to quiver. Then she was dancing about like a kitten on her hind legs.

"Look! Look! Tag, honey, look! I *been* up there! I been *all the way up there*! Ain't that a life! Ain't it a *life*?"

Then the jet was gone. The sky shut behind it like a door. Sealink became more thoughtful. "I been tiny like that," she said quietly. "So tiny you'd be like to lose me in a snail shell." She shook her head in wonder. Then she said, "Tag, I just got to get to Russia before I die!" And, as if the two concepts were related, "I smell weather." Clouds were running in from the north on a cold dry airstream. They were deeply folded, white on top, undersides gray and scuffed. "Can't say I like the way the wind sits. We should go back." She stared up a minute more, then shook herself regretfully. "Don't keep too many things from me, hon. I like to know where I am."

"I'll try not to," Tag promised.

Sealink hurried him back through the dense, souk-like alleys of Piper's Quay, returning now and then to the canal—which she crossed and recrossed by its narrow ornamental bridges—to orient herself. If she seemed fraught, that rarely prevented her from making sarcastic comments about the architecture. Tag was content to follow her. She had made him happy again. Her very presence grounded him and gave him back the Tag he knew.

As she had predicted, the weather closed in on them. The sun went in. The wind got up, bringing air from the arctic. The temperature dropped so suddenly that fragile, transparent flowers of ice bloomed on the surface of the canal, and puddles froze where they stood. Suddenly, the air was gray and full of hard, dry pellets of hail. They bounced and scuttered across the cobbles in the wind. Thunder growled, away to the north. The sky darkened further. "Thunder and ice!" grumbled Sealink. "Something not right here, hon. Let's hurry!" And the hail thickened even as she spoke, hissing and sputtering furiously on the pavements. It stung their faces. It lodged next to their skin. "Come on, kitten!" They plunged down a narrow cut between empty-looking apartment buildings, scuttled across an intersection. They quivered for a couple of minutes beneath a wind-racked awning. Lightning flashed. The thunder chimed out. The familiar line of lampposts drew into view at last, and Tag was beginning to race toward it, slithering on the ice.

"Stop!" called Sealink. "Tag, stop!"

They stood panting on the far edge of the piazza. Tag was soaked. His skin twitched and winced at every gust of wind. All he wanted was to get under cover and be warm.

"What?" he said.

"Look!"

Not twenty yards away stood a brand-new ice-white vehicle. It was tall with sliding doors, darkened windows at the rear, and a heavily ventilated roof. On its side was a smart-looking design featuring a hand cupping a flower, under which ran the words RED ROSE LABORATORY SUPPLIES. It was parked directly outside the building in which the animals had spent the night. Water vapor rose from its exhaust. Faint music came from its cab. Other than that, and the mumble of its engine idling, everything was quiet. Between Tag and the van the piazza was veined like a leaf with shallow drifts of hailstones that had frozen hard.

"This isn't good," said Sealink.

Tag said, "The others! They're inside. They need help!"

Sealink was deadly calm. "It's too late, hon," she said. "I've smelled this before. Cat catchers! We go in there, they'll take us too—"

"What do you say about human beings now?" Tag asked her bitterly. "I don't think they've come to give us some *pizza*!"

As he spoke, fierce cat yowls broke out from inside. One for Sorrow could be heard croaking with rage. Loves a Dustbin barked loudly once, then began to snarl and growl like a dog that has got something in its mouth. There was a prolonged shriek, human in origin, followed closely by curses and shouts. At this, another cat catcher got out of the van.

Its body was broad and awkward looking, thick across the shoulders but carried with a serious grace. It moved quietly and smoothly. In the wintry light its face was hard to see. More shrieks from inside. Turning up its coat collar against the weather, it stood a moment at the door of the building, listening intently to the noises within. As soon as it was certain what was going on, it walked quickly but calmly back to the van, slid back the driver door, and took out something that looked like a short iron bar.

"Help me!"

At this cry, shrill with fear, there was a renewed outbreak of snarling from inside. Wet light licked across the piazza. Thunder rolled. The driver did something to the iron bar in its hands—*click!*—then with a practiced pirouette swung on its heel and barged shoulder first through the door. There was a yellow flash and a loud bang, followed by a series of high, whining yelps. Renewed yowling, in which Tag could detect the voices of Mousebreath and Ragnar, was muffled suddenly.

Presently two dark forms appeared in the doorway, one of them half supporting the other. In its left hand the injured figure clutched a sack. Its right arm dangled uselessly at its side. Something had ripped open the sleeve of its jacket and then done rough surgery on the white forearm beneath. Blood trickled down in a steady stream, melted the hard drifts of hailstones, then drained away as diluted brownish trickles of water.

The sack moved agitatedly. From within came a bubbling angry moan.

The driver kicked out. Silence.

"Come on," it encouraged its companion. "Not far now."

As they reached the vehicle, One for Sorrow exploded from the doorway to fill the air between them with mayhem, battering with his wings at their heads and shoulders, striking for their eyes with his beak. They ducked. The injured one swore and swiped at the bird so hard with the sack of cats that it lost its balance and half fell. "For God's sake," said the other impatiently, trying to get far enough away from the bird to shoot without hitting its accomplice. "Keep still." At that, the magpie changed his tactics, perching suddenly on his victim's head and digging in his claws until it shrieked. Then he swung his own head down savagely and buried his beak in its left ear, like a woodpecker addressing a tree.

The cat catcher let out a scream of pain and fear. It dropped the sack. It clapped its hurt hand to its ear and screamed again at what it thought it had found there, its face shocked and chalk-white in the feeble illumination. The bird was still fastened to its head. Blood ran down into its eyes.

"Oh God, it's really hurting me!"

"Right, that's enough," said the driver calmly.

It stood back and let the shotgun off again. The magpie, who knew when to quit, rocketed up into the dark air and vanished.

"Oh God! Oh God! Help me!"

The driver slid the van door open, threw the gun in, dragged the injured man around to the passenger side, and stuffed it in too.

"For Christ's sake, shut up," it advised.

Then it went back for the sack, which was lying on a heap of melting hailstones soaking up black water. The sack convulsed furiously and the face of the Mau appeared, all trembling and huge green panic eyes. "Would you, my sweet?" said the driver, and made a lunge for her. "Run off? I don't think so." She was almost free when its short hard fingers clamped on her rear legs, pinning them together and immobilizing her with pain.

"I can't stand this!" Tag told Sealink.

He raced across the piazza and bit the driver as hard as he could in the calf. It dropped the Mau and pivoted almost delicately on one large foot so that it could kick Tag in the head with the other.

Tag stiffened.

He thought, But I—

He tried to say, Sealink, help—

Consciousness writhed away from him like a strip of white light.

"Sealink, help the Mau!"

The last thing Tag saw was Pertelot Fitzwilliam, running blindly across the cobbles in her fear and falling into the canal. The last thing Tag heard was his captor saying amusedly, "He'll be well pleased to see this one again." The last thing Tag thought was that "he" could only mean the Alchemist. How did he know we were here? thought Tag. How did he know where to send them?

Blackness.

Part Two

Signs Among the Stars

The Third Life of Cats

I am born of the sacred She-Cat, and thus I am the
son of the Sun and the daughter of the Moon, the
Pupil of Ra and the Eye of Horus . . . I am the one,
born of the She-Cat, the double-guide, walker in
the ways of the living and realms of the dead: I am
the Cat, the divine Cat of the Spaces of Heaven, the
sacred Cat of Creation and the End of the World.
—THE EGYPTIAN BOOK OF THE DEAD

*O*f course, the humans came out of their caves, eventually.

They spread out across the Great Cat's creation, and
though their litters were often tiny, their numbers swelled to
fill the world.

Most of the Felidae avoided them; but Felis cattus, known
for its curiosity, drifted closer and closer to their cities. There
we found rat and mouse running well fed and unchecked
through the markets and the grain stores. They were up for
anything, those rodents. They lugged away whole children in
the evening. There were more of them than there are hairs in
the Great Cat's coat!

So we were like a gift from the gods when we came at last:
scourge of rats, death of mice! Oh, we got them running, all
right, through storehouse and silo; we put the light of panic
in their beady eyes! They had all but forgotten us. But we
soon reminded them—with sharp tooth and razor claw!

Were the upright ones grateful? I should say so! Those
families bade us welcome, and we went into their homes of
our own free will and stayed on our own terms. They treated
us like deities, each cat a god in its own house—gifts and offerings, and prayers for a share in our fertility and health, for
they were a sickly and superstitious lot.

Before long, they were raising temples, drawing our image
on the walls like their ancestors before them. In the new
drawings we were guardians of the doors of night, guardians
of the realms of the dead. We sat at the frontiers of the shadow

169

kingdom; we watched over the spirits of the dead, to guard them in their long sleep.

The same old fears, the same old hopes.

Still, for a thousand years they treated us well. Too well . . .

The priests and priestesses of the cult brought us more food than we could eat. We slept on beds of linen and silk. We were pampered, perfumed, exalted, and venerated; and we enjoyed every moment of it.

We were cats, after all.

Soon they had devised a ceremonial day. From far and wide the upright ones traveled to worship at the great temple at Bubastis, spiritual home of the She-Cat, the Great Mau, Mistress of the Eye—ah, the heavenly Eye! It was a solemn occasion: all processions and offerings, prayers and divinations. Nice and quiet and reverential.

Then they started to bring in any cat that had died—an offering to the favor of the Goddess. They interred them, embalmed and mummified in sacred receptacles, in the temple or—when things got crowded—its grounds. They shaved their eyebrows in mourning, and brought us thousand upon thousand of our dead kin.

It was a popular event from the beginning. But what had started with some decorous cymbal and flute music and a few symbolic religious dances was soon an excuse for both men and women to drink potent brews, sing, and fling up their garments to expose themselves along the banks of the Nile. Cats were all but forgotten in the fun of that. By the time the celebrants finally reached the temple at Bubastis, half of them had lost the offerings they started out with.

It wasn't long before the priests found a way to profit from that. Cats began to go missing. One here, another there. Soon they were going down by the tens and twenties, then by the hundred. Toms and queens, brindled and sorrel, spotted and fawn: before long, the area around Bubastis was devoid even of kittens as the priests captured every cat they could lay hands upon and—with a smart tap to the neck—helped them on their journey to the other world. After which, they were hastily embalmed and swaddled in linen and sold as instant offerings in the name of Bast.

The brighter ones among us caught on and survived. The others, I suspect sadly, did not. It was another lesson to learn about human beings: Sometimes they can love you too much.

Chapter Nine

THE CITY AT NIGHT

A cat bitten once by a snake will dread even a rope.
— OLD ARABIC SAYING

*W*hen she knew the Alchemist had found her, Pertelot Fitzwilliam put her head down and bolted. Her breath came hard and ragged. Cobbles bruised her velvet pads. Across the square she hurtled, a streak of sorrel in the indigo night, only to sail in a long, elegant arc straight off the side of the dock. For a moment her feet pedaled wildly in the chill night air, then she fell.

There was a brief silence, a splintering sound, and she was in the water under the ice.

Pertelot had spent most of her life in a cage, where water came small and confined in a clean metal bowl. Down here, it was some other thing. The whole world had given way beneath her paws and now this malevolent *thing* was wrapping itself around her and thrusting itself in through her open mouth. She choked and struggled, tired in an instant. Grimly she fought toward the surface—legs kicking, eyes shut tight in panic— only to find that she had come up under the ice. The momentum that had propelled her up drove her back down again into the choking darkness, where her feet sank instantly into the soft bed of the canal. A frantic maneuver disengaged her from the embrace of the mud. Exhausted, she hung in the water, and the bubbles streaming from her mouth spiraled to the surface like tiny silver fish. She followed their progress with a detached curiosity. Above her, the light appeared faint and impossibly far away; whatever she did would make no difference. Air now rose from her mouth in a continuous stream. She let go of herself and sank, soundless and still, like a cat in a dream of silent

172

flight, into the waters that closed possessively around her and pulled her down.

Another time; perhaps even another place. Something heavy, pressing hard. The sound of water gushing in little rills. Darkness again, to be replaced eventually by a sense of something warm gathering itself firmly around her. Pertelot moved her head cautiously to examine her new environment. She seemed to be wrapped in a great fur blanket, of which the piazza's lamps made a neon patchwork. It was black and white and a gorgeous, flaming orange. Each strand was precisely delineated, so that she felt for some moments as if she were enfolded in the warp and weft of the world itself. Then the blanket shifted slowly and redefined itself as another cat—large, female—the black pupils of whose eyes were outlined in amber.

It was Sealink.

"What was that stuff?" asked Pertelot.

The calico blinked puzzledly. "It was water, hon. Are you awake?"

The Mau shuddered and retched dryly.

"Ain't nothing left to come out," Sealink advised after a moment or two, "so you may as well stop that. Didn't no one ever tell you cats and water don't mix? Once had me a tom called Muezza—sweet guy, Turkish Van cat—he kinda liked to swim. But this ain't Turkey, hon, and you ain't him."

"I didn't get in there by choice," Pertelot said. "Do you think I did?"

"And that's to say nothing about ice. You tread real careful, but that stuff just keeps on creaking there. Whoa! Darn good job I got a long arm is all I can say, 'cause I surely wasn't going to dive right on in."

She added, "Hate getting my head wet."

Pertelot groaned. "Ragnar. Where's Ragnar?"

"They've all gone, sugar. Don't ask me where, 'cause I don't know."

Pertelot's eyes grew huge and round. In her agitation, she began kneading the calico's foreleg, her claws, translucent and pink in the sodium light, flickering in and out.

"That hurts, hon," said Sealink briskly.

She extracted her punctured leg and rearranged herself around the Mau.

"Ragnar'll be just fine," she advised. "That old guy of mine wouldn't let him come to no harm. Let's get you warm. You're full of canal water, and there ain't enough flesh on your bones to make soup."

Pertelot closed her eyes for a moment—the piazza light explored tenderly her ancient mask of pain and fortitude—then struggled blindly upright, bracing herself against the calico's flank.

"No," she said hoarsely. "Mousebreath was hit. They hit him on the head because he was shielding the little tabby. They put both of them in a sack, and Mousebreath *didn't move*. Sealink, he didn't move! When I saw that I ran. I ran."

Sealink digested this, her eyes distant and unfocused.

"I'm sorry," the Queen said. "I had to run. There was nothing I could do."

When Sealink failed to respond to this she added in a forlorn singsong, "Nothing any of us could do."

The calico shook herself. "Well," she said briskly, "he's a strong old tom, that Mousebreath, and he's taken a knock or two in his time." She stared across the piazza. "Skull like a stone," she reassured herself. "Always loves a fight. All the flying fur. All the hissing an' spitting, he loves that stuff better than food, better than—" Her voice became contemplative. "Well, not better than *that*, of course," she decided. She fell silent.

"I hope he's okay," she said eventually. "Sure, he'll be okay!"

"You love him," said the Queen.

"I love 'em all," said Sealink. "But he's a tough old tom and he'll be fine. So will Ragnar." She considered Ragnar for a moment. "Big, strong cat that one, hon. Hung like a lord and a real neat butt. Pity he's spoke for."

"He is a lord," said Pertelot. Then, less complacently, "And he is spoken for."

Sealink gave her an amused look. "They got that Tag with them too," she said. "It was him saved you from the sack. I seen him bite one right in the leg. Gave you plenty of time to run off and drown yourself"—here, the Queen looked suitably admonished—"at any rate. He's got a long old road to go, Tag, but he's one of them goes it all the way. Once he gets the idea."

"Tag isn't his true name," said the Queen.

"Call him what you like, hon, but he's one of them goes all the way with it. I seen enough of them to know. Scary stuff." She laughed. "Why, the three of them are scary stuff, and—bet on it!—they're having a nicer time than us right now. You'll see!"

"When will I see?" said Pertelot grimly.

"Hush now, babe. Let's get you warm an' dry before we worry anymore."

She went about this task without speaking for a while. All that could be heard was the rasping of her rough pink tongue. Then something occurred to her, her ears pricked up, and she said, "You know, there's a place where we can get some help. I know a load of cats hang out there. Anything happens in this town, they'll know about it."

She transferred her attention to the back of the Queen's ears. Pertelot allowed her eyes to close for a moment in a reflex of pleasure and submission. Then she forced them open again. "Will they help us find Ragnar?"

Sealink regarded her a little wearily. "Sure, babe. Sure they will. Try to be calm now. And, hey, it's a real interesting place, the Old Fish Market. Every cat should visit it once in her life!"

With this, she wrapped her great boa of a tail around the Mau once more and waited patiently for the trembling to cease.

Midnight: Piper's Quay. Wintry breezes drove the river into the concrete embankment with soft, rhythmic little slaps. Scraps of newspaper skittered along the cobbles. Otherwise, nothing stirred until two cats emerged from the shadows.

The first was large and furry. She walked with a long, swinging stride and carried her tail high in the air like an ostrich feather fan over an African monarch. The second moved more sinuously and with greater caution, looking around every few paces to interrogate the darkness behind her. The moon struck her back with a silvery gleam. Not the faintest odor of mud remained. Sealink had been very thorough.

In the dead of night they traveled deserted alley and cobbled squares in which pools of melted hail glinted dully. They crossed Jamaica Square with its rows of empty town houses and disused storage sheds. The river moved like a flow of silent lava at the end of every cross street. And as they crept through the silent front gardens, along the cracked concrete paths where the clothes dryers sagged, they encountered not a single barking dog, not a single feral tom patrolling his duchy. Windows were curtained or boarded up. Everyone was asleep or had gone elsewhere.

After a mile or so, the Mau began to struggle. Sealink failed to notice this. Her pace was robust. Her head was up and her ears were alert. She loved a journey.

Down Cathay Street and along Spice Walk they passed, between Cuckold's Point and Ratting Stairs. Near Pickle Herring Lane, Sealink cut northward. They emerged suddenly on the riverfront, and ahead of them a huge structure loomed over the river in the night. Glowing in its array of lights, the twin towers of a great bridge rose in a mass of struts and chains. It was cold, massive, and forbidding.

"Must we cross here?" called Pertelot fearfully.

But Sealink was already trotting briskly over the paved footpath that flanked the road. The Queen stopped nervously; she raised a paw, dithered. In the end though—more frightened of being stranded on the opposite side of the river from the calico than of this appalling structure with its stink of fumes and machine oil—what could she do but persevere? Halfway across a movement caught her eye, and she stared down through the ornate railings to the dark water far below. By the time they reached the other side, she was trembling with vertigo and exposure, and terror had stiffened her gait. Ahead lay the open paving and rusting chains of Russia Dock; beyond that a great stone keep above a lawned moat.

Sealink sat down abruptly. "Rest here, hon. See that?"

"The tower?"

"Yeah. That's a kind of cruelty place humans have. They been cruel to about everyone in there, one time or another."

They contemplated the tower together.

Sealink shrugged suddenly. "Never been in there myself, of course." Then she said, "I been around, and I seen some stuff, but I never seen anything real scary till I met you folks. The things that happened in that warehouse!" She gave the Queen a direct look. "I don't pretend to understand what's going on and I don't much want to. Sometimes you're best not knowing." She got to her feet. "Developed a *nose* for trouble in my years on the road, hon, and this shit sure stinks." And with this pronouncement she was off again, heading for the maze of streets behind the great tower.

Pertelot stared miserably after her. "I'm sorry," she said softly. But Sealink was already too far off to hear, and all the Mau could do was gather her failing resources and limp along behind.

After some minutes of scurrying between tall glass-walled offices, Sealink stopped suddenly.

"Best take the highway from here," she announced.

They were on the steps of a gray-spired church. She opened her mouth, flehming the air for an accurate scent map. She shook her head impatiently. "You never did get the hang of this," she scolded herself. She faced several directions, her whiskers twitching. Then, choosing a line two or three points off north, she moved a couple of paces forward and started to strain against what seemed to the Mau to be some kind of invisible membrane. Almost at once, her head and left front foot vanished.

Pertelot grew agitated.

"I'm sorry!" she said loudly. "Please go on without me. I shall stay here."

There was a moment of silence from the headless cat, as if she were held in suspended animation. Then, with a *pop* Sealink withdrew her head and paw from the highway and looked at the Queen in disbelief.

"You stop, I stop, hon," she said. "But look here—what's the matter?"

"Please. I just don't want to travel with you anymore." The Mau looked down. "You've been kind," she said, "but we must part now. It's better if I go on alone."

Sealink narrowed her eyes. "Forgive me for being blunt, hon, but I never met a cat less able to look after herself than you. You need me."

Pertelot Fitzwilliam drew herself up.

"I am the Queen of Cats—"

"This is crazy, hon!"

"—and I could command you if I wanted. But I don't *need* anyone."

Sealink looked amazed. "Command?" she said.

She laughed. "I don't think so, sugar. I don't answer to anyone in the world, you understand?" She pushed her face close to Pertelot's. "No human," she said, "no tomcat, and no frigging Queen. Understand?"

To make the point, she leaned up over the Mau like the side of a house. But the Mau stood her ground, trembling with distress, until Sealink, awed by her determination, added more quietly, "Look, do what you want, but don't kid yourself: without me you don't stand a cat in hell's chance."

"A cat in hell's chance," the Queen repeated softly. "Indeed, I am in hell. Even so, I prefer to be there alone."

Sealink stood, looking down curiously at Pertelot for a long moment, then arched her back, flicked her tail, and declared, "Have it your own way, hon. We all got to make choices. See you around."

And with that she was off, her outline so broken up in the moonlight that in seconds she was a few disconnected harlequin patches flouncing away down the church steps and into the shadows of an alley.

The Mau watched this departure with a mixture of fear and relief. She had been raised under bright laboratory lights. Still, she would rather be alone in the dark, in the unknown city, than travel the highway with Sealink. Whether it understood their nature or not—whether it could enter them or not—the creature called the Alchemist would hear her slightest step on the wild roads. The moment it knew she had escaped the cat catchers in the melee at Piper's Quay, it would be relentless.

Such a poor reward for Sealink's bravery and kindness to put her in further danger.

Pertelot scanned the shadows warily. Without the calico— without even the comfort of a voice in the night—how could she survive this inimical place? She lacked the practical skills to find her way to safety.

The buildings here were the usual city mixture. To the east, gleaming towers of glass and steel: no help there. To the west, the architecture of another age, a shambles carved and blackened by hundreds of years of polluted air. Rows of small shops had the air of having been mined out of larger buildings; above them, poky storerooms or smelly curtained apartments where the human denizens of the area slept. Neon signs blinked in the night. It was mazy, jumbled, confusing.

And yet I must start somewhere, Pertelot thought.

She followed Sealink's scent trail until she reached a corner. Here, the calico had gone straight on: not fair, then, to follow her.

Pertelot hesitated, then turned off into a dark lane with tiny shops, each dusty little window crowded with yellowing, handwritten notices, old advertisements, aging produce. A depth of gloom, a quality of inhabited vacancy caused her to quicken her step each time she passed a doorway or an intersecting passage.

In this way she came to a shop full of animals. She stopped, head turned, one paw raised, to stare briefly into its window— where birds slept with their heads tucked under their wings and small, warm mammals ran with a kind of frantic diligence around their cages in the window—shocked by so much captivity. She was about to run on, when something made her pause.

There was some other animal behind the closed wooden door. She smelled power and rank old age. Her nose wrinkled. All along her back the fur began to rise, a prickle of electricity from her ears to her tail. Still as a stone, barely breathing, she waited to see what would happen. Whatever lay beyond was asleep, but its dreams . . .

Oh, its dreams!

She felt the air around her move subtly. Every smell was suddenly distinct and clear. Traffic fumes, humans and animals in close quarters, the dank salt of the river—a sudden sickening wave of decay and waste and teeming life that came up from things as she stood there with her hocks quivering, pressed against the old bricks of Cutting Lane; and, slowly but surely, the dreams of the creature inside the shop overwhelmed her.

First this unspeakable clarity. Then a sudden sense of breaking away from things. The outlines of the very street began to shift and merge until the buildings appeared to be overlapping one another. They stretched away, down the hill, all the way to the south horizon. As far as the eye could see, silhouette lay upon feathery silhouette, shadow and sunlight in a constantly shifting dapple, as if the skies of a dozen different ages were scudding overhead. Ghostly shapes moved up through the layers, quick and slow: a legion of cats, old and young, fit and scabrous, trapped and free. The cats of Cutting Lane!

They all looked like her . . .

Dizzy and disoriented, the Queen slumped to the ground, her paws over her ears and eyes, and tried to shut them out.

She was surrounded by reflections of herself: slanted green eyes, rosy taupe coats with flecks of sorrel, and black feet; tails like whips, and legs with a sharp delicate curve. The ghost cats of Cutting Lane wreathed themselves around her, their silent miaows communicating a terror so profound it could barely be expressed, never be ignored. Yet how could she help them? They were dead, and she was only Pertelot. Was this her heritage? Was this the burden she would have to bear once she set foot on the wild roads?

There in the street, she began to struggle. She fell on her side.

Her little black paws kicked out erratically. Mewing sounds escaped her as she fought to escape her ancestors.

She heard a voice quite near her say, "Come to me. Come to me now, and no harm will befall you."

She shook herself awake and ran.

She ran.

She thought, I will not go into the dark with that one-eyed black cat and his band of ghosts. I will not go with him. My ancestors went with him, and look at them now. Look at them now!

"Come back," called the black cat. "I can help you. You are in danger in this city . . ."

The sound of the voice died away like fading light as Pertelot raced down Cutting Lane and into a maze of randomly selected back streets. She ran, and as she ran, she chanted over and over, "I'm Pertelot Fitzwilliam, Queen of Cats.

"I'm not a ghost," she told herself. "I'm Pertelot Fitzwilliam, Pertelot Fitzwilliam, Queen of Cats."

In this state—less a Queen than a panic fully clothed in one—she hurtled around a corner and into a large, stationary calico cat, who was sitting on the ground and nonchalantly cleaning an extended hind leg.

"You having an identity crisis here, hon?"

"Sealink?"

"Uh huh."

"Oh, Sealink, is it you?"

"Who else, babe?"

"Sealink, I'm so pleased to see you."

"I can kinda tell that."

The Mau hung her head in exhaustion. "I'm sorry I was so rude," she said at last.

"Think nothing of it."

"I was afraid for you."

The calico seemed amused. "That's caring of you, hon."

"Don't laugh. Please listen. It's me the Alchemist wants. You're in danger all the time you're with me. If I go on the highway with you, he'll find me—and you, too." She stared emptily into space. "I've put enough cats at risk already," she said. "I can't bear that responsibility along with all the others."

"Honey, life is choices. You think I didn't know the risk I took? I make my choice; that's a gift you got to be gracious enough to accept from me. Hey, hon, you're a Queen. Ain't that what they *do*?"

There was a silence.

"But—"

"Come here to me."

Pertelot Fitzwilliam of Hi-Fashion bowed her head. Relief washed over her.

At that moment, some streets away, the door of a shop swung open on Cutting Lane, and the black cat called Majicou walked out into the night. He looked up the lane and down it. He sniffed the air.

Nothing.

A dream, then. Only a dream.

A cold, rosy light had just started to touch the east of the city. All along the riverside, pigeons huddling in leprous-looking plane trees examined the winter dawn, then tucked their heads back under their wings. It was very cold.

Sealink padded purposefully through the dead leaves, potato chip packets, and fast-food wrappers strewn across the river walk. She was as immune as ever to the weather. Pertelot followed closely in those comforting footsteps, shivering so hard that her velvet fur seemed to ripple in the cruel new light. They kept an eye out for food as they went.

Junk food was Sealink's specialty.

She would interrogate each paper bag and hamburger package encountered along the way, give a judgmental sniff, and then announce, "Haddock in batter" or "smoked saveloy" or "flame-grilled burger with cheese. Mmm-mmm." This would be followed some moments later by the declaration, "Sure wouldn't mind some breakfast."

She got up on her hind legs to crane over the edge of every waste bin.

"It pays to be big, hon," she advised. She thought, Of course, that's, you know, kind of a genetic thing.

A hot dog came to light, cold and congealed. Pertelot looked on in disgust as the greasy paper and ketchup-stained remains were dragged forth. Down on the pavement, Sealink wrestled briefly with the sausage until she had maneuvered it into a position in which she could chew it noisily with the side of her mouth. Soon there was nothing left but a small red stain on the ground. Sealink licked her face carefully, savoring the last of the mustard, while Pertelot crouched uncomfortably beside the bin.

"Ain't nothing like junk food for filling a corner," said the calico cheerfully. "But I guess a pedigree like yours don't allow the force of that. Well, you got to learn to eat what you find in this life. Can't expect to get that fancy tinned stuff out here."

"I'm not very hungry, anyway," said Pertelot, who thought she was going to be sick.

"Say what?"

"I'm not—"

"Queenie, you *always* hungry out here. Always hungry, always tired. You sleep when you can, eat whatever you find. Even if you ain't hungry you eat when the opportunity arises. Hon, you're already far too skinny for health. Lord knows how you managed to attract that tom of yours! Wait here."

She leapt lightly onto the rim of the bin, teetered there briefly, and vanished inside to begin a further trawl through the rubbish. Time passed. Aluminum cans clattered to the ground, followed by polystyrene cups and chocolate wrappers. Eventually the calico emerged again, to nudge a blue Styrofoam box over the edge. This dropped to the pavement with a damp thud; the top sprang open to reveal half a piece of battered fish in a chewed bun. A gooey white substance was oozing out of the middle.

"There you go," declared Sealink generously. "Real healthy eating, that, real gour*may*. Go ahead, be my guest."

Pertelot Fitzwilliam, Queen of Cats, nosed at the fish doubtfully. Her lips drew back. "It smells a little sharp," she complained.

But Sealink—engaging in a postprandial wash, her big pink tongue following the long fur of her ruff from chest to tip in a wide arc—only said, "Why, that's the relish, babe, chef's sauce. Eat!"

The Mau's nostrils narrowed. She pulled the slice of battered fish out of the soggy bread and bit off a tiny morsel. She chewed thoughtfully for a moment, then sank her teeth in and started to eat it as fast as she could.

She said something unintelligible.

"I beg your pardon?"

"Delicious."

Two seconds later every trace of the filet had vanished, except for a small crescent of tartar sauce across the Queen's nose. Then a small sharp tongue whisked that away too.

Early morning sun was clearing the rooftops as the two cats neared the Old Fish Market.

Sealink abandoned the riverwalk, slipped under some railings, and, pushing once off the stone wall, jumped athletically the ten or twelve feet down onto a dank wooden jetty beneath. Skidding slightly on the weed, she looked back at the Queen.

"Come on."

Pertelot gathered all four feet onto the edge of the wall. The old jetty looked dark and slippery, and much too close to the water's edge. What if she were to fall into the river? Reminded of near death in the canal the night before, she could only teeter uncertainly. Sealink, meanwhile, had given her an irritable stare and was disappearing amid the pilings at the end of the pier.

The Mau looked over the edge. I hate this, she thought.

She closed her eyes and launched herself into space. The old wooden boards came up and hit her so hard she pitched forward onto her nose. She clung on hard for a moment, then, carefully not looking down at the water, ran after the calico. Together they rounded the last of the piers.

There were men everywhere.

Men on the quay; men down on the moored boats, handing up plastic crates of lobsters and cod, crabs, herring, mackerel, and sea bass; men heaving great sacks of ice and huge wooden boxes over to waiting lorries and vans; men packing the open-sided market building, where the fish were displayed in labeled piles and on pallets. There was so much activity that no one noticed the two cats cross the cobbles, slip through the shadows at the side of the building, and insinuate themselves behind a stack of piled wooden pallets.

"Men!" said Pertelot, her ears flattened to her head and her spine raised in knobs all the way to her lowered tail.

The calico cat, though, was in her element. She opened her mouth to capture the rich aroma of fish. Her eyes were narrowed with pleasure. Her toes kneaded the damp cobbles with unashamed sensuality.

"Ain't it great?" she breathed, more to herself than her charge. "Man, I love this place." And, tail high, she sashayed out into the confusion.

"Don't leave me!" cried Pertelot in horror.

"Just wait here, hon. I'll be back directly."

And off through the market she strode, to collect her dues. She was, as she said later, a popular cat in those parts. Two or three paces into the activity, and a young man in dark green overalls had already bent to stroke her.

"Hey there, angel!"

Sealink dipped her head and walked on so that the end of her tail brushed his hand, murmuring, "Honey, you know me. I don't get out of bed in the morning for less than a sprat."

"Well, hello, Furbag!" called her next victim. "It's been a while." He knew enough to flourish a sardine.

"Furbag I ain't," Sealink declared indignantly, "but I'll have that there *fish*."

She reared up on her hind legs and accepted the offering from his outstretched hand. It vanished. She twined herself around him, and by this shameless vamping procured two more sardines.

"Oh my," she chided herself. "You are such a bad girl."

Then she was off again.

The men loved her. In and out of their clumsy feet she wove in a kind of teasing dance. A dance like that required more than grace: it required a constant eye on the crates being slammed to the ground around her.

Pertelot watched through the slats of the pallets until Sealink had disappeared where the crowd was thickest. Loneliness swept over her. She had no idea where she was. Her head ached with the sounds of stamping human feet, raucous human shouts. Where had Sealink gone? In the end, she could only close her eyes and shut everything out. Cats go easily from despair to sleep. She settled back into the shelter of the pallets and dozed fitfully.

She woke cold. For a moment she was looking up into darkness. A shadow had fallen across her. It was accompanied by an acrid smell. When her eyes adjusted, she found herself staring at a huge pair of rubber boots, the tops turned down to reveal a canvas interior splashed with drops of reeking blood and intestine. Dread froze its way through her chest to the pit of her stomach. Above the boots she could see a long rubber apron—and the silver glint of a knife.

The Alchemist!

There was nowhere to run. She would lose Sealink forever if she left the cover of the pallets. If she didn't, the Alchemist would have her and take her back to its laboratories! It moved, so that light fell into her hiding place. Had it seen her? She shrank back. She was breathing so loudly, surely it would hear her!

I won't go back! she thought dully. I won't bear all that again—

She thought, Oh, Rags, where are you? Come back and help me now!

Then the figure turned away abruptly, strode across the market and out onto the quay, revealing itself to be a man in later middle age, gray and balding, white stubble on its florid jowls. Its rubber apron glittered with fish scales. Its boots were old and green, too large for its feet, so that they slipped as it walked. Its face split into a grin as it acknowledged a call from a colleague out on the dock, and then it was away, out into the raw January sunshine.

Pertelot watched it go. "You see?" she told herself. "Pertelot, you're such a bag of nerves. It looked nothing like the Alchemist!"

In her relief, she threw up the fish, which lay there on the cobbles in a warm, accusatory puddle.

"Didn't you want that, then, my dear?"

It was not a voice she knew. Pertelot spun around.

Sealink had returned, looking remarkably cheerful, and with her she had brought an old mackerel tabby with a crinkled coat. He had a squint in his left eye and a grizzle of gray around his nose.

"Meet Pengelly," said Sealink.

"Hello," said the Queen.

The mackerel tabby looked her up and down. "I'm charmed and honored, my lover," he declared. And he looked as if he was.

His coat was thick but short and tufted in places with a density that seemed to absorb light rather than reflect it. When she leaned forward to sniff him, he smelt of tar and fish and brine. It was an attractive odor, both comfortable and bracing. He was sturdy and fit despite his years, and the way he cocked his head on one side and waited for her response suggested both humor and confidence.

They touched noses in greeting.

"You'm the Queen of Cats, I hear," he encouraged her in his measured way.

She laughed rather wildly. She liked him, and he made her feel safe. "Does the Queen of Cats throw up so?" she asked. "I am if she does." Then, "It's been a trying day," she apologized. "You'll have to forgive me."

"My dear, I'd have done exactly the same," said Pengelly, eyeing the remains of her breakfast. "That fish weren't what *I'd* call fresh."

Pertelot gave Sealink a look. "Some people will eat anything," she said darkly.

Sealink laughed. "Strong stomach makes a strong cat," she said. Then she announced happily, "This here Pengelly is going to take us on a sea voyage."

Chapter Ten

RECRIMINATIONS

It's no use crying over lost kittens or spilt milk.
— PROVERB

Tag woke.

Darkness and chaos. Fumes.

He was sliding in unpredictable arcs across a metal surface. At the end of each arc he bumped into something. Brilliantly colored sheets of light flickered behind his eyes. He braced himself and tried to get up; a violent lurch rolled him over. He dug his claws into the floor; it was unyielding. He opened his eyes. Pain and nausea forced him to close them again before he had seen anything.

He drifted in and out of consciousness for what seemed like a lifetime. It was hard to distinguish the waking world—with its booming and shaking, its smells of hot metal and rubber—from the inside of his own head. It all ran seamlessly together, dream to reality, in one long fluid moment of discomfort. This state was interrupted by a single clear image, which he took to be a dream and which he was to remember for some time.

He opened his eyes. He was in a kind of slick white metal room, with ribbed and canted walls, ceiling ventilators, and two blackened windows at one end high up. A little gray light leaked between the double doors into which the windows were fitted. The enameled floor was dusty, rust pocked, stacked toward the back with empty, white-painted cages. There was a long orange canvas bag, a square chipped wooden box. A thick sack lay in its own pool of water, exuding a strong smell of wet cats. In the floor, in the cages, in the very walls, lingered an older, staler smell—cats confined, cats fearful and depressed. The room was stiller than it had been—though it shook rhythmically— and a steady, muffled vibration came up through the floor.

189

On top of the stack of cages sat Cy the tabby. She looked at home.

Her paws and coat were glossy clean; her eyes shone with a kind of amused intelligence; her cobby frame was full of both repose and energy. Around her, tiny lights came and went—little motes, mostly white as ash drifting up from the embers of a garden bonfire on an autumn day, but some colored faintly red and green. She cocked her head alertly on one side to listen. Tag listened too, and thought for a moment he heard a distant voice. Perhaps music. Then nothing. Motes came and went. A sharp smell invaded the room. This was followed by a faint unaccountable blue radiance that, though it seemed to spring from every wall, came from a fixed point somewhere *beyond* them, so that the stacked cages threw acute ultramarine shadows and a pool of shadow grew about the wet-blackened sack. Cy looked around her with delight and began to sing, in a low, crooning unmusical way. Tag had the impression that she was in the room but somewhere else at the same time, as if the new light had imposed some other landscape on the walls.

"Cy?"

She stared at him suddenly. The spark plug in her head pulsed and flickered.

"Sleep now, Ace," she said.

The spark plug drew in motes of light from all over the room. They floated toward it like cinders in a draft, like moths to a lamp. Tag grew confused and could only imagine he was back in some Coldheath delirium—rat dreams, bad food, dirty water.

"Cy . . ."

The tabby smiled. "Sleep," she whispered.

The room snorted. It stank. It lurched into life, throwing everything back toward the doors. Empty cages jumped and rattled precariously. Tag's head throbbed with nausea, and he slept.

He woke soon after. She had gone.

Apart from the occasional lurch, the room was still; it hummed. Bright white light flooded it irregularly from the crack between the doors. Tag realized that he was in the back of the cat catchers' van, racing down some human road amid the roar and rage of human traffic. He had lost the Queen, an unknown number of his friends were in a sack, and he was lurching wretchedly toward an uncomfortable fate in the night.

He groaned and let sleep overtake him.

No more dreams.

Wow! he thought, next time he woke. Still alive! Then he thought, Or am I?

Stiff and bruised from head to foot, he could barely lift his head from between his paws. He was freezing cold; but if he allowed himself to shiver too energetically, sharp little pains crackled up and down his rib cage like flames. Where the cat catcher had kicked him, he felt brittle and swollen at the same time. When he looked down at himself he shuddered. He thought he could see a lump. His coat was bedraggled and wet, stiff with dust and grease it had picked up from the floor of the van. And when he bent around instinctively to lick at the bits that hurt, the effort made him dizzy.

Still, he thought, you haven't had it till you're dead.

Or have you? Anxiety for his friends made him miserable. Anger at his own failure made him bitter.

"When you've let everyone down," he told himself eventually, "the least you can do is get up and help them out of the sack."

This turned out to be easier said than done. In his sleep he had managed to wedge himself between two of the cages. With an effort, he dragged himself upright, stretched until the pain warned him to go no further, and poked his head out.

Nothing.

The sack lay on the floor, wet and rumpled. His friends were nowhere to be seen. When he looked around everything was as it had been. Orange bag. Wooden box. Cages with rusty wire fronts. He dragged himself stiffly out of his bolt-hole and, balancing against the tricky motion of the floor, approached the sack. Lips curled in disgust, he found the open end and pushed his head inside. He sniffed. There was a strong wet reek of sack. Cats had been in here recently, but they weren't there now. He was backing out—puzzled and anxious, and with a growing sense that he was always somehow behind events as they developed—when he heard a familiar voice say, "You done us now."

He stared around. Nothing.

"You really done us now."

"Mousebreath?"

There was a blaring sound from outside. The van swerved and rocked. It slowed suddenly. High up in the rattling wall of cages, a door was dislodged and began banging to and fro. Tag looked up. Curled so tightly together inside the cage that they looked like a single bedraggled animal, were three cats. Out of this undifferentiated mass of damp fur rose a tortoiseshell head with one orange eye and one blue: the orange eye looked angry. Mousebreath got his front legs under him, disentangled himself, sat up. Deprived of his warmth, the other two cats curled tighter together, clutching their paws eloquently to their eyes. "Let us sleep!" Mousebreath blinked. His blue eye was discolored, and there was blood caked down that side of his nose. He dragged the rest of himself out of the pile and stared down at Tag. The cage door opened and shut between them with a mournful, repetitive clang.

"Where's the next stop, eh?" inquired the tortoiseshell.

And, judging the swing of the door to a nicety, he jumped down. He was followed by the somewhat less agile Ragnar Gustaffson Coeur de Lion, whose seventeen pounds hit the floor with an audible thud. Ragnar was favoring his right front leg. Cy the tabby came out last, with a yawn and a neat, composed little leap. She looked a lot less cold than Rags and Mousebreath—perhaps they had kept her warm between them. She looked a lot less disheveled—perhaps they had groomed her as she slept. "Hi, Ace," she greeted Tag, sticking her tail in the air and sniffing his nose. "Nice fur." She gave him a little sideways look that reminded him of his dream.

"Oh, yes," said Mousebreath. "You done us now, *Ace*. Eh?"

Tag thought, I was happy to blame myself for this, but I find it unfair when Mousebreath blames me too. He thought, You learn something about yourself every day. "This wasn't my fault," he began. "How was I to know they would find us? I don't know any more than you do." And then he went on, surprised to hear how hurt his own voice sounded, "You might act as if you were pleased to see me."

Mousebreath laughed sarcastically. "I've already had to sleep in a sack. Why should I be pleased to see you? It was you what got us into all this. Next stop the laboratory."

"What's a laboratory?"

"You don't want to know. Not if half of what I hear is true."

The night passed. The light flickered. There being no sign that the van would stop, the three cats sat swaying patiently as it rattled toward its unknown destination. Tag listened as Mousebreath told him what had happened at Piper's Quay.

"The first thing we noticed was the weather," he said.

The air temperature had dropped suddenly, driving them in from their celebrations in the square. Clouds were roiling in over the old docks. Thunder growled like a dog in the distance. Everyone was hungry and irritable again. Then One for Sorrow, who had been left dozing triumphantly on his perch on top of the lamppost, shot through the doorway at the height of a human head squawking, "*Raaark! Raark!* Close the door!"

It was far too late for that. Instead, they had tried to hide. The magpie fluttered up into the exposed joists of the ceiling and became as still as a carved bird. Cy scampered into a corner and pushed herself under an empty plastic sack. Ragnar got Pertelot by the scruff and began trying to drag her behind a stack of hardwood window frames. But it was too late for Mousebreath, and when the huge shouting figure with the sack burst through, he was caught in the doorway and kicked in the face.

"It's easy to see now," said Mousebreath, "what we should have done. Outside, they wouldn't have caught a one of us. Cooped up like that, we didn't have a chance—" He laughed. "I was half out of it anyway," he said. "I couldn't see well for a minute or two."

But he did see Loves a Dustbin, leaping and snapping in the

bad light, drive the human into the room until he had it cornered. It was an amazing performance. The fox's eyes were glazed and mad. His black lips were drawn away from teeth as white as bone; slobber dripped and flew from his rolling scarlet tongue. He seemed to double in size. The human was astonished.

"They got a dog!" it screamed. "There's a dog in here!"

Hands to face in the reeling gloom, it dropped its sack and backed as far away from the fox as it could go, only to step on the tabby. It had already lost its composure. Now, as Cy writhed and spat beneath its feet, its balance went too. While its attention was distracted, the fox leapt. A streak of red and white in the gloom, and teeth were fastened in its forearm. For a second, man and animal tottered about together in a kind of grotesque dance in the gloom—the fox at full stretch on his hind legs, the man sobbing as it tried to wrench its arm away—while the tabby fizzed and spat like a firework between their legs and Pertelot ran madly about, yowling. Seeing that it would never end unless something was done, Mousebreath forced himself dizzily across the room. He let them waltz backward and forward in front of him until, judging his moment, he could step in and trip the human. It fell on its back with a gasp and a thud, the breath knocked out of it. There was a momentary silence as it raised its head and stared disbelievingly at its shredded sleeve and bloody hand. Then the fox was at its throat, blood and foam around his leering mouth.

It was still shrieking for help when the van driver stepped coolly into the room with its gleaming black stick. There was a huge noise. A stink of chemicals. A short yellow tongue of flame lit up the walls and fixed each cat in the instant of fear. Then the explosion seemed to pick the fox up by his hindquarters and smash him against the opposite wall. He made a high yelping noise like a cub, scrabbled upright, and tried to throw himself back into the fight.

His rear legs folded up under him.

"Majicou!" he said, "I—"

With a string of puzzled little diminishing cries, he collapsed.

"I ain't seen him since," said Mousebreath. "None of us seen him after that. After that it were just kicking and chasing and being shoved in a sack." He shook his head. "We none of us seen him after that."

Suddenly, he looked worn out and sad, a tough old cat who had had enough.

"After that," he said, "they just ran around kicking us, hitting us with sticks, dragging us out from behind things by the legs. We was all in the sack then."

"One for Sorrow tried to help you," said Tag. He added proudly, "And I bit the driver in the leg!"

"About the bird I don't know anything," said Mousebreath, "though I heard him from inside the sack, just before the Queen got out. But I reckon we've seen the last of the fox. I reckon he's dead. He's got to be, after that. I'll tell you what, though," he promised. "He was a hell of a fighter, I'll give him that! Anyway," he concluded, "that's how we ended up in a cat catchers' van in the middle of nowhere"—here he treated Tag to a wry look—"with no plan, no food, and no future."

"Look," said Tag defensively, "I—"

Ragnar Gustaffson had listened to Mousebreath's tale with approval, nodding here and there, but now he seemed to lose interest. He turned instead to a methodical investigation of the inside of the van, working forward along one wall and then back along the other, scraping in the rusty corners, sniffing at the lid of the wooden box, putting his face up close to the gap between the doors until the cold draft there made his eyes run.

He said in a thoughtful voice, "I think we are here as you might say, *for some time*." He limped over to Mousebreath. "In any case these recriminations of yours are unimportant. What should you be asking Tag, in my opinion? Why, this: *After she escaped, where did the Queen go?*" He thought it over, nodded to himself. "Also: How we are getting out of here to rejoin her! Hm," he decided. "Your answer: *Quite!*"

Then he lifted his hind leg and began to lick energetically at it.

"Oh, quaite," said Mousebreath.

"Shut up, Mousebreath," Tag said.

They stared unblinkingly at each other. After a moment, Mousebreath looked less amused.

Tag said, "Ragnar, I don't know what's happened to her. I saw her escape from the bag. I saw her run away." He paused, bewildered by his own sadness. "It was dark. The weather was bad. Ragnar, I saw her fall into the canal!"

The King stared ahead. "Ah," he said.

After that he went off and sat by himself for a while and wouldn't talk.

The van bumped and swayed along, its tires booming in the night. While the tabby slept with her front paws curled up like neat white shells, Mousebreath and Tag tried to make sense of their situation.

"Where are they taking us?"

"No idea."

"We're going west though, I'm sure."

"We're going west all right."

There wasn't much to add to that.

"At least the little one seems okay," said Mousebreath.

"She does. She seems okay."

"But I seen this sort of thing. I seen it before. Not exactly like this, but close."

"What *have* you seen, Mousebreath?"

"You don't want to know."

"Everyone tells me I don't want to know. I hate it. I *do* want to know!"

Mousebreath nodded. "I can understand that," he admitted. There was a long pause, as he organized his memories. Eventually he said, "I seen the way cat catchers spoil a life. You been lucky not to meet them before. Spoiled my life before it started," he said bitterly. Then, "Nah. Nah, that ain't true. I made a good thing out of my life despite them, especially since I met that old calico queen—" He shook his head impatiently and tried to begin again. "Look, this is how it is—"

Cat catchers, he explained, worked the feral communities on

a rota. "Come summer, come winter, they'll be there. Take the kittens first, then come back when the older cats have forgot. Get any you missed." Cat catchers worked the garbage dumps, the wasteland, the heating ducts and boiler houses under big public buildings—anywhere there was food or warmth. They worked with nets or traps baited with the barest smell of something good. They gassed the sick and the old after they had caught them and kept only the healthy. "In fact, they prefer domestics to ferals. Your domestic's healthier and generally less trouble to handle. Anyhow, as a kitten, I lived in Coldharbor, on a *barge* . . ."

Scores of barges, he said, huge, rusty, blunt-nosed metal things, placid as cows in a field, were moored on the south bank of the river, just east of Coldheath. Loaded to the gunwales with the waste of the city, they were then towed downriver once or twice a week to the sprawling estuarine landfills at Jubilee.

"You should see them!" enthused Mousebreath. Clustered at their moorings, he said, overhung by a constant pall of brown dust, the barges were like a floating country, always rich, always ripe for picking, disputed by scarred gray herring gulls that wheeled and squabbled above them even at night and by barge cats grown huge but not lazy on everything from butter paper to half-empty tins of ghee or coarse Belgian pâté. "You should smell them boats through the fog on a cold March morning!"

The barge kittens were something to see, black-and-whites for the most part, with markings—as Mousebreath put it—"as mixed as a bag of licorice allsorts." They were born daft. They skirmished with rodents and seagulls three times their size. They were dirty and infested and down by the river. They knew no law. "There were *that many* of us! We run about over them mountains of garbage dawn to dusk, fighting and chasing. Oh, we had some laughs! Half the time we couldn't stop shitting, the other half we could barely see from runny eyes. Oh, but we had a few laughs!" Among them, one little female shorthair stood out for animation and daring and fun.

She had the pelt of a seal, and she loved the river. At the age of two months she fell in and floated back to the bank on a raft of plastic packing, her eyes full of laughter. By three she could swim like a rat. "Smelt like one, too!" By five months, no question of it, she was Mousebreath's darling. Every time he looked at her, she took his breath away. When he looked at her, his own life welled up inside him like a pain, and he could barely breathe with delight. She knew it too! She perched on the rusting prow of the barge in the dawn, trying to see her own reflection; the mucky river water rippled away like gold beneath her!

"Her name was Havana."

"Was she beautiful?" Tag asked.

Mousebreath considered. "She was *brown*," he decided with satisfaction, as if that said it all. He said, "There was nothing like her on the barges. I never seen anything like her before or since." For a moment it seemed as if he might add to this, but in the end he only shook his head. "Brown," he repeated.

It was enough.

"Anyway—" he said. But instead of beginning again he let a silence draw out.

"Anyway."

Coldharbor. July. Late afternoon. The sky was brass. For once, the herring gulls were out to sea, planing in the maritime air, dreaming of cold silver fish like coins spilled from a net. An unctuous, appetizing rankness lay on the barges; the cats lay in a stupor. Everywhere you looked, there were silent parliaments of adults blinking at one another in the drowsy buzz of flies—the sound of the summer sun—cabals of kittens with fat little bellies turned up to the light. Then engines! Doors slamming! Shouts! Men in waders, plowing through the thigh-high garbage!

"Oh, we scuttled and ran," said Mousebreath, with a kind of amused bitterness. "You should have seen us run!" He was silent again.

"They got the lot of us," he said eventually. "Everyone except me. I hid. I never forgave myself for that."

"Anyone would have hidden," said Tag.

Mousebreath looked at him emptily. "Would they?" he asked. "Anyway, they got the lot of us."

"They got Havana?"

"They got her last of all. I never seen a cat so frightened or so brave. She ran; they was always there. She hid; they found her. She's calling out for me—*Marsebref! Marsebref!* She waits as long as she can. In the end, when I don't come, she jumps in the river and swims out into the middle. Brave? That brave!"

"She escaped!" said Tag.

Mousebreath shook his head. "You'd think she'd be swept away," he said, in the voice of someone talking to himself. "That great huge river that cares for no one. You'd think she'd lose her strength eventually, paddling out there while they waited for her on the bank. Drown or be swept away. But no. She's too alive for that."

Silence.

"Mousebreath! What happened?"

"They waited her out," he said simply. "It was a big joke to them. They sat there on the bank and waited till she got cold and hungry and swam back in again because she couldn't think of anywhere else to go." He looked at Tag, and his mismatched eyes were full of despair. "Then they hit her on the head with a stick and took her away."

"And that was the last you saw of her?"

"I wish it had been." After a moment he asked himself, "What could I do after that? I did the only thing I could do. I made a life without her."

After Havana, the barges smelled of wet ash, and all Mousebreath could hear in the morning was the groan of the conveyor belts that filled them. Human shouts. The shriek of an angry gull. He traveled with the barges up and downriver. He grew into a strong young tortoiseshell tom who never lacked for mates—mostly cheery black-and-white queens who adored his mismatched eyes and didn't remind him of her. He fought a lot. He got a bad reputation among the barge cats. He threw himself into anything that was going, but—at least to begin with—left it all every evening to sit and watch the sun go down over the up-stream reach, to dream of Havana and wonder what became of her. In the end, though, life worked its magic, and he did what any cat would have done: he forgot her and went on. Then one morning—it was perhaps six months later—he got up in the dawn to inspect the new garbage. It was colder now, and the sky was a paler blue. The barges had returned the day before from Jubilee, and were still riding high in the water. The great fixed conveyor belts roared and shook and poured the rubbish into them. Over them the gulls wheeled and fought like scraps of rag on a blustering wind.

"I went to have a look at what had arrived. It were black bags."

Black bags. Hundreds of fat black garbage bags, pouring off the belts; and in the very first one he tried, cats. All the cats he had ever known. He ripped it open and there they were. They had lost legs or eyes, or their jaws were bolted together. They were shaved in patches, drilled in the head. They had ab-dominal scars held together with rough black stitches like zip-pers. Among them was Havana. She had grown since he last saw her, and her body was long and beautiful as she spilled stiffly out of the ruptured sack in front of his face. Her fur was a lighter brown than he remembered, and her skin beneath it a tremulous pink. "She had the most beautiful *paws*," said Mousebreath. "That's the change you noticed most."

That, and the snarl of pain, the empty eye socket, the pro-truding wires.

"All them poor buggers," he said.

Then, after a silence, "At least she were dead. Two or three of them were still alive. If you can call it that. That's when I first heard *laboratory*. I heard that word over and over again from one of them till he died. It was all he could say."

"What did you do?"

"I stood there a long time," said Mousebreath. "I had one more look at her. It was getting dark by then. I 'ad one more look at Havana, then I walked away and never went back there again."

He thought for a moment.

"I loved them barges," he said. "But I was never a kitten again."

In the silence that followed this story, Ragnar spoke up. "People would not do this," he claimed. "No one would do this to another animal."

Mousebreath stared at him.

"Got you there," he said. "Because human beings aren't *animals*, are they?" A kind of morose triumph swam in his orange eye; while the blue one still contemplated with sad delight his beautiful brown friend of long ago. "They ain't got the decency of an animal."

"Some have," insisted Ragnar. "I must believe this."

"More fool you."

Midnight. White light shifted and flickered. The van sped on.

Dispirited by the story of Havana, worn out with fear and motion sickness, Mousebreath, Ragnar, and Tag sat silently staring into nowhere. Soon, two of them slept.

The tabby cat looked down on them from her perch and purred.

Mousebreath's paw, dabbing at his face, woke Tag to confusion, darkness, bitterly cold air. The van seemed to be swaying and lurching its way through a maze. He slithered helplessly about for a bit, then the two of them managed to wedge themselves across a corner, eyeing with anxiety the cages that tottered precariously above them.

"Not far past midnight," said Mousebreath, "and we got a problem here."

It was darker than it had been, but not too dark to see Ragnar Gustaffson crouched at the back of the van, where he was patiently attempting to lever the metal doors apart. He wasn't the cat they knew. With his powerful haunches braced, his back arched, and his tangled, dirty fur sticking out against the cold, he looked like something much wilder.

"Ragnar!" called Tag.

Ragnar glanced up briefly, only to give a kind of bubbling snarl and return to the doors. He had split a claw to the quick. Blood was caked in his paw and smeared on the metal.

"Help me here if you are anyone," he demanded.

"Ragnar!"

"No help for this," said Mousebreath.

When they tried to draw him away, he stared sightlessly at them. When they insisted, he spat. His size made them cautious, but the misery in his eyes was worse. "Don't you see?" he appealed. He plucked and plucked at the doors. "She may still be in the water. Or by now they may have put a wire into her eyes. *We must find her!*" While they slept Ragnar Gustaffson had lain awake, staring straight into the darkness at his worst fears. With no one to talk to, he had dreamed awake; and in his dreams Pertelot Fitzwilliam's fate had become inextricably entangled with that of a barge cat called Havana.

"What's wrong with him?" Tag said.

"He's lost someone he loved," Mousebreath replied, "and he wasn't sure what that meant till I told him."

"So what do we do with him now?"

"I don't know."

It was a decision they never had to make.

As Tag spoke, the van stopped so suddenly that for one strange, extended instant everything inside it seemed to be floating. The air was full of loose, incongruous things—nuts and bolts, dirt from the floor, some grayish wooden wedges, a blue metal box snapping its lid and spilling shoals of rusty objects. A length of frayed blue rope writhed past, curling and uncurling sensuously. Cat cages clattered in strange orbits through the pitch dark, flapping their wire doors like poorly thought-out wings.

Tag had time to see Cy revolving solemnly among this stuff—dabbing at one thing and another with velvet paws and an expression of puzzled delight—before the van crashed to earth again with a tired groan and slithered to a halt, catapulting the three male cats in a single writhing bundle toward the front. There Tag lay, the breath knocked out of him, trying to make himself as small as possible as the reluctant cages gave up their brief fantasy of flight and exploded into the bulkhead wall around him.

There was a long, stunned moment of silence.

What now? thought Tag. What are they going to do to us now?

Chapter Eleven
THE WIDE BLUE OPEN

The sea is calm to-night,
The tide is full, the moon lies fair . . .
—MATTHEW ARNOLD

"*B*ut why?"

Pertelot Fitzwilliam, Queen of Cats, had never been to sea, could not understand the need for a voyage—nor indeed the reason to travel anywhere without Ragnar Gustaffson Coeur de Lion. Her green eyes were brilliant with anxiety. Her thoughts went around and around and ended nowhere.

"Because," said Sealink, "it's the safest way to go."

Pertelot stared obstinately away. "Go where?" she said.

"Tintagel."

"I won't go there." Then, "Oh, I feel so alone, and no one will help."

Sealink sighed. "Don't be spoiled, hon. We been through this. We don't know where the rest of them are; we don't know what they're doing. We don't even know if they're alive, but Tintagel was agreed. Tintagel's all we got."

"I won't go any further without Ragnar. You said that if we came here we'd be able to find out what had happened to him." Pertelot looked around with contempt. "But these are only the same human beings I've been running from for weeks." She transferred her verdigris gaze from the Fish Market in general to the back of Pengelly's neck in particular. "And anyway, it appears you had other plans."

If that brindled old salt felt anything, he wasn't going to say. Neither was his hearing good at this time. As for Sealink, she only shook her head.

"I asked all over, hon. No one's heard about no cat catchers operating on the quays. And nobody seen anything last night. People see a fox, a magpie, and a bunch of cats, they'll re-

204

member that. You know? We don't know anything; so I suggest we move along before the Alchemist comes sniffing around you again. I got your interests in mind. You don't want to look down that long nose of yours at me because I meet an old friend."

Pertelot dropped her head.

"I'll never see Ragnar again."

"Don't be foolish, hon. This ain't no soiree. It ain't no cat show. We ain't got time to be cast down. You got the chance to take a boat trip—which you ain't done before—away from the Alchemist, away from all your worries. As for that tom of yours, he'd rather see you at sea than putting yourself at risk looking for him. Take my word on it."

The Queen thought.

"Pengelly?" she said.

"Yes, my dear?"

His gaze was unwavering, if skewed. She wasn't sure which eye to focus on—the one that seemed to be looking right at her or the one that glanced to the side. In the end she chose the former.

"What do you suggest?" she asked him.

"Well now, my dear," he mused, in his soft West Country burr. " 'Tis clearly a situation requiring some thought. But I reckon I've always known which I'd choose, when it came down to the devil and the deep blue sea."

Pertelot shivered.

Down at the dockside ships of all sizes bobbed upon the water, ropes creaking, lines rattling in the breeze. Huge, barnacle-encrusted iron hulls reared up alongside tiny boats with varnish peeling off their decks. Arrogant-looking seagulls, their feathers clean white and gray, their yellow beaks sharp and avid, adorned the booms and bows. They eyed the three cats beadily, and their cries rent the morning air.

Pengelly paid them no attention, but some way down the dock, he stopped and scrutinized the bobbing vessels.

"See that little beauty out there?" he said proudly. "That's the *Guillemot.*"

He was indicating a trim fishing boat moored beyond the renovated barges and pleasure cruisers. Her black-and-white paint was old and flaking, but her lines were clean and serviceable.

"I see Old Smoky ent back yet. Tender's still tied up to quayside. He'm probably getting rat-arsed."

All he received from Pertelot was a blank look.

"Never mind, my lover," he said.

And with an agility that belied his age, he leapt lightly down from the dock onto the deck of the first boat out from the quay. In quick succession he had made three more leaps—across a trench of murky water onto the bows of a larger craft whose decking was covered in piles of rope and net, then several feet onto the stern of a pleasure cruiser whose gleaming white fiberglass and polished wood contrasted sharply with the workaday craft around it, and from there, in one final huge neat bound, onto the deck of the *Guillemot*.

It was a bravura performance. The fishing boat rocked gently at its buoy as if welcoming him aboard.

"Well, hon," Sealink murmured to the Mau, "off you go, now. And try not to miss your step. I could do without another ducking."

Pertelot looked out across the river in dismay. So many obstacles and so much water between them. She looked back at the calico cat. Sealink's expression was closed and unhelpful. Of Pengelly there was no sign at all.

She could remember in clear detail the sense of sailing through cold air before hitting the ice on the canal, the sensation earlier that morning of sliding on the weed of the rotting jetty. Neither memory was encouraging. She considered the problem again. Then before she had any conscious idea of how she had gotten there, she found herself among the nets on the first boat, already poised for her second leap. With a considerable sense of surprise, she was in flight, sure and elegant and economical as only a cat can be—muscles bunching and flexing, limbs out-stretched, skin taut with effort, legs bending slightly to absorb the shock of landing on the rigid fiberglass. By the time she had arrived safely on the deck of the *Guillemot*, her body felt fluid and agile—a delight to move in. A surge of well-being coursed through her, a sense of achievement and pride. Her bloodline might have been attenuated through centuries of calculated design, but she was still Felidae; and no amount of breeding to purpose could erase her essential nature. Beautiful, lithe, and vital, she was the Queen of Cats.

What fun! she thought. Oh, what fun!

When Sealink arrived, it was via a series of efficient, powerful jumps, her long coat bouncing and rippling as if she were loosely enclosed by a completely separate animal. Movement was bread and butter to her. As soon as she touched down she was off about the boat, nosing about among the crab pots and netting, around the engine housing and out onto the foredeck, where ropes lay in coils like vast, rough, sleeping snakes and steel cleats gleamed among the wood and hemp.

Pengelly's efficiency was conservative. It lay in knowing to a hair how much effort was required for a task. He already had made himself comfortable out on the bow. At first, you thought he was asleep, but a glint of light in the slit of his left eye showed he was still open for business and watching the distant quay with lazy attention.

Sealink flopped to the deck beside her old friend and gave herself a wash. Then she rolled heavily on one side and turned her amber gaze upon him.

"What now, babe?"

He squinted at her. "We wait till Old Smoky comes back. Though if he'm drunk, my handsome, he won't be getting back here tonight—too ockard to get the rowboat out across the river to old *Guilly*. So he'll kip down on the dock. Or pass out, more like. Now, if he's only had a few, he'll probably reel down here and make it on board somehow. But mebbe he'll not have made enough from his catch to wet his throat at all. In which case he'll be back shortly. That being so—" here he winked confidingly "—he may not be the best of company."

"Keep your voice down, hon," said Sealink.

Too late.

Crouched in the shadow of the wheelhouse, Pertelot listened to this ominous exchange. Her newfound confidence ebbed away. How had she let herself be stranded on a leaky fishing boat in the middle of the water, awaiting the arrival of some angry human being?

Oh, Ragnar, she thought, where are you? Ears flattened to her skull, she fled below.

Down the dark steps she went, into the cabin, where she burrowed her way into the darkness beneath Old Smoky's berth. There, she turned her back to the world, curled up, and pushed her face into the tangle of bedding—faded woolly blankets, a quilt made up of hundreds of tiny crocheted squares in different patterns and colors—that had been stored there. It smelled of tobacco and Pengelly. Hairs, human and feline, had woven themselves into it over the years until you couldn't tell one from the other.

The conversation above was comfortably muffled by layers of wool and wood, by the creak of the timbers and the gentle sloshing of water in the bilges below.

Soon she was asleep.

Hours passed. The sun slipped between dull layers of cumulus cloud—lending them a muted, opaque light that seldom broke the surface—and arced its way methodically across the leaden sky. With each hour's passage, a new corner of the cabin was illuminated, and the light made its acquaintance with Old Smoky's eccentric accommodations.

It glinted off a pair of gimballed brass oil lamps on the wall and found beneath them a basic galley: a blackened stove smelling strongly of charcoal and stale food, pots and pans restrained in bulging mesh nets. Farther down the cabin, it investigated a sink and a cubicle clad with a piece of old toweling, after which it passed on to a jumble of clothbound books, their covers feathered with salt and mildew, and to a wedge of oilskins and tarry jumpers that had been stuffed into the gap beneath the cabin steps. It examined all these things, then turned and shifted and lay as quiet as the cat beneath the bunk.

Pertelot woke lulled; smelled fish, diesel, nicotine, ammonia. Drowsily she began to groom these odors from her fur, beginning with her velvety tail and haunches. A minute or two later, she sighed and fell asleep again.

Out on the foredeck, Sealink and Pengelly were also dozing. They had curled together, face to tail among the ropes, in a shellacked yin and yang.

The sun went down slowly behind the far bank of the river, outlining the spires and tower blocks in a wicked red light, and winked out suddenly, like the closing of a lizard's eye.

As darkness fell steadily across the city the lights came on one by one along the quayside. Some were streetlamps, with their gauzy haze of sodium. Others were small and quick and low to the ground—a glint here, a glint there, then gone into the night.

They were like the dreams of the city.

In her dreams, the Queen was running for her life, and someone who might have been Ragnar was running with her.

Behind them swelled a sea of farouche cats, ghostly gray and white, translucent and shifting, their limbs writhing in pursuit, faces bleak with menace. They were dead. The moon shone out of their cold and empty eye sockets. They wailed and wailed at her, but no matter how hard she tried she could not understand their warnings. Then, out of the midst of them there rose a vast, forbidding shape. Pertelot's paws were hobbled. She could not run away. Her companion was gone. She twisted and fought, but the dead cats held her fast. Darkness towered up. A great cold shadow fell across her—

And then she woke, her chest fluttering with sharp, ragged breaths. Her feet were caught up in the folds of blanket. It was dark, and for several moments she did not know where she was.

The smells of the cabin tranquilized her, the subtle rocking of the boat at anchor, the quiet of night falling. But no sooner had she calmed herself to a point just south of panic than there was a lot of splashing and swearing outside the boat, and a commotion broke out on deck, and two faces appeared at the cabin hatch.

"Are you okay, hon?" Sealink inquired.

Pengelly ran down nimbly and jumped on top of the berth.

"Here comes Old Smoky," he declared. "Best hide your-selves for the time being, I'd say. Never know how he'll wel-come company when he's had a few jars. Sometimes he'm companionable, and sometimes he ent. If he'm really doddered, he'll probably set sail tonight. He don't much like towns."

Sealink romped cheerfully down the steps. "He'll have brought some stores, though," she explained to Pertelot. "Pengelly says he never forgets, no matter how drunk." She wriggled underneath the berth beside the Mau. "Babe, I could eat a whale."

Thumps and crashes from above. Pertelot looked up anx-iously. The *Guillemot* rocked, once, twice, and the water in her bilges slapped and gurgled. Heavy breathing. The sound of wood dragged along wood, then a further thud and a curse. White light scythed across the hatchway.

"He'll have dropped his torch," Pengelly said matter-of-factly. "Bit cackhanded at the best of times. I do hope he ent going to cook. Can get a bit fierce around here when there's fat flying."

A pair of huge boots appeared in the torchlight at the top of the steps.

"Pengelly?"

A grizzled white head dipped into view, the hair as thick and crinkled as Pengelly's coat.

"Pengelly? Where you be, boy?" Then, "Ah, there you are now."

Pengelly had jumped lightly off the bunk to mark his human with much enthusiastic rubbing of cheek on boot.

A massive, calloused hand reached down and kneaded the Rex's head so roughly that Pengelly's eyes briefly took on an unusual and Oriental slant. To Pertelot's amazement, he seemed to enjoy this. It made him purr blissfully and cast himself at the fisherman's feet, where he proceeded to roll on his back with his front paws tucked up like a rabbit's. The hand buried itself in the soft fur of his belly, and Pengelly's eyes closed in delight.

It was an extraordinary display for a grown cat.

Crooning meanwhile, "How's my lad, then? How's my lad?" the old man straightened, thumped up the steps, reached blindly around on the deck, and brought down a paper-wrapped package that smelled strongly of fish. His warm, beery breath filled the suddenly cramped confines of the cabin. He sat so heavily on the berth that its horsehair stuffing compressed with a sad sigh and the underside bulged down upon the two cats beneath.

"I brought us a fish supper to share, boy."

From the moment it appeared, Sealink had been unable to take her eyes off the parcel. Now she was drooling. Pertelot stared at her, then realized that she was drooling too.

There was a lot of rustling, then a crumpled square of greasy paper landed on the slatted floor by his boots. Little flecks of white fish and golden batter were stuck to its edges. The calico cat fixed upon these alertly, her toes flexing with greed and intent. Pertelot shook her head—No. No.

Sealink ignored her and got ready to pounce. The situation was saved—like many another, Pertelot guessed—by Pengelly's sly paw, which steered a sizeable lump of fish over the edge of the bunk and into the shadows beneath. Haddock! It landed softly and in an eyeblink had disappeared.

Three cats and an old fisherman chewed contentedly in the darkness.

The tide rose with the dawn and found the *Guillemot* chugging slowly downriver through clinging mist, her navigation lights a soft green and red haze at bow and stern. Sounds were muted, visibility poor, but Old Smoky maneuvered his craft without incident between buoy and barge. Moored pleasure craft—long since past their best—bobbed gently in their wake, paint feathering off to reveal old timbers silvered by the passing seasons. Fenders and buoys, once startling neon orange, now hung limply over gunwales, faded to a flat, bleached apricot.

Out in the starboard channel, where the water moved more freely, the elderly diesel engine began to strain. Sealink and Pertelot crouched beneath the bunk, wincing at the noise it made. Pengelly lay sprawled on the wheelhouse chart shelf—a position he would often take up on mornings such as this, when the weak winter sunshine was barely warm enough to penetrate his fur. Behind him, the fisherman stood with one hand on the wheel and drew on a cigarette. Its end glowed briefly in the damp air, and, drawn out of the companionway by cool air off the water, the exhaled smoke spiraled lazily upward. January sunshine filled the mist—evaporating the fine detail of the riverbank into a luminous plasma—then eventually burned it away to reveal a clear sharp morning and a cool, dove-white sky.

The city passed slowly by on either side, increasingly far from the boat across an expanse of sluggish, oily-looking water. Tower blocks and mirror-glassed office buildings gave way gradually to low-lying warehouses and acres of desolate concrete patrolled by iron gantries and huge, vigilant cranes, where rusting signs adorned the blackened brick walls of the abandoned warehouses.

Now rotted pilings, dark with age and weed, emerged along the banks. Upon them, shaking their wings out in the new light, the gulls lazily surveyed the scene: the passage of the *Guillemot*, the water churning and spooling behind her; a police launch on its deliberate way upriver—no crimes, yet, to attend to; a smartly painted black tugboat making good headway against the current on a mission to usher some great container vessel into its dock.

The morning passed like this, and as it passed, the landscape spread and flattened toward the far horizon. As the sun rose higher, it illuminated a panorama as inimical to cats as to humans—estuary waters, out of the unforgiving shallows of which rose gleaming banks of mud, glistening like the backs of whales in the sunshine. Reed beds fringed a wide shoreline beyond. There was no sign of life. Not even the gulls bothered with this part of the river.

At last Pengelly stretched and yawned, toes spread, head back. He jumped down between Old Smoky's feet and down into the darkness of the cabin. Two pairs of eyes glinted at him.

"How you doing, my dears?"

"About time," Sealink complained. "When do we get out of here? This ain't too dignified for a cat of my proportions. I ain't used to skulking around when I travel, Babe. I like to take the air. Where's the sense in moving if you don't see where you're going?"

She explained, as if he had asked her, "Where you been ain't so important. You *been* there."

Pengelly blinked. After a moment he said, "Best wait till Old Smoky gets us out to sea—don't quite know how he might react to stowaways. Least if we're out beyond land he won't feel so disposed to turf you off." Motes of humor danced briefly in Pengelly's uneven tawny eyes. No," he concluded, "he may be a grumpy old bugger, but I never seen him harm a cat. I doubt he'll throw you overboard. Leastways, not without the life raft . . ."

Sealink failed to take the bait.

"I'm up on deck in five minutes' time, babe. And your human had better get used to company, unless he wants me to take a crap in his bed."

At the word *crap*, Pertelot groaned.

"You sound a bit crook, my handsome," Pengelly told her. "Can get a bit fumey down here, I know. Bloody old engine probably needs a look. Ent been serviced in my lifetime—" he winked lopsidedly at Sealink "—and that's longer than I'd like to admit with ladies present."

At this, Sealink rolled her head in apparent unconcern, proceeding to strip the old sheath from the claws on her right front paw.

"Huh," she said.

The Mau did, in fact, feel rather ill this morning. The light hurt her eyes and her mouth was dry and furry. Moreover, she seemed to have eaten something that disagreed with her.

"Oh dear," she said.

"I'm sorry, I think I—"

And she shot out from under the bunk and dashed un-heeding up the stairs onto the companionway, where she was violently sick.

At exactly the same moment, there was a clanking of steer-age chains below as Old Smoky, sitting in a gentle hungover doze at the wheel, took action to avoid an iron marker buoy. The boat swung promptly to port. Pertelot felt herself slide at forty-five degrees down the companionway, toward the railing and the waiting river.

She stared down at the sucking eddies barely two feet below. Her claws fastened themselves into the old rope-and-cork fenders strung along the side of the boat. No good: the depths beckoned avidly. Then she felt a set of teeth fasten themselves in the scruff of her neck, and she was carried without ceremony—her feet bumping like a kitten's on each step—back down into the cabin.

Pengelly set her on the slatted floor and stared at her.

"I can tell you ent been at sea afore," he muttered. He was barely bigger than she was, but he had a thick, sinewy neck and his feet were steady as the *Guillemot* rolled.

"You got to listen to the boat—you got to feel the way she moves herself in the water, specially when Old Smoky's got a sore head. You all right now, my lover? Can't have you getting seasick this early on; it won't do at all. You this bad now, you'll be terrible out on the briny."

Sealink extracted herself from the space under the bunk.

"Ain't that the truth?" she said. "Lord, honey, this here's as peaceful as a puddle, and you go throwing up your good fish. What you gonna do when we're out on the ocean wave? You get yourself used to it soon, hon, because there's some stuff you're gonna see out there. Oh yes," she said, and her voice had a sudden dreamy quality, the soft daze of the enthusiast. "The best and the worst, hon. The best and the worst." She shuffled until she was comfortable on the slats and had settled herself to her satisfaction in the feather boa of her tail. "I like an airplane, I truly do, but I came to your country on a boat—"

"This ent my country," Pengelly declared crossly. "Cornwall is a country all its own; you should know that, being as *well-traveled* as you are."

Sealink barely noticed the interruption. "And Sealink is the name I got called here, so I guess I got a soft spot for them if for no other reason. But I've sat on a thousand rails if I've sat on one, watching those waves go past just like a New Orleans

marching band—and, honey, I just don't tire of it. All the sky
and the sea stretching away the same color till you barely know
which way's up; and the land turning all faint in back like it's
going to just disappear, so that there you are—like a little boat
yourself, alone in the middle of all that air and water. Honey,
you're gonna love it too."

Pertelot considered this. It made her feel sicker than ever. "I
don't—" she said.

But Sealink was off again.

"Man!" she exclaimed. "Travel! You know what they say?
They say: *Move, and the world moves with you.* What do you
think of that? Best saying I ever heard. Troubles behind you,
and a whole new future out in front!

"Hon, you gotta stop looking back over your shoulder at the
bad things. That's what traveling's for—putting distance between yourself and your past will save you from many a sorry
situation. The Alchemist, he ain't gonna find you out here. Ain't
no way anyone's gonna do that. So you just focus on having a
good time and forget about all that stuff. We'll cruise on down
to Tintagel and you'll meet up with your old tom, and I'll meet
up with mine, and we'll be just fine. So relax, enjoy the trip.
Take it easy, and you won't be seasick at all. It's an attitude of
mind, babe—just take that from me. Now, if you'll excuse me, I
got to make a short visit up on deck."

Before she could suit actions to words, Pengelly had nipped
neatly in front of her. They confronted for a moment. Her fur
was so thick and massy that for a moment it looked as if two
Pengellys would be needed to make up one Sealink. But he was
not so easily outfaced.

"I'll come up with you, take Old Smoky's mind off things
while you do your doings," he offered. "Since you're not entirely inconspicuous, my handsome."

And he ran lightly up the steps.

Sealink was forced to follow, in a flounce of calico. "Ain't no
call for you to talk so familiar," she told him.

"No offense, my dear. I like a bit of meat on the bone."

"Well, find another bone to chaw on, Cornwall, cause we's

only ever pals, and you ain't gettin' them loose old implements of yours into me."

Pertelot watched them go, then sought comfort beneath Old Smoky's berth, where things seemed to go up and down less. Was that possible? All things were possible, she had heard, at sea.

Old Smoky had retrieved his bedclothes the night before, the better to snore away the hours until high tide. But he had left a single soft crocheted blanket in the far corner, where it was gathering fluff balls and dust. She pulled at it with her teeth, trod around it again and again to mark it with the scent glands between her toes. Then she sat in the nest she had made, tucked her head under her paws so that the noise of the engine receded to a comfortable thud, and fell into a blessedly dreamless sleep.

Once having escaped the constrictions of the cabin, Sealink was determined not to go back. She quickly made space for herself in the litter of crab pots, lines, and buckets behind the engine housing in the stern of the boat.

From here she had a view of the passing world.

They had cleared the estuary by now, and their surroundings had become the blank canvas she had so recently described. The nose of the *Guillemot* tilted down to meet a wave head-on. White spray flew up from her bows. As the horizon—a barely discernible tonal change from sea to sky—dipped and rose with this motion, Sealink was filled with a quiet joy. Birds wheeled overhead, too far up for their cries to carry. The sun was the half-kept secret of a bank of cumulus clouds, tingeing their edges with silver and gold as it traveled westward with them.

On the move again! She gave a deep, contented sigh.

When she woke it was dark and cold.

The engine had stopped. The *Guillemot* rocked gently on the swell, making no headway. There were lights in the distance, banks of them, rising in serried rows. They had put into port, and she had slept so soundly she had missed it!

She looked around. No other signs of life. No one in the wheelhouse. No other boats close by. She stretched herself with languid thoroughness, taking the same pleasure as ever in the presence of her flesh. A satisfying group of dorsal extensions was followed by front, then hind legs. She arched her back luxuriously. She sat down again to attend to her toilette. Paws first, then haunches, flanks, ruff, ears, face; finally her proudest possession—the much-admired tail. Grooming complete, she shook out her coat like a white and orange flag in the moonlight.

"Hey!" she told herself quietly. "You look good! You look glowing! Oh but, honey, how come you're so *hungry*? Well could it be because you didn't eat since last night?"

She nosed hopefully among the nets. She would try anything. She would welcome the head of some week-old mackerel, staring puzzledly at the stars; she was prepared to meet the intricate challenge of a discarded lobster shell.

Nothing.

She trotted down to the wheelhouse in case the fisherman had left the crusts of his sandwiches behind. Not a crumb. But while she was there, something made her pause on the edge of the stairway and listen.

It was quiet down there but not silent. A soft, rhythmic sound was issuing from the cabin. Someone breathing? Hard to say. But her curiosity was up. Transferring her weight stealthily from paw to paw, she descended the steps.

The darkness in the cabin was thick and warm with life. Old Smoky lay curled fetally on the berth, with Pengelly nestled in the hollow between his bent knees and his chest.

They were both asleep.

The sound continued. It came from the galley. Sealink's pupils widened. There! There! On top of the draining board! A most peculiar shape! An elegant, whip-thin *thing*, its clean lines marred by a strangely bulbous head. Sealink approached, trying not to breathe.

Then a passing light gleamed momentarily at the porthole; and for that split second, the apparition was limned in silver.

Pertelot.

The Queen of Cats stood with three paws braced on the galley work surface. The fourth, along with much of her head, was inside a jar of peanut butter. With every rasp of her tongue, the jar scraped lightly against the Formica, to produce the noise Sealink had heard.

Pertelot was so absorbed in this task that when the calico landed on the counter beside her, she leapt a foot into the air in terror. The peanut butter jar sprang from her head and bounced across the floor. Old Smoky leapt from the bunk and lit the nearest gas lamp in a panic, while Pengelly sprang from the bed-clothes and simply ran about. Shadows reeled upon the walls. Further unnerved, Pertelot bolted beneath the berth and bur-rowed under the crocheted blanket. But when Sealink tried to follow suit, she could only fit her head and front half into the space. Her rear end stuck out into the air, tail waving helplessly like a flag of truce—a view Pengelly, who had recovered his natural calm, took in appreciatively.

"What are you lot doing on my boat?" roared Old Smoky, and he grabbed Sealink's waving tail in a calloused fist. Sealink dug in and tried to haul herself to safety—to no avail. Huge hard hands closed around her midriff. Slowly but surely she was pulled out, hissing and spitting and promising murder.

"Don't fight!" Pengelly warned her. "Not if you want to avoid a swim, at any rate. He do like cats, honest."

Sealink gave Pengelly her hardest stare. "You better be right, hon," she said. She gave up the struggle, withdrew her claws, and gazed upward insincerely. "Hi," she said. "I'm Sealink."

The face that loomed over her was tanned and lively. Light glinted from dark eyes caught like fish in a mesh of wrinkles. He held her at arm's length and surveyed his catch with kindness.

"Well, you're a beauty, ent you?"

"People have often noticed that," she said.

"You old devil, Pengelly." The fisherman chuckled. "Stash-ing your girlfriends on my boat now, are you? This one looks big enough to eat you alive!"

Sealink glared up at him. "I ain't a *girlfriend*. And I'd be obliged if you'd put me down."

Old Smoky stared at her almost as if he had understood, and set her on the floor. There, she composed herself majestically, keeping an eye on his hands.

Meanwhile, Pengelly was urging the Mau. "Come out, my dear. May as well get hung for a ham as a sausage."

"Hung?" said Pertelot.

"Sorry, my lover. Figure of speech. He'm in a good mood now; we may as well take advantage."

"Lord lumme," said Old Smoky, as Pertelot Fitzwilliam of Hi-Fashion emerged cautiously into the light. "You're a sly one, Pengelly. Two females in one night, that's plain greedy. And this one as scrawny as t'other one's fat!"

"This," said Sealink, *"is muscle."*

Pertelot stood near the fisherman's boots, sniffing timidly up at him. She was ready to run. But he extended his gnarled fingers to her, and they smelled of tobacco and sealife. It was a good smell. To her surprise, she found herself rubbing her cheek against the hand. She retreated hurriedly.

"You'm a bit jumpy, my lady, ent you? No need to fear me. Come up here now so's I can see you proper."

He lifted her firmly but gently onto the bunk beside him and ran his big hands over her tiny frame. They paused for a moment over her belly. He probed solicitously.

"Ent been eating proper, have you, sweetheart? That won't do at all. You sit here and I'll see what I can find."

He made his way down the galley, noting the broken jar on the floor.

"Peanut butter, eh? A bit rich for you in your condition, my dear."

He extracted some tins from the cupboard beneath the sink.

"Better start feeding you up," he said, "if you'm going to carry them kittens to term."

The Fourth Life of Cats

*Beloved of the gods, from Bast and Heliopolis we came;
from Attabiya markets where the finest watered silk was sold,
named for the beauty of a moiré tabby coat, from Abyssinia
and Persia* Felis cattus *ranged across the world.*

Thousands of miles away, on a promontory above the sea,
a chieftain had made his court at Tintagel in the ancient
country of Kernow. And for reasons best known to himself, he
had made known that he promised his only daughter, and a
considerable bride-gift, to the first man who brought him a
pair of cats.

A young Phoenician trader planned to be that man. Cats
were rare and prized—but the Daughter of Kernow with her
bright red hair! Now, there was something to think about. He
had just acquired a superb pair of cats, a pair that had
walked right up to him in the middle of the marketplace and
sat before him, blinking in the sun.

Atum-Ra and Isis were those cats: the King and Queen of
Cats in their time, and they had a mission of their own. They
were to bring the magic of the Ancient Kingdom to the lost
highways of the north; to revitalize the old roads made by
sabre tooth and Panthera, now fallen into disuse, and to popu-
late the cold lands once more. And with her, the Queen carried
her own precious cargo on this journey away from lands of
heat and trembling air, to eternal mist and rain.

In their well-appointed quarters Atum-Ra and Isis lay and
listened to the chatter of the crew as they sailed the wide
ocean; while the sailors, intrigued, stole below decks to peer
at them.

220

One said, "See how at dawn the apples of their eyes are long and thin; while at noon they are quite round; and at night the entire eye shines like a lamp!"

A second replied, "By day they soak up the light of the sun; at night they use it to see as if it were noon. Thus it is they secretly stalk their prey!"

And a cabin boy laughed and said, "They lie so sweetly there together!"

But the ship's Christian would only say, "I heard they fell to Earth like Lucifer. Eyes like those can see forbidden realms." And he crossed himself.

There was an Egyptian on the ship. He had once owned a cat himself, before he lost his home and went to sea. He loved to look at Atum-Ra, whom he called "the Little Son of the Morning." "In Egypt," he said softly, "the cat has been for centuries a sacred animal, bringing life and fertility. Like a little god, the cat walks the paths of the living and the dead." He smiled at the Christian. "No other animal can do that." Then he said, "The roads of Morning and of Evening—are those your forbidden realms?"

The Christian stated that cats were demons in animal form. The Book of Revelation referred clearly to a cat with seven heads.

The Egyptian said, "I heard cats were first created on Noah's Ark. The Ark became infested with rats. Noah sought God's advice. 'Go seek out the Lioness,' said God, 'and strike her upon the muzzle.' Noah struck the lioness and she sneezed forth a pair of cats. It is not recorded what she thought of that."

"Heretical rubbish!"

"It's your mythology, not mine," said the Egyptian with a shrug; which incensed the Christian so much that the pair fell to fighting in the hold and had to be doused with buckets of seawater before they could be separated.

The Queen of Cats licked her belly anxiously.

The ship sailed the quiet waters of the Middle Sea. Three days more, and they were beating north against the restless waves of the great ocean with the Pole Star their guide by night. The weather was cold and turbulent. The King and Queen shivered and slept. The cabin boy stroked them when no one was looking.

At last the ship made land, and Atum-Ra and Isis were carried up the steep steps to the cliff-top fortress of Tintagel.

The chieftain welcomed the Phoenician and his sailors with great delight. The bargain was made: a great feast was spread before them. But it was clear the chieftain was a troubled, sleepless man. There were lines etched deep in his face. His eyes were dark.

That night, when the marriage feast was at its height, he took Atum-Ra and Isis to his chamber and released them from their cage.

He addressed the pair. "I am a haunted man. Every night the spirits disturb my rest. I have not slept for six long months. Yet I cannot identify my tormentors and make amends. I killed many, to win this realm. Which of them rests so uneasy they will not depart to the Isle of the Dead? Cats live in both worlds, I know, and the image of a spirit will remain for a moment or two in a cat's eye. Stay with me tonight. Help me name these ghosts, and I will free you forever to come and go as you will."

Atum-Ra and Isis listened to his plea. Territorial wars are hard, as all cats know, but they must be fought. "And it is a good offer," said Isis.

They took up positions at each end of the great bed. The chieftain swathed himself in furs and rugs and lay between them. No sooner had the moon sailed free of the clouds outside the window than the after-walkers began their nightly visit.

First the clattering upon the roof, like iron heels on the ribs of a dead horse; then gusts of chill air that blew down the hangings and tore the chief's hair from its gold band, so that it was like a fiery nimbus around his face; and, at last, shapes that danced about the chamber, throwing down trays and chairs. Only the cats saw figures in an icy mist, grinning with the glee of their horrible wounds!

Atum-Ra saw a man. Isis saw a woman. Both wore saffron-dyed cloaks. One carried his head.

The King and Queen of Cats stared at these visitants; then calmly—though the icy wind was in their fur—they padded across the bed, stood before the trembling chieftain, and gazed upward.

He stared into tapetum lucidum of their eyes. There! Something woven deep within!

The spirits were named, and fled, never to be seen again. The chieftain was true to his word. He made amends to his enemies, erecting to their memory an ogham cross. And he gave the cats their freedom and decreed that none should harm them, or their offspring, on pain of death.

And so the King and Queen of Cats, Atum-Ra and Isis, enjoyed—as cats prefer to do—the best of both worlds. At Spring Equinox their kittens were born, at the heart of the wild roads, and golden light spread across the land. Which is why the headland at Tintagel is for cats a sacred place.

Chapter Twelve

LOSS

Never stroke a cat backward
or your luck will turn bad.
— OLD SAYING

*F*or a moment, after everything stopped moving, there was silence and darkness in the van. Then Tag heard indistinct human voices outside.

"Hide!" he urged.

The cats burrowed into the nooks and crannies formed where the cages—all dreams of flight abandoned—lay piled in confusion where they had come to rest toward the front of the van. They curled up. They tucked in their tails, then anxiously curled up a little tighter and tucked in a little further.

The rear doors of the van were opened and flung wide. Icy air and brilliant moonlight flooded in. Tag raised his head a little and had a look out.

The city was a long way behind them.

A cobbled square. Silent houses on three sides. Across darkened porches the moonlight projected vague, lacy shadows. Off in the dark on the fourth side, a strip of open grass stretched away to a village pond, where slurries of ice were forming and dissolving under the hesitant fingers of air. Everything was muffled up in snow—roofs slathered with it, eaves plastered. Every hedge and tree, every thin reed at the pond's edge, had its soft, damp windward coat, its shining plastrons of snow. As Tag watched, clouds obscured the moon. More snow began to pour down upon the center of the square. Four swathed human figures appeared at the open door and blotted out the view.

One of them jumped clumsily into the van, stared straight at Tag's hiding place for a moment, kicked one or two loose cages out of the way, then called out in an impatient tone. Outside, its companions grunted and muttered. After a pause, they began to load the van with large square objects. Feet scraped and scuffled. The air seemed to warm up a fraction and fill with the rank smell of human effort.

Tag risked a look.

More cages!

He stared, then—worried that the moonlight reflecting off his eyes might give away his position—withdrew.

More cages, he thought. But why?

"What is happening?" hissed Ragnar Gustaffson. "What is going on?"

"Hush up," Tag warned him.

"There are cats in these cages," said Ragnar. "What are they doing to them?"

"Ragnar, shut up."

"There are cats in these cages," Ragnar repeated obstinately. Then he was silent again.

The new cages crashed and rattled into position, until they were stacked high on both sides of the van. There was a brief argument, as the human that was in the van dusted its hands together and, breathing heavily, tried to get out again. The others pushed it back in. It shouted, but they shouted louder. It spat on the floor. Then it stamped its way to the front of the compartment and, with violent, overstated gestures, began to unload the original cages.

Now we're in for it, thought Tag. It's the one I bit.

For a while they remained hidden. Rage made the human incompetent, and there were a lot of cages. When two or three of them became tangled together by their doors, it wrenched and hauled at them, and threw them across the van. Finally, it picked them up again, and with a massive effort, tore the doors off them. There was laughter from outside, but it soon stopped when the cages were thrown out. This action seemed to calm the human down. Thereafter, it addressed itself efficiently to the task, carrying the cages to the open doors, from which position the others carried them off into the night.

Each time a cage was removed, Tag and his friends ran about behind the diminishing pile, looking for new places to hide.

Each time it got more difficult.

Eventually, the human looked down. It stopped. It bent forward.

"Well now," it said.

"Run!" called Mousebreath. "Run for it!"

Tag ran.

Long before he reached the square of icy moonlight at the end of the van, he felt hard hands catch at the loose fur behind his head. A great, round, pale face, pocked with open pores and stubble, loomed above him. He smelled its breath: very old food. He hissed and darted his head at it, teeth bared. The face disappeared. The hands slipped for an instant, then fastened around his body just below his ribs, where they tightened cruelly. He writhed and spat. He shrieked and bit. There was a yell and he was free again, scrabbling toward the doors. He fell over the edge and out into the night, where he found his companions trying to evade the other cat catchers: three gross human figures doing a kind of quiet, savage dance in the falling snow.

A thin fog of their own breath blurred their outlines, gave to their actions the ponderousness of slow motion, dampened their dull cries. Between their feet, tangled up in their legs, always managing to slip desperately out of reach, were three spitting cats. In a moment, Tag had been spotted, and there were four.

Amused, the fourth cat catcher watched this dance from the back of the van. Then it reached into a pocket of its coat and carefully shook out what it found there.

"Run!" Tag gasped, when he saw it. "Run!"

But by then—although they tried—it was too late to run anywhere.

The net was already over them.

Tag felt himself lifted into the air. Thin nylon mesh cut his face. He got one of his front legs out, but this only allowed the mesh to slip over his elbow and embed itself in the soft skin beneath. The more he struggled, the worse it hurt. The four of them were crushed in together, with Mousebreath at the bottom, howling in fury and terror. Tag felt him kicking out repeatedly like a dying rabbit, to no point or purpose. The net began to spin, drawing the visible world out into a gray blur. Tag got glimpses in quick succession of the frozen pond, a house standing on its own, a big raw hand reaching up. Then the van again.

From inside it, a smell of imprisoned cats welled into the cold night. Stale fear, stale urine, inadequately covered feces. Tag got a confused impression of the new cages, stacked up against the walls so that only a narrow aisle was left between them. Cat faces stared rigidly out at him in a brief moment of hope. Then the net spun and he was looking across at the pond again.

An irregular fifty-yard oval, fringed with spiky reeds and trees whose trunks were leaning and grotesquely split. The water, gray and glistening, flush with its flat grassy banks, looked sugary, inert, part frozen. He had time to see a movement out there—time to wonder what it was—before the motion of the net turned him to face the van. Hard human hands reached down. Human smells immersed him. He was pulled in, and the doors began to close. But not before Mousebreath's struggles had spun the net one last time.

The snow had stopped. A bleak yellow moon licked the racing clouds. The square was silent and still. Dull reflections seemed to flicker at the far end of the pond, where the wind was moving something to and fro. A leaf or a branch. No. It was something too big and vague for that, some kind of motion the brain couldn't easily grasp. Tag narrowed his eyes. His heart began to race.

Because he was a cat he understood what was happening long before the human beings did. It was too late for them. All they heard was a grunting roar, echoing off the trees. All they saw, as they turned to one another in horror and dropped the heaving net, was a black cat bounding toward them across the surface of the pond, its teeth bared, its big hard pads throwing up sprays of water, its glossy shoulders and haunches moving like a machine. It was *diminishing* as it came but was still larger than any cat a human being ever saw—

The Majicou!

It was the Majicou, caught in the instant of his power, emerging from the highway like some vast Brazilian jaguar from its arboreal gloom, his breath as hot as iron smoke in the frozen air!

Mousebreath, by now in a very dangerous state of mind indeed, finally got a claw into the net and gutted it like a fish. At exactly the same moment, the cat catchers dropped it and jumped out of the back of the van. Majicou bore down on them. Unnerved, they jumped back in, only to be confronted by the tortoiseshell, snarling up at them demonically as he tore off the remains of the net. For a moment they were paralyzed. Then they broke. There was a brief struggle for the driver's seat of the van. The starter scraped. The engine caught. The vehicle raced out of the square, wheels spinning, rear end sliding, back doors hanging open. Tag, Cy, and Mousebreath tumbled out into the road like lost luggage, but Majicou barely let them get their breath.

"Quick now! Follow me!" And he turned and sped off toward the pond.

"Wait!" called Tag.

"No time!"

At the edge, Tag halted uncertainly.

Mousebreath ran into him. Cy tumbled past them and slithered a little way across the ice on her bottom, looking aggravated.

"Wait!" they called.

But the black cat wouldn't listen.

"No time! This ice will bear you as long as you run!"

And he sped out in front of them, ten, twenty, fifty yards into the distance, growing larger as he approached the strange, smoky flicker on the far bank. A dozen cats spooled out onto the ice and streamed away in the night air after the one-eyed cat, bowling Tag over in their haste to escape.

There was no option. "Come on then!" cried Tag. Suddenly they were bounding across the ice together, throwing up spray like tigers in a rice field. Moorhens woke up and scooted for the bank. Startled mallards took to the air left and right. Tag ran. The ice held him up. Tag ran; they all ran; far in front ran Majicou. Their breath was hot in the freezing air. Cold and hunger meant nothing to them. They shed without thought the iron heat of their lives. On and on they seemed to run until the pond became a gray nowhere and movement all that had meaning—They were cats. They were *cats*!—then the highway had recognized and accepted them, and in one seamless gesture they were some-where else. "We're safe here for the moment," said Majicou. His voice was hollow and echoing. Out of immediate danger, and with the whole world to choose from, the other cats from the van were already wandering off in different directions. Majicou watched them go. He focused his single eye on Tag. "Now tell me quick!" he said. "The Queen—where is she?"

Tag stared at him. "She's not here." He was bewildered. "You can see she's not here. She fell in the canal."

He sat down tiredly. He admitted, "I've lost Sealink too."

"And the fox?"

"The fox died," Mousebreath offered. He asked the black cat, "Who are you?"

Majicou ignored him.

"Pray that she is with the fox," he said. He lashed his tail, paced to and fro. "If he's not there to help, the Alchemist will have them both!"

Mousebreath shrugged. "He didn't look as if he could help himself last time I saw him. Let alone anyone else."

The great cat stared.

"Then the game is lost. This afternoon I dreamed she was near me—or have I yet to dream it?—but then she was gone again. Why didn't I act then? Why didn't I *act*?"

Tag looked round bemusedly.

"Where are we?" he said. "And where are Cy and Ragnar?"

"I'm here," said Cy. "I'm me."

"Ragnar? Ragnar!"

"Ragnar!"

Their voices no longer echoed. They were off the highway, in a bleak-looking spot on the downs above a village. They stared at each other anxiously; they stared anxiously about. They stopped calling out. There was no comfort to be had up here for city cats. Only Mousebreath had seen anything like it before, and even he was shocked. Everything was harsh black and white in the snowlight. It was bitterly cold. They felt their small size under the wheeling arc of the night. The wind made them cling together and press close around Majicou as he led them down a short steep slope, through a gate and a thicket of elder and hawthorn, to the door of an empty barn. Downslope was dead bracken, an earthy path winding away, the beginnings of fields. Upslope, back through the gate, Tag could see a great ridge—but not yet the two iron-hard ruts at its summit, worldly markers of the wildest road of all, stretching away under the moonlight to Tintagel in the deep west. In the end he had to admit, "I think we've lost Ragnar too."

Majicou sighed exasperatedly.

"This is all my fault," said Tag, hoping that Majicou would say it wasn't.

Instead, Majicou asked himself wearily, "What else can go wrong?" He looked frail and old now—a one-eyed cat worn out by long responsibility. "Nothing," he concluded. "We had better go in where it's warm." But a few moments later, when they had got inside the barn, he found that he had lost Tag too.

The bracken was hard work. But after a mile or so it gave way to beechwoods, a little beaten path, and rather easier going.

By then, though his pads were numb and he was already tired, Tag had begun to enjoy himself. The moon was low. The path ran here and there across little empty ditches and exposed root systems. There was no shelter. In the tunnel between the tall trees, the snow had been too powdery to cover; instead, a light salting picked out the line of a gnarled stone here, a broken branch there. Tag trotted and loped; stopped to listen, one paw raised; told himself, "Better be off!" and fled across the view, quick, silent, barely visible, until the edge of the wood brought him up short, and he was looking straight down into the valley.

Everything was laid out so clearly for him!

A mesh of steep-sided little lanes each with its handful of houses. Gardens, asymmetric and overgrown. Spinneys thick with dog rose and rhododendron. A tall gray building with an ivy-covered tower at one end. If Ragnar was down there, he could be found. Everything was so close that Tag could hear the ducks, grumbling sleepily from the pond. He stood—haunches down, front legs straight, every nerve alert—on a fallen tree and watched. A minute. Two minutes. Nothing was moving. There was no danger. Thirty seconds more, and he would go down there.

But he never did.

As he launched himself off the damp black trunk of the dead beech, he heard his name called.

"Tag."

"Ragnar! Are you here?"

Nothing.

"Where are you?"

"Tag," said the voice again.

There was a laugh.

Just out of sight, something moved quietly between two trees. Tag looked around puzzledly. "Majicou? Who's there?"

"Tag."

It was a kind of whisper.

This time he heard it move—whatever it was. It made the noises you would expect of a large animal trying to shift its position silently in thick cover: a rustle, a furtive scrape. Tag shivered. The moon was down. Even so it was easy to see that the woods were empty. Beeches are cold, elegant trees, and nothing grows beneath them. The ground rose away, open and scoured, limned here and there with dusty snow. There were only roots and stones to see. There was no cover in the woods. There never had been.

"Who are you?" he said.

Scrape.

"I'm you."

There was a hot, fetid smell.

"I'm—"

Something huge, stalking something small: a terrible incongruity. Something stalking from an undergrowth that wasn't there—

Scrape.

Behind me! thought Tag. He whirled around.

Nothing.

"*Tag.*"

Scrape.

Did he see it? Did it allow him to see it?

He was never sure. A twist of light—of less than light—fell on something as it poured itself around the tangled roots toward him. A smell of ammonia and rotten meat. It was almost as if he were watching it stalk someone else. He wanted to warn them, but he couldn't speak. Panic raced up through him, and he went off like a rabbit in the night—"*Tag*"—a flickering white blur making desperate—"*Tag*"—figure eights around the bases of the trees and then—"*Tag, Tag, Tag*"—straight out of the wood and down the slope and into the village, crying, "Help! Majicou! Help!" until he saw the icy surface of the duck pond in front of him and flew across it without a thought, to the safety of the highway.

Night on the highway, as iridescent as reflections on oil. Here, Majicou had said, time had some other meaning. Echoes sped away in all directions. To the north, the great chalk ridge loomed against the sky. Above it burned white stars. All along it the smoky ghosts of cats streamed east and west. On its lower flank lay the village, vibrating faintly with a thousand years of itself. A village viewed by cats—barns and butter churns, open windows for them to come and go. And beyond it the pond, its banks debatable and its willows sketchy. Tag looked around. The compass wind lifted his fur, cooled his fear a little. It was familiar enough. He had come this way an hour before, running like a proper cat with Majicou. He was an old hand now. He looked behind him once, shivered, turned his face into the wind, and trotted forward slowly at first and then faster and faster as he felt the highway move in him and bring him in touch with that tireless, burning, interior gait.

"We run!" he called to his friends the ghosts. They streamed past silently and silently agreed, "We run."

He had come this way an hour before. He remembered a vast sweep of downland cupping the village, the barn beneath the ridge. He remembered woods, but not these . . .

Every stride took him further in. The air was thick and oppressive. It smelled of mold. The trees were close, tangled, strung with vines and moss. Many of them had fallen down and lay across his path rotten with beetle larvae, plated with thick white bracket fungus. But he still had his confidence, and he leapt them with contempt. His great heart beat within him. He loved to stretch his legs and leap. He was Tag: a cat. When the ground turned black and boggy, his broad pads bore him up. He splashed through hidden pools and streams. Dense growths of bramble and thorn tugged at his fur—he felt nothing. Ashen glades, gray trees, the trickle of black water. He wondered when the highway would begin again. He heard a voice.

"Tag."

It was a thick whisper. It filled his mouth like dusty fungus spores. It filled his nose with the smell of rotting meat, the smell of something caged by its own appetites. It was at his elbow, yet it filled the whole wide wood.

It was the whole wide wood.

"Tag!"

The highway had trickled away from him into groundwater and sand. He was his own size again, and something was pursuing him between the moldy trunks of trees. When he ran now, it was not the oiled gait of the predator but the sudden terrified scramble of the prey.

"Tag."

He ran until he couldn't run any longer. Then he nosed into the undergrowth and crept through the root systems where the earth smelled dank and decomposed until he could push himself into a damp cranny between two stones like knuckles.

"Tag—"

It couldn't follow him into such a small space. But it knew where he was. It settled down. It would wait patiently for him to come out again, whispering his name now and then in a disappointed but cajoling fashion. Confusion and fear lay on him. His pads were split, his face grazed and cut. His fur lay on his thin pink body in dirty tufts and draggles. He had forgotten Majicou. He had forgotten Ragnar. He had forgotten why he left his friends. He had forgotten who he was. He couldn't stop shivering long enough to lick himself, or stop listening long enough to rest. He didn't dare curl up. Instead he stared and stared ahead, his eyes black, his lips drawn back in an endless snarl.

"Oh, Tag."

And that was how Majicou found him, just after dawn, in the lee of a beech tree less than a mile from the barn. A cold milky light fell through the woodland in slanting columns. It picked things out in pastel colors, diffusing them at the same time so that they seemed to overspread their own edges. It questioned everything it saw.

Majicou thought he had stumbled across a dead squirrel.

How can a sound be muffled, yet at the same time echo? How can a voice you have never heard seem like your own? At first, all Tag would do was huddle like a kitten into the warm curve of the black cat's body and repeat, "It chased me. It chased me."

"Did it name itself?"

"It said it was me."

"Hush," said Majicou. "You're safe now."

He said, "Old forces have been awakened, and are traveling the highways again, out of control—"

"What are they?"

"I don't know how to describe them, Tag. Discarded things. Bits of the ancient life that went astray and were somehow never subsumed. Now the Alchemist has woken them without knowing it. They might yet be his downfall."

This meant nothing to Tag. He was hungry. He licked energetically his disordered fur.

"Are they gods?" he said.

"You might say that," agreed Majicou. "If cats had gods, I suppose that is what they would be like." He thought for a time. "They are ourselves," he said. "What you met was some old fragment of the cat life. Some ancient experience of hunting, perhaps, cut loose from its rightful place and time."

"Or some experience of being hunted," Tag said. He shuddered. "It made me feel so small!"

"These things have no real force of their own, though at times they can be—" Majicou sought for the right word "—marshaled. You were a little young yet for an encounter like that. Perhaps you shouldn't have looked for Ragnar on your own."

"I felt responsible. He's such a fool!"

"You haven't been so clever yourself. Did you find him?"

Tag hung his head. "No."

"He is not here," said Majicou gently. "I would know if he was."

"Then he must have got shut in the van again! Oh, Majicou, how will he get home? He misses the Queen." Loneliness swept over Tag suddenly and made him add, "How will any of us get home? We none of us have homes anymore."

"Homes are made," said Majicou without much compassion, and took him back to the barn. Inside, it was four whitewashed walls covered with dusty gray cobwebs like letters in an alphabet, two or three low wooden partitions whose function was unclear, and in the corner a pile of ancient bits and pieces made of leather, wood, and rusty metal. It was barely warmer than the hillside. One for Sorrow was hopping about in the rafters, croaking glumly to himself. Mousebreath, hunched up on some old straw, stared angrily at Tag and refused to speak. Only the tabby seemed happy to be there; and she was rooting so busily about in the corner that she hardly noticed them come in.

Majicou looked up at the bird.

"Is there any news?"

The magpie descended, his wings loud in the confined space.

"It's an hour each way from Piper's Quay," he said. "Fly at a decent height and your main coverts ice up. Try it. It's winter out there, Majicou. At least ask me if I'm alive."

"No news, then."

"No more than before."

"Hello, One for Sorrow," said Tag.

"Come and join the party," the bird greeted him. "You can dance with your cheerful friend." He jabbed his beak in Mousebreath's direction and, receiving only a deadly look in return, hopped away. He was never still—always bobbing up and down, turning his head from side to side, fluffing up his feathers to produce a brief dry rustle that made Tag shiver. Seduced by this sound, Cy backed out of the clutter—from which she had been trying to extract a bit of blackened leather smelling of horse and linseed—and, flattening herself quietly on the dusty floor, began to inch forward with her bottom in the air. "Don't even think about it," the magpie warned her.

"Majicou," he reported, "there was nothing. Blood on the walls, some tracks in the snow which were filling as I got there—might have been the fox, might equally have been a stray dog. If he was alive, he didn't stay around to be hurt again. As for the other two—" he shrugged eloquently "—nothing. If they hid, they're still hidden. If they're together, we don't know."

"Why did I bother to send you back?"

Like the other animals, the magpie had been disoriented by the violence of events at Piper's Quay. Suddenly unsure of himself, a condition he barely recognized, he had flown aimlessly over the city—erratic sweeps and sorties that added nothing to his understanding of the situation. Conditions were bad, even for Corvidae, known to be clever and daring flyers: overlapping fronts, masses of cold northeastern air, turbulence. Contact with Majicou had proved difficult. Then—more by luck than design, blown west by an airstream as brutal as black glass—he had spotted the cat catchers' van! As a reward, Majicou had promptly sent him back to Piper's Quay to look for the fox. This search had to be abandoned in the small hours. By the time he returned to the barn, just before the arrival of Tag and Majicou, One for Sorrow had been flying for eight hours without rest. At one point, a pocket of low pressure over Hounds Low had dropped him eight hundred feet straight down, like a ball of cleaning rags thrown out of a tenth-floor window. Normally, that would have been something to boast about. Now he was only aching, hungry, and depressed. He sighed.

"Master," he reminded Majicou gently, "there was no one else to send."

"I'm sorry," said Majicou. "A *vagus* is loose on the highway for the first time in four hundred years. Who knows what else it will liberate before I can put it back? Things become less and less dependable. I sit at the center of it all and watch the wild roads turn into a knot of snakes. Yet the Alchemist is still vulnerable. I could stop him now, if every tool did not break in my hand—"

"I'm not your tool, mate," interrupted Mousebreath suddenly. "And neither is the calico. We come along for decency's sake. Every turn, we done the decent thing—"

"Mousebreath—" Tag began.

The tortoiseshell gave him a bitter look.

"And not one of *you* had the decency to explain what we was into—"

"Mousebreath, I—"

"And now you've got her killed."

Majicou stared absently at Mousebreath, as if he had forgotten who he was or why he was there. The tortoiseshell turned away in disgust and began to lick his behind ostentatiously.

The old cat blinked. "We have this comfort, at least," he went on. "The Alchemist knows as little as we do. He too has lost the King and Queen. His means of locating them are as limited as ours. His proxies are as scattered. He cannot enter the highways."

"Yet," said the magpie.

Majicou acknowledged this. "Oh, if he cultures the Golden Cat, everything is finished. But until then, we are all only kittens shuttling wool between the legs of a chair." This idea seemed to put him in a better mood. "Rest as long as you need," he invited the magpie. "Then go out and find them for me!"

The bird flew back up into the rafters and began to peck about savagely in its wing feathers.

"I knew you were going to say that."

Mousebreath, it was clear, hated to be ignored. Resentment, hatched in his orange eye, soon swam into the other, where it froze in blue ice. But he waited until Majicou had finished his exchange with the bird before he said, "This Alchemist of yours. He's here, he's there, you don't know where he is. All *we* know is it's personal between the two of you."

Then he added quietly, "Kittens shuttling wool."

At this, Majicou drew himself up. "It's not a game," he said.

"You called it that yourself. Not two minutes ago."

"I've already explained what's at stake."

"Oh, you have. And how that entitles you to play with other people's lives. Just like him. You've explained all that." Mousebreath got up and stalked toward the door of the barn, brushing contemptuously past the black cat as he went. "I admire you. You've fought the good fight, cat and kitten. My word. How impressive. A fat bird gets to call you 'Master.' "

"Be careful," warned the magpie.

Mousebreath laughed. "Make me," he said.

"Wait!" ordered Majicou.

"Stuff you," suggested Mousebreath.

For a moment it looked as if they would kill each other.

"Please!" said Tag.

He got between them.

"Mousebreath," he begged, "I'm sorry I couldn't tell you what was happening. But now you know, won't you help? Sealink—"

"Sealink! What would you know about *her*?"

"She was happy to join in."

Even Mousebreath's blue eye was angry; the orange one didn't bear looking at.

He said, "Look where it got her. She'd been all over the world, that cat. Get out of my way."

Tag felt as if he had been pushed aside by a bag of concrete. But he followed determinedly.

It wasn't the sort of morning either of them had expected. Whether Mousebreath wanted it or not, they were forced to stand together for a moment while their eyes adjusted to the brilliant light. The sun had broken through a lid of ruched gray cloud and reached down with huge fingers to dapple the fields and hills. The red brick walls of the barn glowed warmly. Drops of water glistened on the barren elder twigs where the snow had melted. The bracken was a pale fire. A little way above the woods proper, a young tree stood alone in a circle of green grass and dusty beech mast. All its elegant gray limbs but one were posed as if it had just that minute raised them to the sun; that one had broken near the trunk, and now hung down near the ground. Mousebreath went and crouched beneath it, staring out toward the village. Every time Tag tried to sit down near him, he got up and moved away. Tag wouldn't be put off.

"Mousebreath."

"Stuff off."

"Mousebreath, please!"

"Tell you what: if you'd been a bit more forthcoming it wouldn't have hurt."

"I'm sorry."

"I'm sure."

"Sealink wanted you to help!"

"Well, she's dead."

"You don't know that. Look, Mousebreath, come with me to Tintagel! She knew we were going there. She'll make her own way, I know it!"

Mousebreath regarded him grimly. "Nah. They shot the fox. For all we know, they shot her too. She's dead. That's all."

"Mousebreath, this is silly!"

"She's dead, and I'm off back to town."

Frustrated and wretched, Tag watched him walk away down the hill. "Oh, Mousebreath," he whispered. "You never did leave the barges." After a moment or two, he sighed and stretched out beneath the broken branch with his head on his front paws. The sun was quite strong. As the beech mast warmed, it gave out a tarry, almost appetizing smell. Birds sang. Insects began to buzz past, on long, sleepy trajectories. It was winter. Why were they flying? They had no idea. Tag dozed. Before he knew it, he had slept, and Majicou was waking him gently.

"Tag, I must go."

Tag looked around. The sun had gone in. It was cold again. The whole short winter day was passing, and soft gray flakes of snow were falling through the glassy air.

"Was I asleep? Majicou, I—"

"There is work to do, and I can do none of it here. The magpie has already gone."

"How will I get to Tintagel?"

"With ease."

"I'm no good at all this."

"Rubbish."

"You had to save me from the *vagus*."

"The *vagus* was gone when I found you. I think you bored it." Majicou laughed grimly. Then he admitted, "If I had been forced to confront it there and then, I don't know who would have won the encounter."

"But you are the Majicou."

"The Majicou was once a cat like you. Tag, Tag. None of this was your fault. In fact most of it was mine. In a way, Mousebreath is right. Fear and confusion make us all arrogant: Why should I be immune? I chafe. I expect too much of others. But nothing is lost unless you despair. Tag, look!"

Majicou stood up suddenly on his hind legs and, gripping the end of the broken branch in his teeth, pulled it down so that Tag could see. Among the twigs were clusters of empty beechnut husks, flared, hard, juiceless, brittle, used up. But inside the nearest, Tag glimpsed a speck of red. "Majicou, what is it?" He peered in. Huddled together in the old shell were six perfect ladybirds, their legs curled tightly beneath them and their glossy backs so bright they seemed to send a light of their own into the gray air as they waited patiently for the long winter to end. For a moment, the world was full of weight and order and magic.

Majicou released the branch.

"Tag, you must continue west. Look after the tabby. Wait at Tintagel for your friends. All this will end well. I know it!"

"It didn't end well for Mousebreath."

Majicou laughed.

"Mousebreath is sitting down there in the wood, sulking. I can see him from here."

"I don't understand."

"Then you don't understand his heart or yours. Mousebreath may yet be defeated by his own life, but not if you or his calico queen are there to change his mind! I'll apologize to him as I leave. Make him come with you to Tintagel. *They will be there.* The magpie will bring news. Take care!"

And the black cat was off through the flying snow.

Tag watched for a long time, wondering what would become of them all. Slowly, it grew dark, and the stars came out over the ridge. Silence prevailed, but Tag sat on. Eventually Mouse-breath returned. For a while the two of them stood on the cold hill's side, not knowing quite what to say to each other. Then the tortoiseshell suggested, "May as well get in out of the cold."

"May as well."

Inside the barn, the tabby offered them a share in her piece of leather.

"Have some," she encouraged. "It's good."

Chapter Thirteen

THE RAW AND THE COOKED

*My cats are compromised. I do not entirely trust
them—they may be spies, like dolphins, reporting
to some unknown authority.*
—JAN MORRIS

*T*hey slept in the barn that night. Mousebreath woke Tag about two hours before dawn.

"Listen!" he said. "Look!"

The air was bitterly cold. The darkness had a faint, hard luminescence to it, as if it had been lacquered. Flakes of snow were blowing in through the partly open door, then floating toward a peculiar smoky twist of light that had established itself between the cobwebby walls of the opposite corner. Every so often this apparition fizzed quietly and shifted on its axis, an adjustment accompanied by a small convulsion that raised dust from the floor beneath it.

"What is it?" said Mousebreath.

"You don't want to know," Tag told him. "How long's it been here?"

"I been awake fifteen, twenty minutes."

They watched for perhaps another five. Nothing else happened. Then the light flared up with a kind of silent crackle, a current of warm air passed across the floor of the barn, and everything returned to normal. Warily, Tag approached the corner. A few snowflakes had been left blowing about the concrete in the drafts. When he tried to touch them with his nose, they turned out to be little gray sparks of light. There was a faint smell of burnt cobweb.

"I've seen this before," he told Mousebreath. "It won't come back tonight. But we should leave as soon as we can."

Mousebreath curled up, grumbling. Alone with his thoughts, Tag licked his paws until his eyes closed of their own accord. The tabby, who had followed all this with lively interest from the darkness, waited until she was sure they were both asleep again. Then she crept carefully into the empty corner, sniffed it thoroughly, and sat there like a china ornament on a mantelpiece, her eyes wide open and alert. After a moment, the snow began to drift in through the open door toward her.

First light, Tag led his little band up the side of the ridge.

The snow had consolidated itself while they slept, piling up quietly on an east wind so that in places it was higher than Mousebreath's shoulder. Through it protruded the occasional thin shaft of reed grass. Powder, whipped off the crest of each drift, hissed away across the empty fields. At first it was fun to bound and tumble through the cold spindrift. But they soon grew tired—especially Cy, who could hardly keep her nose above it—and settled for a steadier pace. Tag and Mousebreath took turns to force the way. They were soon soaked to the skin and panting for breath. Their feet grew numb and somehow at the same time tender. When they stopped an hour later, two hundred feet below the crest of the ridge, Tag saw that they had ploughed one long, untidy furrow across the flank of the hill. Either side of it, acres of unturned snow glowed frail pink and gold in the rays of the risen sun. He shivered in delight. He wanted to race away into it forever. No streets, no walls, no gardens or houses: just a great snowy sweep of downs as far as you could see. He felt bigger than his own body.

"Look at that, Mousebreath! Isn't it beautiful?"

Mousebreath gazed anxiously around.

"Let's get going," he urged. "We stick out like a sore foot here."

Up on the crest, emptiness roared away in all directions. No track was visible, only the ridge, which curled and dipped like the scarp of a huge snowdrift. The sky was bitter and endless, blue-gray. The airstream broke and roiled across the path, encasing everything that stood above the snow in transparent ice. It was as if the very vastness of it all had sucked the warmth away. As they arrived, the weather tightened its grip. Thick gray clouds drew in. Spindrift was whipped off the ridge. Tag felt ice forming on his whiskers. The wind was so loud he could hardly hear himself think, but he held his ground and looked it in the eye. The colder it blew, the taller he felt himself stand. Mousebreath stared into the west in shock; the tabby huddled close to Tag's shoulder for comfort, rubbing her face repeatedly against his fur and advising him, "It's raw-John blind here; it's rime-eyed-Jack! I see white iron ahead. Ice time, Tiger! There's a wide wind up here!"

Tag barely noticed her. They were in a bad place for small animals. He wondered why he felt so little fear.

After a moment, he shook himself. "We must run," he said.

Easier said than done. They floundered along, stumbling into icy ruts. Balked by gusts of wind like walls, they rocked back yowling on their haunches or flattened themselves in fear. The ridge had vanished. Only the weather was left. How could they find the highway in this? How could they be *cats* when they were cold and scared and soaked through like this? When the air was full of the voices of dead animals? Everything streamed to white before their eyes. They ran and ran, and nothing happened. Then the spindrift parted like a curtain, and Tag glimpsed a ghostly tiger of the ice, loping out purposefully ahead of them in a hollow in the wind! What journey had *he* been on, so long ago? His thick white pelt was gray striped, tipped with pewter. His huge paws were silent and sure. His breath smoked in the freezing air. He was soon gone; but while he lasted, he had filled the world with a rank, careless heat, a jungle in the snow, and Tag, suddenly running and jumping like a kitten in his wake, was filled with joy just to have seen him. Tag raised his face to the blowing ice.

"This way!" his friends heard him call. "Come on!"

Their hearts lifted. The highway had recognized them, and welcomed them in.

Chalk hills echoed away east and west, their features blurred and indistinguishable beneath the ancient lives that flowed across them. Only the land endured; everything else was a living, shifting knap, and if there were towns, weather, people, it would have been hard to point them out. Metallic light lay across these ghost lands, as if someone had long ago tipped a silent cup of sky over everything. It was a color none of them could name: not Mousebreath, not Tag, not Cy. Though the tabby warned herself when she thought no one was listening, "I never said I'd walk on this apple-tree moon. Whoo!" It was a million skies, a million days and nights, a million colors running into liquid bronzy-gray.

That first day on the old wild road, they didn't know how to stop. By noon it was clear they would never find anything to eat there. Neither would the road let them rest. If they halted for too long, they soon began to feel anxious and ill, disoriented by the echoing spaces, the impatient wind, the dizzy rush of ghosts . . .

Eventually, it was late afternoon. They had no idea how they knew. They had no idea how far they'd come. More by luck than judgment they got on to a little local trackway and later found themselves tumbling down a steep bank, earthy yet overgrown, outside some downland village. They had left the weather behind. The air was damp and raw down here, but it smelled of rain and earth. Twilight crept out of the tangled roots of holly and hawthorn and crab apple. The remaining light lay in streaks of peach and ruby across the western sky or shimmered, trapped for a long moment, in the unearthly bright green of lichen. When the three cats looked back, they shivered to see the great chalk ridge to the south of them against the horizon. They could hear the wind bumbling across it; and it was capped with snow.

"We'd better walk," said Tag, and so they did, past slumped old wooden gates, fields softly glimmering with the last of the sunset, half-timbered houses draped with ivy or half hidden in thickets of leggy hydrangea. The lanes were narrow, winding, steep. The afterglow—a sudden enthralling flare of peppermint—gave itself up to darkness. There was a smell of coal smoke. At the curve of a lane, latticed windows lit up, warm and orange-yellow. But the houses were few and far between; and in any case, Tag's band didn't dare go near. Local cats stiffened and slunk off evasively in the dark or sent them on their way with raucous threats. "And don't come back!" By now, they were hungry and tired. Mousebreath grumbled. The tabby sang tunelessly to herself or pulled great loops of old man's beard out of hedges, which she tried sulkily to eat. Suddenly, with a roar and a cough and a soft explosion of actinic light, a car rounded the corner in front of them. For an instant they were in its path. Its tires rumbled and stank. Its white glare turned every shallow pothole into a trench, and cast paralyzed feline shadows infinitely long on the gray lane.

Tag and Mousebreath shouldered the tabby out from under the wheels. They fled, spitting up the bank with her, and stood, trembling blindly together and looking away as hard as they could, their spines in the curve of fear. Behind them the thing slowed down briefly. A human hand waved out of one of the windows. There was a faint shout of laughter, and something white and heavy flew through the air for a long moment before it burst in the empty road. The car accelerated. The cats followed its progress as it went away from them, around all the corners, up all the little hills they had already walked. Eventually the night was quiet again, though the lane still stank of petrol.

Mousebreath was the first to disentangle himself. He approached the object in the road, gave it a smart tap with his front left paw, jumping backward in the same gesture in case it was alive, then touched it cautiously with his nose.

He laughed. "Well, look here," he said in a low voice. "Will you just look at what we got here—"

Sandwiches. It was a packet of sandwiches, wrapped in greaseproof paper.

Mousebreath sniffed. Tag sniffed.

They looked at one another in wild surmise.

Tuna fish and mayonnaise.

They ate the sandwiches. They ate them, bread, crusts, and all. Even the tabby ate some. They licked and licked the paper. They licked their lips. Then they slept in the hedge with their faces buried in each others' fur, and early the next morning they were on their way again.

This became the pattern of their lives.

They were never sure how far the wild road would bring them each day or where it would bring them to. They often abandoned it out of simple anxiety; yet somehow it never abandoned them. The wild road is the Old Changing Way, and it knows its own. Days came and went, like the shadows of clouds passing quickly across the slope of a plowed field. Snow came and went. They saw many extraordinary things. Chalklands stretched out before them, hillock and tumulus, sweet high valleys carved long ago by ice, shallow quarries scattered with flint cores . . .

And there! A single thorn tree on the skyline, with a rainbow curving away from it into black cloud!

However long they ran, they never grew tired. After all, the Old Changing Way *is* to run, and bound along in that endless stride, and never tire. But toward the end of each day some part of them began to hunger for the real. "You feel," as Mousebreath put it, "*as if you was being run away with*. You begin to wonder where it'll all end." Paradoxically, after all that running, they wanted to stretch their legs. Fed up with being tigers, they wanted ordinary ground beneath their feet, ordinary air to breathe. So, though they could have traveled vast distances, they settled in the end for a few miles a day. They slept in barns and spinneys. Mornings and evenings they searched the lanes and villages on either side of the Ridgeway for food. Food was important to them. They were just ordinary cats, after all. Or Tag and Mousebreath were.

The tabby was another matter.

Tag caught her looking at him with an expression bold as brass. She brought him things from ditches. She sang him lullabies in languages of her own invention. He woke at night and she was watching him. "Sleep now, Quicksilver," she would whisper, as if she had care of him, and not the other way around. He grew fond of her despite himself. He watched her washing in the endless chalkdown dawns; composing herself for sleep under the glimmer of starlight. In return, she collected and assembled objects for him—wafers of silver paper, mirrors, anything that held water. Small discarded bits of motor cars from verges. All of them made one sign, and it was this:

$$\female$$

If he tried to join in, she bit him smartly in the head. He didn't know what she wanted from him. She liked Mousebreath, but it was Tag she wanted to be near. When Tag walked away, she followed. When he followed her, she boxed his ears. The tortoiseshell watched them with the kind of gentle amusement you reserve for kittens, and when Tag tried to talk to him about her, would only say, "Have to sort it out yourself. Eh? Sort it out!"

But how? thought Tag.

She was a mystery to him. He liked her smell.

Things came to her, on and off the highway. In the deep night she was often surrounded by lights; at midday, when she thought herself unobserved, by tiny colored birds of no species Tag recognized. Up on the ridge, ghost kittens danced along beside her, only to fade sadly away after a mile or two, as if to say, This was where we lived, so long ago. This was our village. See?

Tag woke in the small hours and there she was, sitting quite still a little way away from him, looking attentively upward, her head tilted to one side. Her ears seemed bigger than he remembered. Her spark plug glittered brass and diamond. Around her the air was crowded and vibrant, aflutter with the most glorious summer moths, their massive blunt brown-and-cream heads thick with fur, their eyes like cheap red jewels. From the tabby's eyes poured a light the color of streetlamps in the city. One by one, the moths were flinging themselves into it, to crackle and vanish. She was so preoccupied she couldn't know Tag was awake; yet he thought he heard her warn him softly, "Don't watch me now, Silver. Nothing to see here." Suddenly he felt very tired, and the world began to spin.

He awoke the next morning to find himself under a bush: stiff, wet through, and with an animal of unknown origin snuffling about on the grass only a yard or two away from him.

* * *

Leaving the highway late, lost in a maze of subsidiary tracks, they had done without supper and stopped for the night in the first place that looked acceptable. In the wet gray light of the winter morning it turned out to be the garden of an empty bungalow. A newish birdbath, a lichen-stained patio, two shallow flights of steps. At one end, a lean-to conservatory with two panes gone from the roof. At the other, sleet billowing through a gap in the bleak *leylandii* hedge.

At first Tag thought the animal was some breed of cat he had never seen before: long-backed, reddish, brindling toward its hindquarters and long tail. It moved haltingly, close to the ground, full of nerves. After a minute or two it found the birdbath and, standing with considerable difficulty on its hind legs, lapped from it at length, staring around every so often. Then it moved into the middle of the lawn, where the autumn leaves had been left to rot. There, it scraped a few times at the acrid mulch with one foreleg, got down stiffly, and tried to roll about on its back. This movement only caused it to yelp out loud. It sat up and yawned. Its tongue was long and red. Suddenly Tag realized what he was looking at.

A fox, with tawny yellow eyes.

A big dog fox, which blinked and stared vaguely into the *leylandii* hedge and called, "I know you're in there."

"It's a free country," answered a voice like a ratchet.

"I can see you quite clearly."

"I'm not trying to hide."

The fox digested this.

"Hah!" he said. Encouraged, the voice from the hedge went on, "You need help."

"I don't care," said the fox. "You're not coming near me with that beak."

He got to his feet and limped hurriedly across the lawn. Close to, he looked emaciated. Clumps of his fur had fallen out, to leave dusty gray skin. He stank—but not of fox. One of his haunches had been flayed to a kind of angry-looking raspberry color, with soft yellow scabs the size of grapes. Lower down, the hock joint was stripped to bluish-white bone. Only one fox in the world could have injuries like that. Aghast, Tag jumped to his feet.

"Loves a Dustbin!" he cried. "I thought you were dead."

"I'm not sure I'm not," said the fox.

He sat down in a flower bed and began to shiver violently. His eyes were clogged with mucus, and his entire muzzle had gone gray. "I'm quite glad to see someone, actually," he said. "Majicou's not here, is he?" A squall of rain splattered across the garden. The fox regarded it bleakly. For a moment it looked as if he would try to get up and seek shelter. Instead, in a gesture of simple unapologetic weariness, he put his head down in the flower bed near Tag's feet and closed his eyes.

"Just don't let that bloody magpie near me," he begged.

But in the end they had to.

He lay like an old fox fur all morning, like a skin from which the fever had burned every ounce of flesh.

"Stay calm," he advised himself.

Then, "Where is this?" like a puppy in the dark. "Help me!"

The cats gathered around him in the flower bed. He called their names. He had saved his strength until he met them, then let go. They didn't know what to do for him. Cat spit cures all, their mothers had taught them. Lick it on! But who would lick a dog? Then Tag discovered they could enter the conservatory through a broken pane low down behind the water butt; and Mousebreath found the strength to drag the fox inside. Loves a Dustbin woke up and snarled at him.

"Don't think I've forgotten you," he warned.

"Any time you're ready," Mousebreath reassured him patiently. "For now, could you at least try to walk?"

After that, there was nothing more they could do. They stared at one another helplessly. They stared at One for Sorrow, who by this time had hopped down out of the conifers to stick his narrow head and beady eye diagnostically into the fox's face.

He shrugged. "I don't *want* to do it," he said. "But if I don't he'll die."

"He *is* unconscious," Tag pointed out.

"But how long for?"

In the end, they had to do it.

"You've only got to smell him," reasoned One for Sorrow. "We'll be okay as long as he's unconscious."

Tag sat on the fox's head. Mousebreath sat on his emaciated ribs. The magpie stropped his pitted black beak back and forth a few times on the sour concrete floor. He took a deep breath. He took aim. They all got ready to bolt if the fox woke up. An hour later, twenty-three lead pellets lay on the conservatory floor. They reeked of death. No one would go near them but the tabby, who liked the heavy rolling sound they made. She patted them about desultorily, then grew bored. The fox's leg looked as if it had been eaten by rats. But the wounds were draining, and he hadn't stirred once.

When he regained consciousness six hours later the fox's eyes were clear, however, and the fever had abated. He dragged himself out to the birdbath for a drink, then back in again for a sleep. Then he told them what had happened to him after the fight at Piper's Quay.

"I don't remember much about being shot," he said, "just flashes of light. Shadows on the walls." Shock had put everything at one remove. "Everything went quiet," he said puzzledly, "after the bang. But at the same time—" he looked around at the assembled animals as if they might confirm this experience "—it was all still going on in my head." Flashes, lines of sudden white light. The fluttering shadow of the magpie, the shadow of a raised human hand. Cats being stuffed into sacks. "This filthy smell." Anyway, he said that he had lost all feeling in his back legs and for that reason alone was afraid to move. "There was blood splashed up the wall, all mine. I thought it was still there," he said, meaning the human. "I was terrified it would find me." He looked around the conservatory, shivered with horror. "Does this seem stupid? I didn't want it to kill me *again*."

After a long time, understanding at last that he was alone, he had dragged himself out into the sleet.

"The piazza was dark. I could hardly stand up, but I could smell the river."

For the next three days, he had wandered dazedly about Piper's Quay, hiding if he heard a sound. Pain and fever moved him slowly and steadily away from the piazza into the abandoned, weedy spaces of the old docklands. His wounds became infected; by the third afternoon, he was hallucinating, too weak to eat, licking up rainwater. He found himself in a factory yard, then in a tiny back garden with a young human female backing away in horror from his smell. "I think it wanted to help me, but I didn't know how to stop baring my teeth." For thirty-six hours he lay like a dead thing on the edge of a shallow industrial pond, his muzzle just touching the water, while a heron watched him ironically from a rotting log. He had no idea how he had gotten to any of these places. By now, his voice was but one among many in his head. They all told him something different, but in the end he found a highway entrance—a blur of light between ragwort and broken bottles at the base of a wall.

"It opened onto a maze. I was hoping to find the pet shop in Cutting Lane—the way through to Majicou—but every time I moved, I only got pushed further away. All but the biggest highways are knotted up now, wriggling like half a worm. Once, I was on the seashore, *and it was summer*. Was that delirium? I don't know."

Since then, he said, he had been traveling at random, pursued latterly by the magpie, who had come upon him—quite by chance, as he searched the city for Sealink and the Queen— lying in a puddle of his own urine between two cardboard boxes in a rainy street. He reeked of infection. He was raving. Above all, he was alone. His spirit, so at ease with pain or danger, had wasted under the impact of loneliness.

To make things worse, something was following him.

"I sensed it as soon as I entered the highway. Something dark, shapeless, and never far away." He shivered. "I never saw it, but it follows me still."

"A *vagus*!" cried Tag. "A *vagus* followed me, too," he claimed proudly.

The fox stared out of the rain-slashed windows.

"I don't think it is a *vagus*," he said bleakly. "I think it is my death."

Then he shook himself. "We must go on," he said. "We must all go on." He looked around. "I'm starving," he said. "Is there anything to eat?" He laughed. "I tried to eat the bird when he found me," he said. "But we got along well enough after that."

"Don't be so sure," said One for Sorrow darkly.

Mousebreath winked at him. "Tandoori bird," he said. "Eh?"

"In your dreams," the magpie promised.

"Behave yourselves!" ordered Tag.

"Tandoori bottle top," said the tabby. She had juggled one of the shotgun pellets into a corner until it became wedged behind a fat terra-cotta pot, then—bored perhaps by the fox's story— spent the next twenty minutes trying to lever it out again. Anything she couldn't have, she wanted immediately. "Tandoori bedstead." She carried the pellet over to the fox and dropped it in front of him. "Eat that," she said.

"I nearly did," the fox said.

"Whoo!"

He was some time recovering. They looked after him as best they could, and kept to the conservatory, which was dull but warm and dry. The wind dropped. The sun came out. After a day or two the magpie had to leave.

"Majicou will expect to hear about this," he said.

Tag went out to see him off.

"Must you go?"

"I'll leave the fox. He's no use to us until he's well again."

Tag, who had expected the black cat's agents to solve his problems, not add to them, said, "What can *I* do with him?"

The magpie cocked his head. "You can make him feel he's alive again," he said. He added, with a kind of patient scorn, "Have you got anything better to do?"

"I suppose not."

"Look, when I found him he was babbling to this thing he thinks is following him. He'd given up. He's never been so low, and I hate to see it."

"I'm sorry," said Tag.

"He's my friend."

"I can see that."

"Well, just remember it."

"I will."

Mollified, the bird prepared to fly.

"Wait!"

"What?"

"What about Sealink and the Mau?"

One for Sorrow looked grim. "I've never seen Majicou so at a loss. But none of us can do anything until we find them."

"No sign then?"

The bird bobbed his head. "I'm sorry," he said.

He took off in a clatter of wings and shot low over the *leylandii* like an errant firework, heading east.

"Look after the fox!" he called. "And try not to lose anybody else."

Half an hour after the bird had gone, Mousebreath, who had been dozing on a saggy old canvas chair in the conservatory, jumped down, shook himself with a stately energy, and winked his blue country eye. "Have a look 'round, perhaps," he said to Tag. "See what I can see. Eh?" And off he wandered, across the garden and through the hedge.

Tag watched him go, tail high, haunches confident and furry, past the birdbath in the spitting rain. Beyond the hedge the fields began. They were small and eccentrically shaped, sheltered by high untended hawthorn hedges—each field like a high-sided tank of rough grazing darkened with patches of thistle and gorse. A shaggy-coated pony stood, one leg bent, in a muddy corner, looking boredly over a gray wooden gate. Curiously tunneled and undermined hummocks of chalky soil lay among the nettles. Wood pigeons whirred overhead by day; there was a sound of owls at night. It was a small country, self-contained and welcoming despite the winter wind, and Mousebreath had quickly made himself king of it. To start with, he had taken Tag along with him. But Tag's coat was the wrong color for that kind of work. It wasn't that he had no talent, or that he didn't love the quiet disciplines the tortoiseshell had learned from his uncle Tinner. But, "You stick out a bit," Mousebreath was forced to inform him apologetically in the end. "That's all, mind. I'm not saying you wouldn't be good at it. You just stick out a bit."

So Tag watched him set off in the promising gray dawns and dusks—and for that matter, mornings and afternoons—and felt a little sad. This time, when Mousebreath returned, a full-grown doe rabbit hung limply from his mouth, her head lolling at one side, her back legs at the other. She was huge. Her brown eyes were sad. A little blood had leaked from her nose, but otherwise there wasn't a mark on her.

"Never try to catch anything more than a quarter your own size, eh?" boasted Mousebreath, panting a little with the weight of her. "Look at this stuffer!" And he dropped her on the conservatory floor in front of the sleeping fox. After a moment the fox's nose twitched in a lively way, and he woke.

"What on earth's that smell?" he said, sitting up rapidly.

"Rabbit, mate," said Mousebreath. "Get some of that down you, you'll soon be fit."

The fox stared at him.

"I—"

"Well, go on!"

"Don't you *like* rabbit?" said Tag. "I do! I really like it!"

The fox stared down at the doe.

"I don't know what to do with it," he admitted. "In the city—" He shrugged defensively. "Well, the fact is that I've never eaten anything raw before."

Mousebreath chuckled quietly.

"Have a go," he said. "I'll fetch you something in a tin if you can't manage it."

Shared out, the rabbit made more than enough for everyone, even though the fox, quickly getting the idea, ate twice his share. They crunched the bones; they cleaned themselves. Then Mousebreath boasted a little about how difficult a rabbit she had been to catch, and Tag boasted about the difficult rabbits he would catch if his color didn't make him stick out so, and one by one they grew silent and fell into deep, satisfied dreams.

Two or three hours later, a lean moon raised itself over the roof of the bungalow; a light wind moved in the *leylandii* hedge. There was a quiet scratching noise from behind the water butt, and out of the conservatory came Cy the tabby. She wandered onto the bright rustling lawn and posed by the birdbath, washing her bib. The brass plug glimmered between her ears. Every so often, she lifted her nose and smelled the night. She listened. She raised her head and stared at the moon, and the moonlight filled her eyes. One by one, the little white garden moths came to her and began to circle her face. She crooned to them. They were sparks. There was a flicker in the air near her. A soft, apologetic cough. A popping sound. A twist of grayish smoke, which grew and grew and parted suddenly with a creak like a cat jumping onto a canvas chair, *parted* suddenly, like a zip in the fabric of the night, and out . . . came cats. There were perhaps a score of them: black cats and white cats, tabbies and marmalades, longhairs and shorthairs, and two cats with no hair at all whose faces were like the little sad screwed-up faces of demons in the night. The last good place they could remember was Tintagel Court. Now, puzzled and deformed, with bumps and buds and lumps, with wires and implants, with flaking skin, eyes a funny color and legs an awkward length, they barely knew who they were. *He* had given them names, but they weren't names a cat would speak. *He* had sheltered them, but it was not proper shelter for a cat. *He* had given them food, but they were dull with hunger, because it was not food a cat should eat. They were his best subjects. They had no real idea why he had sent them here, along the highways, to find the singing tabby and kill her companions. Unaware of their own wretchedness—their own pain—all they knew was to break across the lawn like surf, part briefly around the birdbath, and pour toward the lean-to conservatory in the quiet dead of the night . . .

Chapter Fourteen
A VOYAGE OF DISCOVERY

You can't catch a fish without wetting your paws.
— OLD SAYING

Old Smoky's revelation was received with varying degrees of enthusiasm.

Sealink stared for a long moment at the Queen, her eyes blank, the top lid a flat, grim line across the pupil. Then she turned her back deliberately and without a word applied herself to one of the bowls of tinned food the old fisherman had set down on the slatted floor.

Pengelly watched her with hooded eyes. Then he turned to Pertelot.

"Ma'am, I'm delighted. May your young 'uns be many and as handsome as their mother." He chuckled to himself. "Seasick!" he said. "Shows how much I know. That Old Smoky, though, eh? Observant old buzzard!"

The Mau gave him a distracted look. Her eyes were bewildered and hurt.

"Thank you," she said.

She said in a low voice, partly to herself and partly to Sealink, "Oh, what can be the matter now?"

She said sadly, "You're very kind, Pengelly."

If Sealink heard any of this she ignored it. She cornered the bowl against the wall, finished off what was left in it, and then jumped lightly up onto the galley surface. There, she positioned herself carefully, head away from the other two cats, wrapped her tail around her, and fell asleep with her paws tucked in.

Within seconds, a rhythmic snoring filled the cabin.

"Don't you pay no attention to she," Pengelly said softly. "She'm just jealous."

Pertelot looked surprised. "But why?"

"You best ask her yourself, when she'm in better odor," returned the Rex, cryptically. "It ain't really my business, though I known her longer than some. Don't worry about her." He gave the Mau a wink. "Look here!" he said. "Old Smoky knows what I like: that's the best turkey dinner you'll have out of a tin, bless him. Get some of it down 'ee."

Pertelot ate. Pengelly ate. Sealink snored on. The old fisherman watched them with a curious expression on his weather-beaten face; then he went up on deck with a mug of coffee to watch the stars.

In the quiet cabin, Pertelot watched flickering patterns of light and shadow cast by the oil lamps. Her eyes were half-closed. Her flanks rose and fell with her breathing. She looked composed, but thoughts were tumbling chaotically through her head.

Kittens. An extraordinary, terrifying miracle. Kittens! How could she not have known? Surely, something inside her *had* known and made her abandon Ragnar and sent her out here where the Alchemist would never look. She missed Rags. She felt the loss of him. She missed his awkward attentiveness, his benighted, unwavering love. She missed him. But kittens! Pregnancy had her now. It swept through her in a warm tide; it was a drugged glow in her belly. Now she knew they were there, she could feel them stirring. Tiny lives were *moving* inside her. How could she not have known? How long was it now? Already weeks—

She was not naive. She was a Queen. Like the rest of them, she'd witnessed enough selective breeding in the Alchemist's laboratory to know the cycles and patterns.

Sixty days from coupling to birth, or thereabouts. She tried to remember. When had she and Ragnar mated? Their time in Tintagel Court was a daze of pain and fear, the confusing frenzy of estrus, raised temperatures, bizarre dreams, wails that Ragnar had gently tried to stifle, in case she brought the Alchemist's proxies down on them.

She remembered how he had fought off the feral toms attracted by her heat, her cries, the musky scent of her that filled the court. Her mind was full of images—tangled, dark, and muddled. A thread of silver, twined with one of gold: together they danced through the center of the knot, bright and elusive. She fastened on them, she drew them out and pulled them free.

Silver. Mercury. Tag. He had come to them like a blessing, a savior, a catalyst. The food he had brought them had saved them, had made her well enough to respond with sudden abandoned delight when one afternoon Ragnar had nosed at her uncertainly, then nipped her firmly in the thick skin of her neck.

A few days of decency and hope, before the Alchemist had found them again. Powerless, she had run from it, and left Mercury to face the madness. It was her story. She drew the Alchemist to her like a shark to the feast, then fled. Others dealt with the consequences, if anyone could.

"And yet," she told herself, "I was able to run away in the first place. If I hadn't, there would have been some kittens for me!" Not from a mate of her own choice. Not kittens she could hope to cherish and raise away from hurt and harm. Alchemical kittens! she thought. Well, what was done was done. She had found her own mate and broken the bloodline, and in just a few weeks the kittens would be born. There was no point in guilt or recrimination. Kittens are the important thing in the world; hers would be the most important of kittens. She would face the new future with hope not because, as Sealink said, it was fun to travel and always be someone new, but for their sake.

At least I know my pursuer, she thought.

What was Sealink running so hard from?

The next day was bright and bitter. Sunlight licked off the wave tops but barely warmed the chilly timbers of the deck. Pertelot watched Pengelly's breath wreath and spiral into the air like the old fisherman's cigarette smoke. Old Smoky knelt at the stern, hauling something over the side.

"What's he doing?" Pertelot asked Pengelly.

"Pulling up the pots he set last night when we were at anchor."

"Oh."

A gull shrieked and wheeled overhead. Then all was quiet again.

A bit later she remarked, "He seems very kind."

"Oh, aye."

More silence.

At last she asked, "How did you meet?"

Pengelly stared out to sea and said nothing.

Pertelot dropped her gaze. Events had made her uncertain. Had she offended Pengelly now? But the old cat had only been thinking, and after a minute he turned to her and said, "Picked me up out of the harbor at Mevagissey, he did. Me and my sister, too."

"You have a sister?"

"I did. She was drownded. I was luckier."

"Oh, Pengelly."

When she thought about what he had said, it became clear to her what he had meant. "Someone tried to drown you?"

"That's what humans do with kittens they don't want," said the old cat. His tone was factual, but his expression was tight and closed. "No one's taught 'em better."

She stared at him. "But that's so cruel."

"Aye. Still." Pengelly contemplated the scenery for a few moments, then seemed to come to some sort of decision. "Old Smoky pulled the sack out of the water with a boat hook, emptied us out onto the deck. I staggered around a bit, choking and coughing up seawater. Poor little Wriggle, she warn't wriggling no more. Dead as a dog's brain. Cold as clay."

Old Smoky, he said, had picked him up—"I warn't no bigger than a mouse"—and sat him in the palm of his hand and scrubbed the life back into him with a piece of cloth, until his strange little catch writhed and spat and sneezed with it—all the pain of feeling, all the thawing nerve ends.

"I thought he were trying to rub my fur right off." Pengelly fixed the Mau with a wall-eyed grin. His wicked eyes looked in different directions. "Probably why it looks so odd now." Pertelot didn't know what to say. He did have odd fur, it was true. It was curly and lay close to his skin like a dog's.

Sensation had overwhelmed him: fish scales, human sweat, the salt off the water, and a curious aromatic spiciness. It was all over the old fisherman's hands and on the handkerchief he held.

It clung to his huge woolen sweater. And suddenly the little Rex could smell it on his own fur.

Tobacco!

"I didn't know what it were then," he confided. "But I loved it at once; and every time he lights up now it takes me back to that day.

"I been at sea all my life with Old Smoky. No kits or mates to speak of. Old Smoky's all the family I got, and all the family I need: he's father and mother, brother and sister to me, and I care for he as much as I could any cat."

Pertelot looked out to the far horizon where today the sky met the sea in a sharply defined line. For a moment she felt the most dreadful sense of pain and loss. Then she saw how the sun winked off the surface of the water as if a handful of stars had been trapped just below it. She thought suddenly, What will my kittens make of this extraordinary, beautiful world? Stars! She looked over the edge of the boat for them. But close in like this, the light barely penetrated, and the water showed murky and opaque like some semisolid substance filled with weed and foam—darkness beneath translucence.

Pertelot drew back hastily. She combed the deck for a secure spot and settled herself deep in the middle of a twist of ropes and netting. She thought about her near death in the canal. She thought about Pengelly's near death in the sea. She shivered. It was a wild world—gaudy on top and deep beneath. The cold, dark sea extended away below her and her kittens, down and down and down.

All at once Sealink's head appeared out of the wheelhouse door, followed by the rest of her shining bulk, the sun striking orange highlights into the glamorous calico coat. She yawned and stretched languidly.

"Morning, shipmates!"

Just as if nothing had happened the night before. The Mau stared at her.

Sealink bustled past Pengelly, trotted around the deck, rubbing her head against the old fisherman's legs in passing, then came and settled herself next to the Queen, where she reclined casually, extended a long hind leg and proceeded to groom it with long, careful strokes of her big tongue.

"Pengelly was telling me about himself," Pertelot said quietly. Perhaps it was better to avoid the subject of kittens for now.

"I'm sure he was, hon. Let's see now: traveling the seven seas, a queen in every port, exotic foods from the far Orient? That it, hon?"

Pertelot was at a loss.

"Well, no. He was telling me how, when he was a kitten, the fisherman saved him from drowning."

Sealink lifted her head. Her ears pricked up. Her tail twitched and thumped on the deck as if it had a life of its own. "You ain't never told *me* about this," she accused Pengelly.

"You never asked. It's a long, long time ago now. And don't you always say, my lover, *'Why, history don't mean nothing, babe, when we make our lives anew each day'*?"

His rendering of Sealink's honeyed southern tones was eerily exact.

For a moment the fur along the calico's back bristled and subsided, bristled and subsided, as if disturbed by a passing breeze. Her eyes glittered and, without turning round, she said to the Queen, "Why don't you tell us about *your* early life, babe? We can have a real sharing time with that, I'm sure."

But she was really talking to Pengelly; and when Pertelot looked up, she saw that their eyes were locked in some challenge she didn't understand. She felt their history going back away from them like a corridor closed to her.

"I'd rather not," she said.

"Now don't be so *elusive*, sugar," Sealink chided. "It's attention getting, and we love you without you need to do it."

The Queen hunched unhappily. She stared down at the coils of rope that surrounded her. The fibers twined and coiled intricately, hundreds of tiny threads to make a single rope; each thread delicate and fragile, yet so robust in combination. When she spoke, her voice was low and emotionless.

"I was born in a laboratory. I know that now. Then, it was all I knew. I thought the smell of fear and despair, the whimpers and howls, were what it was to be alive. A normal life for a cat!"

She laughed bitterly.

"He took me from my mother before I even opened my eyes. But I felt the softness of her fur, and the rasp of her tongue . . . and I remember that, I do. Then, a hard white hand, huge and powerful, and the scent of another cat, her love and despair, falling away below me . . . Now heights make me feverish and I dream of a world that topples endlessly away . . ."

She took a breath, closed her eyes.

"Of course, I was the lucky one. I lived. Pampered, they said. His special one. The Mother. The others hated me. No one made *me* shriek with pain. But it was pain of a different sort, outliving the others. Every day, more cats, brought in, taken out. They arrived, confused, afraid, but optimistic. I could hear them, though I could see nothing but white ceiling from my cage. *'At least,'* they would say, *'we shall be fed. After all, that's what humans do for cats, isn't it? Feed us.'* "

They were fed. For a time.

"Then the cries . . . oh, the cries . . . I never knew what was being done to them. I never wanted to know. I crouched in my cage and tried to close my ears. Even then, I heard them in my head."

Pengelly stared at her in horror. But Sealink's face was hard to see.

"Time went by. How long was I there? I grew—I could see that much. But the lights stayed on by day and night. I knew the difference. I'm a cat, and I could tell the night! And all the time more cats came and went. The Alchemist acquired them all over the world. Things were done to them, and they were thrown away. It used them up, I know now. It sold the coats; it sold the meat—"

She broke down.

Pengelly bore this for a moment or two. Then he slipped up among the ropes and curled himself around her.

"Hush now, my lover. Don't say no more." He stared angrily at Sealink. "You knew about this, didn't you?"

Sealink turned away to groom her other side.

"Why did you make her tell me this? Why?"

Sealink finished her toilette. She stood and arched her back.

"Didn't guess the details, babe: now I know. She's the Alchemist's pet, and she's here with us. I never signed on for that. I got a gift for staying out of that kinda trouble."

Pertelot gave her a bitter look. "How weak you are!" she said. "I'm sorry you had to get involved in my life. I didn't want you to be, if you remember. You said then that you chose to take the risk. You said I should respect your decision. Oh, how weak you are, under all that!"

Sealink looked away. "You kept stuff from me, hon," she said in a dangerously soft voice.

"I didn't know I was pregnant. I didn't know!"

"She didn't know," Sealink told the boat.

"I didn't! I knew nothing until Old Smoky picked me up last night. The kittens moved! I didn't know until a human being showed me!"

She said, more quietly, "Ragnar Gustaffson Coeur de Lion is the father of my kittens. They have nothing to do with the Alchemist. Listen.

"In the laboratories it is like this: the male kittens are killed. The females are bred from, then disposed of. The same blood goes down and down the generations, for hundreds of years. All to find—I don't know what. The Alchemist speaks of a Golden Cat—some magical creature that he believes will bring him the knowledge of the world through the freedom of the wild roads. He thinks the Golden Cat will come from me. It is in his calculations. And so he wants me back. I'd rather die."

She stared out to sea, her face tight with misery.

"Now you know the story," she told Sealink. "I am a Queen. I am a foolish cat. I am a snare and a delusion: a trap. Ragnar Gustaffson is caught in me. Pengelly and his decent fisherman are caught. You are caught. I warned you. When we put into harbor again, I will leave and make my own way to Tintagel."

Pengelly jumped up. "You'll do no such thing! I don't care whose kittens they are. I'll not let you nor they come to harm. Neither will Old Smoky. We ent having you jump ship at the next port, nor anywhere at all till we reach the old country."

He glared challengingly at Sealink.

She was silent.

"As ship's cat," he said, "that's my final word."

For the next couple of days they occupied the *Guillemot* in an uneasy truce.

Sealink spent much of her time promenading tail-up around the boat, and made so much of Old Smoky that he was often heard exclaiming, "What a beauty you are, my handsome. A proper treat." He called her *"moes fettow teag,"* his pretty little maid.

"Well, you got one out of three right, hon," she congratulated him.

He crooned old Cornish songs to her as he tended the wheel.

> *"Ha mî ow môs en gûn lâs*
> *Mî a-glowas trôs an buscas mines*
> *Mes mî a-droucias ün pesk brâs, naw ê lostiow;*
> *Ol am bôbel en Porthîa ha Marghas Jowan*
> *Nerva na wôr dh'ê gensenjy!"*

This broke the feline stalemate, when Sealink, unable to stand it any longer, was forced to talk to Pengelly.

"What *is* all this stuff?" she asked one morning as the *Guillemot* chugged along through rising seas. "I can't make head nor tail of it. Does he, like, make it up or what?"

Pengelly grinned slyly. " 'Tis a secret language—the ancient language of a secret, ancient land. Only a few old throwbacks such as me and Old Smoky use it at all anymore. It's probably of no interest to a modern cat like you."

Sealink, immune to ironies unless they were her own, persisted. "But you know I love to learn, hon. You know I love new stuff!"

The old Rex winked and reeled her in. "Well, let's see. Proper old nonsense song that is. Tells of a fisherman who goes out looking for a nice big shoal, but instead of the pretty silver fish all he got was one great big one with nine tails! 'Tis a riddle, a puzzle, a chimera. There's plenty of mysteries in the seas around the old country and plenty more on the land, too."

"Tell us, Pengelly," said the Queen, who had appeared quietly from the cabin, where she spent her time out of sight. "Tell us."

Pengelly licked his black lips gleefully. "Why, there's the giant hare of Polperro, my dears, an elusive creature that runs across the cliff tops at the end of spring. Woe betide any who see it, for it foretells the death of a loved one. And there's the knockers, one of the many races of Small People the land of Kernow has hidden for thousands of years—wicked little beggars they be. You'll find they sheltering from the rain under the butterbur down by the rivers. Best watch they," he warned. "They'll give a cat a nasty nip."

Suddenly, he crouched down in a silent pantomime of stealth, then reared up again and pounced on the empty deck, leering at the two females as he did so.

"And then," he said, "there's the wild old Beast of the Moor, eating his way through travelers foolish enough to pass by in the night."

The *Guillemot* rolled as it met a wave head-on. Somewhere in the background there was a gush and a clatter. Sealink snorted with amusement. "Hey, hon, you want to get hired out to mothers—keep their kittens in line." Her voice took on a sepulchral tone: "Beware the mad Beast of the Moors, with its taste for the flesh of fresh young cats. Don't move off the path, my kit, or he'll catch you and skin you and eat you right up!"

"Oh, this ent no beast, really. 'Tis but a local cat, takes the form of a big jungle cat when he goes on the wild roads. Old and mad with pain from his teeth, he is now. He can hardly remember who he is half the time. Human beings been trying to find he and shoot he for years." He thought. "Don't suppose that improves his temper."

During this story, little furrows of fear and puzzlement had appeared in Pertelot Fitzwilliam's nose and forehead. By the end of it, she was staring angrily over Sealink's shoulder. Her ears were flat to her skull and she was snarling.

"Hey, babe, it's only a story," said Sealink.

Then she saw what the Mau had seen.

"Oh my—"

An object the size of a small cat was scuttling toward them across the deck of the *Guillemot*, legs clacking incongruously on the wooden slats. Legs! It had a lot of legs, and they were all moving at once. Mottled pink and umber with reddish patches and bone-white spikes, it bore down on them, two vast arms raised.

Pertelot yelped and without a second's thought leapt on to the wheelhouse, where she slithered on the sea-wet surface, spitting and hissing. Sealink bristled, filled with fighting chemicals, stood her ground. "Touch me, fishbait," she explained, "and you're history." The intruder never paused but, joints clicking, opened and closed two giant fingers on the empty air.

Pengelly seemed to be convulsing, lips drawn back off his fine white teeth.

"It's the beast!" he cried. "It's the beast! Oh, Sealink my lover, the beast'll have 'ee now!"

Sealink turned and nipped him sharply in the head.

"What the hell *is* this?" she said.

Pengelly was laughing too much to feel anything.

"Oh, you want to watch those claws . . . wicked pinch . . . sharp pain in the arse, my love . . . right through that calico fur . . . soon have 'ee running . . . been all 'round the world . . . never seen a crab!"

"Crab?"

"Spider crab, my handsome."

Sealink was incensed. She skipped neatly over the bold crustacean, tapping it sharply with a forepaw as she landed. The crab scuttled under the netting, its eyestalks swiveling this way and that.

"Crab?" repeated Sealink incredulously. "Honey, I was *raised* on crab. Ain't never seen anything like this!" She thought for a moment, eyeing the creature warily. "Not alive anyway." She considered further. "Not whole. Hell," she admitted, after a pause, "I ain't never seen more than the claws, and they was pink."

Old Smoky, alarmed by this ruckus, abandoned the wheelhouse—where the wheel spun wildly this way and that—assayed the situation with a curse, and staggered off around the deck to half fill a big old black bucket with seawater. Armed with this, he advanced determinedly upon the crab. It had draped itself in netting. He reached down, unwrapped it deftly, and grasping the rough shell behind the waving claws dropped it with a splash into the bucket.

"What's the use," he asked himself, "of a bloody dinner that walks? Bloody thing. Bloody cats."

Later, he found a sheltered bay, dropped anchor, and cooked the valiant spider crab in a pot of boiling water. As he hammered it open to get at the meat, little bits flew off the worktop and scattered across the floor. The cats nosed around hopefully, drawn by the appealing stench. Sealink got part of a claw. First she chased it around the galley in some cheerfully contrived game. Then, hunting instincts appeased, she settled her body around it, gripped it tight with her forepaws, and worried at it expertly. A gobbet of white flesh popped out and into her mouth.

"Hmm hmm."

Sealink ate. Pertelot and Pengelly ate. Old Smoky ate. They all ate. The *Guillemot* rolled in majestic sympathy. Water gurgled in her bilges. Night drew on. Sealink gave a sudden, resounding purr and began to lick the scent of crab thoroughly into her fur.

"Ain't ate like that," she said, "since I left my own hometown."

"Tell us about your home," said Pertelot shyly, anxious to mend the friendship.

Sealink seemed brusque but amenable. "New Orleans, babe," she said. "Finest town in the world for a cat that enjoys cuisine. You got your crabs and crawdaddies, and the biggest, juiciest shrimp you ever tasted. You got chicken gumbo could make your eyes water. Why, I've ate blackened catfish that—"

"Catfish?" Pengelly looked alarmed. "You don't want to go eating those. They're sacred to the Great Cat. I heard of they, 'round the coast of Kernow, sitting on the rocks, licking their fur, and howling at the moon to warn the sailors off the rocks."

Sealink rolled her eyes. "Hon, it's just a fish with whiskers—

nothing divine about that 'cept the sauce they serve it in." She licked her lips.

"Sounds too fancy for me." Pengelly yawned hugely and took himself off to the bunk where he promptly fell asleep with his head and front paws on the fisherman's legs. It was a gorged sleep, a sleep benign with crab. Old Smoky grinned and reached under the bunk. "Well, my handsome," he said, "what next?" He stroked the tabby once or twice, then unscrewed the top of the bottle he had found and swigged from it appreciatively.

"Oysters," Sealink was saying, "so fine the juices spurt right down into your ruff. And the smells! Walkin' down through the Vieux Carre at midnight you could just die of the smells!

"I was born," she explained, "under the Mississippi boardwalk in the town of New Orleans . . ."

Down there, she said, safe in the sand and the marram grass, a kitten could look out across the whole wide steel-gray river at the shipyards and warehouses of Algiers, and dream. She could watch the big ships forging their slow, powerful way upriver to the docks and refineries of Baton Rouge. "Foreign ships, hon, flying them colored flags, flags from a hundred different countries! That's where I learned the names—Sierra Leone and Senegal, Trinidad and the Ivory Coast. They's all changed now." She could watch the garish splendor of the paddle wheelers bearing a cargo of tourists out into a steamy creole afternoon—tourists who would later wander the boardwalk as the moon came up over the city to shine benignly down on the French Quarter. And every night, whatever the weather, the human being known only as "Henry" would come from his apartment in one of the shuttered and refurbished town houses on Ursulines Street to feed the cats of Moon Walk.

Those tabby toms and shellac queens, those saints and sinners and wheeler-dealers—all those wide-eyed, longhaired, crossbred products of a thousand noisy moonlight assignations who would gather along the boardwalk to receive their daily blessing of redfish heads, catfish tails, and softshell crab. "And, hon, they was little bitty things—all greeny-gray and succulent, two bites and a gulp; a very distant cousin to that monster this afternoon. It is surely unnatural for any crustacean to grow so large and self-determined!"

Born into this cosmopolitan community of itinerant felines, Sealink had soon discovered an appetite for three things: travel—"Those ships looked so fine, honey, sailing huge and proud out into the world, I just wanted to leap right up on the first one I saw and breathe the air of a different continent"; food—of which there was plenty and more; and the vagrant toms, the more glamorously scarred the better—who wandered down each day or two from the delta; who strutted up and down the boardwalk with swivel hips and narrowed eyes; who were loose and fine and on the lookout in the Big Easy, ignoring the halfhearted threats and hisses of the local lads, on the lookout for impressionable females to arouse with their tales of foreign climes and sensual delights.

"Honey, I'm tellin' you there was no finer place to grow up in the world. Loved those traveling cats with a passion, babe. They was—" she sought for a word to convey their irresistible charms "—free . . ."

And so had she been: free to wander through the enticing stalls of the market; free to leap the crumbling brick walls of the Marie Laveau Cemetery and sing to the moon with a ragged band of cronies; free to range the balconied streets of the Quarter and watch the sun go down behind the towering skyline of the modern city, a distant, hazy vista glimpsed between brackets of curlicued ironwork and terra-cotta-tiled roofs. Free. Until, that is, falling prey to a weakness for catfish tails, she had been lured into a *house*.

"What can I say? They was real nice to start with. The lady, she could pet you just right. You'd fall over in the street for her—I seen cats do that. Well, then it come to food, an' food'll get you every time. They took me in, and they fed me the best food I ever ate, before or since. Course, I was carrying at the time—couple weeks more advanced than you are now, I guess—which maybe excuses me a little.

"So they fed me, and I got larger, and they patted themselves on the back. They're parading me to their friends—*See our fine pedigree Maine Coon, ain't she* ador*able?* and like that. I mean,

I ask you, babe—pedigree? Me? I don't think so. As for Minouche: do I look like a Minouche? Where was I? So they start keeping me in, they get me this *litter tray* for my toilet—*très* degrading. And I go, 'What's going on here?' but I'm too stupid to see the answer, until—

"Well the next thing they know is that their cher Minouche has sprung a surprise on them, and there's five little Minouches curled up sucking on their momma. You shoulda heard the cries, babe. Human beings can be *real* raucous when perturbed."

Sealink paused in her narrative to stare emptily away into the cabin. Pengelly snored, and moved his feet in his sleep. The fisherman tilted his bottle high and drank the dregs.

"And then what?" prompted Pertelot anxiously. "Did you leave your kittens? I don't think I could leave kittens, even to travel the world!"

Sealink's face was closed and stiff. "You think I could? They took them from me."

"Took them? Where?"

"How do I know? I never saw them again." She stared into the brown, warm fusty air with an expression that might have been puzzlement or pain. "Thing is, I ain't never been able to have kittens since." She turned to Pertelot. "Can you say why that is? Can you say why that happens to someone who was no more'n a kitten herself? Hon, I was no more than a little boardwalk queen."

"Oh, Sealink."

"You don't have to say nothing, hon."

What could either of them say? The calico stretched and yawned. She got heavily to her feet. "I think I'll go on deck. You coming?"

They made their silent way up the steps and up to the bow, where the wind ruffled their fur. It was a sharp northerly, bearing promise of rain. The sea moved dark and uneasy, furrowed into troughs and peaks. Even in the shelter of the bay, you could feel the *Guillemot* rock. The moon was obscured by a mantle of cloud; away over the headland, thunder rolled ominously through the leaden sky.

"Storm on its way, babe," observed Sealink. She scratched her ear.

For a time Pertelot watched the sea building its walls of water outside the bay.

When she thought of Pengelly, half-drowned in a sack, or of Sealink, rootless and solitary in the world, her heart contracted. Drops of rain fell unheeded on her coat, darkening it in streaks. She was lost in the deception of things: how bewildering they were, how complex and cruel. Then thunder crashed, nearer than before, and a brilliant streak of lightning brought her back to herself. She blinked in terror as it blazed across the sea to landward. Silver afterimages replayed themselves on her closed eyelids.

A wave caught the *Guillemot* broadside and sent the two cats sliding toward the companion rail. Rockets of freezing brine shot up and burst over them.

"Sealink! Look!"

"Time to go below!"

But the Queen was standing stock-still at the rail, her elegant lines intent and quivering; all her senses were focused on a single point, somewhere landward beyond the foam.

"Hon?"

She was staring at the cliff tops, where all was dark and inchoate.

Thunder rolled. The skies cracked open.

In the fork of lightning, in the instant of the strike, in the kindled radiance of electricity, they saw, clear and present and undeniable, the black, heart-stopping silhouette of a gigantic cat.

The Fifth Life of Cats

The fifth age of Felidae history must surely belong to the Troll Cats, or Forest Cats, of Norway, most ancient of breeds but for the cats of the Nile.

Hedinn and Finna had traveled with their Viking companions far from Norway, a land full of forests and lakes and plentiful game, to Greenland—thus named by the deceitful upright ones to attract new colonists but known by cats as the Cold Land with No Trees—and they were less than impressed by their new surroundings.

One night in the fire-hall while lazing beneath the benches, they overheard the Vikings talking of a new land discovered far across the ocean. There was much chatter, but since we Felidae take account of human language only when it contains something of interest to us, all that Finna noticed were the words "rivers full of salmon," "fields full of self-sown wheat"—thus field mice and other snacks—and "forests full of game."

So when, some weeks later, a great longship sailed into the fjord and was filled with supplies and livestock for the settlement of this new land, the Forest Cats, eager to go a-viking themselves, stowed away.

For three days the ship sailed through calm seas; but then the fair wind failed and they were becalmed in fog. After two days of northerly winds, which drove them off course, the mists cleared and they sighted land that looked green and wooded so that the cats were eager to put ashore. But the Vikings sailed past with barely a look. Three days later they

passed land again, but this time it looked freezing and moun-
tainous, and glaciers came right down to the sea. The cats
were relieved to sail past this land, but there had been no
fresh catch for a while and they had to steal the Vikings' dried
fish, which took a great deal of chewing and tasted very stale.
They were now beginning to worry about the existence of this
fabled land.

It was some days later when the horizon yielded sight of
a white shoreline backed by low-lying green hills. The up-
right ones made strange squawking cheers and Hedinn ran
to the bow and popped his head over the gunwale. They
sailed into a wide estuary where the trees came right down to
the water. The land looked most promising: birds called in
the branches and the bow of the longship parted shoals of
fish that gleamed and sparkled in the waves.

The boat was beached and the humans leapt off, splashing
to land through the shallows. They laid planks to the sides for
the livestock, but as soon as they had crossed, the planks
were hauled off.

"I can't swim," confided Finna, staring into the water.

"The Felidae are the most adaptable of the Great Cat's
creations; I have no doubt that we shall prevail," said Hedinn.
"Follow me!"

He launched himself off the side of the ship and swam with
considerable style to the beach, where he stood, shaking his
coat like a dog. Water droplets radiated from him like a
bright halo. Finna gathered her courage and followed with a
great deal of splashing.

Hedinn grinned. "It's a good land," he declared. At his
feet lay a silver fish, its bright scales shining in the sun.

The humans built shelters from stone and turf, raised fences
for their livestock, and traded for a time with the brown-
skinned natives; and the cats ranged widely across the land.
In the forests they encountered wildcats—fierce, striped crea-
tures—and struck up an uneasy acquaintance. Then Hedinn
lured one young queen away and mated with her among the
cool roots of a lodgepole, to produce some nine weeks later a
rumbustious band of brindled kittens. He was immensely

proud of them and one day was, as ever, boasting of their fear-lessness and the unusual beauty of their mother to a bored Finna, when a voice came from high in the branches. "Fat foreign cat, your yammering hurts my ears."

Hedinn puffed out his chest, pulled in his stomach, and stood tall. "My name is Hedinn Haraldsson," he declared, "and cats who hang around in trees listening to others' conversations may overhear things that have little to do with them."

"It is very much my affair," replied the wildcat, spiraling headfirst down the tree trunk. "For Pine-Scented Fur is one of my females."

"Where I come from," Hedinn said, "a female makes her own choice of mate, and woe betide any male who should gainsay her."

The wildcat smiled from ear to ear, displaying an alarming array of sharp white teeth. "That suggests to me that the males of your country are of little account."

"Where I come from," cried Hedinn, "any cat who might suggest such a thing would have to be able to run very fast."

"I have no intention of running," said the wildcat. "Instead, I think it is you who should run, for you are outnumbered."

Hedinn turned to find another wildcat being faced off by a determined Finna. The wildcat's wide jaws grinned out of a striped face, and his muscular body was tensed for action.

"I see that you are not confident of your ability to fight me single-pawed," Hedinn declared coolly. "Maybe you have had your balls chewed off by a troll."

The wildcat spat in fury and hurled himself at Hedinn. At this, Finna leapt upon the other wildcat. There was a great deal of snarling and tussling, the wildcats' speed and wiry strength matching the Troll Cats' weight and power. Once, the wildcat chief pinned Hedinn beneath him, but Hedinn raised his strong back legs and raked his opponent's belly. They sprang apart and set to again; first one gaining the advantage, then the other; and so it went for a time. Eventually it became clear that neither side was prevailing and after a while all four cats drew apart, gasping for breath.

"If even the females of your country fight so well, it must be a remarkable country," conceded the wildcat chief.

"This is also a remarkable country," said Hedinn, "and we should like to stay here on good terms with you and your fellows."

"I have no objection to your staying," said the wildcat chief, "for it seems to me that your breed must be very strong to produce cats of your size, and the mixing of our bloodlines would give advantage over our enemies. I should like to test my theory with your female!"

"This female is not mine, but her own," reminded Hedinn. "It must be her choice or none."

But Finna stepped forward and raised her rump before the wildcat chief, purring deep in her throat. Hedinn's preference for the native queen had annoyed her; and her blood had been heated by the tussle . . .

Soon after the Felidae had formed their amicable contract, the Vikings and the brownskins set about one another with a howl and a hurling of weapons. The dead fell everywhere. Eventually the Vikings decided to abandon the settlement and return, not to the Cold Land with No Trees but to Norway, Land of Fine Forests and Food.

The Troll Cats sat down to consider their futures. Hedinn's kittens were now well grown; but the queen who had borne them had died during the winter at the teeth of a bear, so Hedinn decided to rejoin the ship and return to his homeland. But Finna was heavy with the wildcat chief's brood, and she had grown fond of the brindled natives. And so it was that one Troll Cat stayed, and one returned across the sea; and thus Hedinn Haraldsson came to be known as Hedinn the Wild, ancestor of Ragnar Gustaffson, and his fame spread so widely that he had his pick of fine Norwegian queens, a situation in which he reveled; and many fine litters did he father.

And so it was that the offspring of Hedinn the Wild and Finna the Brave colonized the New World in an amicable manner where the upright ones had so signally failed.

Chapter Fifteen

THE STRANGE ADVENTURES OF RAGNAR GUSTAFFSON

A cat pent up becomes a lion.
— OLD ITALIAN SAYING

*W*hen Ragnar saw Mousebreath, Tag, and Cy spill out of the cat catchers' van and disappear into the night behind him, he thought, So. I am alone. Well then.

Then he thought, It does me credit that I can think at all, with all this noise.

Every time the van accelerated, its doors swung apart. When it slowed, they crashed together again in front of Ragnar Gustaffson's nose. Still half tangled in the rags of the cat catcher's net, he could barely prevent himself from sliding between them. If that happened, he would certainly be guillotined before they spat him out into the road. What a gloomy joke that would be! was his next thought. Clinging on for dear life, he managed a brief look around the inside of the van. Well, my friends are certainly gone. He missed them already. But if this is how—as one says—I "find" myself, then I must do my best. He was, after all, a King. He would make his way. But first he would make a mental list.

Much needs to be done. And the *Norsk Skogkatt* is rather good for work of this sort!

By the time he had accomplished the first item from the list— "free self from the net"—a particularly violent lurch had slammed shut the doors of the van. This allowed him to carry out the second task with less effort than he had expected—"find ways to close these noisy doors!"—and move straight to the third and perhaps most important—"examine surroundings." These he found familiar, if not reassuring: odors of hot metal and rubber, the metal floor with its bashed and dusty wooden slats, the dented ceiling and metal cages, the light falling intermittently as the machine lurched along through the night. The new cages rattled less than the old ones. They were painted a different color. They were all closed.

They were all occupied.

He looked up.

Cats stared emptily down at him.

He thought, When a kitten dies, the King dies with it. Then Pertelot Fitzwilliam of Hi-Fashion—the look of her, her cinnamon smell, the dry hot feel of her fur against his face, her eyes at once tender, ironic, and shy, her voice, her, "Oh, Rags. Really!"—rushed into his mind until there was no room for anything else.

Pertelot! he silently called to her.

Madness filled him. He was a full-grown *Skogkatt* who weighed seventeen pounds in his winter coat, and—as Sealink might have put it—he occupied his own space like a concrete block. He reared up, spread his powerful front paws, and launched himself bodily at the first cage he saw. There was a ringing crash. His wounds opened. Blood came forth. He stared at it, so red in the bad light. The King is not an ordinary cat. "Our blood is a book," he heard his Egyptian wife whisper. Even now, they were running a wire up into her brain. "Our blood is a book, whether we like it or not." These were the wounds of a king. They were the wounds of his responsibility. If a single kitten falls, the King falls with it. A cat in a cage cries out to the King. Ragnar Gustaffson—Coeur de Lion!—raised his great sad head and howled.

He threw himself at the cage again.

"Take it easy," someone advised.

But the other cats, impressed, set up a babble of encouragement and advice.

"You don't want to do it that way—"

"You want to do it this way!"

"Like this, with a—"

"Hook! Like this! See? Hook at it!"

"No, leave him! I seen it done like that! Go on, friend! Go on!"

In the cage in front of him, huddled up in the farthest corner she could find, sat a white female cat about ten years old. Her nose was pink, her eyes blue. Her name was Cottonreel. She had not been outside much in her life; her home was in a quiet street in Cartonwell Green, and until now she had always worn a nice collar. She was as deaf as a post, rather confused about what had happened to her, and almost as frightened of the King as she was of her captors. She had been single—not for want of trying—all her life. But she had clever feet, and she could slide back a bolt. She had learned how to do that by the time she was six months old. Didn't everyone? What a fuss about nothing!

"Excuse me," she said.

Ragnar Gustaffson hurled himself at the bars of her cage. He had found the bolt, but he seemed to have no idea what to do with it.

Perhaps "frightened" was not the word for what Cottonreel felt. Ragnar Gustaffson's tangled mane—which could have been so impressive if someone had looked after it—was full of oil, small sticks, and flecks of white. His paws were simply the biggest she had ever seen. And he did seem very upset. But there was something fine about his leonine profile, something comforting—as she expressed it to herself, as well as rather exciting—about his smell. She sensed in him some great sorrow. So she crept toward the front of the cage and re-peated, "Excuse me!"

The huge cat regarded her for a moment, his green eyes glazed and rounded with the solemn lunacy of the very royal. His anger had heated the air around him, emphasizing its pow-erful flavors of testosterone, blood, and rusty metal. Cottonreel swallowed her anxiety and spoke up.

"I think you push down first," she said, "*then* pull." She winced. "I'm sorry," she said. "It's no use shouting. I'm a bit deaf. But I think if you push it down first you'll find—"

Ragnar Gustaffson blinked at her.

He raised one devastated paw and examined it. Then he reached out, lined up the bolt, and slid it gently back. The little white cat pushed open her door and walked out purring under his nose.

Nothing would satisfy Ragnar then but to go around the van and let everyone out. In the case of the cats in the top cages, this proved difficult. But—as he told them later at some length—the breed-standard of the *Norsk Skogkatt* requires a powerful and determined climber; and eventually they were all assembled on the floor of the vehicle, purring and rubbing against him, only congratulating him more when he modestly gave the white cat credit for her idea.

"Good," he said. "Good. But I must say we are not yet out of the woods. We are still in this van!"

They stared at him hopefully.

There were perhaps twenty of them, all different. Or perhaps not so different. Few of them were strays. Like Cottonreel, they had led decent, well-fed, fireside lives. There was a half-Aby with fur like Middle Eastern sand; two or three shiny short-haired blacks, one of whom claimed to be from Bombay; the most extraordinary bicolor blue longhair who looked like the marbling in the front of an old book and who could barely spare time to raise her head from grooming. Many of them, like Cottonreel, were pure white; and among the whites two perfectly matched Orientals stood out—tiny, emaciated, sinuous creatures with huge green eyes tinged dove gray near the pupil. Their voices were so high, and so similar, and they echoed one another so, that you never knew which one of them was speaking.

"No escape—"

"For us!"

"They'll make us into gloves—" they sang "—into gloves—"

"Into gloves."

It was Ragnar's turn to stare. But Cottonreel gave the Geminis a no-nonsense look.

"Thanks to Mr. Ragnar," she announced, "I don't think

anyone *here* is going to be made into gloves. But we do need a plan. And what I suggest we do is this . . ."

Toward dawn—as Tag, now many miles away to the north, huddled beneath a tree root in fear of the *vagus*—a rather battered white van drew up outside a large detached house in the suburbs of a town fifty or sixty miles south of the city. There were twelve inches of soft snow in the road, and the plane trees were pasted with it. Two tired-looking human beings from the fur industry, so swathed against the weather that their arms were pushed out from their sides and their movements limited and slow, climbed down into the snow from opposite sides of the cab. Their breath steamed in the cold air. It had already been a bad night for them. Leaving the engine on, they ploughed their way around to the back doors, which they opened. In an instant, twenty cats had spilled out around their legs and scampered off in nineteen different directions. Gemini and Gemini had decided they would stay together, come what may. The humans stared dully. If they ran after one cat, they would lose the rest. While they were thinking about it, of course, they lost the lot.

Ragnar Gustaffson, who had been last out—a certain amount of overcrowding and panicky behavior in the doorway had left him hard put to it—peeped around the base of an ornamental cherry while he got his breath back. He had enjoyed confusing the human beings. It was satisfying to watch his new friends scatter over garden fences, beneath cars, up and down the silent road. But what would become of them now?

While he was pondering this, Cottonreel appeared by his side.

"I came to say good-bye," she said shyly. "And to thank you. You certainly saved my skin! No, don't say anything, I shan't hear if you do!" She looked away from him suddenly. "This is such an attractive little place," she said quietly. "Don't you think? Nice houses. Oh look, there goes the bicolor! How she hates the snow!"

"Mm," said Ragnar. "I can only ask: What will their lives be now?"

She couldn't hear him, but she saw how anxious he was. "I shouldn't worry too much about them," she advised. "They'll find a place and fit in. Cats are good at that. In a month's time, some of them will hardly remember all this." Her face took on rather a firm look. "Those absurd Geminis, for instance. And others—well, you know, domesticity doesn't suit everyone. They'll make a life for themselves!"

Ragnar Gustaffson looked down at her. "And you?" he said.

She purred. "Oh, don't you worry," she said. "I shall scratch at the first door I see and ask for warm milk." She shivered, then gave his bulky shoulders and tangled ruff a sideways glance full of awe. "I'm not like you, I'm afraid, born to be wild!" She laughed. "I'll probably end up as the post office cat!"

"What is a post office?"

"I can't hear you, my dear. Good-bye!"

And before he could thank her for her help, she was gone.

He was a little bit sad as he left the town. But dawn gladdened his heart with images of a beloved if unvisited country and eased his anxious thoughts of Pertelot.

The suburbs gave way to winding lanes. The houses thinned out, became larger and more relaxed looking. Fields appeared, grew broader, sloped cheerfully into shallow valleys between ivy-choked copses of oak and holly—the valleys full of haze, the haze full of the promise of sun. Transparent winds had varnished the snow; a gliss of ice stretched away pink and gold and full of mirages in the feather dawn. A quarter of an hour, and the haze had parted like a curtain. Church towers dissolved in a blaze of light he couldn't bear to look at. An incense of coal smoke rose into the clear blue air. Children emerged, delighted, their cries full of laughter and energy.

As for Ragnar Gustaffson . . .

It was one of the best days of his life. He had been given, at last, the opportunity to test every aspect of the sturdy, good-looking *Norsk Skogkatt* design! Comfort. Durability. Practicality. The paw tufts for warmth and grip. The ear tufts for insulation. The stylish double coat with its high-speed drying characteris-

tics. The versatile all-leg drive he had so often tried to demon-
strate to his good friend Mousebreath.

Snow!

He chose a steepish slope; stood for a prolonged, delicious
moment at the top; then charged joyfully down it, sliding, rolling, bounding, and panting until he tumbled head over heels into
the fat white drift at the bottom. Snow! He wriggled about in it
in a frenzy. Snow! He rolled onto his front and went through the
drift like a mechanical shovel, tossing clouds of it into the air
with his head and then batting out right and left at them like a
kitten. Snow, snow, snow, snow, *snow*! Suddenly, remembering
that he must also test one of the least known but perhaps most
interesting features of the Troll Cat breed, he rushed into a plantation of young conifers and dashed up the trunk of the nearest
tree. His heart was an engine. His powerful claws, adapted for
rock and ice, gripped the resinous bark. He was a feline machine. Turning around carefully at his high point, he was easily
able to descend *headfirst and in a spiral*. Then he leapt to his
feet and sprinted—eyes bulging, ears back, tail curled over—
through the plantation, his passage dislodging explosions of
powder from the feathery lower branches where they swept
the ground. Snow flew up into the sunbeams like spray from a
torrent! Snow! He swam in snow. He breathed up snow and
sneezed it out. It was Norway, larch and pine. It was—

Well, of course, it was snow.

Snow.

Afternoon found him tired but happy. At his own guess, he had
covered ten or fifteen miles. He had been able to experience the
great stamina of his breed by eating nothing. As he went, the
sun reddened the snow and began imperceptibly to descend. In
the great wide fields the ivy-thickened trees looked like plumes
of smoke. A big male hare crouched in the open, watching him.
He saw its breath, pink in the graying air. He felt its love of
life—its strong blood, its dignity, its grave determination to
wake the next morning—like a vibrant line drawn in the air between them.

"Good-bye!" he whispered when it ran off at last across the glorious blood-red smear of sun. "Come home safely!"

The surface of the snow would soon begin to freeze again. For now, it made difficult walking; one or another of his paws broke through the crust at every stride. "This could tire the patience—even of a king!" He began to avoid the drifts and the little coppices where he could only flounder along. Pellets of ice had formed between his toes, and in the fur of his ruff and belly. While he was still dry on top, he was soaked underneath. "Well," he advised himself drolly, "the *Norsk Skogkatt* is known to love hardship and cold!"

The sun set. Lamps came on in the villages around him. A bitter frost settled in. The stars glittered in black shellac above, and he could hear the very water cracking in the ponds. The snow hardened into ruts at the junctions of the little lanes. Dozing a little on his feet, Ragnar Gustaffson turned a corner in the night and found himself in a steep graveled driveway.

Comfortably obscured by its overgrown front garden, out of which grew a single magnolia tree fine with blossoms of snow, the house was L-shaped and pebbled-dashed, with black-painted drainpipes, overhanging gable ends, and yellow-lit dormer windows in a pantile roof. Ragnar, attracted by the warmth and light, gave it a wide berth nevertheless. He wanted to leap up onto the nearest windowsill and call, "Let me in! Me in now!" He wanted to roll on the doormat. He wanted to race into the house. He wanted to rub his face again and again on someone's legs. Instead, he made his way cautiously around into the back garden.

There he found parterre flower beds cakey with snow roses, snow lavender. He was hungry, but he would wait and see. He sat for some time beneath the variegated holly a few yards from the house, studying the lighted French windows. Muffled silence reigned. Then a small icy wind scraped the black branches together; and a human being appeared from the road. Its head was a black woolen blob. Its breath steamed fiercely. It muttered to itself. It banged its hands together and stamped its feet to dislodge the snow. It went inside and forgot to shut the kitchen door. Ragnar rushed after it. Halfway down the parterre, he lost his nerve and scuttled back to his refuge; but hunger drove him out again almost immediately, and soon he was standing in the human footprints, lifting his feet uncomfortably, kneading the snow. Everything seemed quiet. He approached the back door. He nudged it. It opened inward perhaps two inches. Warmth and light poured out over him.

"Excuse me?" he said quietly.

No reply. Ragnar squeezed his head into the gap until his shoulders touched the edge of the door on one side and the door frame on the other. He had a look. A kitchen lay before him, equipped with white square objects that hummed. A strange, pungent smell hung about the red-tiled floor and deep yellow walls; and over by the sink, on clean sheets of newspaper, a large steel bowl of tinned food had been placed next to an equally large enamel dish of water. Ragnar stared helplessly at them. Saliva filled his mouth.

"Excuse me!" he said. "Anyone home?"

There was a roar from the rooms beyond, and a large black dog flung itself into the kitchen.

"*My* house!" it said.

All Ragnar saw was a vast red mouth with yellowed teeth and a disgusting tongue; a nose like a black leather boxing glove, wrinkled up and dripping wet; eyes popping and white-rimmed with rage. He backed out of the kitchen as fast as he could. But that very action pulled the door shut on his own neck. "Yow!" he said. He was wedged. The more he pulled back, the more wedged he became. The dog shook its head, close enough to spatter him with spittle, its bark a kind of endless hysterical *rowrowrowrowrowrowrow*, its smell enfolding him, rank, powerful, even more frightening than its teeth.

This is the end of me, thought Ragnar Gustaffson. Then he asked himself, "Is the *Skogkatt* so easily dismayed? I think not!" He opened his mouth wide and closed it on the dog's nose. Through clenched teeth he told the dog, "I am sorry to have to do this."

The dog yelped and ran.

Ragnar's legs began to *chase* it.

What am I doing? he thought, halfway across the kitchen floor.

The back door had opened itself again as soon as he moved forward. Fur up on end with panic, he skidded in a half circle, dived through the gap, and pelted off down the garden. Without being entirely certain how he had got there, he found himself in the lower branches of the holly tree. There, he bubbled and spat for some minutes. "Safe now! Safe!" he assured himself. "No one can see me now!"

Commotion filled the house. Doors were slammed. Human voices were raised. "Then *go* and have a look, Libby," said one of them reasonably. "I'm not going out again!"

A minute or two later, a female human being issued from the kitchen, wearing a long quilted waistcoat over what looked like a woolen dressing gown. There were green rubber boots on its feet. "Do come on, Arthur!" it urged, and began to drag the reluctant dog around the snowbound garden on a lead. "Show some spirit, for goodness' sake." It shone a torch into each bush and flower bed, then up into the holly. It shouted excitedly, "Oh! Eyes! Eyes! Something's looking at me from up this tree! I think Arthur's been bitten by a fox!" There was a silence, during which even the dog looked confused. Less certainly, the woman called, "Do foxes climb trees?"

Slowly and carefully, Ragnar Gustaffson Coeur de Lion put the trunk of the holly between him and them, and climbed higher. He waited uncomfortably, with his paws on different spindly branches, until the cold drove them in again. For a long time after that, cold and exhausted, he crouched in the boughs of the holly, looking across at the warm windows of the house. He tried hard not to feel excluded. After all, he thought, I am a forest cat. A tree is good enough for me. Then—optimism being one of the breed's great virtues—Perhaps tomorrow we shall have a lovely morning. With that, he slept.

He dreamed of snow—in the dream he was a kitten, dashing and tumbling, while his great uncle Wulf looked proudly on. He dreamed of Cottonreel and the Geminis, nosing sadly among the collars their captors had discarded on the floor of the van. In that dream, guided by the familiar smell of home, each lost cat could find its collar but never get back into it. He dreamed of Tag and Mousebreath and their little Cy. In the dream they were in some dark place, moving forward into danger because chaos lay behind them. A pale, determined light was in their eyes.

Finally he dreamed of Pertelot Fitzwilliam.

Tintagel Court. Cold light flickered on the walls of a cold room.

The Mau smelled of civet, cinnamon, and tar—bizarre spices in the night. The whole of Egypt was in her eyes. She was as soft and clever as a bird. She loved him. "Ragnar!" she wailed at him over her shoulder, and raised her elegant haunches. It was deep music. Before he knew it, he had bitten her suddenly in the loose skin of her neck and mounted her. With that lurch of pleasure there went through them both the dislocation of every promise they had ever made—*Never mate. We shall never mate!*—and they were like two other cats there in the gloom, driven by the blood, soft and savage, delighted and fierce.

Then the light shifted and changed, and he was looking at her from far off, under a blinding white light, where she was etherized on a table, eyes gone, rosy limbs pinned down, and the wire snaking up into her brain, and he could hear her whispering over and over again, "If a single kitten dies, the King— If a single kitten dies, the King—"

From this nightmare he woke, cold and appalled, to find that it was almost morning and he had fallen out of the tree. He walked dazedly about on the lawn in the dark until the dog began to bark from the house.

With that, his days became the search for her. Ragged and hungry, he wandered the human roads of the south. He had no plan. He listened to his blood or to the voices in his head. The roads were white at first, then churned to slush. A raw wind blew from the east, to blacken the lime trunks. It brought freezing rain—and then, before the snow could melt—more snow. Ragnar trudged from one dawn to the next, carrying his ice-hung coat like a burden. The wind made his eyes water. Tears froze on his face. He avoided houses and people. He was the Troll Cat now. He had a real sense of this creature within him. It was enduring, empty, dull of mind, determined, a voice that said, "Go on!" because to stop would be to die. He ate from dustbins. He ate dead animals stuck to the roads. He became so hungry that late one afternoon in the gathering dark he found himself gnawing frozen turnips in the corner of a field. He was thinking, Good! Good! and growling to himself. His coat was shaggy and knotted. At a distance, making his way slowly and patiently along some frozen stream between induviae of butterbur and willow herb, he could be mistaken for a pony in a winter field. Then he stopped and raised his head, and his eyes flashed like a signal, brilliant green.

Three or four days after he bit the dog, his instinctual drive south was balked by the broad, willow-stitched meanders of a river. Sheets of broken ice, piled up on the outside of the curves, had refrigerated the air until he could barely breathe it. Well then, he thought, at least I shall be able to go over. But halfway across he encountered a thick black channel of unfrozen water, its glossy back freighted with broken branches and huge but swanlike structures of plastic packing material. It was as muscular as a snake. He studied the powerful eddy and swirl of it. He looked over at the far bank, which was hairy with birch and alder. Then he backed carefully off the thinner ice at the brink and resumed his plod across the water meadows.

Conditions were bad, even for the Troll Cat. Snow whirled around him so thickly he couldn't tell whether it came from the sky or the earth. His sense of direction failed. He was afraid to stop in case he started off again in the wrong line and ended up back on the ice. After a few minutes he heard muffled cries nearby. There was a tinge of color to the snowy air. Nacreous pinks and yellows—agitated like summer leaves or weed curling under water—developed to red and orange and gold. There were smells: acrid, aromatic, unfamiliar. The cries, thin and urgent, redoubled, then died. Ragnar flattened himself to the ground. He crept cautiously forward, step by partial step. Had the air grown warmer? He wasn't sure. Snow surrounded him, opaque as fog. Then he seemed to step free of it, as if blundering out of woods into a clearing.

It had been a pleasant summer cottage of rosy-orange brick, with a weatherboarded upper story and dormer windows. Now—miles from the nearest town, isolated by winter, the water meadows, the cruel cold loops of the river—it was on fire. Long flames roared out of the dormers. Black smoke boiled off into the night. The blaze had started at the left-hand gable end. This it had already reduced to a tissue. No flames could be observed there, only an intense gold light filling the ghosts of rooms. Heat resonated through the freezing air and across the faces of the human beings standing on the lawn. They were pale and shaking. They had saved nothing from the disaster but the nightclothes they stood up in. They had given up trying to do anything.

They were watching a cat run backward and forward between the house and the lawn.

She was an ordinary domestic black and white, and perhaps the kittens were her first. They were about eighteen days old. When Ragnar arrived, she had retrieved two of them. By the time he'd understood what was happening, she had fetched out a third. Because the fire had begun upstairs, its claim on the ground floor was, as yet, tentative. Even so, no human being could survive the heat and fumes inside. Quiet and determined, quick and clever on her feet, mining a layer of good air five inches deep, the black and white was fetching her litter. The fourth kitten took longer. She dropped it gently with the rest, and when she looked up at the human beings—calmly, as if to say, This is hard work!—Ragnar could see she was exhausted, filthy with soot, and already burned. By the fifth kitten, her ears had become a kind of blackened frill on her skull, and she had to sit down for a moment before she went back in. She was careful to sit well away from the people, in case they tried to stop her. She stared at them thoughtfully. But when the kittens mewed for her, she would not look, in case their need sapped her determination. When she came out with the sixth kitten, Ragnar had made up his mind and was waiting on the garden path.

"Two more inside," she said. "Help me."

The sixth kitten was dead. She put it on the pile with the others and began licking it, looking about her every so often in a puzzled, irritable fashion. It was clear to Ragnar that she could no longer see. Her eyelids had gone, along with the fur on the left side of her face.

"They will be dead now," he said gently. "You have done enough."

"No," she said.

She lurched toward the house.

"They will be dead," said Ragnar.

"No."

"Then let me fetch them."

"All right," she said.

She took two steps back toward her litter and fell over on her side. "Thank you," she said indistinctly, as Ragnar walked past her and into the house. "I don't feel well." She smelt powerfully of scorched hair and worse.

Ragnar was no fonder of fire than any other cat. After the fight with the Alchemist, dread had filled him to see the flames burst from the warehouse. He stood for a moment in the doorway. Cold air rushed past him. Convection currents raged within. He could see fallen timbers at an angle across a passage, bellying brown darkness shot with carmine, and thick yellow particulate smoke. If the fire on the second story had purified itself beyond flames, something darker and less formed lived down here. He shrugged. He had said he would help her, and now he would. He ducked beneath the smoke and into the hallway. The fire welcomed him. Even in the good air he could barely breathe. Cinders bit him through his fur. His eyes ran with tears, then dried out as the tear ducts gave up. His ruff sizzled suddenly under his nose. Nuzzling the cinder out, he burned his mouth.

Room to room he went, scuttling from pocket to pocket of air, as flat to the ground as a wood louse. The tough *Skogkatt* coat brushed the floor. All weathers, he thought. All purpose. Room to room, alive to the noises beneath the voice of the fire, the smells inside the black breath of combustion. He was so alert he could almost see through the smoke. He was all nerves. He had never felt so alive! He found them in what had been the kitchen. She had been keeping them among the tablecloths on a shelf in the linen cupboard. Their age had prevented them from crawling off into the fire in panic, but one was already dead of smoke inhalation and the other, a piebald little thing with not much to recommend it, lay with its face on the shelf, blinking and mewling feebly.

"I hurt," it said, trying to look up at Ragnar Gustaffson. "I hurt."

"Well, then," Ragnar Gustaffson told it. "We should go out of here, I think, you and I. Cheer up. As my tough friend Tag says—'You haven't had it till you're dead.' "

And he picked it up in his mouth.

You would have thought this was a signal. Fire flashed over in a roiling, glittering cloud a foot beneath the kitchen ceiling. The linen cupboard exploded. Ceiling beams creaked and fell. But Ragnar Gustaffson Coeur de Lion knew exactly where he was going. He reached the doorway, took a moment to look up and down the passage. "That way fire. This way the open air. No contest, I would say!" He got a firmer grip on the kitten, put his head down, and ran. As he went, he cast quick glances from side to side. My, he thought, this is some story to tell!

Outside, he gave the kitten to its mother. The black and white lay on her side staring into space, suckling her family. Fire had stripped raw the left side of her face. Her mouth gaped open on that side in an unintentional snarl. She was quivering a little with shock but ignoring it. That was only her body. She waited until the last kitten had wormed its way to a nipple, then said, "What's your name?"

"Ragnar Gustaffson Coeur de Lion," he told her.

"Well, I can't call her that," she said. "She's a female." After a pause she said, "You sound a bit of a toff to me. Come 'round in front of me, I might be able to see you there. No. Ah well."

"In any case I am a Norwegian Forest Cat."

"I don't know what that is. You sound like a bit of a toff. I suppose I could call her Rags." She tried to moisten her lips with her tongue. "The other one died then," she said.

"Yes."

"Six out of eight isn't bad." She let the silence grow between them.

After a time he asked, "Will you be all right?"

She laughed. "Yes," she said. "They look stupid, but they'll take care of me."

The human beings were still staring up at the house in disbelief. One of them had wrapped the other in a scorched blanket. Sometimes they put their arms around one another and looked disbelievingly from the cats to the flames and back again. They looked at the blowing snow. The man shook its head and said, "I turned everything off, I know I did." The woman said, "Oh dear, oh dear." It began to cry. There they stood, awkward and shy—the way human beings often are—in front of the disaster they had made.

"If you're sure—" said Ragnar.

"Oh, I'm sure."

"Because I am looking for someone. She also needs my help."

"Go on," said the black and white. "You go on. I'll be all right with them."

"Well then. Good-bye."

She lifted her head as if she could watch him go. "Good-bye," she said.

"You could call the kitten 'Cottonreel,' " Ragnar suggested.

"The other one was definitely dead, was it?"

"Yes."

After that, he walked and walked. He walked as hard as he could. He crossed the river by a bridge. He crossed it back again. He welcomed the bitter wind that sprang up to blow the snow into his smarting eyes. Whenever he thought of the black-and-white cat, he was filled with an energy he couldn't control. Something about her courage—which was not courage but some blind determination of the organism—made him quicken his stride. Awed and elated, raw with misery and anger, he was trying to outdistance the knowledge of life, which is also the knowledge of death. Ragnar Gustaffson walked and walked to leave the burning house behind. But he had not eaten anything for two days, and not even a cat as sturdy as the *Norsk Skogkatt* can go on forever. Not even a king can march without food. He had lost his friends. Tired and hungry and trembling in the wake of events, he had no idea where he was. He felt his legs go from beneath him.

In that exact moment he remembered his dream of Pertelot, and understood what his life to date had been trying to tell him.

He thought, And what if I am a *father*?

He tried to rise. Nothing happened. He looked up, and the stars were spinning.

He woke suddenly, much later. It was still night, but the snow had let up. The moon was bright but low. Not far away above the flat river valley, set on its own among wide avenues and ter-raced lawns separated by broad shallow flights of steps, stood an elegant white mansion, its tall windows and roofed portico limned with snow. Ah, thought Ragnar, who despite his situa-tion felt oddly warm and relaxed. "A house. Good." It took longer to get there than he had expected because he kept falling over on the way.

The terraced lawns were furnished with balustrades and urns. Many leaden statues—life-size human figures, naked or draped, alone or in groups—cast precise moon shadows. In places a thin mist lay across the snow between these figures, so that they looked as if they had waded out into water up to their knees and then stopped in wonder to look around them. Ragnar approached them with a sudden lightness of heart, but fell asleep again before he got there. When he next woke the mist had risen further, so that it reached up to the thighs of the statues. They didn't seem to care. They stood around, looking more or less intently toward the elegant house.

Strange! Ragnar thought.

As he watched, one of them moved. It seemed to shake itself out of a dream, look around in surprise. "Oh dear!" it said clearly. And then, "Damn!" It shivered, bent down quickly, and from out of the milky fog around its legs fished a pink toweling bathrobe. It wasn't a statue after all, but an elderly woman. "Damn cold!" it said. "Woo." It was frail but still tall and straight. Its long gray hair fell thickly around its shoulders. Its skin had a dignified luminous whiteness in the night. It belted the robe quickly, looked around, shrugged. "Oh well," it said, and made off toward the house.

Ragnar, warm and comfortable, his eyes already beginning to close—so that there came up on his eyelids a dream of sunshine flickering on water—thought nothing of it. But he must have made some kind of noise, because the next thing he knew the woman had come back and was kneeling beside him in the snow, quietly extending its fingers for him to sniff. He couldn't get up, but he could lean forward a little and touch its hand with his nose. After that, he closed his eyes again. They were both surprised, when the woman reached cautiously down and picked him up, to hear him purr loudly.

"So," she said, "who are you, you splendid animal, and how did you get in this condition?"

She had fed Ragnar Gustaffson on cod—poached with a little milk and butter, very good—and given him a drink. She had washed him gently in lukewarm water, tutting over his scabby front paws and wasted limbs; dried him with a towel; then gently brushed out some of the lesser tangles in the *Skogkatt* coat. She had dressed his burns with ointment. On Ragnar's part nothing had been required but that he sleep a little more, then finish the fish. For a cat who had so recently returned from the edge of hypothermia, he felt remarkably strong and well. He jumped up on the sideboard and began, "That is, as you would say, 'a long story.'"

"The first thing to learn," she interrupted, picking him up and setting him on her lap, "is to stay off the furniture."

He didn't hear her. He had fallen asleep again. In the next few days he would sleep twenty hours out of twenty-four.

Her house was full of rooms. There were six or seven on every floor, connected by long corridors and broad staircases. Large old chairs inhabited them, grazing alongside overstuffed chintz sofas, leather stools, and glass-fronted cases full of ancient porcelain and stuffed birds. The old lady had upholstered them years ago in brocade and velvet, favoring deep greens and petroleum blues, russet browns. The morning sun glanced off a hundred mirrors and onto a scatter of dusty brass objects—coal scuttles, fenders, fire irons, little brass lizards that seemed to flicker with movement. The rooms smelled of dust. They smelled of mice. One of them smelled sharply of turpentine and new wood. It was a narrow room but very tall. A window at one end reached from floor to ceiling. There were no curtains. Light poured in across a floor of bare gray boards onto the easel in the middle of the room. There the old lady went in the mornings to work.

"You aren't welcome here," she informed Ragnar. "Cat fur and oil paint don't mix." And she pushed him out of the door.

"Meeargh," said Ragnar.

"No."

In the end, though, she did let him in, and while she worked he watched the garden birds or slept the morning away on an old brocade cushion by the window. In this room the old lady wore a paint-spattered white overall. She did her hair up with a piece of silk or chenille. She painted the same picture again and again. It was a view of a young man's head taken from two or three very small, brownish photographs pinned to the easel. They were curled with age.

In her parlor was a polished round table covered with silver frames of every size and description. They were full of the young man's photograph too. She sat in there in the afternoon, and at four o'clock ate buttered toast or crumpets by the fire. She fell asleep with Ragnar on her lap. One evening she woke up with a gasp. It was six o'clock. The room was lit only by the dwindling coal fire, which cast faint shadows and glimmered in the brass fender.

"Joseph!" she said, with a laugh.

"I thought he'd come back with me," she told Ragnar. "I thought this time he would." For a moment she was as full of delight as a girl. "Oh, Royal," she said. "*Can* we meet the people we once loved? In dreams? After death? I'm sure we can! We can go back to all the things we've done." She sighed. She said, "I loved him so." And then in a quite different voice, "That man completely overshadowed my life."

Ragnar yawned. He stretched one foreleg out in front of him in the firelight and extended its claws. Then he got up, shook himself, and jumped off the old lady's lap. "I love someone," he told her. "And as soon as I am strong again, I must find her."

The old lady treated him well. He was always warm. When he watched the snow flurry across the garden, it was from the right side of the window once more. But she had her disadvantages. Oh, she called him "my little lion." But she seemed more frightened than proud of his energy and liveliness—and sometimes quite angry with it. One morning, leaping up onto the kitchen table to say hello to her, he knocked over the milk jug.

"You silly cat! You silly, bad cat!"

Snow whirled across the terraces in the dark afternoon, curdling the brown air and settling on the heads of the statues like a white fur hat. In the morning the lawns were a dazzling fresh expanse, across which hopped a single thrush like a bird in a painting. Ragnar spent his time staring out of the studio window. He ate only half his breakfast.

"Dear me, Royal!" said the old lady. "Don't you like cod after all?"

She was amused.

"How can a cat not like fish?"

While she worked, she talked about Joseph.

"You would have liked him, Royal—"

"I am looking for someone too. I go south because that is what I feel inside. You know?"

"And he would have loved you."

"I've walked a long way already. The world is a bleak place. Cats only have other cats."

"He loved cats with a passion. He drew them to him with that marvelous voice, those marvelous hands. When he stroked them they couldn't resist."

"I go south and keep looking for her. I hear her say the things she used to say. 'Rags, you are exasperating.' And, 'Come here this instant!' "

"None of us could resist him."

Joseph's portrait filled the walls of the room. He looked out from canvas after canvas, old and dull, fresh and new. His face was sharp yet placid. His hair, a darkish brown tending to chestnut at the sides, curled gently into the nape of his neck. His eyes were a musing green. The old lady had painted them so that they looked at you wherever you sat. They had a lazy, amused expression. They weren't quite so gentle as his face.

"His friends said he filled his pockets with catnip to attract the cats." She laughed. "What did he fill them with to attract us?" she asked herself. "What indeed!" She sighed and put down her brush. "Well, Royal, my little lion—"

"The world is a bare place without her, and now I have something new to wonder about."

"Shall we try you on haddock for lunch?"

"What if I am a *father*?"

That night Ragnar watched her make her way down the stairs, open the back door, and go out into the garden. Her eyes were wide open. She was fast asleep. She wore only her pink wrap, and her feet were quite bare. Her skin already had a translucent waxy look, as if in anticipation of the cold. She often got up like this—especially if she had been agitated during the day—found her way down the stairs, and walked across the lawn to stand and hold a dialogue with the statues. These conversations were diffuse and full of vague regrets. She took up a listening posture, as if she could hear the statues' reply.

"How could you, Joseph?" she would plead. "I would never have done that to you." She added, "You were always a torment."

And then suddenly, after a pause of almost five minutes: "My, but we did have *fun*, didn't we?"

Ragnar looked out across the lawn. The surface of the snow, silvered by frost and thaw, frost and thaw, shone like water in the strong moonlight. Everything looked very clear, but so cold. The old lady's misty breath hung about her own shoulders. Suddenly, she began to take off her wrap.

Despite himself, he slept, and he dreamed; and what he dreamed woke him very suddenly. The hearth was cold. The room was chilly. Ragnar was so disoriented he barely recognized it. His heart pounded. Noises had followed him out of the dream—a kind of leaden, sickly buzzing in his ears, human shouts, and behind both a distant panicky caterwaul that for some reason he associated with Pertelot. A voice repeated over and over, "Not the kittens! Not the kittens!"

It was his own.

After a moment or two he was himself again—or imagined he was. He stretched. He sat down and licked one hind paw. Then he went over to the window and pushed with his face at the velvet curtains for a while until he found the gap between them. He had a look out. He blinked. Terraces stretched away down to the water meadow in the distance, where he could just see a sketchy line of willows. Moonlight slipped away across the snowy lawns, slithered off the slick of ice that glossed each balustrade and urn. Everything looked frozen and fixed, although one of the statues seemed to have fallen down, and lay at odds among the others, its arms thrown out. Ragnar looked closer. It wasn't a statue. It was the old lady. In a flash he was across the room, down the stairs and, with the weight of his seventeen pounds, pushed open the door.

She had a slight, puzzled smile, as if she had not quite expected to fall. She lay beneath a statue with a young man's face. It was the face of Joseph. It was the face she had been trying to paint. At the same time, it was neither of those things, but the face of a human being, individual and in the end unreadable. A half smile lay on its lips. Its eyes were a little cruel. It was sure of itself; it was unsure. It was proud of itself; it was a little ashamed. It had put catnip in its pocket to attract cats. It had been alive, and now it was dead. It had loved the old lady in its way. Did she know this? Perhaps. After all, she had a smile on her face too. She looked less cold than sculpted, and her body had a strange, transparent grace.

"Dreams are sometimes worse than nothing," said Ragnar. "Best is to find what you are looking for." He sat for a while, staring intently into her face. She showed no sign of moving. Eventually he said, "I'm going to find Pertelot Fitzwilliam now. You would have liked her, and she would have liked you. She is brave enough to be out there while I sit in your house with you and eat your very nice food. I miss her. My nights are full of her. My dreams urge me on."

The memory of his dreams made him get up.

"Good-bye," he said. "Thank you for taking care of me."

He walked away from the house without looking back. Over in the east, above the line of willows, the day was beginning. Later, the sun might spill itself in a kind of golden, rosy-orange shimmer across the icy lawn; for now it was only a tremulous graying of the sky over there, which picked out the features of the waiting statues. It lighted an eye, the corner of a smile.

Compelled by a knowledge he couldn't explain, he went southward, and the weather began to improve. He woke beneath a hawthorn hedge one morning to the steady drip of water. All around him was melting snow! White gulls wheeled and called above the plowed fields in a sky a bright, aching blue. The air was sluiced and splashed with sunshine. Through every bar of light that penetrated the hedge a million drops of water seemed to flash and fall. He was already soaked, but he felt heartened. He felt hungry.

His luck changed with the weather. Wherever he went, there was food for him. Housewives left it to cool on windowsills. Housecats left it unfinished in nice ceramic bowls on clean back doorsteps. Off its guard in the sunshine, it wandered into his welcoming clutch at roadsides and at the base of hedges. He liked the mice best. Moles he tried to leave alone. Some of them were as determined as the Troll Cat itself, and a lot angrier.

There were dawns—frosty, iconic, heartbreaking. Mornings so windy the crows had to climb out of the air and into the branches of the trees. Afternoon sunlight like crystallized sugar down the side of a blackened telegraph pole. He loved to travel now. He was sure he would find her. He thought he smelled her sometimes in the lanes, a resinous Egyptian perfume so intense—so bizarre—it couldn't belong among the drab smells of this northern winter. He expected to come upon her around the next corner. Or the one after that. Instead, he came upon new companions, new vistas. He spent a night in a barn with a tiny but well-tailored female named Treslove, who soon told him hopefully that she was no better than she should be. "If you like Egyptians, darling, you can always call me 'Cairo.' " He fell in, then out, with a couple of muddy young marmalade toms— brothers on the Old Changing Way—out for rats and anything else they could find. He walked for two days with a traveling cat from Calderdale who never stopped talking about Stilton cheese.

Then, at the turn of a lane where a disused track went off by the side of a wood, he was attracted to a flicker of light among the couch grass, thistles, and young sloes. It was like finding a glittering glass marble between the tangled stems. But as soon as he put his nose in to sniff it, he realized he was *looking into* something. Or somewhere. Some vaguely seen but very real place, where—*things*—rushed to and fro. Were they animals? Wait! Were they cats? That was where Ragnar Gustaffson Coeur de Lion, a King in his time, had his first glimpse into the wild roads—a strange, secluded, rural little tunnel in the matted grass, where farm cats had hunted voles a hundred years. Entranced, he watched their shadows pouncing to and fro under the changing light. Why not? he thought. I should see this too. I should try all these things! Then—because he was the King, and he had no fear—he had slipped inside and been welcomed. He thought he heard a whisper, a shiver through every branch and pathway: *At last!* Then the ghost winds took him up and propelled him south.

"That was a ride!" he would boast later. "I can tell you!" All curves and re-entrants here, like a river in a valley bottom, the highways drew him in and pulled him along and passed him from one to the next at such breakneck speed that his fur flew back in the airstream and he felt as dizzy as a funfair cat on a Friday night. "I could steer, but it was as you say 'a damn near thing'! It was more like flying than running!" Empty of traffic, echoing with speed, they smoothed his way south, to the coast. There they spat him out. He staggered a little in the teeth of the wind at the top of a crumbling chalk cliff. A huge storm was in progress. Clouds roared past the moon. All around him, the night danced and flickered and multiplied itself with lightning. In the instant before each discharge could be heard a wheezing, sputtering sound like drops of water vaporized on a hotplate. Each great forked blue-white bolt left the earth a-tumble with phosphorescent yellow sparks cooling to red as they fell. The wind cracked like a wet sheet. The rain blew in almost horizontally from the sea.

The sea!

Benighted, heaving, cold and unforgiving, licked with fitful gleams of light, it stretched away to meet the boiling clouds, the gibbous moon—and then, he knew, away again. The sea went on forever. It was cold, and it moved as if it was alive. He could smell it, as salty as blood. He could hear it, like part of the storm, smashing on the rocks two hundred feet below him in the windy, lunatic dark. Ragnar was appalled.

His southward drive had led him nowhere.

"Pertelot!" he cried. "Pertelot, where are you?"

He stood there on the wild cliff top in the wind—a new King, a creature of the highway, still massive with all his journeys— and felt in quick succession puzzlement, despair, anger. But a sudden optimism replaced them all. He stared out across the water.

After all, he thought, the one place she can't be is out there! At least I needn't worry about that. That is not a thing to worry about.

And he began to walk west along the cliff top.

The Sixth Life of Cats

Kettie and Vinegar Tom watched the scene below from the boughs of the oak tree in the pig field.

The humans from the farm were behaving oddly again.

They had taken off their clothes and were dancing around the field in the early light, their big bare feet tracing dark patterns through the dew-pale grass. They had found and eaten some mushrooms in the fallow field that had somehow convinced them they were invisible and capable of flight. Some whirled and flapped; others leapt and pounced in strange parody. The cool morning air had raised gooseflesh along their limbs.

"Whatever are they doing?" Kettie asked.

Vinegar Tom shook his head sadly.

"They've prayed to Mahu the Great Cat. They've asked for the power to travel wild roads. They've shed their human skins, they think, and now they think they're animal enough to make the journey."

This bewildered Kettie further. "But the upright ones can't use the highways."

They watched in silence for a while.

"Perhaps," said Vinegar Tom, "they're on heat and this is a mating rite."

"Oh, you," said Kettie.

The humans were slowing down now. The farmer's wife had collapsed puffing onto the grass, her face red and shiny with unwonted exercise. The dungboy was warding his head confusedly from some unseen attacker; while the kitchenmaid and

303

her master had taken to coupling, oblivious of the thistle patch in which they lay.

"*I told you so,*" *said Vinegar Tom.*

Suddenly, there was a great commotion. A crowd of fully clothed people burst into the field, shrieking, "Witches!" They laid about the bemused revelers with cudgels. Failing to detect the menace in the air, the dungboy laughed and wiped his nose.

The two cats looked on. "Let's go now," begged Kettie.

"*They won't climb up here, Kettie," said Vinegar Tom. "We're safer here."*

But the little tortoiseshell was already climbing warily down the oak. Belly low, she slunk through the long grass at the edge of the field and trotted swiftly out into the lane. Straight into the waiting arms of a man in black.

Poor Kettie! She was grasped firmly by the scruff and waved above his head so that her paws swung wildly in the air and her mouth opened in terrified protest. "Behold the fiend!" the man shouted, as the farm folk were herded out into the lane. "See here the demon they summoned during their evil rites: a vile, sneaking feline which insinuates itself into the world to promote fornication and madness." And with his free hand he touched himself four times: forehead, belly, and twice upon the chest.

Kettie squirmed.

Vinegar Tom trembled on his branch, afraid to show himself.

"*Know ye the face of the Devil himself! This is the very creature worshiped by the ancient pagans, which came into being when Satan tried to ape our Lord God's creative powers. This—" Kettie howled as his fingers dug deeper "—is all that Satan's will could spawn. It owes even the fur that conceals its nakedness to the gentle pity of St. Peter himself: for when that saint saw the mewling creature Lucifer had conjured, shivering in the Lord's world, he made for it a fit covering. But though the hand of St. Peter has touched its outward body, still its soul belongs to its master, whose bidding it does when conjured by such dangerous fools as these." He gestured wildly at the prisoners.*

The disoriented farm folk tried to cover their nakedness from chill morning and prurient eye.

An old woman ran forward, finger outstretched at the cowering kitchenmaid. "I saw her leap in at my son-in-law's window when he lay a-bed; and when I looked in on him next his spirit had departed." She looked around at her neighbors. "His body were covered in boils," she said. "It's true!"

The growing crowd muttered. A neighboring farmer pushed his way forward. "Six of my herd lie swollen and rotting. Cats have sucked on their teats and infected them with the Devil's taint."

After that, everyone started shouting.

"I've been wracked by terrible dreams—"

"My babby perished in the cot. The cat got its breath."

"A man climbed into my room last week and forced himself upon me. He bit my paps, he were in such a frenzy. When he were done he leapt from me in the form of a great black cat. I've the scratches to prove it!"

"Such bad dreams—"

"Burn them!"

This cry came initially from somewhere at the back of the crowd but was soon taken up by all. "Burn the witches and their foul imp!"

"Jesus himself wouldn't know where to turn from such dreams—"

"Burn the cats wherever you find them!"

The next day a vast bonfire was made in the town square. Eight stakes stood upon it: one for the old farmer and his wife and two for their daughters; one for the dungboy; one for the milkmaid; one for the cowherd and two for the serving maids, barely sixteen and wetting themselves like children.

People gathered from far and wide, crying damnation down upon their erstwhile friends and neighbors, for fear that they themselves would be accused. And as the man in the long black robe flourished the silver cross on the chain around his neck and proclaimed that the scourging flames would sanctify the souls of the nine humans they burned alive that day, Vinegar Tom bore silent witness from the bell tower of the church.

He watched, too, as they brought in the cats: cats from farms that earned their keep freeing the barns and foodstores of vermin; cats from homes where children petted them; cats from the streets, who did a service no one understood.

Cats—black-and-white, ginger, and tortoiseshell; striped and spotted and tabby—were flung, shrieking in terror, onto the fire. He watched as flesh and fur caught light. He heard them perish, his friends, his enemies, his family, and little Kettie who never did a moment's harm in the six sweet months of her life.

He watched as the fire sent their souls down the wild roads to the Great Cat. He watched the clouds of smoke that billowed into the air to coat the nearby buildings with a squalid film of blackened, liquid fat.

He watched, and then he ran.

Down the stairs from the bell tower, swift and silent, through the deserted streets away from the square—visions of horror in his head, his ears full of cries. He ran away and left his Kettie, and he carried the news far and wide, and behind him fires sprang up from town to town.

They drove the Felidae to the edge of extinction in those days.

Vinegar Tom escaped the slaughter, and carried the news, and died quietly at his proper time in the roots of a beech tree two hundred miles from his home.

Though he witnessed the death of his Kettie, he wasn't there to witness the Festival of St. John, held every summer in town squares the length and breadth of the civilized world, in which the upright ones burned alive hundreds of thousands of cats on iron grates in the name of their religion.

Nor was he there to watch the creeping tide of plague that rode the backs of the rats those cats would have eaten, had they lived . . .

Chapter Sixteen

CY FOR CYBER

Contemporary physics is based on
concepts somewhat analogous to the
smile of the absent cat.
— ALBERT EINSTEIN

*W*hen Tag woke up and saw the Alchemist's cats swirling across the dim lawn toward him, he quickly woke Mousebreath and Loves a Dustbin.

The conservatory was furnished with a scrubbed deal table and a stack of cardboard boxes. There were some well-kept but dusty gardening tools, and one or two terra-cotta tubs packed with hardened dirt. The trunk of an old vine made its way out of one of these tubs, up the back wall, and across the glass roof. It was contorted and muscular, dead-looking but of a rich gold color in the moonlight that broke between the high quick clouds.

Easy enough for the two cats to climb the vine and make their way out through broken panes onto the roof of the conservatory.

Not so easy for the fox.

Instead, he skulked quietly among the cardboard boxes, his yellow eyes turned away from the room so they didn't pick up the moonlight. All he could do was wait.

Motionless on the glass roof, Tag stared down at the alchemical cats.

They flowed backward and forward along the base of the conservatory like water up and down a trough. On every pass one or another of them would jump up silently and look inside. Then they found the hole and poured through it. Once inside, they nosed about perplexedly. They stared up at the vine. Encumbered by their experimental limbs and add-on senses, they knocked over a garden fork. Instead of running away from the noise like proper cats, they just stared owlishly as the fork

307

bounced and rang on the concrete floor. Their acid, unfeline odors wafted up through the broken panes.

Though they hadn't found him yet, they were all around the fox, raising their heads to sniff, nosing about in the cardboard boxes. He bore them patiently for a minute. Then a spasm of disgust made his lips peel back. Canine teeth glittered in the moonlight. There was an explosion of snarling and barking, boxes tumbled one way and another, and the fox shot out of his hiding place and fell down. He got up with an effort and began to drag himself across the conservatory floor. Half a dozen cats were fastened onto his face. They had jumped on his grin. They were silent. Their eyes were like mirrors. Every so often one of them shifted its grip.

Tag was so appalled he couldn't move.

"They're pulling him down!"

"Come on!" said Mousebreath, and gave Tag a rough shove. "We can't just let him die."

Surprise wasn't the issue now. They ran down the vine stem, yowling and spitting and making as much noise as they could. Distracted, the alchemical cats looked up from their victim. He threw them off and laid about him with the same white teeth that had given him away. He was like a dog with rats. A quick dart forward, a snap of jaws, one quick shake of the victim before he tossed it over his back and passed on to the next.

Mousebreath was impressed. "Stuffing hell," he said. Prudently, he remained out of reach, four or five feet up the vine. "Look at that."

Tag had let the rush of adrenaline carry him all the way to the floor. Now he found himself backed into a corner by two Sphinxes and a large silent yellow tom whose smell was almost as frightening as his mouth. The Sphinxes regarded Tag steadily, almost curiously, pulses flickering and racing in the webby blue veins under their bald, folded skin. The tom's mouth had been wired open on an experimental denture. They were a team. He was blind, but they had eyes like fishbowls.

"Mousebreath," said Tag.

"What?"

"Would you mind fighting and not just watching?"

"Oh, yes," said Mousebreath absentmindedly. He leapt down. "Didn't I know you once?" he asked the tom. But it was the Sphinxes who answered, in unison. "You'll know us now," they said.

Behind them, the fox could be seen running around and around in a tight circle, trying to throw off the single cat that remained fastened to his face. The rest of the intruders had left him to it and were quietly packing the corner in support of the yellow tom, who now gargled at Mousebreath round his new teeth, "You know me. I'm the king!"

At that moment, Cy walked into the conservatory. Motes began to pour out of her eyes like grayish-yellow snow and drift about the room. Wherever they touched one of the alchemical cats, it stopped what it was doing. One or two of them wandered aimlessly off until they were halted by a wall or some other object that claimed their attention. The rest sat down suddenly and stared at the tabby. Soon, she was surrounded.

"Now listen to me, boys," she began.

Suddenly, she seemed to lose control of her head, which shook itself rapidly from side to side. She said, *"Brrraugh!"* She reached down suddenly and bit one of her own front legs. "No. Gar. I— Quick, Silver!" Bits of white foam appeared at the corners of her mouth. She whimpered. "Quicksilver, I—" A few more motes issued, slow and stale-looking, from her eyes. She blinked and fell on her face. "Go home, boys," she said tiredly. "This ain't the way we do things in *Gunsmoke*." At this, the Alchemist's cats stood up, gathered themselves, and— whirling around her unconscious form like cornstalks in a hot summer wind—poured out of the conservatory.

Tag ran after them, nipping at back legs.

"Let them go," said the fox. "They won't bother us again tonight."

Even so, they sat up until dawn.

Tag and Mousebreath talked. The fox inspected his new injuries. The tabby remained unconscious where she had fallen, sprawled on the sour concrete floor like a road accident, her eyes disconcertingly open, her mouth open, too, in a quiet gape of astonishment. She wasn't dead, but she had about her a feel of distant travel. Mousebreath huddled up to her on one side, Tag on the other, as if their warmth might sustain her wherever she was now. Occasionally, one or the other of them tried to groom her. Puzzled and, in the end, unsure what had happened, Tag asked, "How did she bring them here? And what for—"

"Don't ask me."

"—if not to kill us?"

"All I know is that it weren't her fault."

This was so palpably untrue Tag couldn't think of a reply. The fox looked up from his bruises and bites. Before he could speak, Mousebreath had added quickly, "She can't help herself. She could never help herself."

"She is a proxy of the Alchemist," the fox explained to Tag. "What she does—the thing with the lights—is a kind of magic. We're at risk now every minute she remains—" he paused "—with us," he finished, although clearly he had planned to say something else.

"But the cats—" began Tag.

Mousebreath intervened. "We're not leaving her," he told the fox.

The fox ignored him. "The cats were a scouting party," he said. "Now the Alchemist knows where to find us, they'll stay close. They'll never harm us badly—only enough to remind us of our plight—but they'll follow us down the wild roads forever. Or until we meet the King and Queen."

Mousebreath said, "We're not leaving her. She's not to blame for the thing in her head."

"Blame's not the issue," said the fox. "She's a proxy. I believe he can see through her eyes. He was watching us at Piper's Quay. He knew the Queen was there. I would never forgive myself if he found her again that way." He was quiet for a moment. Then he added, "Majicou would never forgive me, either."

Mousebreath said, "The Queen's not here."

"But she'll be at Tintagel," said the fox. "Do you want to lead him there?"

"Tintagel," said Mousebreath scornfully.

"I'm trying to talk to Tag," the fox said.

"Talk to me," said Mousebreath.

"Shut up, Mousebreath," ordered Tag. Then he told the fox, "Cy's been with us all along. We look after her. If you can't agree to that, too bad. But there's something else. Majicou always knew about this. I think he wants us to keep her." The fox tried to interrupt, but Tag wouldn't let him. "I can't see why, either," he admitted. "But it will be my responsibility if this turns out to be a mistake. Not yours."

"And who are you to take responsibility?"

Tag looked as directly as he could into the fox's yellow eyes. "I'm Majicou's apprentice," he said.

Loves a Dustbin shrugged and turned away. "You are indeed," he was forced to agree. "We should stay off the highway," he added. "That will make things harder for them."

So they walked.

It was a slower way to travel, but Tag rather enjoyed the change. It was important to get the fox well and to decide what to do with Cy. Her internal weather raged. Bouts of delirium alternated with a kind of unconscious panic in which, rigid as a length of wood, she would cry out, "It's all white tiles, Jack! It's all white! Oh! No wires! Not the wires!" If you looked into her eyes during these episodes, Mousebreath claimed, whatever she was seeing left you in terror too. But for the most part she remained unconscious. They took turns to carry her, and this time the fox helped too. She was heavy and inert. They walked mainly in the dark, a few miles at a time, heading west on their natural compass, resting up at dawn.

Mousebreath fed them.

He had discovered a talent for fishing that he demonstrated one morning by taking ounce-roach out of a deep little stream under some willows. He looked awkward, leaning precariously out from the muddy bank, up to his armpit in water. But his blunt, cobby paws were quick and surprisingly deft. He seemed to hypnotize the fish with them before he struck. Then—flip!—there was an arc of living, wriggling silver in the air, almost as if the water itself had turned into food.

"Learnt it on goalfish—" he explained. Whenever he talked to the fox he thickened his accent until no one could follow what he said. "—in a garen ponged."

"Ponged?" said the fox.

"Yeah. *You* know. Farntin and all. Ponged in a lorn. Goalfish. Very tasty."

"These taste of mud," said the fox.

"Don't eatem then," advised Mousebreath gently. "More for us." He added quietly, "Ponce."

But he must have regretted this, because a few minutes later, when he thought Tag was asleep, he strolled over to where the fox was sitting glumly in some wet grass, eyeing the dinner he didn't know how to eat. They sat there for a minute refusing to acknowledge each other, and they really looked rather alike—the battered old feral, odd-eyed survivor of a thousand turf wars and the dustbin fox with his bony undependable grin and patches of bare black hide. After a moment, Mousebreath rummaged about in the slime and innards of the half-chewed roach. "Darn eat this," he suggested, as if he were teaching a kitten. "See? Or this. Try the rest. Go on."

"This?"

"Go on, try it!"

Tag listened for a moment or two, then curled up tighter and went to sleep. It was a bitter morning, but he felt warm for a change.

The fox did well. His injuries healed, though he still limped, especially at the end of the day. He got on better with Mousebreath. But he never felt less than uncomfortable in this traditional habitat of foxes, where fields were muddy, nights were frosty, food ran away from him, and journeys were long.

One evening, they rested on a tall hill before their night's march. On three sides, mile after mile of farmland spread away into the shadow of the rolling westward hills, above which a long winter sunset streaked the eggshell sky with layers of thick red, dirty orange, and gently fluorescent green. On the fourth side, immediately below, sprawled a town. Streetlights and shop lights switched themselves on in groups as the animals watched. The lights of houses sprang on only to be dimmed immediately as curtains were drawn. The air darkened imperceptibly; the streets were revealed as a great lacy wing of light under the dulling smoky colors of the sunset. Tag, who had been carrying Cy, put her tenderly down. He licked the top of her head. Today she smelled of mint; tomorrow it would be an old bus shelter in the rain. For a long time none of the animals spoke.

"Lot of people in the world," said the fox at last. "Aren't there? Do you know what I miss most when I think about the city?"

"What?" Tag asked.

"I miss the lights."

"I know what you mean," Tag said. "The streetlamps, the neon, the great advertisements flashing up against the night . . ."

The fox stared carefully at Tag for a moment, as if he thought Tag were mad.

"I miss the *traffic lights*," he said.

"Oh."

"How else do you know when to cross a road?"

"Ah."

There was a long pause. Then Mousebreath gave a slow, rich chuckle.

"Had you there," he said to Tag.

The animals continued to stare. Three counties were visible. Moor, pasture, long gently rolling slopes of plowland, black copses and hedges, misty distances out of which stood a single farm or a hawthorn tree, and above it all that strange sunset, which had evolved strong delicate greens and a blue-gold afterglow high up. In deep black silhouette, Loves a Dustbin curled himself down and around so that he could first lick the base of his tail, then scratch vigorously under his chin with one back leg. He shook himself. Tag, full of a sudden happiness, saw the tawny hairs fly up in the last of the light. A strong smell of fox filled the cool still air. "Yes," said Loves a Dustbin, after a pause. "I miss those lights."

"Had you there all right," said Mousebreath. "Got you dead to rights there."

On the Ridgeway, though the snow had melted, the weather was still wintry and undependable. Tag would have avoided it for that reason if no other. He felt safer in the lanes, where it was warmer and easier to hide. Eventually, though, sick of being balked by the rivers in the winding valley bottoms, he led his party above the spring line again.

At midnight the moon was a slippery illumination behind tissues of high white cloud. An hour later, the wind was still light, flirting either side of west, never quite in their faces. The air remained dry and a degree above freezing. But by two in the morning the wind had veered north and become squally. Periods of harsh moonlight—in which the shadows shifted and jumped, razoring the nerves of the two cats and putting the fox into a poor temper—now alternated with heavy cloud. The air was damp and raw and full of electricity. Suddenly, from the north, came the first growl of thunder.

The fox sniffed the air.

"Not good! Not good!" he told himself. He hung out his tongue—as if he could taste the danger—and panted. "We should go down!" he advised Tag. He hated the ridge anyway. "It's like walking in front of an audience!"

"Make your play, partner," said Cy indistinctly from Tag's mouth. She laughed.

Tag put her down and examined her.

Nothing.

He looked around.

The Ridgeway had turned south. Further along, he could see the path descending between earth banks and straggling, wind-eroded hedges. Here, though, they were seven hundred feet up on the bare ridge. There was nothing but sky between them and the next county.

He opened his mouth to reassure the fox, "We'll take shelter as soon as we can." But before he could close it again the moon went out like a popped lightbulb and the storm roared up from the slopes under the summit as if it had lain in ambush for them there all along. Black water filled the air. With a long, tearing hiss and a hot bang, the world lit up white. Sparks fizzed and splattered. Something picked Tag up and dropped him four yards away among stones. As he got shakily to his feet, he saw the unconscious tabby bowling past like a wet rag mop. The fox was struggling after her, his body canted at a strange angle to the wind.

"We've got to go down!"

"I can't hear you!"

"We've got to go down!"

"I can't hear you! We must go down!"

"I said, We've got to go down!"

For a minute or two they could only run aimlessly about in terror of the lightning, crouching and ducking and trying to slink away under the thin cover of tangled couch and thistle. Then Mousebreath narrowed his eyes. He set his scarred face into the storm. "Come on!" he said, and began to shoulder his way down the hill. Tucked in behind him câme the fox, with Cy dangling from his jaws. Tag followed, hindquarters close to the ground. Their eyes were wide and scared. But Mousebreath leaned into the wind and broke a trail for them like some great old horse, until, five hundred yards on and fifty yards north of the track, a bleak earth prominence came into sight.

In the constant flicker of the lightning, white chalk paths made their way around a ring of eroded stones, itself surrounded by tall beech trees in a circle. Rain hissed off the ancient structure that could be seen within: more stones, tumbled about, a long grassy mound with a dark and massively linteled doorway about the height of a human child. Tag and the fox stood nervously outside the ring of beeches in the raw wind while Mousebreath jumped up on a section of drystone wall between two pillars.

"It seems to go straight down into the ground," he said. "But I can't quite see—" He had a closer look. "It's not my idea of home," he reported.

But Tag said, "It's what we've got."

The fox shuddered. "I won't go in," he said. "My death awaits me there."

"No it doesn't," Tag told him. "Your death awaits you out here."

Mousebreath laughed. He seemed to be enjoying himself. "He got you there," he told the fox, "and no mistake. Now, will you bring Cy," he asked Tag, "or shall I? And who's going first?"

"You are."

They left Cy and the fox sheltering among the contorted roots of a beech tree, and entered the ring of stones. Cold, musty air came up out of the mound like ancient breath to meet them. Mousebreath stuck his head across the threshold— chalk, compacted by a million human feet, slimy and puddled and scattered with flints—and entered an inch at a time, while Tag stood by uncomfortably in the flare and bang of the storm. Rain dripped from the lintel onto them both.

Mousebreath vanished. There was a silence. Then he said, "Seems all right. A bit dank." He wasn't far inside, but his voice already sounded distant and echoey. "I'll just go a bit farther—"

"Be careful," Tag reminded him.

"It does go down," Mousebreath said. "Wait, I can see something—" His voice changed. "Out!" he called. "Something's in here! Let me out!"

Too late.

There was a noise like the wind gathering itself across miles of moorland before it bursts upon a lonely village. A long pulse of bitter white light poured out of the mound, projecting Mousebreath's shadow across the ring of beeches *and onto the clouds in the sky beyond*. Then it picked him up and—with the soft contemptuous "pah!" of expelled breath— hurled him backward, his limbs extended rigidly and every hair of his coat raised as if he had been electrocuted.

Tag ran away. Then he ran back again and stared into the mound.

"Struck!" he shouted. "We've been struck!"

But he saw immediately that they hadn't.

Lightning comes and goes in an instant. This light took forever, passing from station to station of the spectrum until it was the color of old blood, and only then winking out. Tag trembled. Something had *arrived* in the mound. Silhouetted by the dying light in the doorway in front of him, as black and massy as any of the sarsen stones in the rain, was the figure of an animal. It sat alertly, head raised and proud. It was five feet tall.

It was laughing at him.

"Hello, little cat," it said.

It opened its mouth. Roared. Dwindled, and became Majicou.

The storm raged on. Cloud boiled over the ridge. With every flash of lightning, the trunks of the beech trees seemed to glitter and shift. Raindrops danced and splashed like fish in the standing puddles between the root systems, among which Tag and Majicou found Mousebreath. He was half conscious, muttering indistinctly to himself. Majicou picked him up and carried him into the mound. Once recovered, he seemed pleased with his adventure.

"Look at that!" he kept boasting. "Not a mark on me! Eh? Not a mark!"

Tag was impressed. But Majicou only said, "You were lucky." By way of explanation, he added, "A small highway emerges here. When I arrived, some of its energy found a way out of the chamber."

This must have seemed like an understatement to Mouse-breath, who responded, "Well, we could do with some fire here!"

"You couldn't do with *this* fire," Loves a Dustbin assured him. "A little more and you would have died of it."

Mousebreath was right, though. It wasn't much warmer inside the mound than out, or much drier. Air circulated in the largest of the three chambers they had found; but the other two were as musty as caves, their walls velvet with damp. In all three, human visitors had left tributes of flowers. Some they had placed carefully in little vases; most were wilting on the worn earth floor. Among these curious out-of-season garlands— bright red, blue, and yellow—Cy lay with her eyes filmed and her mouth open. Majicou paced the chamber, his tail lashing, while the fox hung out his tongue and with tawny eyes followed his master's every movement. Tag watched them all and shivered, but not with cold. This was his life now.

"What was that?" he demanded. "I thought we'd been struck! What was that fire, Majicou?"

But the black cat wouldn't answer. He took the fox to the other end of the chamber, where they were soon deep in talk.

Tag felt left out. "What a laugh!" he said loudly to Mousebreath. "Eh, Mousebreath? I thought you'd had it then!" Mousebreath was dozing, though, and only chuckled. Tag went and sat as far away from Majicou and Loves a Dustbin as he could. Curling his front paws up under him and his tail around him, he stared hard at the seeping wall. He was so tired he fell asleep immediately.

At that point, the tabby had not stirred.

Snatches of talk wove themselves through Tag's dreams as Majicou and the fox argued away the rest of the night, their voices heavy with anxiety.

"No way forward."

"But if we—"

"Impossible!" And then, "All avenues closed, the highways undependable and dangerous."

"You cannot know that!"

"Danger—"

"You are at risk every minute you remain away from Cutting Lane!"

"Did he always know more than we assumed?"

"Danger."

"In a froth of fire, highways cracking like whips. My death awaits me there—"

"*Danger!*"

There was a lot of this. Drifting in and out of sleep, Tag seemed to miss the crux of every sentence. Then he heard Cy's name, and a little later the fox exclaimed, "But she is a proxy, Majicou!"

"Even so."

"But, Majicou—"

"You do not know everything."

"Then it won't be my fault if everything goes to ruin!" returned the fox angrily.

"Sleep now," Majicou told him. "You have a long way to go in the morning."

"Majicou—"

"Sleep now."

Tag was never quite sure which of Majicou's eyes was the sighted one. It was no ordinary eye. It had the prismatic quality of the bar of light you see on the bevel of a mirror. He knew that. But whether it was the right or the left eye he had never been able to decide. He woke an hour before dawn, determined to find out. Everyone else was asleep. He could hear the fox's restive yips and moans; Mousebreath's catarrhal snores; the deep, even breath of Majicou. He crept across to the old cat and stood looking down at him. Both eyes were closed, and nothing was revealed. Even in sleep, Majicou's face looked tired and anxious. Even in sleep, it kept his secrets.

I'll probably never know, thought Tag.

Just then the eye opened and stared at him. Tag jumped back in alarm. When nothing happened, he came close again and leaned over. Was the eye aware? Was Majicou awake? He gave no sign of it. Slowly, the eye closed. Tag crept guiltily away. He had got as far as the center of the chamber when Majicou said clearly, "Come back, Tag."

"I'm sorry," said Tag. "I couldn't sleep."

Majicou sighed. "Why not?" he said gently.

Tag looked around the chamber, then at Majicou. His mentor's eye blinked back at him. Tag couldn't admit that he was jealous of the fox or that curiosity had got the better of him. So he said, "This is such an old place."

Majicou lashed his tail contemptuously.

"Nothing human beings have built is old. The world is old. *Cats* are old." He brooded on that. "Constructed things were new in Egypt, perhaps a little before. By then, cats were already ancient." He gazed into the shadows, as if he could see them there, those ancient cats—the pale sandy cats of the desert, the sleek domestic cats of the Lower Nile: small gods. The cats of Egypt! "They slept by the water without fear," he went on eventually in a low, wondering voice, "and at dawn watched the pelicans rise pink-breasted in the new light. In the afternoon their mouths were full of the soft white doves of the Nile. At dusk they looked about them. They heard the hyenas bark from the night villages. Moonlight had entered their eyes forever."

He seemed to shiver and come back to himself.

"Human beings? We know their dreams. Feeble and self-defeating. Look around you in the world, Tag. What do you see? Time for a new dream; time for an old dream. Human beings have done enough dreaming for now."

"Am I still your apprentice, Majicou?"

"Go back to sleep."

Tag could do nothing else. He returned to his corner and curled up. Which eye had it been? He had forgotten again. Just as he was dropping off, an amused voice advised him, "You are not quite ready to see as I see."

A little time later, the tabby woke.

Delighted by the flowers, she sat for some minutes among them and washed her face like any cat, dreamily licking her paws and wiping her ears.

During this process she touched the plug in her head. A little tremor went through her. It was as if she had woken up again. This time she was more alert. She stopped washing, one paw held up. She raised her head. She seemed to listen. Her gaze went from one sleeping form to the next: Mousebreath, Tag, Loves a Dustbin—on whom she dwelt a moment, as if trying to remember something. When she came to Majicou, her mouth gaped open and a few pale motes trickled out of it to fill the chamber with a faint sticky radiance.

She shook herself and closed her mouth. She washed again, attending busily to the fur beneath her chin with long, awkward movements of her tongue.

* * *

When Tag woke the next morning, the first thing he heard was a purr like a broken lawn mower. The first thing he felt was Cy, rubbing her face against his to mark him. "Mine. My cat." She smelled of thyme and old damp carpet, and her eyes were full of impudence.

"Hi, Silver," she said. "I'm Cy! Cy for Cyber." She wriggled. "*You* know me. I'm the Bakelite Baby! I sit on your sideboard, I sleep in your seasons, I dance in your hat!" She assumed a listening attitude. "Tango Delta callin'! Wow! How nice!" She licked his face until he spluttered. She said, "I miss you when I'm not here. I do!"

"Get off," said Tag. Then, surprised, "You're clean!"

"Yes," she admitted proudly, "I am."

She caught sight of Majicou. "Wow!" she said. "A *highway* cat, with nerves of steel! I must see this!" And she rushed off to examine him, pausing only to glare resentfully at her back legs, which had begun making decisions of their own. The old cat looked down. The tabby stared up. Mismatched as to size and intellect—but not, perhaps, loudness of purr—they regarded one another companionably.

"I'm broken!" boasted Cy.

"So?" said Majicou. "Soon you'll be fixed again. What a life you'll have then!"

"This is madness," said the fox to Tag.

He had that minute come in from the rain.

"Things have gone badly for me," admitted Majicou a little later.

Mid-morning in the main chamber. Outside, the wind still whistled under a low cloud base. Complex weather fronts, one overlapping the next, had raced south all night to lower the temperature and bring hail where there had been rain. Thunder growled somewhere at the edge of it all, waiting to make a comeback. Distant lightning lit the chamber, where shifting gradients of humidity caused the withered flowers to give off ghostly odors of spring. The old cat's voice echoed a little in the cold air.

"While I waited all that time for my apprentice to be sent to me, the Alchemist was pursuing his ends. It was ever thus: Hobbe broods, his master acts. Now Hobbe's old master has knotted the wild roads until they bulge like broken veins."

Tag, Cy, and Loves a Dustbin sat listening on the drafty floor. Mousebreath, who had elected to keep watch, could be heard shifting about uncomfortably in the mound entrance, fluffing himself up as he watched the hailstones jump like grasshoppers in the sodden beech mast and winter-bleached grasses. Meltwater dripped on him from the lintel. Every line of his body was as gloomy as the day.

Majicou continued. "They wince from his approach. They become undependable. All their ghosts spill out and are lost. Ghosts that writhe and call—Oh yes, Tag, I hear them: the million voices of the dead, the rising wail of panic on the night!—then dissipate like smoke while the *vagus* and worse make free of the Old Changing Way. Meanwhile, I have no knowledge of the King and Queen. Where are they? I don't know. I hear nothing from the magpie. I sit by night at Cutting Lane and hear nothing from anyone.

"All is chaos," he concluded. "I have only one throw left." He looked up. "I must take the highway to Tintagel and hope that Pertelot and Ragnar will have made their own way there."

The fox got to his feet. He said heavily, "Majicou, you're mad to do this."

He went to the door, sat down next to Mousebreath, and stared out.

"Funny old day," they heard Mousebreath murmur.

"I know the arguments," Majicou called. "I listened to them all night."

"Majicou, you didn't listen to a word."

There was a silence in the chamber. A draft stirred, then scattered the dried flowers. The tabby chased after them with the wobbling, bandy-legged gait and short jumps of a kitten, tumbling over her own feet. That left Majicou with Tag. The old cat sighed. "I'm not keeping my audience today," he admitted. "Tag, the job of apprentice is still open. But you have to agree with everything I say."

"Will you tell me something, Majicou?"

"Who else have I got to talk to?"

"You came here on a highway, but I can't see it."

"Then you shall see it now."

He led Tag into the smallest of the three chambers, which smelled strongly of chalk earth. Its walls were white with crystals of niter, streaked black where groundwater had run down through the mound above. The air here was so damp it dulled their voices when they spoke.

"Look carefully," said Majicou.

Tag looked. A twist of air glimmered in the angle between two walls. It was the color of watered milk, and it seemed to turn and shift like an insect's wing dangling from a rag of spiderweb in the corner of a window frame—memory of a frozen struggle, unwelcome reminder of time passing. Yet at its heart something danced as gaily as spring morning sun in a drop of water!

"Approach with caution," said Majicou, "and tell me what you see."

"A light! The outside!"

"But not the outside of this place," said Majicou.

"Majicou, look at the light!"

"You and I will use this entrance when the time comes, along with Mousebreath and Cy."

"And the fox," said Tag.

Majicou regarded him.

"Mousebreath, Cy, and the fox," said Tag.

"The fox has other errands," Majicou told him grimly. "He must take a different road."

"I see."

Back in the main chamber, Loves a Dustbin was waiting for them.

"Majicou," he said, "I hate this. You know that he is watching you even now, through—" he indicated Cy, who was still jumping about among the flowers "—that *thing*. It will tell him every step you take."

"And yet we must be there," said Majicou simply.

When the fox only stared at him, yellow eyes full of impatience and love, he added, "She is a cat, not a thing. Look, she's playing. Beyond that, she has no idea what she is. Do you want me to abandon her just to save myself?" He laughed. "I'll live!" he said. "You know I will!" Something in the fox's expression made him look away. "Take heart, Loves a Dustbin," he said softly. "You can't be everywhere at once."

The fox sighed. "Then I'd better leave now, Majicou," he said.

The cats assembled outside the mound in the falling sleet to watch him go. He wished them all good-bye, even the tabby, who said, "You smell!" and wouldn't look at him. When he came to Mousebreath, he caught the feral's orange eye and inquired, "Is there any business unfinished between us?"

Mousebreath considered. "I don't think there is," he said, "mate."

"Good," said the fox.

"Just don't forget howter eat fish."

The fox chuckled. "How could I?"

He turned to Tag. "Well then, Tag. Don't look so sad!"

But Tag remembered how the fox in his pain had stared out of the rain-slashed conservatory windows, whispering bleakly, "I never saw it, but it follows me still. I don't think it is a *vagus*. I think it is my death."

He wanted to say, Oh, Loves a Dustbin, will we ever see you again? He wanted to say, Don't go! But all that came out was "Good-bye."

"Good-bye, little cat. Take care of your friends. Remember who you are. And you too, Majicou: take care!"

It looked as if he wanted to say more. But he turned abruptly, made his foxy way over the drystone wall and between the beech trees, and vanished from view. Soon they saw him two or three hundred yards off, quartering the ridge. He was limping a little, trotting three-leggedly about, nose to the ground among the thistles. At that distance he looked rather small, and his russet coat was already blackened with melted sleet. Then he seemed to catch a scent. His ears pricked up. He looked back. "Come safe to Tintagel, Majicou!" they heard him bark. Then he sprang forward like a greyhound. His brush streamed in the wind. His limp vanished. His coat turned from russet to shining red-gold. His body lengthened and blurred as it went, shedding strange, expanding rings of rainbow light, and suddenly he was no longer there.

The highway closed behind him with a faint popping noise.

Majicou led them back inside.

Tag went and stared hard into the corner of the smallest chamber. A few minutes later the old cat found him there, and asked him, "What do you see?"

"I'm not sure."

I see spring light! Light on water!

"What you see is not often what you find."

"Shall we go now, Majicou?"

"No," said Majicou. "The fox's errand couldn't wait. I sent him into some danger, Tag. A storm will make the wild roads difficult even at the best of times. We'll set off when the weather's changed."

"Ah."

So they waited. Mousebreath and the tabby huddled together, dozing in the cold. Majicou placed himself at the entrance of the chamber, narrowed his eye, and stared off down the Ridgeway, as if that way he might follow the fortunes of his fox.

After a while, unable to sleep, Tag asked him, "What have you liked best in your life?"

The old cat thought. "I can't remember," he said.

"I liked being a kitten best."

"Did you now? And what did that entail?"

"Food, mainly. And bubbles! Majicou, you must remember being a kitten!"

No answer but a laugh.

Tag tried to doze. It was hard.

"Majicou?"

"What?"

"Majicou, I heard you say, 'Hobbe broods: his master acts.' What did that mean?"

Majicou sighed. "That is the trouble with being a one-eyed cat," he complained. "The apprentice won't let you sleep." But he relented finally, and told Tag the story he called "The Seventh Life of Cats."

The Seventh Life of Cats

*W*oolsthorpe-by-Colsterworth, the upright ones called it. A pretty rural hamlet in the back end of nowhere. No sign there among the warm barns in which we slept and played of the horror to come.

I recall highways full of autumn sunshine, the scent of hay and apples and bowls of warm milk. Harvest suppers when the dogs were tied up and the house was thrown open to the cats. No witch-hunts in this pleasant place, where folk understood the value of a good mouser. Thus was I born into my seventh life; though some months were to pass before I met the author of the events I was born to witness and to attempt to divert.

I found that author in one of the outhouses. At that time it was little more than a boy, a silent lad with clever hands. It was always occupied with something to interest a kitten: bits of string, wood shavings, lenses and mirrors that threw a dancing light upon the walls.

You might think that by now I would be more wary of the upright ones, but it is never so simple. At the beginning of a life, my past returns to me in undependable flashes, darts, dreams, patterns like light upon a wall. One minute a kitten chases the dust motes in a sunbeam; next, the Majicou, burdened by the weight of what he knows, confronts the wry harmonies of the world. I was once a cat like you.

I was drawn to it, the boy with the clever hands. I followed it around. It named me Hobbe. It made for me an ingenious door-within-the-door that allowed me to pass at will between house and kitchen garden. It scratched the spot beneath my *chin I could not lick. It watched as I stalked the mice in the barn. I used the little highways that crosshatched the barn-yard. I heard it murmur, "Empty space cannot only be filled by material substance, but also by spiritual substance."*

It shone a light into my eyes, and while I blinked and shied away, it wrote in a book. "What a wonderful work is a cat! The ancients were wise before their time."

Wisdom has its own time.

It jabbed my paws with an instrument. I had a piece of meat for my pains, but became shier of its rooms.

It said, "The aether is surely created by the animal spirit, the workings of brains such as these, the mystical firing of each nerve. Are not rays of light very small bodies emitted from shining substances?"

It walked briskly around the room, wringing its hands.

It said, "Surely this is the true matter of the world, the fine aether that affords and carries out into the atmosphere the so-lary fuel and material principle of light that feeds the very stars and planets!"

In the spring of that year it packed its belongings—books, pots, devices, vials, and Hobbe—into a horse-drawn cart. The journey was interminable. In the city, among the roil of foot and horse traffic, the noise and the stench and the chaos, a million miles as it might be from the trees and cornfields of my home, I was to discover the true nature of my master's calling. And with that, the nature of my own great task.

We settled into our new quarters—a tiny house in the lanes with a tiny yard at the side leading to a foul-smelling jakes. Curiosity soon overcame my fear of the new smells and sounds; and once my master had cut my door-within-a-door I was able to patrol wall and alley or follow the tangle of high-ways down to the fetid, fertile river.

My master toiled. I watched the ghost cats skeining past to wharf and rooftop meeting place. I lazed in the city heat. Young cats should seek pleasure. They should seek experi-ence. I sought rats, which were numerous there, due to an un-explained scarcity of my own kind, and queens, who never complained. It was a pleasant way to idle away the hours be-

tween dusk and dawn. By day I slept before warm embers in the house.

All the rooms were open to me but one.

In there my master chanted, "Dissolve the volatile Green Lion in the cuprous salt to distill the animal spirit. The Blood of the Lion to be mixed with the powdered ashes, then fermented with the double white vitriol of Mercury and purified with saltpeter for the glorious Regulus that will unfold the Net!"

It complained, "The Egyptians had the art. Oh, that it is lost. Perhaps some magic remains in these ancient windings . . ."

And, "Oh, the stony serpents!" *it would cry.* "Lord, give me the Animal Stone, give me entrance to the mysteries of the natural world!"

None of which meant anything to me. However hard I tried to get into that room, I failed. When I looked through the keyhole, stretch up as I might, all I got was an angle of the ceiling, where colored lights played with no clue to their origin.

It was a hot summer that year, hot and humid. The flies swarmed over the river; the fish rotted before they could be landed at the market; the fleas multiplied on the rats.

"Plague!" was the cry that filled the air.

Soon you could hear them shrieking in the streets. Women and babies at the windows. Men mad with pain staggering down the road. They clutched the swellings in their armpits. They threw themselves from upper rooms or shot themselves in full sight of their neighbors. Many chose the river. Its fetid smell pervaded everything.

Meanwhile, the curious or criminal wandered the streets with their heads swathed in vinegar turbans and carrying nosegays of rue. Some watched the misery of others and failed to act. Some acted, and were sick next day. King Mob ran down the alleys, stealing whatever was left to steal, murdering without let.

Plague burned its way through lanes and alleys, single

*houses and entire streets, until a hundred thousand had per-
ished. Corpses were stacked on corpses in the great stinking
pits. A million rats swarmed across the common graves, and
only Felidae could keep them down.*

*Ordinances went up. No public gatherings. None to leave
the city. Cats to be slaughtered in case they carried the disease from house to house.*

*The building that backed onto my master's was a bakery. I
often sat upon its roof. The sun shone in the afternoon; sparrows came after the spoiled loaves the baker tossed out at the
end of the day. I was out there one evening, tired of the scenes
below, when the baker's cat approached me.*

*"They've appointed an Executioner of Cats," he said.
I stared at him.*

*"It's your master," he said. "The one they call the Alchemist."
"Rubbish."*

"He asked for the job."

"Why should I believe that?"

"And anyway, this is my roof."

*You can be sure I showed him where his error lay. But I
watched my master after that. I watched its comings and go-
ings. One night it fixed shutters across the windows and
closed up the door-within-a-door so that I could not leave the
house. Brimstone, rosin, and pitch burned in the hearth with
such a strong smoke that my eyes watered and I lost my sense
of smell. My master went into the scullery, filled its mouth
with garlic cloves until it gagged, and with a sack in its hand
made for the front door. I slipped out under its feet, leapt the
wall next door, and followed it down to the river. There, it
hired a boat and an oarsman. The moonlight glinted serenely
on the water. The boat diminished toward the opposite bank. I
dozed. I slept the night away and missed the boat's return.*

*That morning, I had to break into my own home. I went
straight to the door of the forbidden room and listened. Silence. Then a wail, a cry! Cats! Other cats in my house! I
veered between extremes of jealousy and rage, between in-
quisitiveness and desire, for not only was it the cry of cats I
heard . . .*

It was the cry of females.

For the next few days, they called in my dreams. The imagined musk of them drove me to a frenzy. In the forbidden room of my imagination, they lay rolling on their sides or waggling their delicious rumps in the air. They were waiting for me. And so I waited too, until my master—dawdling down the corridor absorbed in a book that spoke of Democritus, Homer, and the Adeptists, of al-chemeia *the Egyptian art: how a magical stone might make known the perfect nature of things—opened the forbidden door without looking down. In a flash I had scuttled in between its feet and was instantly crouched out of sight beneath a bench.*

Thus the world was changed by the curiosity of a cat.

There I sat. Everything smelt. Bottles and vials, crucibles and retorts. Chemicals, herbs, hot coals—and something else. Something smoldering in the hearth. It was fur. The fur of cats . . .

I looked for them, and I soon found them.

Every wall was shelved. Every shelf was stacked with books and papers, articles and instruments, untidy bundles of stale old cloth—parched yet dank and feeble with age—lenses and charts and weights and eyeballs in bottles. And below the shelves were the cages: cages full of cats. Cats of every size and age and color and shape you could imagine: tabby and tortoiseshell, silver and striped, tawny and black and orange and gray; kittens and queens; toms and thin, dry old fellows with fur scoured by mange—all thrown in together willy-nilly. And all of them were staring at me with misery drawn upon their faces, defeat and accusation in their eyes.

Every shameful thought fled me.

My master laid down its book. It opened the window to create a draft and stoked the fire, then set a pot to bubble fiercely upon the trivet. At first I thought it engaged upon making tea; but then it reached into a cage and extracted a skinny male, his brown legs pumping with the sudden strength of terror as he felt the steam from the pot scald his skin. The next moment he had been plunged into the boiling water and the air was split by a cry of the purest agony, out-rage, and desperation. It was an evil sound. I recalled then, in a flash, other lives, the cries of poor Kettie in the flames.

He wailed, that small cat, for the Great Cat's mercy, for his suffering to come swiftly to an end. He fought the cauldron, and at one point succeeded almost in clambering from it, and I saw for one terrible moment how livid was his skin, with the fur falling away in patches, his paws opening and closing in awful spasms as they clutched the rim. Then my master pressed him back into the pot with a silver stick, and all went quiet. An unearthly howl filled the chamber. It raised the hair all over my body and I found my own voice joining, in-voluntarily, with the lament. I watched as his lifeless body, dripping and pathetically scrawny, was hauled out of the pot. I watched as my master severed the head and burned it to ashes in a crucible. Acrid smoke filled the air, more caus-tic even than the unholy mixture burned in the hearth up-stairs that had made my eyes water. And now, through a veil of tears, I watched as it mixed the ashes to a paste—and ate them. Then it snuffed out all the lamps and stood before the mirror, examining its face with a candle flickering before its eyes.

"Grant me entrance to the wild roads," *it breathed.*

In that instant the knowledge and the power of my seven lives was distilled into burning rage. I knew then that my master was the worst of its kind, that I must save the Felidae from its madness.

There came a knock at the door.

"Be damned!"

"Please, sir, Mister Newton, 'tis a fellow from the Royal Society for Improving Natural Knowledge, come to ask you questions about your theory of gravity, sir . . ."

It was the maid. It did not like me, and I did not like it; but now I blessed it in the name of the Great Cat and prayed that it would take my master away.

And indeed away it went, cursing the failure of yet another experiment, and left me in the darkness.

The cages were not difficult to open.

Out they flooded, the cats of the city, caught by the Official Executioner, out into the room, across the floor, around the walls. Mad with unexpected freedom, they knocked everything from the shelves—pots and vials, papers, and musty old bundles of cloth. One of these bundles tumbled out in front of me and split apart, revealing what appeared at first sight to be a handful of old twigs. But when I bent my head to sniff at it, I saw clearly that it contained a tiny, well-preserved rib cage and spine covered with strips of leathery skin, four long bony legs, front paws crossed upon the chest, an exquisitely fragile skull resting on a broken vertebra, the eyes gone and the mouth drawn into a rictus; and I leapt away, for the power that shimmered from it was ancient and fine.

The chamber was now ablaze. Volatile chemicals crackled and sputtered. Papers and books and mummified remains added fuel to the conflagration. The cats were escaping through the open window, an arcing spectrum of furry color, and I lost no time in joining them. As I leapt upon the next-door roof of Thomas Faryner, the baker, I stared back at my erstwhile home. Flames were gouting out of the basement window—orange and green and blue—flames of deeply unnatural hues. Explosions within sent great billows of smoke out of the window, and then its thick panes shattered with a clang like a broken bell. The bakery, too, had caught light—so much dry timber in such close proximity, so few able-bodied humans to fight the flames.

Chapter Seventeen

IN THE EYE OF THE WIND

If a fish is the movement of water embodied,
given shape, then a cat is a diagram and
pattern of subtle air.
— DORIS LESSING

Gusts of wind exploded into the *Guillemot*'s loose canvas as she heeled and swung at anchor. Rain fell steadily in huge silver drops that penetrated directly to the skin.

"Let's get out of this!" urged Sealink.

But Pertelot Fitzwilliam, wet fur pasted to her trembling muscles, stared into the landward darkness as though her whole life were out there somewhere. Little involuntary movements passed through her, tremors betrayed by a set of the head, a flexing of the toes. She wanted to run but could only remain rooted to the deck.

"Come on, hon. Hurry!"

Lightning flashed.

Unfamiliar colors flared briefly in the bright tapestry of Pertelot's eyes: copper and sea green, a corona of lapis and amber around a pupil like a tiger's claw. Then the third lid slid like an ill-fitting shutter across the complex lenses, and she fell upon her side, ears flat to her skull.

She was still conscious. When Sealink tried to grasp her by the neck and drag her out of the weather, she twisted and bit. Sealink, bewildered, withdrew. Pertelot tilted back her head and howled. "It would make your hair stand on end," Sealink would say later, "a noise like that." The Mau kneaded weakly at the air in front of her, claws extended in a confused gesture of submission and resistance.

"Light," she said. "Light. Oh, now he bears down on us, ancient and fierce, ancient and fierce from his own sky, his own north. Aiee! The old roads! The frozen stars!" She strained up toward the darkness, then fell back.

334

"Save us," she appealed quietly. "Save the kittens."

Her cries brought Pengelly out of the cabin.

"Whatever is it? Whatever's going on up here?"

"Pertelot bit me!" said Sealink. "And I didn't do nothing to her 'cept try to get her out of the rain. She's staring at the cliffs. Staring and staring. Can you see anything there?"

They waited, faces upturned in the dark, for the next flash of lightning. When it came, nothing was revealed but a headland bleak with rain.

"Seems to have gone," said Sealink with relief.

"What's gone?"

"I ain't sure, hon. Might have been the Wild Cat of World's End; might have been a tree." She sighed tiredly. "The light will play you tricks."

Pengelly listened to this with his head tilted to one side. Then he began to dance.

Up and down the deck he went, whirling and pouncing in tight little circles—back paws off the floor, front paws off the floor—as if trying to catch his own tail. His paws thumped wetly, and he accompanied the dance with some odd, garbled cries, like a cat trying to talk through a mouthful of food.

Sealink stared at him.

"I've had enough of this," she said. "Is this some Old Country thing?"

It was.

Pengelly completed his dance and stared hard at the cliffs. A rasping sound, as of hairball displacement, came from deep in his throat.

"Begone, begone, begone," he said.

He spat.

Then he said, "The black cat has a gale of wind in its tail. We're in for a proper bad blow. Black cat means the weather, see? And that's how we calm un."

"I knew that," Sealink said.

She turned her attention to the bedraggled and by now unconscious Pertelot and, firmly grasping the scruff of her neck, hauled her into the shelter of the wheelhouse.

* * *

The black cat had its tail up now, and the wind was beginning to find its strength.

Armies of breakers hit the beach, each company of boiling foam hurtling up the shingle before being sucked raggedly back down the line to recoup. Gouts of spume crashed up from the seaward stacks. The bottom had dropped out of the barometer: above the bay, streams of cyclonic air whirled and collided with a crack like washing on a bad Monday. It made your head spin and your ears itch.

As above, so below.

Currents wrestled and recoiled—the *Guillemot*'s anchor rope creaked—she bucked and rolled. She was fretful but eager to be free.

Accustomed to such nervous displays, Old Smoky, visible now only as the bright coal of a lighted cigarette, made his tranquil way around her deck. His Wellington-booted feet were as sure as any cat's on the slippery planking. If a stray lanyard flailed in the rigging, he caught the ends and made them fast. If canvas flapped and struggled, he furled the sails tight. The boom swung dangerously. Alert to a new movement of air, he turned as it bore down upon his head, grabbed and neatly secured it. Slowly and surely he moved around the vessel. He bade her be calm. He stowed the fishing gear, then swept Pengelly up in his arms.

"What d'you think, old cat?" he asked.

"Wind's northeast and proper nasty. Force six heading for seven and if we stay moored here we'm right in her path."

He ruminated on this. "Night after full moon, so the tide's running strong. Stay here, she'll turn we over for sure. These cliffs ent tall enough to give us shelter. Out there—" he surveyed the miles of braided troughs and foam-topped peaks, piling up now into walls of water as the wind caught them "—it'll be worse. So best try to outrun her, keep in tight along the coast. Ay, Pengelly, that's what we'll do, eh, boy?"

He looked down into Pengelly's grizzled face. He winked. Pengelly stared back. Then down he jumped and ran for cover.

Thunder rumbled, louder and closer. Cloud roiled overhead, hectic with electricity and moonlight. The fisherman hauled up his weed-tangled anchor.

The *Guillemot* plunged joyously forward.

In the wheelhouse, Sealink and Pengelly watched the storm nervously. Pertelot lay panting in her sleep upon the chart shelf, where Sealink—with the determination that bespeaks hybrid vigor—had dragged her, safe from the foul weather and the fisherman's substantial rubber boots.

Now the diesel engine rumbled into life in the bowels of the boat. Old Smoky was suddenly at the wheel, water streaming from his oilskins. Rain dashed against the windshield as the *Guillemot* breasted the waves. She reared gallantly at every peak and trough. Her timbers creaked and flexed.

Thunder cracked overhead.

Every cloud, every wave and surge and breaker, was burnished with light, each detail distinct for miles around. They seemed to be the only living things in sight: no other boats out on a night like this, no gulls about the waves or in the air. Only the tiny vessel in the storm, a thin skin of paint and wood between life and death. Three cats and an old man, bumping across the ocean.

"Well, hell!" said Sealink. "*This* is what I mean! See?"

No one was listening.

Thunder and lightning were inseparable now, as if light could be sound, and sound light.

The lines on the old fisherman's face stood out starkly. His teeth gleamed, and his hands were clever on the wheel. He stared out into the flicker and bang, the pupils of his eyes contracting and dilating to the rhythm of the storm. The *Guillemot* wallowed helplessly a moment, then righted herself and plowed on with the wind behind her. The dark, humped coast swelled past to starboard, barely distinguishable from a solid mass of churning air and sea. There was a kind of pause. Then the wind flung raindrops the size of pebbles into the wheelhouse, the thunder cracked, and directly above them the world split apart.

Cat lightning flashed in the sky.

Out of the chaos, out of the night, out of the clouds that wreathed the waning moon, legs and heads and tails and bodies—all the lithe alchemy of *argentum vivum*—quicksilver cats who cavorted and capered in the dark! They leapt and sprang and twisted. They raked the clouds with fang and claw, and fire streaked from their terrible eyes. Great sky cats, electric cats at play! A smell of sulfur filled the air.

Pengelly stared, aghast.

Even Sealink, that collector of intense experience, looked disturbed. Her ears quivered. She couldn't think of anything to say.

She was still trying hard when something outside caught her eye.

A ragged scrap of black and white was being hurled about above the waves. The storm buffeted it one way then another, lost interest, took it up again. It vanished for some moments behind a wave the size of a hill. Then it dropped like a stone out of nowhere, onto the deck of the *Guillemot*.

Without a thought, Sealink was out into the driving rain. The wind filled her coat like a sail, blowing her fur up the wrong way so that the sharp bones of her hocks were clearly visible. Her tail streamed in the gale, and the long hair of her ruff whipped across her face.

When she arrived back in the wheelhouse, she had something large and piebald drooping from her mouth. She deposited it gently on the slatted floor and shook herself vigorously. Pertelot Fitzwilliam woke up and gazed down from her shelf. "Look here, hon," Sealink invited her, and prodded the object with one huge paw. It remained motionless. "Just look what we got here."

It was a magpie.

"Don't touch he!" cried Pengelly, visibly agitated. "Beware the Corvidae, the *byasen!*" he warned. "Oh, they's birds of ill omen, particular when they come in ones." He lashed his tail. " 'Tis terrible luck that it's landed here, terrible."

He spat three times to avert calamity and chanted,

> "One's sorrow, two's mirth
> Three's a matin', four's a birth

> *Five's a naming, six a dearth*
> *Seven's heaven, eight is hell*
> *And nine's the Devil, his own sel'."*

Sealink received this performance with a snort.

"Pengelly," she told him, "you spend altogether too much time among human beings. This here is an acquaintance of mine, if I'm not mistaken. Though I have to say—" she peered so closely at the still form that her nose almost touched its beak "—all birds do look awful similar to me."

With a gulp and a splutter, the magpie shook itself. Its feathers rustled like dry leaves. Light glinted from the uniform black-ness of one beady eye. Finding itself face-to-face with a cat, it let out an earsplitting squawk and tried to fly. Old Smoky was distracted from the wheel.

"What the blazes!"

He lunged at the magpie, but Sealink was faster. In a moment she had grabbed her catch between her jaws and was pelting down the stairs.

"If you kill me," the bird said faintly, crushed but not quite bitten, "you'll never know the secret I carry."

She set him down on the bunk, leaving a firm paw upon his chest to prevent escape. The cabin gaslight revealed a scrawny specimen, body feathers cemented to his skin, main coverts in disarray. He struggled weakly. The effort seemed to drain him.

"Eat me then," he said, and closed his eyes. "I'm too tired to care."

The bird Sealink remembered had been larger. Feistier too, she thought.

The bird she remembered had worn with pride his oily irides-cent black and blue, in rakish contrast to the creamy white of his neck. The bird she remembered had never stopped talking.

"Hon?" she inquired softly. "Is that you?"

The magpie squinted up at her. The gaslight seemed to be giving him trouble.

"Oh yes," he said sarcastically. "I give the wrong answer and you go looking for the salt and vinegar. 'Honey, is that *you*?'" he mimicked. "Who do you want it to be?"

The calico removed her paw.

"It's you all right," she said. "I wish now I'd et you."

She thought for a moment.

"I still could," she warned him.

"You can't eat the people you know," the bird said in livelier tones. He rolled over onto his front and pushed himself upright with his beak. His claws gripped the blanket. Eyeing her nervously as the boat pitched sideways, he added, "I hate the sea."

At that moment, Pertelot came into the cabin.

"One for Sorrow?" she said. "Is that you?"

The magpie swiveled his head.

"Who wants to know?" he said. Then he gave a low chuckle. "Well, well, well. Who says magpies have bad luck?" He cocked his head. "You fly for weeks. You fly your wings off. You call in favors from every rookery between the city and the South Coast. Never mind that," he told himself. "You call in favors from *sparrows*. What do you get? Nothing. Finally, you have to admit it: they can't all have been staring in the wrong direction at the right time."

He looked Sealink up and down and mimicked puzzlement.

"How could they miss a cat the size of a horse?" Suddenly invigorated by his own cleverness, he hopped from foot to foot. "Because *she isn't on the land*!" he crowed triumphantly. "And the moment you think of *that*, you've got to think of boats. I rest my case," he said. "Here she is, off on a sea cruise. Surprise, surprise: the Queen of Cats."

His eyes shone with self-congratulation.

There was a silence, as the cats digested this. Then Pertelot asked timidly, "But how did you find the right boat?"

"You might well ask," said the magpie. "Ever been in an up-draft? Ever been *stuffed* up some godforsaken cliff in an electrical storm, with every feather stalled out and no more ideas? No? Well, I'll tell you what you think. You think: 'I'm alive. Starved, stalled, and struck by lightning, *but at least I'm still alive!*' "

He bobbed his head up and down excitedly.

"So, I'm in the turbulence at the top of the cliff—rooks call it 'the roller,' and no one flies like a rook—and I look out to sea.

I'm upside down at the time." He paused to judge the effect of this on his audience. Pertelot, at least, looked impressed. "And there! This boat!" He laughed. "Boat—?" he asked himself. "A leaf in a weir. I'm upside down, two hundred feet up in the roller on this heap of chalk, waiting for the hammer to fall—and I'm thinking, 'I bet that's them.' Intuition, or what?"

"Or what," Sealink responded with wry amusement. "It couldn't be, hon, that you lost your way—"

"How did you escape from the roller?" interrupted Pertelot excitedly.

"—and got caught by the storm and fell onto the boat by accident. Could it?"

The magpie regarded her sorrowfully for a moment or two. For a moment or two more he stared across the cabin, avoiding eye contact. Then he buried his head under his left wing.

"Eat me, then," he said in a muffled voice. "I fly a hundred *miles this afternoon alone* and that's all the thanks I get."

"Have you seen Ragnar Gustaffson?" Pertelot asked shyly.

"Go and look for him yourself."

Fatigue had finally gotten the better of him. His head bobbed once or twice. Then he toppled backward into Sealink's luxuriant fur and fell asleep. With his blind-looking eyes, his feathers pasted to his chest, and all his self-assurance gone, he looked tiny and vulnerable against her warm, mammalian bulk.

He slept. He slept through the tempest, which showed no signs of easing. He slept through a visit from Old Smoky, who had come down to feed the cats on beef and kidney casserole. They had pushed the magpie under the bunk. He was still asleep when the new day broke, barely brighter than the night. He slept for seven hours, and then he slept again. Sealink slept on the bunk above him, her head tucked under her tail. Pertelot, filled with a sudden optimism, went around licking all the empty bowls.

Pengelly, though, sat sourly on the worktop, peering suspiciously down at shadows.

"Why would the calico save a *byasen*?" he kept asking himself.

.

"Pardon me?" said Pertelot.

"Byasen! Byasen!" said Pengelly irritably. "Byasen's a bird of ill omen: a black stain on a white feather. Never trust a spotted bird nor a spotted dog nor a spotted cow."

"Cow?" said the Queen.

"Never mind that," the old cat said. "Byasen's the thing to get in your head."

Pertelot frowned.

"But we *know* One for Sorrow," she said. She was silent for a moment. Then she reminded him, "Sealink has black patches, too."

Pengelly regarded her darkly.

"You'm right there," he said.

At the sound of her name, Sealink stretched languorously and yawned. From where she sat on the floor of the cabin, Pertelot could see directly into her friend's open jaws. A great, dark blemish marred the pink roof of the calico's mouth.

"Something wrong, hon? 'Cause if there ain't, do you mind not staring? When you stare so, it unsettles me." Then she said, "Stop that, you old Cornish fool!"

From under the berth, a long, curved black beak had emerged, followed by a tilted head and a beady black eye, which blinked once, twice in the gloomy light.

This was enough for Pengelly. Eyes narrowed, legs bunched up under him, belly slung low, backbone straight and parallel to the worktop, and a curious bubbling snarl issuing from his mouth, he was preparing to spring.

The magpie caught sight of him and ducked back under the bunk.

"If you kill me," he said somberly, "you will never learn what message I carry."

Pertelot Fitzwilliam positioned herself between Pengelly and the bird.

"A message!" she said. "Who is it from?"

One for Sorrow looked thoughtful. "There isn't one. The reason I always say that," he explained, eyeing Pengelly with malice, "is that it slows them down for a second. Gives you a chance to get airborne."

Pengelly gave him a disgusted look and trotted off to join the fisherman in the wheelhouse.

Sealink peered over the edge of the bunk.

"You gonna tell me about Mousebreath, babe?" she inquired.

The bird dipped and bobbed.

"Not before I eat," he said.

They found him something Pertelot had missed, and watched in fascination his eating style, which was to eye and stab, eye and stab, as if he were in a field. It looked odd, but it was efficient, and he soon finished. He stropped his beak once or twice on the floor, then cheekily flew up onto the worktop the old sea cat had so recently vacated. There, he got to work on his feathers, his feet, and his endoparasites, while the two female cats waited expectantly.

"Well?" urged Sealink.

The magpie regarded her coolly, decided he was unlikely to come by further nourishment until he had unburdened himself of what he knew, and said, "What would you like to hear then? Speak up, speak clearly, and don't confuse the bearer with the bad news."

"Hon," promised Sealink, "much more of this, and you are pie. We ain't heard nothing about nothing since Piper's Quay. It was fighting and rushing and falling in the canal for us. It was dark. So you tell us what happened after, and how Ragnar and especially Mousebreath are doing now. And you tell us nice, 'cause we ain't got hearts of stone."

So the magpie told them.

He told them how their friends had escaped from the wreck of the cat catchers' van. How Majicou had rescued them in the snowy night, and taken Tag, Cy, and Mousebreath to the barn on the Old Changing Way. How Tag had returned to look for Ragnar Gustaffson and fallen prey to the *vagus*.

He told them how Mousebreath had been—as he put it—alive and well and as full of bad temper as ever, the last time he saw him.

Sealink closed her eyes, and the tension went out of her like a breath.

"Well, thank heavens for that," she said.

There was a long pause, as Pertelot Fitzwilliam stared at the magpie and summoned her courage. "And where is Ragnar Gustaffson now?" she whispered.

He bobbed and dipped and looked away. He couldn't meet her eyes.

I'm only a messenger, he was thinking. He was thinking he had never seen such need and fever. I'm only a bird.

He looked down at his feet. They were big and black and scaly, the claws long and gleaming. He found that if he dipped and tilted his head so that the gaslight was behind him, he could see his beak reflected dimly in the curve of an outstretched talon. I'm only a bird, he was thinking. I shouldn't have to do this.

He said, "I don't know."

Then louder, "No one saw him leave. They think he got shut in the van again. They didn't see him again. Maybe I'll track him down somewhere," he added softly. "After all, I found you."

Pertelot was distraught. "But I'm having his kittens!" she wailed.

The magpie looked startled. "Kittens?" he said. "Kittens?"

Possibilities were cascading through his narrow head: images of disaster impossible to bind. Words; hieratic, formal. Prophecy and the warnings of his one-eyed master.

"This is the worst thing that could have happened," he declared. "Is Majicou aware of this? He must be told. I must fly at once—"

Sealink was preparing to tell him, You'll do no such thing! when there came a loud cry from the deck above, followed by a splash and the sound of scurrying paws. Then Pengelly's voice, raised in distress.

"Oh my," breathed Sealink. "It's all drama today. You," she ordered the magpie, "stay here. And you," she advised Pertelot Fitzwilliam, "stop howling. It don't mend nothing." And she thudded off up the stairs.

There she found the wind still blowing fiercely across the deck. Pengelly was running up and down in an agitated fashion, leaning over the side and dabbing at the water with one paw, while he made the strange clicking and wailing noises of a hungry kitten separated from its mother.

Everyone's mad today, she thought. Then she thought, Uh-oh.

Off to the wheelhouse.

It was empty. No boots to rub against, no oilskin in sight. Out of the wheelhouse she ran and around onto the bow. Nothing. She quartered the deck in panic, quartered it again. All she found was a discarded cigarette end still glowing wanly in the yellow-gray afternoon light.

Of the fisherman there was no sign.

"Where is he, old cat?"

Pengelly stood dejectedly at the starboard gunwale, staring down into the water. He was unable to speak.

"Oh, surely not, hon—"

A hundred yards away across the churning water, slaty cliffs dipped slantwise onto a broad shingle beach where breakers crashed and roared. Toward the horizon lay an endless repetition of swells and troughs, topped with lacy foam. There was nothing amid the rolling waves that remotely resembled the old fisherman's yellow oilskin.

Pengelly said suddenly, "My fault. All my fault. Oh, oh, oh."

He stared desperately at Sealink.

"My fault," he said. "My fault."

When she couldn't think what to say, he looked away and recommenced pacing the rail—ears low, whiskers drooping, eyes fixed on the water in a frenzy of despair. At each end of the boat, he would switch to the opposite rail and repeat the search there, murmuring all the while, "My fault. Oh, oh, oh."

Sealink had soon had enough of this. She planted herself in front of him. The wind filled her tail like a pennant. Scatters of rain dashed against the wheelhouse.

"What do you mean, 'It's my fault'?" she demanded.

For all the attention he paid her, she might have been a figment of his own anguish. When he spoke, it was only to Pengelly, whose tragedy had become Pengelly. "How can I ever forgive myself? Oh, if only I hadn't been in the way. My fault! Oh, oh, oh."

He stared dully along the rail, calling, "Old Smoky? Old Smoky?"

He considered the murky depths.

"The boat lurched just as he tripped over me. My fault, all mine. He saved my life, and now I've took his. He can't *swim*."

"This is no good," said Sealink to herself. "Who's sailing the boat?" She gave Pengelly a sharp nip. "You stop this now, hon," she said. "I can't think."

But she could, and before she knew it she was down the cabin steps, hot-foot and high-tailed.

"Come with me," she said briskly.

The magpie regarded her with alarm.

"If you eat me," he began, "you'll never—"

"You come, or you're chicken supreme," said Sealink. "Make your choice."

He opened his beak to protest.

She grabbed him between her teeth. His convulsive grip fetched the blanket off the bunk. It trailed behind them for a step or two, then fell away.

"Raaark!"

Pertelot watched this exchange in bewilderment, but it took her out of herself.

In two bounds, Sealink was on deck beside Pengelly. She dropped the magpie at his feet. One for Sorrow sprang up and shook himself, chattering with rage.

"No call for that! No call for that!"

"This bird will help us find Old Smoky," Sealink declared. "He'll fly up, look down from the sky!"

But Pengelly was filled with rage.

"It were him brought us to this in the first place!" he said.

He spat. "Byasen! Byasen!"

"You see?" said the magpie to Pertelot, who had followed them up on deck. "This is what I have to put up with." He stuck out his thin chest. "No favors from me," he told Pengelly, "until you stop the bird-of-ill-omen stuff."

He gave Sealink a look.

"It's medieval," he complained. "Surely you can see that?"

Pertelot, meanwhile, stood up on her hind legs and, with her paws placed on the rail, studied the situation of the ship.

"One for Sorrow," she said, "forgive the rudeness of these two cats. Will you search for the fisherman for my sake and the sake of the kittens? The wind is strong and the rocks are close, and I fear for us all if Old Smoky cannot be saved."

The magpie was pleased.

"You see?" he told Sealink. "A bit of politeness is all it takes. I'd go anywhere for her now."

He turned on Pengelly. "I'm not doing this for you," he said.

He extended his wings. They were shot through with an oily purple-green iridescence. The fierce wind riffled through his main coverts. He only laughed approvingly when it pushed him back a pace or two; then, without moving a muscle, allowed the solid air to lift him from the deck. He had learnt that from a crow.

Once aloft, he rode the wind, wingtips flared to bank and glide. He soared and circled. He swaggered a little. He had learned loops from the same crow, but he was keeping them in reserve. Then he stalled out, folded the aerofoil surfaces, and went down like a thousand feet of bad air. A pass over the deck of the *Guillemot* took him a foot above Sealink's head.

"What do you think?" he called.

"I think you still got to land somewhere!" she warned him.

"Raaaark!"

In moments he had become a small black speck veering toward the cliffs.

"Last we shall see of he," Pengelly said grimly. "And good riddance. Bleddy maggot pie."

He resumed his pacing around the boat, as if by now the ritual was as important as its purpose, while Sealink and Pertelot watched the skies.

Time passed. The *Guillemot* drifted with the tide, pitching broadside into the waves so that water gurgled and slapped noisily in her bilges. Details of the land became clearer by the minute: seabirds roosting on ledges in the cliffs; whitewashed cottages dotted among the gorse and furze; stands of low, sessile oak and leafless thorn; little tumbles of scree and reddish earth; tiny footpaths snaking down to sheltered coves. They passed a village, sheltered in its steeply wooded valley—slate roofs that shone with rain, lights on in the gloom of the afternoon, colorful boats bobbing at anchor in the safe confines of a walled harbor, and not a soul to be seen. Further along the coast, an expanse of sand dunes rolled down to the stormy water, marram grass blown horizontal by the gales. They passed dark, narrow zawns dripping with water, rocky headlands jutting into the restless sea. All the while, Pengelly's plaintive cries gave back an eerie echo to the sound of the herring gulls wheeling above the nearby cliffs.

The rain stopped.

The old sea cat gave up his vigil and without a word collapsed beside his friends, trembling with exhaustion and despair.

The three of them sat silently on the rolling deck, fluffing out their drenched fur in the dull afternoon light. There was nothing else to do. The sun appeared briefly between gold-rimmed clouds. The ocean sparkled, deceptive friend, dispassionate foe. The storm seemed to have played itself out. But fitful gusts still made the sea choppy, and they were driving the *Guillemot* inexorably landward.

Here, the cliffs had become low-lying and haphazard: a tumble of rock and earth and grass, dotted with the black and white of kittiwakes and gannets. The waves roared farther and farther up the shingle beach, so that strands of black seaweed deposited by the previous tide were sucked back into the foam, to be cast up again ever closer to the cliffs. Jagged reefs lined the edges of the bays, gray and crisscrossed with veins of quartz, as if spatters of the sea foam leaping around them had become crystallized within the rock itself. Water sucked and boiled around the base of these boulders, creating miniature whirlpools down which the driftwood and flotsam disappeared, never to rise again.

Sealink shivered. The sea looked cold, the currents inimical; but, if the worst came to the worst, maybe she would be able to battle her way through to the shore.

I'm fit, she thought, and strong, and maybe anything's better than sitting here doing nothing at all as the ship goes down.

She wasn't worried about Pengelly. He had been a ship's cat all his life.

But the Mau?

"Think again, hon," Sealink told herself. "That's one pregnant mother."

She searched the skies again. No sign of the bird. And where was Old Smoky by now? What chance did he have?

Ahead and to the west, the sun, now free of cloud, had started to dip to the horizon, streaking the sky with pale pastel colors that soon deepened to opulent carmine, coral, and gold. Sealink was inexplicably saddened by this.

"I like a journey," she said aloud, "but I hate this drifting life."

"Look!"

Pertelot was gazing into the dusky air behind them. A distant black mote had resolved itself suddenly into the shape of a bird, its mouth already opening and shutting on words as yet unintelligible.

"One for Sorrow!"

The magpie landed in an inelegant flurry of wings. He bounced across the deck.

"You aren't going to believe this," he said, "because I don't believe it myself!"

"What?" said Pertelot. "What is it?"

But Pengelly said, "Have you found un yet?" And then, "Till then, bad luck's all I'll believe."

The magpie shrugged. "So wait and see," he said.

"Bird," said Sealink threateningly, "you tell us what you know."

The magpie glinted at her. He said, "You can wait too.

"They'll be along soon," he promised.

And before she could move, he had flapped up into the crosstree, where he preened gleefully. Nothing would persuade him to say more.

The coast drew near.

Pengelly returned to his obsessive patrol of the deck, stopping only to turn tight little figure eights and call the old man's name into the growing gloom.

Pink with the sun's last light, surf boomed in over the reefs. Sealink made out a tideline of limpets and barnacles, and above them clustered circles of orange lichen. She could hear the water boiling and sucking and crashing, and see how the swags of weed were lifted and then dashed down by each succession of waves.

"Man," she said, "that's us, we don't *do* something."

She stood and shook herself vigorously, to dispel the image. At that moment, there was a flicker at the extreme edge of her field of vision.

She turned and focused on it. There! Some object moving, behind the boat!

"Hey!"

She ran to the stern, stood up on the polished wooden seat, and, planting her front paws solidly on the gunwale, craned her neck.

There was something swimming in the wake.

Not something. Several somethings. The wake streamed out, glimmering deceptively in the last of the light. Were they fish? Maybe dolphins? She dilated her pupils.

Not fishes or dolphins.

"What?" she said, as if they might speak.

Then one of them breasted the waves quite close.

It was a cat.

Sealink opened her mouth and found that no sound would come out.

She stared.

"Hey," she whispered.

Its fur was as sleek as a seal's, its movements lithe as an otter's; its whiskers sparkled with water droplets. But its muzzle was a cat's muzzle, and its coat bore a discernible tabby pattern. A little way behind it swam another, and another. They streamed back with the wake, as fluid as an eddy, as elusive as a reflection. There were nine of them, and they carried a heavy burden.

A wondering voice beside her said, "*Mes mî a-droucias ün*

pesk brâs, naw ê lostiow; but I found *one* great fish with *nine* tails . . ."

It was the old sea cat.

"Silkies," Pengelly said.

He was enraptured.

Then he saw their burden.

"Old Smoky!"

There he was, in the midst of them, borne up flat on his back with his head safely above water: the old fisherman, alive and well and grinning from ear to ear!

Pengelly ran up and down the stern in delight.

"Old Smoky! Old Smoky!"

Sealink stared. "I thought I'd about seen everything, till I seen this! Cats hate the water!—I except my old friend Muezza, of course, but he was *odd*—Swimming cats! Ain't nine swimming *cats* in the whole world, you ask me!"

But Pengelly only said complacently, "The seas hold many mysteries, my lover," and seemed restored to himself.

Pertelot, gazing over the stern, gave a soft cry of surprise.

"How beautiful they are!" she said.

While the magpie cawed and clattered cheerfully to himself from the top of the mast.

Now the silkies swam in close to the boat, their eyes like deep water on a moonless night, and bore up the old fisherman so that he was able to clutch the gunwale and haul himself over the side. There he lay, flopping about in his own boat, gasping on the slatted deck, while the salt sea ran out of his clothing like water from a great wet sack of fish. He had lost his boots and his sou'wester, but he looked happier than Sealink had ever seen him.

"Pengelly! Pengelly, old cat!" he called. "There's no cat like you, but you nearly did me a wrong un there! What d'you think to this?"

But Pengelly wasn't listening.

Suddenly he was half in and half out of the *Guillemot*, while Pertelot Fitzwilliam of Hi-Fashion, Queen of Cats, struggled to keep him from going farther by hanging on to his back legs as if her life depended on it.

"Help me! Help me!" she sang out.

And then to Pengelly, "You can't go with them. Pengelly, dear, you can't!"

The silkies trod water, their black eyes as flat and dead as any shark's. Then eight of them turned and dived beneath the waves; and the ninth swam up to the *Guillemot*. Water cascaded from the close Cornish curls of her wiry fur as she reached up and touched Pengelly's warm nose with her own bitterly cold one. They looked into each other's eyes for a moment; then she dropped back down into the chill gray sea and with a sinuous flick of her body vanished beneath the waves.

"Wriggle," Pengelly called softly. "Wriggle, come back!"

Chapter Eighteen
PARTINGS

*A cat has nine lives. For three he plays. For three
he strays. And for three he stays.*
— OLD PROVERB

"So what did you do then?" asked Tag.

Majicou thought for a while.

"I took the wild road to the other side of the river," he said eventually, "and I watched as the Great Fire ate the city."

"How did you feel?"

"Oh, I smiled."

It was almost dark when the storm blew away south, leaving the sky a washed-looking greeny-blue, empty but for a few fast-moving rags of cloud very high up.

In the villages below the spring line, the wind had blown down the chimneys, the fences, and power cables. Torrential rain had flooded the lanes, leaving sand spits and moraines of gravel at every junction. There were raw scars on hillsides. Strange new shapes had arrived in copse and spinney, where chalk earth, caked in the roots of fallen trees, now made the silhouettes of wild creatures in the growing twilight. Up here none of this was visible. The world stretched away forever, colored the rosy gray of pigeons' wings; and a single star burned above the horizon.

"Time to leave," said Majicou at last.

Things went wrong from the start.

The first path, by way of which he had hoped to connect with one of the Great Roads, led only to a garden in some downland village. The next turned back on itself and emptied itself six feet in the air less than two hundred yards from the point they had entered it, so that they tumbled to the ground among apple trees

353

in an old orchard. The third sent them to a shallow valley between shoulders of woodland, along which a lane and a stream ran side by side. Mallards clucked softly from the water.

Majicou followed the valley for an hour or two, stopping in order to examine the twist of reflected light from a broken bottle or the shadows at the edge of a spinney. Tag followed Majicou, trying to learn what to look for. A little way behind, playing I see, I jump, came Mousebreath and Cy. The stream glittered and winked at them. Moonlight licked the curve of a branch. Majicou darted into a farmyard and nudged his way under the flap of old sacking he found behind a tarred wooden shed. The farm dogs barked sleepily.

"Something here?"

The old cat raised his head so that his eye caught the moonlight, flat and green. "I can connect nothing to nothing," he admitted. It was as if the highways themselves were unwilling to go anywhere that night.

The valley deepened, and the stream fell away from the road, and the cats followed the stream by an ash-strewn track. The water slowed and deepened, turned the color of petrol. It was fringed with elder. A single house loomed out of the night, square, stone-built, slate-roofed. Guinea fowl—making a strange penetrating squeak, like someone obsessively cleaning a window—first huddled in its shadow, then fled like shadows themselves between the lichenous gray trunks of the aging fruit trees. "No need to wait for me," Mousebreath advised, as he slipped off after them. When he caught up again half a mile later, his eyes were amused and bright, and something soft hung from his mouth, one specked gray wing trailing in the dirt. A warm iron smell was in the air.

They rested by some abandoned workings—a tall, rusty metal bridge, served by spiral steps; a sagging chain-link fence; a few concrete tanks in pairs, surrounded by rubbish and bare stems of pussy willow—to eat the guinea fowl, crouching in a circle around a little mist of their own breaths to shear the salty, willing flesh from its flexible bones. They licked their chops busily for a minute or two in satisfaction. Then, despite the cold, they felt like sitting down and having a rest.

"I love this life," Mousebreath said, staring at the stream and already thinking of fish.

"I do too," said Tag.

But it was there, under the lemony moon, that things really went wrong, and fate began to find them out. While Majicou slept and Tag discussed with Mousebreath the finer points of a life outdoors, the tabby wormed her way under the chain-link and began rummaging about between the tanks. "Still sharp-set then, the little devil!" Mousebreath said fondly, as they watched her drag out a number of items, some of which were quite large. There were two rusty springs, something that might once have been a human garment made of white cotton, and a spoon corroded to the color of aluminum. There was a small tin lined with hardened silver paint. These items she arranged in front of her audience, as if for a demonstration, and eyed them for a while with her head on one side. When she wandered off in search of some final element, Tag and Mousebreath stopped paying attention—though they were drowsily aware of her, pottering about behind them amid the tangled stalks of last year's growth.

"Yes," Mousebreath concluded, after a few minutes' quiet talk, "it's the way to live, this. Uncle Tinner always said so, and he were right."

" 'Sharp-set!' " said Tag with satisfaction. "Is 'sharp-set' one of the things your uncle Tinner used to say?"

Behind them among the tanks, things had changed. The thin, elongated shadow of a cat moved across the white concrete walls in the moonlight.

"Sharp-set's only a manner of speaking," explained Mousebreath. "It's to mean you're hungry, see? If you're hungry, it's 'sharp-set' till you eat! But he knew some things, that cat."

A low, crooning song issued from the undergrowth. The branches of the pussy willow were suddenly thick with little white moths.

"Oh, he knew some things!"

While up between the rusty metal girders of the bridge a twist of light had appeared, to spin and dangle like a chrysalis in a hedge.

Mousebreath said, "When all this is over I'll stay out here. I won't go back to the city. Find that old calico again, maybe, fetch her out here."

Tag said, "I might stay too!"

Mousebreath laughed. "I'd ask the tabby about that," he said, "if I was you."

Tag meant to say, What do you mean, "ask the tabby"? I don't understand! But as he opened his mouth, a cloud covered the moon. In the sudden darkness there was a sound like an empty canvas bag being unzipped, and a host of eyes—pale oval feline eyes, green and yellow like lamps in the night— poured silently over the bridge toward him. He leapt to his feet, calling, "Majicou! Majicou!"

Too late. While the Majicou struggled up out of dreams, Tag could only watch in astonishment as two score alchemical cats swirled down the spiral steps like dirty water down a pipe and fell with quiet ferocity upon his friend Mousebreath.

Mousebreath gave a monumental screech of surprise and lashed out. Soon he was rolling about at the center of a dark melee—cats' backs, black and brown; paws spread and ra- zored; teeth bared; eyes as pale as death; an ear laid back, ex- tending and accentuating the curve of a feral grin. It was wet work in the night for the tortoiseshell. His assailants were not only silent; their concentration was appalling. From the start they had no interest in anyone else. Tag seemed to embarrass them. Each time he hurled himself to his friend's aid, five or six of them would lean toward him, surround him, and use their weight to steer him away. They were big animals. Given a choice, they pushed him toward the bridge; but anywhere would do. By the time he had disentangled himself, swearing and cutting out, he was twenty yards from the fight; and by the time he got back, the rest were ready for him. Each intervention gave Mousebreath some respite; but they backed him up steadily, until he felt his tail in the stream.

"Stuffing hell!" he called. "What's going on? Tag, I don't think I—"

"Majicou!" cried Tag. "Help!"

But they wouldn't fight the one-eyed cat either; and anyway Majicou—too long away from his center of power among the highways—seemed reluctant, hard to wake, confused. When they needed him most, he had been emptied out, just as the fox had anticipated, by the effort of remaining in the world.

"Mousebreath!"

"Tag!"

Mousebreath's hind legs were in the water. There was no-where else for him to go. Cuts had closed his blue eye; the orange one glared sullenly.

"Tag! I—"

Tag was in despair. He ran around in a circle, shouting, "The fox said they wouldn't hurt us! The fox said they wouldn't hurt us!" Then he lost his temper with the tabby. She had been watching since she called them down, her mouth a little open, her eyes lambent but vague, as if her "magic" had exhausted her intelligence. Tag stormed over and bit her ear. "Stop them!" he shouted. "You stopped them before. Stop them now!" She shook her head and stared at him in surprise.

"Steady on, Silver," she said. "I can't sing if it's Wednesday. That hurt." She became aware of the melee. Jumped in surprise. "But what's this!" she exclaimed.

Mousebreath was up to his belly in water. Blood ran into his good eye, streamed away on the current from wounds that had opened in his chest. Sometimes he looked down at himself puzzledly. He had given as good as he got: cats lay here and there among the shallows in postures that suggested they would not get up again. But Mousebreath was unsteady on his feet, and they wouldn't leave him alone. For the first time since Tag had known him he seemed lost and uncertain. The tabby scuttled and slid down the muddy bank toward him, making strange, sad little mewing noises. He heard her and looked blindly about.

"Be careful, little un!" he warned. While his attention was diverted thus, a Sphinx—eyes reddened and bulging, skin as wrinkled as a lizard's—slunk up under his guard, sank its yellow teeth into his shoulder.

"I'm here," whispered Cy. "Hang on."

She sat down in the mud. Her eyes rolled up into her head. Her voice rose in a strident caterwaul, demanding and eerie, edged with sounds sharp as knives. Motes poured out of her mouth and busied themselves among the alchemical cats. Up went their heads. They took uncertain steps this way and that. Mousebreath stood blinking and shivering, while the blood ran out of his fur into the stream; then he lunged clumsily forward and got his front paws on dry land.

For a moment, it seemed as if he would make it. Then the tabby toppled forward onto her face and began to roll about. She hissed and spat. Her eyes changed color rapidly. "Oh no!" she cried. "Wrong cat! Wrong colors!" The strange lights floated out over the water in aimless processions and were doused. All over the bank, alchemical cats shook their heads and leapt forward again. Mousebreath went down tiredly beneath them.

For Tag, it was like fighting air. "Mousebreath!" he called. They parted in front of him. They let him reach the water's edge. He stood there with his paws in the black mud, but he couldn't see his friend. Only something brown and already waterlogged, all the life going out of it as it was whirled away by the stream. "Mousebreath!" He thought he saw legs kick feebly. A head was raised above the water. The moonlight licked off one orange eye, fierce with the determination to live. Then the tortoiseshell sank beneath the surface.

The alchemical cats turned as one and rushed silently away upstream, where they vanished like a cloud of smoke in the darkness.

Cy leaned out over the water, rocking backward and forward in her misery as if she might try and follow Mousebreath wherever he had gone. Tag stared at her with such emptiness she winced away from him and hid in some brambles, crying, "I'm sorry! I'm sorry! I'm sorry!"

Majicou raced up onto the iron bridge. He called down, "Quickly, Tag! Do you want to be next? Follow me!"

Tag ran after him angrily.

After a last look at the willows, the remains of the guinea-fowl feathers and the hurrying stream, the tabby followed them, her eyes confused and sad.

Everything had changed up there. A sourceless silver light now limned the iron girders. There were echoes suggestive of a tunnel. There were smells as cold as rust in January, and distant smells of lemon peel and coal. Tag said, "I want to know what *happened* here!"

"Listen," said Majicou. "The Alchemist is almost ready to face us—"

"I don't care! Mousebreath—"

"Tag, at Tintagel Court he had you in his hands. Have you ever thought why he didn't kill you then? I'll tell you: he didn't think you were worth the effort. He spared you tonight for the same reason. Mousebreath seemed like a threat; but you were just some kitten I had adopted in my old age. Soon he will see his mistake!"

"We can't just leave Mousebreath."

"Mousebreath is dead. Do you want to be next in the river? If not, come on!"

And, turning his back on Tag and Cy, Majicou addressed the highway from which the alchemical cats had issued. During the fight, it had swollen to the size of a dustbin. All its shy qualities had gone. Presenting as a hard, polished sphere in which they could see their own distorted reflections, it was like no highway Tag had ever encountered. "This can mean nothing good," Majicou told him. "Yet without it I don't know how we can pass." He rocked back onto his haunches and jumped. The surface of the highway seemed to roil and swim like oil patterns on water. He vanished.

"Follow me!" they heard him call a moment or two later, as if from a great distance. But Tag dithered, approaching, then turning away in confusion. And the tabby refused to go near it at all. For some minutes they got nowhere. Their breath made cold patterns in the air. Their paws shuffled quietly in the tingling partial silence. Their noses twitched at the thin, persistent odors. It was easy enough to lead Cy to the edge. There, though, everything twisted away from you and at the same time pulled you in. It felt like falling. It felt like being gassed. As soon as she sensed that, the tabby would veer away, her eyes obstinate and empty, and—without appearing to have changed her plans—head off toward the spiral steps.

Tag sighed and fetched her back. "Come on," he encouraged. "It can't be so bad."

But she only whispered, "I'm not going. It's snakes inside and all. I only want soul and beautiful things. See?"

"It scares me too," said Tag.

She stared stubbornly down at the stream.

"Well then," he said suddenly, "I'll have to go on my own."

"No!" said Cy. "No!"

She scuttled around in a tight circle in front of him. She pushed her face into his—Look at me! Look at me!—She was vibrating like a wire. "Please, Silver! It's such bad things. I—" Suddenly, she gave up. "Carry me then."

Before she could change her mind—and without giving himself any time to think about it, either, because he *was* a bit afraid—Tag snatched her up by the scruff and sprang through.

It was hardly more than a leap into greasy water, a slither across rotten ice. But as soon as he had done it, he wished he hadn't. When he looked the way he had come, whatever direction that was, it was fog and gray moiré. Ahead was worse. It was a field of shadows. It was the color of silence. It was nothing much at all. It seemed to have been left to itself, like some empty building long ago.

"Majicou?" he called anxiously. His own voice came back to him. "Majicou?"

Nothing.

Had Majicou come through in the same place? Had he come through at all? Tag shivered. He didn't even know if he was on a highway. Easy to picture himself alone in some endless gray space, soft yet full of hollow echoes, without even the compass wind to guide him. Too easy.

It was too easy to remember the *vagus*.

"We'd best go on," he told Cy.

When he looked down, she had gone too.

He stood there passively. In some measure, he felt as he had the first time he tried to use the highway, in the days when he lived in his garden shed. He was equally disoriented. He was equally afraid. All he could see was fog. He had the illusion of it streaming past him. He was stationary and the cold fog was moving past him: that was how it felt. The moment went on and on, but this time he didn't panic. If he panicked he would be lost. He began to call out regularly, "Majicou! Where are you?" He called, "Cy!"

Suddenly her head and shoulders popped out of the fog two or three feet above his head. "Here, kitty kitty!" she called. "Merry Christmas!" She was the wrong color. Her voice, papery and tired, came from somewhere else. Her face was impassive, her eyes clamped tight shut. Was it her at all? She seemed asleep or dead or carved from stone. Where it poked out of the fog, her head was wreathed in ivy leaves and shiny balls. Her mouth gaped open, and a thousand tiny colored lozenges puffed into the air with every dry, faint little breath.

"No!" cried Tag.

He ran.

It was a kind of highway after all. It was every road he had ever traveled, and none of them. It was a long perspective spiral of concrete—Tintagel Court!—and a back alley across which slashed the black adrenaline shadow of a cat. It was sleety suburbs, yellow-lit windows, a faint *miaow* from a cardboard box in a doorway in the rain. It was the *vagus* woods, a muddy slot to nowhere. It was a ribbon of metal. It was *wrong*.

Wherever he looked it raced out in front of him, tipping and banking at ferocious speed. It split and forked and burgeoned like the branches of an enormous tree. At every junction the tabby was there waiting for him, half turned, one paw raised, to call, "This way. Quick, Tag, this way!"

Her spark plug glittered. Lights poured from her mouth.

"Hurry!"

Suddenly the roads vanished, the tabby vanished. Everything went black. Tag's sensation of rushing forward continued for a fraction of a second longer. Then, with a kind of silent *pop*, he burst through some invisible membrane and out into the light again.

He was back on the kind of highway he knew. It ran through a broad shallow combe between the gentle slopes of the downs. Clouds sailed over, their shadows merging with the strange smoky bronze flicker of ghosts, which lay across the ancient land like a patina on metal. A million days—a million lives bright and dark—passed every second. All around the combe, sandstone sarsens stood like human beings twelve feet high. Their surfaces, sculpted by the ghost wind, glowed purple and rose-gray. Smooth and streamlined, pendulous and lobed, they had been arranged, as if by some massive hand, in avenues and circles, complex knots and clusters that defeated the eye. Among them sat Majicou, very upright and proud, eye like a lamp. The wild roads had returned him his power. He was as large as Tag had ever seen him. Tobacco-brown rosettes seemed to shift and flow beneath the oily shine of his fur. At his feet crouched the tabby, looking up at him with lively admiration.

Tag approached.

"Majicou?" he whispered. "I'm afraid of the big stones."

Majicou laughed. "So you should be," he said.

"Majicou, I don't understand anything—"

"Good," said Majicou.

He closed his eye, the better to see.

"Long ago," he said, "the wildest of roads met and merged here. Aflicker with the movement of the Great Cats, this haunted plain attracted human beings from thousands of miles away. They crossed seas to come here. They hardly knew why. They buried their dead, and thought that was it. They held their feasts, and thought that was it. They built, as they always do, and thought that was it. As you see, they built—this thing, whatever it is. Less a work of architecture than of language—a response, a recognition, an answer: a plea.

"They knew we had been here before them, coming and going since the Ice. They entwined their roads with ours, in the hope . . ." He was silent. "In the hope of what?" he asked. "Power? That, certainly."

The highways looped and hissed across one another. Through

them Tag could see dimly the human roads that mimicked them. A faint gray traffic crawled this way and that in its mist of dirt and chemicals. He could hear the distant roars.

"What do I know?" said the old cat tiredly. "Not enough, despite all these years. Edges always leak. Our roads snake beneath and between the human ones. The boundary between our work and theirs is blurred. Everything shifts and changes as if you were looking through a ripple of clear water, through heat shimmer in summer. No pathway—great or small, human or feline, in the world or beyond it—is fixed or definite. The world is what we make it. The world is what they make it. Moment to moment . . ." He sighed. "Power," he said.

He looked down at the tabby.

"Oh, the Alchemist has a special job put by for this little cat. But like all the best proxies, she is hard to manage. She turns in his hand, especially when you are near, Tag. For an instant tonight, he lost control of her to you."

Tag wanted to say, So it's control that this is all about? He wanted to say, But I don't want to control anyone. All that came out was, "Majicou—"

"He knows you now, and soon he will fear you."

"Majicou, I don't—"

"Worse, he will remember that he had you in his hands once and threw you away."

Tag remembered those hands. White pain. Wrong cat.

The tabby, who had been asleep between Majicou's front paws, now woke. She gave a chirping purr at the sound of his voice, stuck one leg up in the air in a jaunty way, and began to lick her bottom. She stopped, tongue out, to gaze first vaguely, then with growing intentness at the clustered stones and the maze of spirit paths that wove between them. "What is it?" said Majicou sharply. "Something there?" She made an anxious noise. "Be calm, little one," he reassured her. "It's only a change in the light: the shadows fall badly at this time of day." But he lashed his tail nevertheless. "Tag," he said, "we used one of his corrupt roads to get here. We had better leave now, before he follows us down it."

It was far, far too late for that.

There were no sparks: no warning. He didn't need Cy's magic to bring him there, and he had come without his cats. There was no need for the proxy, except to help him aim. There was a kind of cat there: but it was him. And again, he was no kind of cat at all. And *there* is perhaps the wrong word, because he had brought his own place with him.

"Hobbe? Hobbe!"

Whatever the Alchemist had become, it was twelve feet tall.

"Come to me, Hobbe."

At first Tag, staring at it in silent horror over Majicou's shoulder, thought that its upper half was draped in the skin of some huge spotted jungle cat. Then he thought that its upper half *was* some huge spotted jungle cat. Finally he saw that somehow both these things were possible at the same time. Cat and cat skin ran together, except where the skin's empty hind legs and tail dangled and flapped around the Alchemist's waist. There, Tag could clearly see it as a skin, weighted down by big white bones knotted into it at intervals. The limbs beneath were human, bent and tortured into the ropy curves of the feline rear leg. Its right arm remained human too, naked pink flesh bulging out of the sloping muscular shoulder of the cat. Its right fist squeezed and squeezed at the alchemical staff prepared from the mummified foreleg of a panther. The whole travesty was bent forward oddly from the waist, unable to walk four-legged but constantly struggling to balance itself upright. Its head— Tag could not look at the head. Sometimes it resembled a cat's head; sometimes it looked like a human head surgically defaced. There were wires and eyepieces. There was a necklace of feline skulls. The head stank. It leaked. It was in pain. The Alchemist had spared itself nothing to walk the wild roads like a cat. Everything it had done to others, it had done to itself. Until it repossessed the Mau, there was no other way. It roared and sang and danced and tottered, and around it—"Come on, my Hobbe!"—around it, the combe heaved and rattled with bad light. How far had it come that night? A hundred miles? Every inch of the way the wild roads, unable to absorb it or the disaster it represented, had tried to vomit it up. They had lashed to and fro like broken power lines. They had writhed and quivered. For seconds only, they had flashed in and out of the world in displays of lightning and colored smoke. They had sprung to life in front of stunned drunks in urban alleys and children walking their golden retrievers at the lonely edges of villages or thrashed for a moment across acres of woodland in the dark. They had writhed over the city like ribbons of magnesium wrapped into a spiral by some pain that only objects feel.

Black winds tore across the Old Changing Way. Ghost light withered to ash. The ash blew about, so that the Alchemist breathed as it came the brief lost lives of cats. It had bent everything so it could enter. It had pulled everything open with dances and chemistry, chants and bones and endless neurological interventions. It was standing still and rushing forward at sickening speeds. It knew how to do that. Every cat it had ever killed came with it, trapped and bottled to move it on its way.

"Hobbe!" it called. "Hobbe, Hobbe, you're the devil!" It shambled down the megalithic avenues toward them, coughing and choking and waving its great staff.

Whatever it had made itself, it wasn't a cat. It was *wrong*.

"You're the very devil, Hobbe, and I know you're here!"

When Majicou heard this, he turned around slowly, and the adversaries faced each other for the first time in hundreds of years. They were silent. The old cat sat. His master swayed and stank. Their heads were on a level. The same light that bleached the Alchemist's string of skulls and marrowbones burned dull emerald in the eye of the cat. The man leaned forward a little on its shattered legs, then rocked back again. Sensors buzzed and whirred in its sockets. It seemed puzzled. "Is that you, Hobbe? You've grown." Then a gurgling laugh. "Oh you're the very devil, for a cat!" Majicou seemed to stretch upward though he remained sitting, front paws placed between rear paws, as straight and alert as the soapstone cat in a Middle Eastern tomb. He seemed to grow a little. He yawned, then said quietly, "Go away. This is too soon. It is too soon for both of us."

"Oh my. Hobbe has learned to speak!"

"You come here like some dead thing and hope to defeat me? Look at yourself. I am the Majicou!"

"You're the devil."

"Go while you can. These roads won't bear you long. Look how they buckle and fade around you!"

"That's what the devil says, is it?"

But for Cy, this exchange might have gone further. At first, terrified by the presence of her tormentor, she had pushed herself into the thick fur between Majicou's hind feet. Now she jumped out and, tumbling forward with the wobbly aggression and misplaced feet of a kitten, bit the Alchemist where his ankle had once been.

"Your head in my mouth!" she hissed.

The Alchemist pointed at her with his staff. "Be quiet," he ordered. A long green spark leapt from the staff to the plug in her skull. Her legs splayed and she fell down.

"No!" cried Tag.

"No, Tag!" warned Majicou.

But Tag didn't hear him.

Even the leap of a domestic cat has grace, power, the signature of danger. In Tag's earliest attempts on the bird life of the gardens, there had been a kind of physical intelligence, the sense of internal forces ordered, compressed, then released as a long parabolic arc. When, evading him, the garden thrushes had murmured, "Nice jump, son," that had not been all irony. He had leapt, in his way, like a small snow tiger, and given them a sense of what it was to be alive. Now, the arc of his leap seemed infinitely prolonged. He rose in slow motion, and kept rising; and as he rose, he shifted and changed and grew. He was the color of pewter above, pure white beneath, and striped charcoal gray in horizontal bands across his great thick forelegs. His paws were armed and spread. His blood was full of fire. In the moment of his epiphany, he measured fifteen feet from nose to tail, and his eyes were like chips of broken ice. When his jaws opened, the roar that issued from them sent Cy the tabby bowling across the combe like crumpled tissue paper.

He had never felt so glorious.

It being too late to halt matters now, Majicou hissed in annoyance and leapt too.

Master and apprentice struck together. Their adversary roared and staggered backward. The whole story was told in a frozen instant. One black cat, one silver. The curve of the leap, the bared white teeth, the paws extended for the prey. The ears flattened on the great heads. But between that instant and the next, the Alchemist had opened its defaced mouth to the endless sky and raised its staff. There is always another instant. A whining Egyptian music filled the air. The cat skin flapped and danced. Bones jigged in the bad light. Shadows, expelled like flocks of birds, fled between the megaliths on winds full of black sleet and ash. The combe itself seemed to fold and buckle like a wet cardboard box in the rain. Unable to bear the Alchemist any longer, the highway writhed, emitted the plangent groan of a stretched catgut string, and broke. Tag was himself again. He fell through grey moiré—

—to land almost instantly in the middle of two lanes of human traffic. It was four in the afternoon, raw cold and dark not far away. Of the Alchemist and his false highway there was no sign. Visibility was poor: low cloud, drifting mist, rain streaming in from the bleak downs north of the road. Everything looked brown and smeared, as if water were running down the very air. Spray, ripped in tufts and plumes from the wheels, obscured things further. Headlamps glared through this, their light rippling away into brassy reflections from the surface of the tarmac. Drivers squinted. Windshield wipers banged uselessly. Horns blared as the huge vehicles drifted slowly back and forth across one another's paths.

Old and vulnerable away from the wild roads, Majicou lay half conscious in the middle of the road, soaked in a sour mastic of dirty water and oil.

The little tabby was trying to pull him to safety from under the wheels.

Three eyes stared bright and blank with fear at the vehicle bearing down on them. It towered up like the side of a house, black water streaming diagonally along its sides to break away into its slipstream in a brown spume. Tag, who had fallen to earth ten yards away, watched Majicou raise himself groggily and then subside. His back legs seemed useless. Had he been hit already? The tabby buried her teeth in his scruff and redoubled her efforts. Losing her grip suddenly, she tumbled over backward and was forced to dance away from the oncoming monster just as Tag, closing the gap, darted straight into its path.

"Majicou!"

Majicou looked up.

"Go back, Tag," he said.

"I've got you," Tag said.

He felt the old cat's fur in his mouth. He felt the old cat's heart race.

"Tag, go back!"

The truck hit them both.

Tag felt a bang and saw things at strange angles. The inside of his head went limp. He hung on to Majicou. Wheels were everywhere, black and shiny as flint. A length of frayed blue rope whipped back and forward in the slipstream of the wagon. For a split second, as the world was tilting away, Tag saw this and remembered a kitten chasing blue string up and down a pink carpet. Then the underneath of the thing, all rust and caked black oil and whirling shafts, was above him. He tugged at the old cat with all his might. He heard, through the roar of the machine, through the terror and confusion inside his skull, the furious screech of a cat in pain.

"Majicou!" he called.

Something picked him up and threw him aside. There was an unbearable pain in the side of his head. The world folded up into it and vanished.

He woke. It was more pain, and he was looking up into a sky of dull, slate-colored clouds. He seemed to be moving, though it was hard to say how. His own legs were quite still. He was lying down motionless, but at the same time inching along slowly under this shifting gray sky. Rain fell into his open mouth. He heard loud, urgent noises, and great shadows passed over him, filling him with fear. Everything stank of oil. Everything was vague but threatening. When he shook his head to clear it, consciousness swung away from him into a soft mass of charcoal-gray feathers.

He woke again.

Dread went through him, and he dragged himself upright immediately. The world spun but held. The side of his head felt as if it had been scraped raw. He was in the short grass at the side of the road, where all was gray with mud and the chemicals of human transport. He had no memory of getting there, but, to judge by the light, only a few minutes had passed since he'd been run over. He wondered where he was and how it had happened. He thought he might be on the Caribbean Road. Perhaps he had been hit as he pulled the tabby from under the passing wheels.

"It's my own fault," he told himself.

He felt vague and detached, as if this stuff were happening not quite to him but to someone else called Tag: a near relative.

"I should never have eaten that rat."

A memory of the rat's dry, intelligent voice and greasy fur caused him to heave a couple of times. He blinked to clear his vision. The road swam as if seen through water. It was not the Caribbean Road. Then Cy was shuffling toward him backward, with her bottom stuck in the air. He dimly remembered warning her, "The next time you go in the road, stay there." Would she ever learn? She had no fear of roads, human or otherwise. She was at home with all of them. Here she was now, patiently dragging something inedible out of this one. He couldn't quite see what it was.

"Were you born yesterday?" he called.

Then he remembered everything.

Together they pulled the one-eyed cat the last foot or two out of the traffic.

He seemed light enough. Everything that made him Majicou was gone. It was like pulling an old fur collar through the rain. Every so often he woke up and tried to help, but his spine was broken and he couldn't get his rear legs under him. He kept trying to help; he kept trying to speak. When they set him down in the bleached grass at the side of the road, he seemed better for a while. Then blood bubbled suddenly from his mouth. He thrashed to and fro in front of them in his anger to live. They darted about helplessly or stood shivering, ignoring each other in their fear of death.

"Tag—"

"Majicou! I don't know what to do!"

"Tag," whispered Majicou. "Listen—"

He lay still, trembling from head to foot with shock, the damp air around him heavy with the iron smell of blood. Tag approached him cautiously, and sniffed.

"Majicou?"

"Come here, Tag. Listen. There is nothing you can do for me now. No. Don't look away. Listen. Listen to me. Don't blame the tabby. She has done her best by all of us, and she has one more thing to do."

"But—"

"Listen! Never blame her, Tag. She must be brought to Tintagel."

"But, Majicou, she—"

The old cat's eye was fixed wide open, so dilated that to him the dull afternoon must have seemed like noon on the brightest summer day he had ever known. He shook his head irritably.

"Do as I say, Tag."

There was a pause.

"It dazzles me, Tag." He said tiredly, "I have failed. All is lost."

"No," Tag said.

"Tag, Tag. You weren't a bad apprentice. What do you know about death?"

"Nothing."

"Good. Listen: we couldn't have life without it." He laughed bitterly. "How would we *know*?" he said. "My last life, too. I shall truly die now."

Tag couldn't think how to delay him.

"Don't die," he said. "You haven't told me my real name."

The old cat gave the ghost of a smile.

"Haven't you understood anything?" he said. "Very well then. So far as your breeders knew, Tag, you were an accident. One Saturday afternoon, their Burmese entered the cage of a visiting shaded silver Chinchilla queen." He tried to smile again, but it looked more like a snarl. "One kitten was born from that short affair. A Burmilla, of course. Bloodlines all confused. Too heavy for the breed standard, and with ridiculous great feet—but a black-tipped Burmilla nevertheless, and a nexus of champion lines. You were 'petted out' to Cutting Lane as an embarrassment. They had no idea of your significance. How could they? But before they delivered you into my care— I who had been waiting so many years!—they had to give you a name worth having, and they did:

"Mercurius Realtime DeNeuve.

"Tag, they called you Mercury ... and you have as fine a pedigree, in your way, as Ragnar or Pertelot Fitzwilliam." The old cat closed his eye. "Now leave me alone," he said.

"What kind of cat is a Burmilla?" asked Tag in wonder. He had turned around and was trying to look at himself.

Majicou laughed. His voice was barely a whisper now, but it was full of unaccustomed warmth. "Look in any mirror. A Burmilla cat has honest green eyes and thick silver fur. A Burmilla cat combines mass with naïveté, sturdiness with a limitless capacity for missing the point. When the highways at Cutting Lane first delivered you to me, I wasn't sure you would serve my purpose. A Burmilla cat does not make the world's most intelligent apprentice, Tag, but it is beautiful, affectionate, interesting, disobedient, and—above all—optimistic. You weren't a bad pupil, but I was an absent teacher." There was a silence, filled only by the harsh rattle of the old cat's breath. He said, with considerable effort, "Somehow you learned anyway. If you have a talent, Tag, it's to be yourself."

Majicou's death was not kind to him, except in the snatches of unconsciousness it offered. These he accepted gratefully. When he woke, he was so weak he could barely move his head. "Tag?" he whispered once. And when Tag bent close, "So many years." Tag sat. Cy calmed down. They were able to be beside the old cat so that he wasn't lonely as the day drew to its close. At the last, the clouds were broken in the west, and a thin line of sun struck down.

"The light!" cried Majicou. "The light!"

A prolonged convulsion took him up and threw him about. Bright blood filled his mouth. He bit himself. He bit the ground. "Tag! Tag! You must be there. It must be done in the presence of—"

And he was gone.

Now I've lost everyone, Tag thought.

"You've still got me," said the tabby.

Tag stared at her.

"I didn't speak," he said.

"You did."

"This is all your fault."

"No it isn't."

"Go away."

She hissed at him resentfully and went to sit a little way away along the side of the road. There, she began to collect things and sing. Every so often she looked up to see if he was watching her. Tag took no notice. He was remembering how it had been when he was a kitten and lived in a wonderful place. The warm kitchen with its yellow walls and red-tiled floor. A red cloth mouse—"*My* mouse!" Meat-and-liver dinner. How could he ever forget? He remembered how his dulls had blown bubbles for him, and how the bubbles had wobbled through the air like little worlds filled with evening light, to burst with a noise that only he could hear. He remembered how he had thought he was a prince. How the garden birds had laughed at him! How the magpie had jeered! He had been so naive he didn't even know what a highway was. I've come a long way since then, he thought. And he wished with all his might he had stayed where he was.

Then he seemed to hear Majicou's voice, faint and distant.

"You don't need the wonderful place, Tag. You carry it with you. Homes are made."

"I'll miss you, Majicou," he said.

He turned his face west and began to walk.

The tabby, busy with her pile of things, looked surprised. After a moment, she abandoned them and followed him.

"I pulled you out of that road, you know!" she called. "When will you ever learn?"

Part Three

Where the Wild Roads Meet

Chapter Nineteen

THE ANCIENT COUNTRY

Why are Freyja's
eyes so bright?
From her eyes it seems
that fire doth burn.
—THE ELDER EDDA

*L*ater that night, down in the warm cabin with their bellies full of tinned food, the cats found themselves on their own again.

One for Sorrow had declared himself fit and well. He had spoken at length of what he called "bullying" and "superstitious rubbish." He had flown landward in a dignified manner, to take Majicou the news of the pregnancy and inform him of Pertelot's intention to make her way overland to Tintagel once the *Guillemot* had docked in the ancient country.

Meanwhile, Old Smoky had dropped anchor in a small harbor town, heaved himself into the tender, and rowed ashore for supplies. He was off, he muttered, to get his clothes dry, and his insides wet, at a local inn.

Sealink lazed full-length on the vacated bunk, one eye on the old Rex, the other on her own coat, which had now been returned to its full luster by an extended period of attention.

Pertelot lay dreamily beside the calico. She felt the kittens float into her mind. They were swimming inside her! She purred softly to encourage them, and let them fill her with their strange, subtle motions as they pursued the long water journeys of the womb. Something made her think, "the unrepeatable journeys of the womb."

She shook herself.

Everything was so fragile. Everything was so strong.

"Pengelly," she said. "The silkies . . ."

Since the rescue of the old fisherman, Pengelly had been crouched on the cabin steps. It was his compromise between being where he wanted to be—up on deck, watching the waves—and being in the cabin, where Sealink could keep an eye on him. The Mau's voice roused him from his stupor. His amber eyes in their wildly skewed aspects were dull with misery.

"Neither cat nor fish," he said. "Why talk?"

"I don't understand."

"That was my *sister*!" he cried.

"Oh, Pengelly. My poor thing."

"No one should have to see that! It fair hurts my soul to think of her down there. Here I am in warmth and comfort, with a kind man to feed me, while she wanders the cold dark sea with the rest of them that drowned. When I die I'll go peaceful down the wild road; but she'll swim forever, looking for land."

"My poor Pengelly."

"Aye, poor Pengelly—his sister's neither cat nor fish. A silkie . . . I never thought to see one, let alone one of my own flesh and blood . . ."

He mused.

"Silkies," he said. "I never believed in them, till now. They say you can hear them howl on stormy nights, warning the big ships off the rocks. I'm told they lie all day in the sun on the high-tide line and groom their fur like you or me, and deck themselves out with seaweed, and live on the souls of fish the fishermen throw back into the sea."

There was an empty pause. Sealink shrugged. She said, gently, "It's a life, hon. Maybe that's a life we can't know."

"Oh yes," agreed the old Rex. "It's a life. What a life that is, eh? She'll never catch a mouse or sleep curled with another warm creature or have kits of her own. And she'll never know this: I wish I'd died that day instead of she. It should be me down there, not her . . . The guilt of it has never left me. And now I shall never see her again . . ."

He raised his head and wailed.

"Never look at a silkie," he said. "It'll be one of your own, and you'll regret it forever . . ."

"Please don't, Pengelly," cried Pertelot.

She jumped up from the bunk and curled herself around him. "Please don't. Wriggle came to save Old Smoky in return for his help all those years ago. She's happy you're alive. She's happy for us all."

"How do you know she's happy?"

"Because all kittens begin in a sea. I have mine here in me. Your silkie sister would not begrudge them a life above the waves. My heartfelt thanks to her. And their thanks too."

She purred suddenly.

Pengelly looked from her to Sealink.

"You're right, I know," he admitted.

But at the mention of kittens, Sealink rearranged herself into a tight ball, her face stiff with some visible but untranslatable emotion.

"Don't dwell on the past, old tom," she advised him. "Never cry over lost kittens or spilled milk. Keep looking forward, take what you can, remember who you are. The world can't trick you then."

With that she refused to countenance any further talk. Crabs, silkies, things in the wild night: they were all one to her, she implied. She would rather be on her way to Mother Russia in a jet.

The next few days brought no drama. With the sail up, they drifted along the coast. As they passed through the shoals of mackerel, Old Smoky pulled up string upon string. Sealink and Pertelot stood over the flapping bodies as the old fisherman tossed them into the boat, fascinated by their sunlit tabby stripes, the fading iridescence of their scales.

They tasted good too.

As the image of his silkie sister waned, Pengelly spent his time following Old Smoky around the boat, rubbing his cheek against the new Wellington boots, until they had a proper place in the scent map of his territory. He was perhaps a little aimless, a little insecure.

By day, the wintry sun offered early promise of spring as it split the last of the clouds and fanned out over the sea in sheaves of golden light. A brisk breeze drove them ever closer to their destination.

All night, the stars wheeled overhead, as sharp as claw marks in a velvet sky. Pengelly sat on the deck and gazed at them. He could never get enough stars. Pertelot stretched out by him, so that the kittens could feel the starlight on her belly. She wanted them to be at home in the dark.

"Stars on the brine," Pengelly told the Mau with a kind of companionable authority, "tomorrow sunshine. That's what they say. Clear skies, see: stars are beautiful bright. Did you know that you can find your way by the stars?"

This bewildered the Queen of Cats.

"But there are so many. How can you tell them apart?"

The old Rex smiled.

"See, there, halfway up the southern sky, a creature with four legs running across the heavens, tail stretched out in the wind?"

Pertelot squinted. A shape sprang out of the confusion.

"It has a glowing eye!" she exclaimed. She was delighted.

"Aye, that's She. That's the Great Cat—Felis Major, my dear, and her they call the Cat Star—humans know it as the Dog Star, for their ignorance. There, in the middle, veiled as it heads for its northernmost aspect, the Eye of Horus."

The Mau shivered; but Pengelly, warmed to his subject, did not notice.

"And just to the east that's Felis Minor, the Kitten. See how close they lie. Unusual, that. And there—" he stretched out a wiry paw "—soaring up landward, there's the Heart of the Lion, guardian to all travelers on the wild roads. Shining faintly down at the horizon, that's the Lynx. You won't see the Wolf or the Leopard for a little while yet; they'll rise later in the night."

He looked perplexed for a moment. "Curious, that," he muttered to himself. "Looks as if they'll converge, come vernal equinox."

Then he shook his head and trotted below deck to curl up with Old Smoky, leaving Pertelot to stare into the skies and wonder.

I feel my kittens turn in the light of the Great Cat's smile, she thought.

But in the dark recesses of her skull, some other idea trembled. She felt it. She pushed it down.

"I am a cat," she whispered defiantly. "I am a cat like other cats; and these kittens will be like other kittens. I will carry them with me to Tintagel and give birth to them like any mother. I shall feed them and guard them—" she lifted her head to the blazing sky "—and not even you will take them from me while I live."

Late the next afternoon they sailed into harbor.

Old Smoky stowed the canvas, started the engine, and threaded the boat neatly between the rocky outcrops that bracketed the estuary. The town rose up on either side of a wide river dotted with moored boats and colorful buoys. Nestling between evergreens at the eastern entrance to the town was a ruined fort, its walls gray and foursquare against the foliage. The remains of its companion guarded the western bank. Houses had been piled, it seemed, one upon another, street upon street, from the water's edge to the top of the hill. Quays and a boatyard passed on one side, a deserted beach on the other. Then a marina full of bobbing pleasure craft. Smells wove a tapestry in the air to catch the attention of the three cats: a distinct but not overwhelming odor of humans and their vehicles, estuarine salt, sharp tang of fish, wood smoke and coal fires—a bustle of life.

Pengelly drew it all down into his lungs and sighed.

"I love this town. It smells like home to me."

Pertelot was curious. "I thought the *Guillemot* was your home?"

"Aye, 'tis, my dear, when we'm away. But when we'm home, well, this is home," he said simply.

Sealink leaned across to the Queen. "Make what you like of that, hon," she said.

"I shall miss it," said Pengelly.

And he gazed sentimentally at the passing jetties draped with emerald weed, the golden light streaming from uncurtained windows.

The Mau gave Sealink a look. "What?"

Sealink shrugged and shook her head. "Aren't you staying, then?"

"How can I, my dear? My duty's clear. 'Twouldn't be right to let two females cross those moors on their own!"

Sealink growled. "My," she said, "this sure is old-world down here."

She stuck her face into Pengelly's.

"I've traveled all my life with no help from males. As for Queenie here, well, she may be thin but she's from old stock, an' they got this far on their own. You been real kind, *sir,* in allowing us to share your boat and your food and all. Even if it was because you fancied the fur off me."

The growl turned into a brief, throaty purr.

"And maybe that's okay, and I'll come by here again when I've visited this Tintagel place. But Pertelot and me'll be on our way tonight, without *help* from no randy old tom."

Pengelly received this diatribe looking at once forlorn and hopeful. The first of these emotions advertised itself in the eye that considered the calico full-on, the second lurked in the one that peered craftily up and away.

"You may have your joke, my dear," he said, "but you'll need all the help you can get. The moors are old and treacherous, and her ladyship here has kits to think of . . ."

Pertelot regarded him thoughtfully.

She would miss his gentle humor and his old-fashioned manners. But he mustn't go with them. He was an old cat, and she would not put him in danger. Of course, he had already sensed that. It was his pride that was at risk, not his chance to dance with a calico queen in her prime. Or perhaps it was both.

"We'll be fine," she reassured him.

He snorted.

She tried another tack. "Look," she said, "we can't take you away from Old Smoky. You belong together. Without each other you'd wither away. I've never believed a human being could really love a cat, nor a cat a human being. All I've known from the upright ones is cruelty and coldness. Yet seeing you together, you look . . . well, comfortable."

Pengelly knew exactly what she was up to. He winked and gave in.

"Aye, well, you could be right there. Two old beggars we are: so gray and grizzled and cranky that no female'll have us and we have to cherish each other. Still—" he brightened "—might get me leg over an old calico one day, who knows?"

"Dream on, sailor."

* * *

The last of the light was draining out of the western sky as two cats, one fine-lined but with a rather distended belly, the other large and furry, with a huge plume of tail, trotted purposefully across the gleaming pebbles of an empty strand. The ebbing tide had left behind it sandbanks etched with a complex pattern of ripples curiously reminiscent of a mackerel's skin. Under the eaves of the shrubs that overhung the riverbank, all was silent but for the furtive scrabbling of some waterside rodent going about its business in the twilight.

"Shouldn't we—?"

Sealink listened for a moment, dismissed the suggestion.

"No need, hon. Plenty of food where we're going," she promised.

Woods rose steeply up the cleft of the river valley. Sallows drooped leafless and pale to the water, their slender boughs rustling in the icy breeze. Sealink led Pertelot up terraces of dripping evergreens and ancient oaks whose gnarled roots twisted among boulders of granite, outlines blurred with moss and liverwort. Hart's-tongue fern sprang up between the rocks, pale green blades a startling contrast to the shadows. The two cats plowed through drifts of curled brown leaves and empty acorn cups—of the squirrels who had emptied them there was no sign—and out onto the top of a hill.

Below, the river snaked and glinted. A narrow creek wound off to the right; beyond it the main watercourse widened and split, both forks fading from view in the dusk. A waning moon crested the far hills even as the sun dipped behind them so that for an eerie moment both bodies seemed to hang in some celestial balance; then the sun sank in graceful defeat into the sea, and in its place the first of the evening stars became visible.

"Look how high we are!" gasped Pertelot.

To start with, she had been enjoying herself. Now she was exhausted and out of breath, and the kittens were dragging at her, and she meant *Let's stop and look*. But it wasn't much help. Sealink didn't stop, and by the time Pertelot could breathe steadily again, the calico was already halfway down the hill, an indistinct shadow among the furze.

"Wait! Wait!"

Two miles later they had crossed the creek via stepping-stones that terrified her, scrambled up a steep bank covered with ivy and thorn, and climbed a rocky outcrop, only to drop down almost as steeply on the other side. They had dodged a farmworker on its way home with its dog. The dog, catching their scent, had strained at its leash, barking eagerly. They had watched a great white owl fly soundlessly overhead, then stoop and vanish from sight. When, a second later, a thin high shriek had announced the sudden end of some small life, Sealink had carried on with barely a pause. They had crossed hard tracks that smelled of diesel fumes and the excrement of some large animal. They had ducked through every hedge, run down every ditch, and surmounted every wooded hill on the way.

"I'm sorry. Please stop. I just can't go any farther."

Sealink, who, cramped by the shipboard life, had been rather relishing the chance to stretch her legs, stared down puzzledly.

"Sorry, hon," she said after a moment. "I guess you ain't used to this. Stay here. I'll go fetch us some dinner."

And she disappeared into the darkness.

Pertelot found herself a niche in the tangled roots of an ash, and from there listened to the life of the woods at night. It was a strange place for a cage-bred cat. Twigs rustled in the breeze. A beetle trudged through dead leaves. A disturbance of air brought information about the slow beat of great wings in flight. Seconds later the barn owl ghosted overhead and came to rest in the uppermost branches of a far tree, a mouse protruding from either side of its cruel beak. She knew when it began to eat. She could hear quite clearly the rip of tendon and warm, rich flesh. These events seemed to make her alert to the quick heartbeat of small creatures near her. They were awake and aware of her.

She started to salivate. Meanwhile, from down the slope came muffled thumps and crashes, the sounds of a great deal of energy being expended to little gain.

"Hang on in there, hon."

Pertelot dozed. Her ears and whiskers were alive to her surroundings even as she slept. The kittens moved comfortably inside her. She dreamed of Ragnar Gustaffson, tall and proud. His long, handsome face, the warmth of his breath on her muzzle, the weight of his body upon hers . . .

Her eyes snapped open. Another animal's breath steaming in the air in front of her!

It was Sealink, empty-pawed.

The next morning they were still hungry. In the wooded strip bordering the river on the opposite side they sat for a while and let the pale sun warm their fur. In that indeterminate season between winter and spring, the earth was still bound by frost. Leaf and bud were locked inside branch and stem. Little animals curled tight into well-chosen burrows, planning their brief, hazardous forays above ground. Nothing stirred. Even the wind had died away. It seemed as though the world were waiting.

By midday, they were making their way through fields of reddish earth. Puckered old berries hung on the hawthorns. Gray clouds had filled the sky. Gulls wheeled over the icy furrows. Pertelot's stomach growled. The *Guillemot* had started to seem like a lost home to her, full of the smells of food. How they had laughed at the crab and its antics! How she had enjoyed eating it! When she looked back, the boat was already like some warm, bright room, seen very small and far away.

At evening they reached a town of dark gray stone.

"We'll eat now, babe," promised Sealink, looking happily at the traffic and people and glowing shop windows. "Will we eat!"

But they didn't.

The dustbins had been emptied that morning. They found a fish and chip shop and hung around it for what seemed like hours. But it never opened. Pursued by its smell, they dodged around corners, down narrow alleys, and across an expanse of waste ground that led down through a children's playground to a stagnant pool scummed with pondweed and candy wrappers.

There, Sealink trawled disconsolately through the waste bins lining the path.

Nothing.

All that was left was the murky water. This she studied

without much hope, while the Mau watched exhaustedly from a broken bench.

"Hey!" said Sealink suddenly.

She dipped a paw into the water. She licked it thoughtfully. She dipped it again. Little muddy spirals spun to the surface. Sealink inspected her foreleg carefully. Shiny matter rolled off her fur, clusters of translucent globules each centered on a single black speck. This she tasted warily, then licked her black lips.

"Well, it's sure got a weird texture, hon; but you can get used to it. Tastes just fine."

Pertelot was done for. All her pleasure in the outdoors had gone. Her faith in Sealink was at a low ebb. She made her way to the edge and stared at the jellied mass floating on the water.

I can't eat that, she thought.

Then she looked sideways at Sealink, who was stuffing it down.

She thought, I don't care what I eat.

And, bending her head to the inevitable, she started to push it about timidly with her paws.

About this time, the calico, having fished out the inshore water, leaned farther out, and promptly fell in.

There was a wail of horror. Then the pond turned into a maelstrom of froth and weed, and she exploded out onto the bank, so wet that an observer would have been hard-pressed to determine exactly what species she belonged to. She shook herself with an energy born of fury, disgust, and embarrassment. Strings of spawn flew from her fur up onto the grass, where Pertelot gobbled them down.

One frog colony would be sadly depleted this spring.

Three days later, they had eaten very little else. More by luck than judgment, Sealink had flushed a bank vole that ran straight into the Mau's waiting paws. Half a vole was better than none, but they were soon hungry again. Earthworms, they found, were edible, if not delicious. But the patience it took to stand over their casts in the cow pasture, while fat wood pigeons flew contemptuously above, turned out to be more than Sealink could manage.

They tried eating beetles. But beetles are a lot of effort for what you get, and by the time they started the climb into the barren uplands bordering the moor, the Mau's ribs stood out like staves. Her pregnant belly was a swollen sac that seemed to bear no relation to the body that carried it. Sealink's fur disguised her condition more successfully. But her boundless energy was flagging, and her humor with it.

Up here, among the close sheep-bitten turf and icy winds that scoured the land, making it inhospitable to tree and leaf, game was even harder to come by. The only relief to the dull expanse of furze, thistle, and fescue were the raised profiles of quoits and sarsen stones. Pitted with age and the corrosive action of rain on granite, they stood proud against the weather. Sheep sheltered in their lee. Sealink regarded the sheep with a cunning, acquisitive glint, but they were clearly out of her league. Crows soared like black rags against the sky. There were magpies, too, but none of them answered to the name of One for Sorrow, and they had no interest in a pair of wandering Felidae.

They crawled beneath fences of barbed wire festooned with wool, climbed over low drystone walls, and moved ever northward with the sun as their guide.

On the edge of the moor they encountered their first wild road.

It buzzed and hummed; but when Sealink stuck her head inside, there was nothing moving on it, and no sense that anything had used it for a while—as she explained to a bewildered Pertelot.

"There was no sense of destination to it. None at all. It was just as if it ended in midair . . . Real odd, babe. Not many cats passing this way at the best of times, I know; but it was eerie in there." She shivered. "Shame, really, hon. I know you don't like to use the things, but we could sure do with some help, you know?"

That night, however, their luck changed, or so it seemed.

As the last of the light went out of the sky, Sealink glimpsed a pair of lighted windows in the distance. A farm or cottage? Humans meant food, and perhaps shelter: an outbuilding where they could sleep out of the biting cold. The two cats cut quickly across the upland valley, over sodden mats of sphagnum and sedge that soaked their paws and bellies, skirting pools of stagnant water that lay between clumps of bilberry, bog myrtle, and cotton grass, their breath steaming in the night air.

The farmyard was deserted.

They dodged warily beneath the wheels of a tractor, slipped around a rusting trailer, a tangle of hurdles and buckets and fraying orange twine, and crouched behind a stack of bales, scanning the scene cautiously.

A powerful cocktail of smells had been prepared for them: machine oil, chemicals, various species of livestock and their waste products, other cats . . .

"Stay here, hon," Sealink breathed.

She dropped into her New Orleans street-fighter's shuffle—a curious, sideways gait designed to present the largest possible profile to any opponent—and crossed the yard.

Everything in the barn was ingrained with the scent marks of the local tom. But he seemed to be out patrolling his boundaries, and nothing stirred but some chickens who clucked and ruffled their feathers at her as she passed.

She regarded them ruefully. Too big.

On the far side of the yard, though, her nose helped her to the discovery of the day: a large ceramic dish full of great chunks of meat in gravy. The area around the bowl smelled rank and strange, but food was food, even if it was a little crusted on top. Without conscious thought, Sealink buried her face in it and began choking it down.

This process—which bore more similarity to inhaling than to eating—filled the night with noise. Pertelot drooled behind the hay bales for a minute or two, then let the biological imperative take charge. She had to feed herself and her unborn kittens, quickly, now, before Sealink ate the lot.

Even as she made this decision, pandemonium broke loose. An explosion of thuds and grunts. A sound like a ceramic bowl rolling across concrete. Snarls, shrieks, hisses, and howls that bounced from wall to wall of the farmyard and echoed off into the night.

The Mau poked her head out and had a quick look around.

Where Sealink had been, there was a blur: a ball of fury-colored black and white and orange. When this broke apart for a second, it resolved itself into a calico cat—back arched and every filament of fur on end, its lips drawn back in malignant defiance—enough to put any normal creature to flight—and a frenzied piebald collie dog three times her size, his scarred old face ruched with hatred and territorial madness.

"My food! My food! My food!"

"Come near me again, asshole, and I'll rip your face off!"

"My food! My food! My food!"

"Oh, grow up, jerk!"

Pertelot watched, rooted to the spot, as they went at each other again in the mist of saliva, obscenity, and murder.

Then a door opened and a human being ran out, shouting. Cat and dog broke apart. Sealink streaked across the yard; and the dog, yowling and yammering in triumph, turned his attention to the Mau. She stiffened. Adrenaline poured through her. Without a second's thought she took to her heels. Muscles bunching and stretching, legs working like pistons, she sprinted after Sealink, who called, "Run, hon! Run!" and caught her up and overtook her.

"My yard! My yard!" railed the dog.

Its gnarled paws thudded into the ground.

When Pertelot turned, she saw Sealink slowing visibly, her eyes wide and blood pouring from a wound on her hind leg.

"Sealink!"

With a curious grunt of despair, the calico toppled over, legs outstretched toward her attacker, claws extended to rake in a last-ditch defense. The collie made little, jabbing, bouncing runs at her, already howling with victory.

The Mau stared, appalled.

Rage flooded through her.

She had no choice. She ran back, stood over the fallen calico, and prepared to face off the ancient enemy.

Something odd happened.

The world shimmered for a moment, and suddenly she was someone else.

This other her was big and old and had no fear. Charged with all the experience of the hunter and the hunted, the wild and the tame, she tested the electric air. All the long, intense years of Felidae washed through her system like a great wave. She smelled prey. Her head buzzed and rang with it. Her fangs bared themselves. Her body swelled with muscle. She looked down upon the dog as if from a great height.

Canidae! she thought with contempt.

A million generations of bad blood filled the space between them. Behind the dog, she saw the landscape stretch and blur. Moor and farmland were replaced by swathes of savannah—burned land, drought land, scrubland—then forest canopies in a green jaguar daze, and at last the great deserts themselves.

She saw the wavering air, the breaking dunes, the line of palms. She smelled the distant water and the sweet blood of the doves!

"Canidae!" she heard herself hiss.

The dog stopped in its tracks.

Where once had been a pair of thieving mogs, there now loomed a great, snarling animal the color of sand. Black stripes ran from its eyes across its wide head. Long, tufted ears were raised aggressively. Its breath was hot and its teeth cold. It spoke a language he had never heard. In the face of such an apparition he could only quiver. His tail, of its own accord, it seemed, drooped suddenly. His ears flattened. Belly low to the soaking ground, he found himself whining in submission.

Hind and forefeet almost overlapping in his eagerness to escape, he turned and fled.

The caracal watched him go.

Canidae! she thought.

Then she took the injured calico between her jaws, lifting it as gently as she might a kitten, and at a stately pace padded into the darkness.

Around her, a highway shimmered briefly in the air. Then she was gone.

A few minutes later, an observer crossing the uplands that night might have seen the incongruous sight of a heavily pregnant, but otherwise tiny, domestic cat, ribs showing clearly through its slick fur, muscles trembling with the effort, lugging the weight of a far larger cat up into the safe recesses of an isolated granite tor.

Sealink's leg was slow to heal.

Teeth had met at the bone from either side. She had lost a considerable amount of blood. Between them, they licked the wound clean and its surface healed over within a day; but this only caused the leg to swell with infection, so Pertelot had to nip the skin with needle-sharp teeth to allow it to drain.

They slept for long periods of time. Neither of them spoke of the Mau's transformation. How much had Sealink understood through her mist of pain? Pertelot, confused and terrified by the whole affair, found herself reluctant to ask. Many of the night's events would remain blurred.

After she had left the highway, it appeared that she had dragged the calico into a cave in the granite bedding planes. There she had found a great jumble of sticks and twigs, arranged in a loose nest and cemented with a mixture of earth and turf, tufts of sheep's wool, and scraps of fur. Tiny bones jutted through the lining, delicate and white as shells. It smelled musty and unvisited, but it provided effective shelter from the elements, and some of the turf was still green. Both cats were able to fit neatly within its confines, curled one around the other.

They wondered what had made this odd collection, but they did not have to speculate for long. Early one morning, Sealink raised a sleep-hazed head and stared right into a large, black, shiny eye.

"Raaaaaark!"

She blinked. This was no magpie.

"Out! Out of my roost!"

It was a bird three times the size of any crow, with a powerful beak, broad jet-black shoulders, and a throatful of long, pointed feathers currently fluffed out in considerable annoyance. He bobbed his wicked head, spread a pair of wings almost four feet from tip to tip, so that they filled the cave, and croaked again. "Out! Out!"

The inside of his mouth, including a large, muscular tongue, was as black as the outside. Though she had woken hungry, she struck him off her list of possible prey. In fact, she thought, I'll go one further.

"Hey, hon," she said. "Don't eat us."

The bird stared at her.

"We were, you know, looking for a little shelter. But we had no idea the place was already took." She looked around. "It's nice, but I don't usually sleep in sticks. Y'know?"

During this exchange, the Mau had roused herself and sat up in amazement. Head on one side, the bird now regarded her swollen belly. He folded his wings down, ruffled his feathers.

"Two Felidae," he told himself quietly, "up here in my roost. *Graaa.*"

He considered Pertelot's thin ribs.

"One pregnant with all her bones showing, and one wounded—she has a big mouth and less flesh than she's used to. *Kaaaark!*" With a rustle of feathers he sailed suddenly off the ledge, slipped sideways on a column of air, and vanished from sight. Some minutes later he was back.

"*Gak,*" he said. "*Graaa.*"

He had brought with him a still-warm starling.

"If you've come to goad us," began Sealink. But the great bird only swooped into the cave, dropped the starling gently in a surprised Pertelot's lap, and flew off once more.

Three times he returned, with an egg, a mouthful of worms, and the not-very-old carcass of a field mouse; all of which he presented to his visitors with a dusty hospitality—as if he knew the gesture but had not had the chance to practice it for a while. The cats, out of equal formality, of course, ate the lot.

"Yes," said the bird, watching closely. "*Graaa.* Can't have a mother starve, no matter what her species."

Pertelot took this as an opportunity to ask the bird its name and family.

He looked offended.

"Don't you know *Corvus corax*? *Raaaark!*"

Sealink, of course, knew a raven when she saw one.

"Met some of you guys at a tower, once," she recalled. "Where was that? Old. Stony. Human beings in parrot costumes. Pretty weird."

"Ah, the tower . . ."

The raven looked wistful. "I expect that's where Thought went," he said.

"Beg pardon?"

"My nest mate, Thought. She went away last year." He nodded back to himself, looked around. "I like to keep the place up, just in case she comes back. Yes. I looked forward to raising chicks here."

The Mau watched him sadly as he picked up a piece of eggshell, studied it for a moment, then flung it over the edge. "My name's Memory, by the way," he said. "Thought and Memory!"

He chuckled dryly.

"Ravens have a mythological bent."

He fed them until Pertelot had gained weight and Sealink could flex her hind leg without the wound opening. He said it was a tradition of ravens. The rain poured down outside, he perched on the edge of his nest and regarded them as if they really were nestlings, and told them stories of the Moor, and the great black Beast that roams it. He seemed to know when they were ready to leave, and at the third twilight bade them farewell.

"Keep to the high ground," he advised. "It's cold up there, but you can see where you are. Lower down, the bogs are treacherous; and mist tends to gather in the valleys."

He watched them go.

"A bad winter this year, and no sign of it breaking yet. Strange things going on too. Keep an eye open at all times."

He called, "*Corvus corax.* Don't forget. And if you should see Thought, tell her I remember her!

"Kaaaark!"

They resumed their northward trek across the ancient country, keeping the sun on their right in the early part of the day, and on their left toward evening. Progress was slow: Sealink limped, though she made no complaint. Pertelot's belly swung low to the ground, and she began to feel the kittens inside her.

They did much better for food now. Pertelot's encounter with her wild self—the caracal within—had released some innate ability to hunt. Toward the end of their first day, she staked out a rabbit warren in a patch of stunted gorse; surprised the doe that cropped unconcernedly downwind; and had made the killing leap, plummeting down from high above her quarry, to dispatch it with a crushing blow and a suffocating bite to the throat. It was almost half her size; but between them they ate it in a night, crunching the bones and swallowing down even the fur and feet, so that not a morsel was left.

In the days that followed Pertelot caught and killed: a short-tailed vole, two mice, a meadow pipit, a second rabbit, and a mole. She was a hammer.

"It ain't seemly in a Queen," Sealink complained. "I'm eatin' as fast as I can!"

When Pertelot laid the meadow pipit mournfully at Sealink's feet she was forced to admit, "I didn't even mean to kill this one. I just caught the movement as it ran through the grass. The next thing I knew, it was in my mouth." She stroked a paw down its soft, spotted plumage, examined its tiny, hooked feet with regret. Sealink watched her sardonically, then took its head off in a single bite.

The weather turned colder. Feathers of snow came twisting and tumbling out of a leaden sky, blanketing the moors with soft deception. Sealink awoke one morning from a hollow in the heather and limped delightedly about, her head turned up to the flying snow and her great, tufted paws making quiet whumping noises in the drifts.

Pertelot found it hard going. Her tiny feet sank down until she was up to her nose in it, and her belly was driven into it and she feared her kittens would be frozen inside her.

She looked like a cat in deep water.

By day, she struggled. By night, her dreams returned: full of flight and capture, torture and anguish. Sometimes she let herself dream about Ragnar and the kittens they would raise together. How could she stop? But if dreams like this visited her in the daylight, she closed herself like a shutter against them, and pushed herself into the weather. Rather drown in snow than face the pain of her loss and her fear of the future.

The snows melted; but the weather remained bitter. Freezing mists swept across the moors and swirled in the hollows. The water in the mosses underfoot froze so that each step crunched beneath them. No bird or animal was to be seen. The cats went hungry. Increasingly they were forced to skirt abandoned mine workings—open pits and the twisted, rusting metal of disused railway lines. They passed through ancient hut circles and tumuli without any idea of what they were. Acres of sedge and furze stretched away from them, as far as the eye could see. The sun made its daily journey, followed by the moon and her retinue of stars. Sealink's leg remained stiff and ached in the cold. As Pertelot's kittens grew, she became increasingly exhausted and needed more frequent rests.

One night, a curtain of fog draped itself across the entire landscape. It was impossible to see more than a body length ahead. The cats shivered and debated—could they go on?—while the fog pressed itself against them like a physical presence, dampening their fur and chilling them to the bone. Bushes poked through it like spiny, sudden, black fingers, to vanish again as they passed.

They reached the shores of a lake.

Everything was deathly still. Pertelot stopped and sat down suddenly on the quartzy sand. "This is awful, Sealink. I can't go on . . ."

Behind her, the calico emerged by degrees: first her great, furry head and burning amber eyes; then her ruff and forelegs. She stood there for a moment, the front half of a cat apparently detached from its hindquarters, then the mist eddied and the rest of her appeared as if by magic.

"Come on, hon. It don't do to despair."

"I'm frightened of falling or drowning, and I'm so tired . . ."

They sat huddled up together in the hope that the weather would change, and for a time even fell into a kind of sleep. But the fog persisted, and despite Sealink's generous warmth, the Mau, dreaming suddenly of white birds over a green river, started to tremble. Sealink licked at the cold gray flesh beneath the rose-gray fur, and tried to warm those delicate ears. She was beginning to say, "I think we better walk a bit farther, babe," when she saw the Mau staring over her shoulder, eyes wide with terror.

"Sealink!"

Behind them the fog was swirling and spiraling, pouring up into the air, settling back down, torn and displaced by the movement of something very large. They watched, transfixed.

An enormous black carnivorous head hung in the air above them. Its eyes were pale moonlight and its breath another fog.

They remembered the raven.

They remembered his tales.

"Oh my," whispered the calico cat, and her voice cracked into a wail.

Nothing like this—nothing like this on any journey she had ever made. All that way and nothing like this.

"It's the Beast!"

Chapter Twenty
GHOST ROADS

For in the morning orisons, he loves the sun
and the sun loves him,
For he is of the tribe of Tiger.
— CHRISTOPHER SMART, *Jubilate Agno*

This soft western earth took badger prints, dog prints, the dainty prints of foxes but held them only the length of a night frost. The air was bitter one moment, warmed the next by the palest morning sun Tag ever saw. The ice was retreating from the ponds where the ruined willows leaned. Bare thorn curled into the hollows, molded by the white winds of early spring that touched the uplands like cold, anxious hands. Lapwings raced up piping from the plowland in arcs.

"Our field," they were calling. "Our field!"

Water rose in the wide rain-dirty valleys in the darkening afternoons. There was a wiry sound of last year's reeds rubbing together in the wind.

Tag's head hurt on the left side, where he had been hit. In the mornings it was a quick dizzying stab that came and went, clouding his vision and causing him to misjudge the distance of things. Later in the day it settled in and became a bare, steady ache as bleak as the fields around. He grew used to it. He grew to welcome it. When it left him for a moment, he looked up, quivering suddenly as if he expected a blow. His eye on that side blinked and watered, and was often half closed. It gave him the appearance of being absentminded and irritable at the same time.

In his sleep he prowled restlessly the ghost roads, and this damaged eye gave him a new kind of sight. He had the privileges of the living and the dead. He had the privileges of motion and stillness. There, in the rushing brown shadows, where the Majicou rolled to and fro in his agony, crying out

"The light! *The light!*" Mousebreath made his good-bye a hundred times, as if his real death had only been one more rehearsal. He looked so surprised. "I can't help you no more!" he would whisper or, "Hey, Tag, mate, I—" and die. Just as his ghost turned to smoke and became indistinguishable from the rest and rushed away, it sometimes stopped and turned and called, "Say good-bye to Sealink for me." They were such real dreams.

Tag followed the lanes and hedgerows in the sudden gray rains. The tabby followed Tag. Dragging along through the afternoon as it closed up like the arc of a door, hungry and fractious, her short legs unable to match his stride, she fell farther and farther behind. But she had always caught up by sunset, when Tag let himself fall where he had stopped. There was a pause, and then she came quietly out of the shadow of cedars or slipped from under a hedge fogged with old man's beard, her bib gleaming deceptively in a streak of light enameled pink and thrush-egg blue, her long, quiet complaint lost for a moment amid the hoarse cries from some rookery.

"I'm starved, Jack!"

"Feed yourself. Find some rubbish. Or a nice stick."

She regarded him mulishly. "I want a friend."

"You can't eat your friends."

Every day for a week, dawn assembled itself under cover of a thin cold mist, which lifted one morning to reveal four magpies convoked in a plowed field. They reminded Tag of something. He blinked and stopped washing, with one front paw lifted to his face. Acres of pale fawn earth swept away from him on a complex rising curve. At the top, the dark hazel coppices hung like smoke. To his watery eye everything had the slow undulating motion of weed underwater. Broken flints glittered hard and precise in each furrow. He was hungry.

The magpies hopped about silently for a time, moving away upslope. Then three of them made noises like a stick dragged along a wooden fence and took flight, flaring across the sky with their long tails as elegant as the sticks of rockets. Tag set himself to catch the fourth, slinking patiently along the deep cold furrows where the shadows lay black and precise. The wind scoured his face. He could smell the magpie on it, stale and dry. As Mousebreath had predicted, Tag didn't make the best hunter; but he was an obstinate one, and, applying with a kind of wooden determination the lessons he had learned, he could maintain himself and the tabby. He stopped whenever the bird's head went up. A skinny, tired-looking creature preoccupied with the effort of feeding, it never saw him coming. It eyed the ground. Stabbed. Waddled off a few yards and stabbed again. Its tail feathers were awry, and it had the oily, unpreened look of a sick pigeon. After a quarter hour, Tag was within a yard or two, forcing himself not to quiver or scold or warn anyone "My bird!" He got upslope of it and waited. The bird's back was to him. A dash and a scuffle and it was in his mouth, beating furious wings in his face and squawking with outrage in his ear. Like all birds, its feathers had a dry, musty, not very pleasant taste.

"Raaark! Haaraaark!"

"Shut up," Tag told it.

At this point one or two of his victims always managed to escape out of sheer hysteria. He was too hungry to allow that today. He shifted his grip and hung on grimly. But, indistinct though it was, his voice had been recognized. The bird began to shout, "It's me! You know me!"

"They all say that."

"You *know* me!"

It was One for Sorrow.

"Oh it's you," admitted Tag. "Damn."

As soon as he got free, the magpie began to hop around in jerky, drunken circles like a broken mechanism, stumbling over the crests of the furrows with one wing trailing, his neck extended, and his beak wide open. After a moment or two, Tag's head began to go around with him, aching and cold.

"Can't you keep still?"

"I'm hurt! You've hurt me!"

"I haven't."

One for Sorrow stopped trailing his wing. He ruffled his feathers and closed them like a dusty old fan. He approached with a kind of sideways shuffle and fixed Tag with one shiny eye. "You wouldn't believe the stuff that's happened to me," he said. Then, "Where's the rest of them?"

"We're all that's left," Tag said.

The magpie didn't understand. "But where's the fox?"

"I don't know," said Tag. "Majicou sent him down the highway on an errand. He feared his death was out there waiting for him. We haven't seen him since."

The magpie cocked his head alertly. "What errand?"

"I don't know."

"Then I must find Majicou and ask!"

By now the ache in Tag's head had blurred the magpie into a black-and-white wash. He stared at it blankly, wondering what he could say. In the end, all he could manage was, "Majicou is dead."

One for Sorrow looked nonplussed. He studied Tag from the corner of one eye. "The Majicou will never die," he said.

"We all die," Tag said. "How else would we know we'd been alive?"

And he turned and walked effortfully away. The tabby gave the magpie a contemptuous look and followed. Chirring and grating like an old rattle, One for Sorrow shot over their heads and bumped to earth in front of them.

"Wait!"

"You don't look so hurt," said Tag.

"Sealink and the Queen are alive!" said the magpie excitedly. "The Queen's *pregnant*." He looked from Tag to Cy and then across the long empty sweep of plowland. He cocked his head and asked puzzledly, "Where's Mousebreath?"

"Mousebreath's dead too."

"He can't be."

Tag walked on blindly. As he passed the magpie he repeated, "We're all that's left."

"Come back!" demanded One for Sorrow. "Listen! I've talked to Sealink and the Queen. Tag, come back!"

"No," said Tag. "You got me into this. I would have had a happy life but for you." He stopped and swung his head painfully toward where he thought the bird was. "I would have had a house," he said. Then he added, "Mousebreath was right."

"You don't look so hurt," the tabby accused the magpie.

They left him standing there, trying to absorb the scale of the disaster. It took them a long time to traverse the field against the grain of the plow and intersect the line of the far hedge. There, two tiny figures shining in a long pale crescent of sun, they began to comb the winter grass for beetles and voles, one watching while the other hunted, always moving downhill, always moving west. One for Sorrow watched them until they had disappeared, then shook himself and flew off.

Later, Tag felt angry with himself. I didn't mean to say any of those things, he thought. I used to admire that bird. And he loved Majicou. It wasn't fair to tell him like that. All afternoon he worried about One for Sorrow and wondered where Sealink and the Mau might be. What was their story? How had they fared? He had lost his chance to ask. "Kittens!" he exclaimed to himself. He couldn't quite grasp that. "Kittens!" He was too used to thinking of himself as a kitten to be able to imagine that. One for Sorrow. Sealink and Pertelot: Pertelot pregnant. How strange! Everything came back to him somehow—though it had never departed. All afternoon his mind worried and picked over in a kind of slow wonder the things that had happened to him since he left his home. He was exasperated. But he did notice that if he worried about the Mau instead of himself, his headache receded. The next morning he woke and admitted to Cy, "I don't know what to do."

They were sitting by a stream with a cat-lick of ice at its reedy edges. He had given her the front half of a bank vole for breakfast, but it was the first time he had spoken willingly to her since the death of Majicou. Straight away she came up close to him and began pushing her face against his. "My cat. My cat." Her purr was like a rough engine breaking into life. She had grown muddy again, especially about the bib, but her eyes were bright.

"I can't think," Tag said. "And I'm afraid of my dreams."

"Whoa, Silver!" she advised him. "Don't despair. We've got CB. 'Hello? Hello?' I'll dream those dreams with you!"

"That will help a lot," said Tag wryly.

But from then on she did seem to be in his dreams, and it did seem to help. The Majicou no longer acted out the pains of his hard death. Mousebreath slipped away, with a sly wink of his country eye and a "Don't wait for me, mate."

Over there on the dream roads Cy was cobbier and more kitten-shaped. She was cleaner. Her ears were bigger. She was always laughing. She was always running off ahead of him, only to wait with one paw raised under a domed sky the color of his coat. She chased everything that moved. She taught him to navigate. She taught him to speak to ghosts: echoes flew about like dragonflies. She tried to teach him about her "magic," and—though he would never have allowed this in the waking world or on a real highway—he tried to learn. Lights did seem to dribble from his mouth— they were hot and cold at the same time; they tasted as musty as they looked—or drift toward him like amber sparks. But after that his efforts only drew shadows out of the shadows, hulking things that, though they had form, reminded him too much of the *vagus*. Perhaps, he thought, magic was a thing only female cats could do. "You got no talent, Jack," the tabby was forced to agree. And when in the deep of the night he heard one of the shadows use his name, he grew afraid and would try no further.

"It said I was the Majicou," he tried to explain to her when they woke the next morning. "But I know that I'm not."

She regarded him with huge eyes. *"Woo,"* she breathed. She said, "You know, Silver: awake, you're a different cat!"

The world was a different world.

As they made their way west the land seemed to shift in sympathy with the tortured highways that crossed it. Long pleasant sweeps of chalk earth fell away to be replaced by a country of complex, intimate little valleys cut into honey-colored stone that, even at the end of a chilly afternoon in early spring, seemed to glow with warm light. These in turn gave way to the deeper, more somber valleys of a limestone upland, where full winter still reigned along the narrow rock-walled riverbanks and the water was gelid blue with cold. There, the day came late and ended early. There was no line of sight. But if their course was meandering and uncertain, it was dictated less by geography or whim or even by the wretched state of the wild roads than by Tag's poor vision. In the end they extricated themselves from the dissected plateau and climbed up onto the rolling granite moors with their poor acid soils, bracken slopes almost scarlet in the sun, and abandoned human workings.

"Whew!" said Cy, looking anxiously back as they crossed a spoil-whitened quarry floor choked with rusty machinery. "I thought that refrigerator was a horse!"

Tag shrugged.

The weather had improved daily, but his headache hadn't improved at all. By now he had seen so many sheep that looked like boulders, so many gray rocks that got up and walked away as sheep, he was quite used to an equivocal style of relationship between the animate and inanimate. As the wild roads grew more tangled and debatable, forcing the two cats to make their way on foot, there were days when he not only mistook rocks for sheep, but when he became so confused he couldn't walk at all.

At these times the tabby had to care for them both. She took her duties as seriously as always, but in practical terms this meant he went without. She would eat "real" food if he insisted. Left to herself, she supplied them with a diet of interesting objects. She fetched acorns, polished by the wind to a lustrous gray-brown. She brought knots of plastic baler twine and sheep's wool. She brought him part of a gate.

"Nice," he said, so as not to discourage her.

"How can you expect to get better," she grumbled, "if you never eat the food?"

And then late one morning things changed.

They had spent the night in a narrow lane constructed like a ditch, with a stone wall on one side and a steep turf bank on the other, which had once been part of some human boundary. Now it gave some respite from the upland wind. Weak sunshine flickered through spindly trees and onto the turf where the sheltered wildflowers cautiously displayed their buds. Tag was curled up in the sun, trying to sleep his headache away, when Cy trotted into view at a gap in the wall. She stopped, looked around, and ran down the bank. She was chattering excitedly through a mouthful of something he couldn't identify. He could tell she had begun talking to him long before that.

"Eat!" she called. "Eat!" His heart sank. "Hold on, Ace!" she said. "I got the dibs!" And she dropped something in front of his face.

He couldn't see her—the world was a wash of greens and browns—but he could smell her. He could smell what she had brought.

"It's a mouse," he said.

It was about as big as one of his paws.

"It's your first mouse!"

"You can have it all," she said.

He hardly knew how to answer. From the beginning, he had cared for her only reluctantly. But her faith in the world—the inner picture of things she maintained despite everything the Alchemist had done to her—made no allowances for that. She had taken Tag at her own valuation. This small gray object, bedraggled and coated with spit, was her thank-you for a love he hadn't known he felt.

"I've never seen a fatter mouse," he said.

"Oh, I can get these any day."

Broad southerly winds blustered out of a blue sky full of sailing white clouds. Birds had begun to sing again in the little woods.

The days grew longer. They grew warmer.

The tabby followed her prey west across the moor. Tag followed the tabby. When his headache allowed, he watched her.

"What do I see?" he asked himself. Only the same small, sturdy, short-coupled tabby cat he had once dumped unceremoniously at the side of the Caribbean Road in the rain. The same symmetrical black marks curled like flames all down her ribby sides. When she tilted her head it was still as if she were listening for a voice no one else could hear. She still had the same white socks. But now, in the mornings, she smelled of fresh egg. She would look up, tousled, at birds moving against a cloud, her little pink tongue still visible and her yellow eyes full of a secret mischief and delight. Later in the day she had a dusty smell. It might have been the dry, licheny smell of the moor itself. Or it might have been the smell of the gold ticking scattered across the thick fur behind her ears. A smell of gold.

She had other smells.

One evening, they found themselves at the top of a little hill in the extreme west of the heathland. All day the still air had been filled with an almost summery warmth, like a glass with honey. Horizontal light sent long shadows across the rabbit-cropped turf, and lent a gentle, tawny resonance to the piled sloping rocks of the tor itself. There, when she turned to him, she smelled of gorse in flower. It was a smell of heat and spice and vanilla, a smell that spoke. He could hear speech in it.

"Come on, Ace," she said. "You never play."

There was that fleck in her eye, that extra color he had noticed in the bright tapestry when he pulled her out of the road all those months ago!

"You never play. Are you old?"

"No," said Tag, affronted. "I'm young."

"Well, then," she said. "Chase me." She thought for a moment. "Mind you," she warned him, "I shall bite."

So he chased her, even though sometimes he could barely see her, and they fought a little and rolled about for each other, and the warm air was the exact color of tabby fur, and she said, "Now I do this: see? Well, come on, then! Now you have to bite me!" So he bit her quite hard, and suddenly he was inside her.

It wasn't anything like looking out of her eyes. But he was inside her.

Later, she said, "Well? Did you enjoy it?"

Tag walked a little way away and sat down to stare west into the golden light.

"I've never done anything similar," he admitted. Then, cheerfully, "I can see better now." While to himself he thought, As well as everything else, she *bit* me, and I liked it. Perhaps *liked* was the wrong word? "No," he told himself. "I liked it."

The tabby purred loudly. "You did like it!" she agreed.

She rolled on her back, keeping her tawny eyes on him.

"I can do that again anytime," she said.

Tag went over and licked her behind the ear. "You're still as dirty as you ever were," he told her. He added, "You can hear what I'm thinking, can't you?"

She looked surprised. "Can't everyone?"

"I don't believe so," said Tag. "We came all this way before I realized."

"Let's do it again now," said the tabby.

Two days later, they reached the sea.

It began as a long line of violet glittering at the very edge of things. Huge clouds, suspended above the water, tugged gently at invisible moorings. Shadows darkened it. Breezes ruffled and scatted its surface. It was every color of gray and silver. The sea! The oyster-silk, mackerel-tabby sea! Standing stupefied and silent before it, Tag remembered the calico cat. "Ain't *nothin'* like the ocean, hon!" she had told him on their last good walk together at Piper's Quay. "You were right, Sealink," he whispered to himself. "You were right." And he hoped she was still alive and would come safe to this ocean.

They made their way off the heath down a steep valley patched with different crops, scattered with cottages painted in pastel colors, and thickly covered with tangled vegetation that looked exotic even in its winter dress. As they wound their way down to the shore the cottages huddled closer and closer, into a maze of little streets and alleys. The air smelled of salt, tidal mud, and weed, a smell that grew pungent and rank. It smelled of fish.

"Woo!" said the tabby.

They stepped around a corner and there was the harbor. Nylon fishing nets were piled like blue candy floss on the setts of the stone mole where it followed protectively a curve of steeply shelving beach. The tide was out. Canted at all angles on the sand—all colors like a box of candy, red and blue with fluorescent pink fenders, green and yellow and white—lay the fishing boats. They were tubby and made of wood. Pennants streamed from their masts in the breeze. Gulls shrieked and skirmished. A young woman in green rubber boots and a head scarf walked across the sand and climbed into one of the boats. It disappeared below for a moment, then returned, to shade its eyes against the sun and stare at the place a hundred yards away where the sea lapped the land like a kitten.

Tag was enraptured. He thought, If I could find somewhere like this, I'd live in it forever. But outside the harbor a northerly wind was ripping the tops off the waves as they broke, so that the spray smoked away like a burning fuse. He shivered. If the Alchemist doesn't kill us all, he thought.

"He won't kill us," said the tabby, sniffing the salty air. "We'll kill him."

She said, "Can I come too?"

Tag tried to find out about Tintagel. He was back to asking cats in doorways.

"You'm a way to go yet," they said. "Oh ar." And went back to their own business, which was gossip. They were plump housecats with wide, satisfied faces, blinking amiably in the sunshine as they polished up already-polished coats. They had never heard of the Alchemist. A little put out, perhaps, by a temporary dislocation of their traditional pathways to and from the fish dock, and wary of strangers as a result, they seemed quite oblivious of the threat that had gathered over their world. And after all, why not? thought Tag. We can't all guard the life we love—or there soon would be no life left to love but being a guard. And he thought, If I lived here, I'm not sure I'd tell my tale to a pair of scruffy nomads. Especially if one of them had a spark plug in her head!

"Belay that," said the tabby, who had been down on the dock conversing with sea cats. And she bit his ear.

They were in the village for two or three days. There was no need to hunt. Cy was up at dawn, scrounging fish heads at the quay. Tag slept late and one morning awoke to find that his headache had gone. It was a whole new world now that he could see again. As soon as the sunshine had fairly warmed the little esplanade, he went to see what the litter bins might hold. They could be unpleasant, but he soon perfected a method of balancing three-footed on the rim of the bin while he raked about inside with the fourth. He rarely had to climb in all the way, and there was no competition for the fine out-of-season haul he made of discarded sausages, chips in tomato sauce, and bits of battered cod. At noon he met the tabby in an empty bus shelter facing the sea and they split their take. They slept or asked questions in the afternoon.

Tag's favorite bin was in a little triangle of waste space at the corner of two lanes, chained off from the busy street and with a low parapet fronting the sea. There were some blue-painted benches and a red-and-white lifebelt. Tag's bin—its characteristic sharp smell compounded of rotten fruit, alcohol, and a slurry of meat fibers dissolved in the dribbles from soft-drink cans—was mounted on the wall just beneath the parapet. He never knew what he might find there. From it he could see the whole harbor—fish quay, lighthouse, mole, and all—and behind that the clustered cottages of Fish Street—windows, roofs, and walls, tumbling up the hill as if gravity didn't apply to them.

Tag ran into the triangle one shiny, rain-washed morning, leapt onto the bench, and got his front paws on the edge of the bin.

Just then, a head popped out of it.

"*Yow!*" said Tag. "My bin!"

"I don't think so," said the occupant pleasantly. And he stayed where he was. "Besides which," he said, "someone got here before both of us today. You can have *this* if you want it," he offered, "because I wouldn't, frankly, eat it with my eyes closed."

After a brief scuffle in the depths, he sprang straight out of the bin without touching its sides, made a neat landing on the bench to which Tag had prudently retreated, and dropped a liquescent brown banana in front of the Burmilla's startled nose.

This gesture revealed him to be a fine young tom, long-bodied and with short, thick, springy ginger fur. His eyes were a color that balanced precariously between yellow and copper. He bristled with stiff white whiskers, and lively upcurled tufts of fur were set like muttonchops at each side of his face. He had long, athletic legs. He had three white socks and a white bib so clean you could barely look at it. Though he was clearly out on his own in this world—rakish and sharp, bursting with health, all burnt gold and red-sienna-bold—some human being had once tied a scarlet and blue silk handkerchief around his neck instead of a collar. Whatever this might have signified then, he wore it now as a challenge.

Who could possibly own me? it seemed to say. *You might as easily own the day, the sky, the sea. Just try!* He was perhaps a year old. "Hey!" he said. "I've smelt you around!"

"Oh yes?"

"In the bins, mainly. I wondered who was getting the good stuff." He looked Tag up and down with an approval that was at the same time brusque and sly. "And I see why now. You're not new at this game."

"I've done a bit of it," admitted Tag.

"I admire you tough old guys. Up early. Out in every weather. Know just where to look."

Tag thought, Old? He thought, Me? "I'm not old," he said.

"I meant 'old' in the sense of 'experienced,' " amended the ginger tom. "Hey!" he added, jumping up onto the parapet above Tag's head. "It's a great morning. Look at the sun! Look at the waves! Let's do the rest of these bins *together*."

He ran along the sea wall, scampered tail-up and tip-curled across the triangle and under the chains. He looked up and down the road, then back at Tag. "What d'you say?"

Tag was fascinated. "Why not?"

"Come on then!" called the ginger tom, and off he went. "We could even get down on the beach and try our hand at a gull," he said. "A couple of hard cases like us!"

"Steady on," said Tag, running to catch up.

They had a profitable morning. A light shower at eleven shone the esplanade pavements so they could see their own faces. They sheltered under an upturned boat, then hung about restaurant doors for an hour. They ate pizza from a plastic bin bag outside the amusement arcade. It was good; though, Tag tried to explain, nothing like as good as pizza *topping*, which he had once had with a friend. They ate a couple of scallops in batter they discovered in a gutter. The ginger tom talked freely, but not often about himself. Later all Tag would remember him saying was, "A gypsy cat like me, he likes to get around." Noon found them sitting in the bus shelter staring amiably out to sea, wondering what to say to each other next. On the tideline, a few oafish young gulls had found, among the soft-drink cans and tubey weed, a small dead dogfish with spotted fins. Next to the bus shelter, the dried-up fronds of a bewintered rag-mop palm were rustling stealthily in the offshore wind. The gypsy yawned and stretched.

"Great morning," he said. "I could make a habit of this. You and I should team up."

Tag felt a little shy. "I'm kind of with someone," he explained.

"Hey!" said the gypsy. "No problem!" And he turned his attention quickly to the gulls, who had given up on the dogfish and were pecking desultorily up and down the tideline again. "Look at that! Just ate a condom! Straight down, didn't even taste it. They're so stupid it's a sin not to prey on them."

"My friend and I?" Tag said.

"Mm?"

"We're heading west—"

"Good move. There's some brilliant eating down there. Not

to mention those peninsula queens with the moon in their eyes!"

"—to a place called Tintagel. As soon as we find out where that is. Do you know the coast 'round here? Only, I've gone wrong so often. Have you ever heard of Tintagel?"

The ginger tom let his gaze rest gently on the gulls, who had begun squabbling over something they had found in a plastic bag. For some time he said nothing. The palm leaves rustled in the wind. The surf was like breath far out. Then he blinked slowly. "Have I heard of Tintagel?" he asked himself. And when at last he turned his strange, sly, polished eyes on Tag, they caught the light like shields. They might have been cut from brass and copper, so little expression was in them.

"I'm going there myself," he said quietly. "Now isn't that a surprise?"

Before Tag could say anything, Cy turned up, irritable from trying to carry two mackerel heads in one mouth. When she saw the newcomer, she made a point of burying them noisily in the loose earth at the base of the palm tree. Then she walked around him twice with her nose in the air; while for his part he lost interest in the herring gulls and gave her a stare of curiosity and admiration.

Tag, rather alarmed by the openness of the appraisal, reminded him hastily, "This is the friend I was telling you about."

The ginger tom laughed. "Is she always this dirty?" he asked Tag.

Cy, who had been eyeing him—and especially his neck scarf—with interest, looked annoyed. "I got these fish," she told Tag. "But he's not having any."

"I was leaving anyway," said the gypsy. He stared thoughtfully at Cy's spark plug, a little dulled by the salt winds but still visible. Then he got to his feet. "I had a brilliant time this morning," he said to Tag. "It was nice to work with one of the real old hands. That other thing, now," he said. His eyes, which had become much livelier when he first looked at Cy, were flat and reflective again. "We might go tonight, if you wanted."

Tag was no longer sure. "I don't understand what you would be doing there," he said.

The ginger tom laughed. "Who knows?" he said. "I heard something would happen there soon." He stared at Tag. "I heard some cats were going down there for something that would happen. I want to be part of any cat thing." He shrugged lightly. "It's no matter," he said. "I'll call by." He winked at the tabby. "About midnight," he said. "Just about midnight."

And he walked off down the seafront, his long tail curled like a question mark. Every line of him was full of life. He seemed to combine action and stasis, motion and repose, so completely that they canceled each other out, and every movement he made—every step he took—was like a dance. He looked new-minted in the sunshine.

"Lick me," said Cy to Tag, as they watched him go.

Tag said, "I'm trying to think what to do."

"No fish until you lick me."

Midnight.

A bright moon lit up a sky full of clouds as thin and iridescent as fish scales. The tide was high, rushing back and forth across the thin remaining strip of shingle and crunching into the sea-wall. Stiff offshore winds tore at the heads of the rag-mop palms, and sent the halyards of moored boats ringing aimlessly against their masts. It was cold in the bus shelter, and Cy was asleep. Tag stared out across the oily black swell, the breaking surf, and they failed to calm him as they had. His headache was back. When the ginger tom appeared, it was from the shadows, and he was a black shadow himself.

"Well?"

"Who are you?"

"A gypsy cat like me has no name. So will you come?"

Tag shrugged. "What choice have I?"

"It's only a walk down the coast," said the ginger tom quietly. "It's a cat thing."

Then he said, "After all, you're a cat."

Cy woke with a jump. "Who's this?" she said. "Oh, him. We don't need him."

"Wake up," Tag told her.

"We're going to Tintagel," he said.

The Eighth Life of Cats

FROM THE DIARY OF MR. NEWTON

A single, ancient piece of paper have I discovered, en-folded in the pages of Walter Charleton's Physiologia Epi-curo, while searching the City Library for texts to bolster my hypothesis regarding the nature of the Æthereal Spirit, with which to quell the criticisms of my opponents, Mr. Boyle and Mr. Hooke. The best of my own books were sadly lost in a ter-rible Fire, along with many of my experimental subjects, and my dear and faithful cat, Hobbe; which I do privately believe to have been started by volatile materials in my Theatrum Chemicum. It is a miracle that my little house has survived, but its bricks are old and thick. Refurbishment has been re-markably simple; and at least now I have no close neigh-bours to interfere with my Work. Others believe that the Fire originated in the bakery of Mr. Thos. Faryner, which backs onto my premises, and I have refrained from advising them otherwise, for the damage to city and population was quite devastating.

This sheet of paper has piqued my interest greatly, for I have long sought greater understanding of the Universe: in-deed it is a quest that burns within my very Soul. So many scraps of knowledge do I hold already—the fluxions of the Earth and Moon, the array of the planetary masses, how colour is created; I know of magneticall attraction, gravity, and levity—but the Nature of the World itself, the fuel which generates the very spirit of the Universe, that has so far eluded me. I have followed the wisdom of the ancient Adep-tists in seeking the Philosopher's Stone, as have so many be-fore me; but I always felt in my heart that the perfect Matter

414

of the World could be nothing so mundane as Gold, a mere and soulless metal . . .

The cat is called in Hebrew, *Catul*; in Greek, *ailouros*; and in Latin, *Catus, felis*. The Egyptians named it *mau*, for the sound of its voice, and gave it worship. To the Northern peoples, it is a Creature of fertility and fortune; but the Romany call it *majicou*, and abhor its presence.

All Cats are of a single nature and agree much in one Shape, though they be of different Magnitude; each being a Beast of Prey, the Wild and the Tame, it being in the opinion of many a diminutive Tyger.

The most miraculous of Beasts, it walks invisibly and silently the highways of the Earth, and many believe it invested with the Magick of the World.

The Ancients have prophesied that in every eighty-first generation of the most ancient of the Felidae there shall come a Cat of Power, which shall not be greatest of Magnitude, but possessed of the most exquisite Soul. And the greatest of these shall be the Golden Cat, which shall come only when the ancient north joins with the Eye of Horus, and it shall have the Power to harness the Sunne and the Moon and the Wild Roads, and may render to any so lucky as to possess it the very Key to knowledge of the Natural World.

—William Herringe, *The Diminutive Tyger*, 1562

I had already stumbled on the magical properties of the Brain of the Cat, which the Adeptists have for years used to cure a variety of ills from the Web, the Pin, and the Pearls, to Madnesse, Gout, and even Alopecia. I have myself discovered that the digestion of certain parts of a Cat's anatomy may further one's appointed time in the World; a welcome discovery to one with so much knowledge to seek. Yet, despite the proximity of my experiments, I had not made the obvious connection! Indeed, the magick of cats must be a source of the Æthereal Spirit that fuels the very World . . .

The Golden Cat!

The key that will open to me the mysteries of Nature itself!

Chapter Twenty-one

BEASTS OF THE MOOR

*And let me touch those curving claws of yellow
ivory, and grasp the tail that like a monstrous asp
coils round your velvet paws . . .*
— OSCAR WILDE

The great beast came to an abrupt halt. He rolled his head, sniffing the air as the pressures changed.

He had been running.

He sensed an unfolding, a falling away, as if the highway were closing, fading, dispersing itself into the entire moor.

He had been running.

He felt the world come back to him, second by second. Wildness eased out of him. It eased out of his spine as movement ceased.

He had been running, and the highway was still there, surrounding him with brown air and an endless coppery plain. But now everything before him was indistinct. It was a swirl of white fog, and then what?

It was something else. It was something open and fluid: a scent on the mist, wild and tangy. It made his head feel heavy. He was aware of himself as a creature cased in his own head. He was aware of his head—the ropes of muscle at the hinge of the jaw, the thump and rush of blood around the great skull, the sabred fangs that cut the air.

He had been running the highway.

First there was something unfamiliar about himself; then there was something familiar in this alien place. How did he find himself here?

A familiar thing: and an unfamiliar self.

It made his whiskers twitch and his thick blood race, tiny electrical messages running the length of his spine so that a ridge of fur sprang up from the wide space between his ears to the very tip of his tufted tail. A sudden craving washed through him, a hunger so sharp it felt like a physical pain.

Prey?

No. It was a scent more delicate. It was a scent more terrifying.

He bent his head further.

Predator?

No. It was an ancient, complex scent. But what he felt was not fear so much as awe. A huge and terrible awe.

Attar and civet. Spice and blood.

All at once his heart was afire. The scent of the blood filled his body, so that his own pulsed in response. As if it, too, were joined in this purpose, the highway twitched and sighed around him. A golden light filled his eyes, and thoughts tumbled through the echoing spaces of his ancient skull. "Our blood is a book!"

The beast lifted his head and roared. The air trembled at the sound. His world dwindled and fell into focus, yet became, in the same gesture, diffuse and colossal; and as the mass of his flesh melted away, he found himself nose to nose with a creature of heat and fire: a female cat! Fine-boned with fur of delicate rose-taupe stretched taut across the barrel of her body. Her ears were laid flat back at the sight of him. Her eyes snapped with fear, and she stood high on her toes in defiance.

The blood roared through his head as Ragnar Gustaffson felt the rags of the highway fall away from him, and he was himself again after another unknowable journey, exhausted and cold, trembling with shock and delight.

"Pertelot . . ."

The Queen of Cats beside Dozmary Pool.

At last the terror went out of her eyes.

"Ragnar . . ."

King of Cats: he stared at the beautiful apparition before him—swollen belly, sodden fur, bedraggled paws, and all.

They huddled together—Ragnar Gustaffson, Pertelot Fitzwilliam, and Sealink the calico in a comforting heap of multicolored fur. Ragnar gently licked the mud from Pertelot's face, then carefully groomed her coat from top to tail, inhaling the familiar scent of her with wild joy. When he reached the swell of her belly, he lingered to trace the tiny forms there. In their turn they moved beneath the pressure of his great, rough tongue, and a vast rumble of pride and pleasure rose from his throat.

All his trials, all his journeys, had prepared him for this discovery.

"Now I feel like a King at last," said Ragnar. And he tried to explain to them how his adventures had brought him to this moment.

He told them how he had journeyed with Tag and Mousebreath and the little tabby until circumstances had split them up. How he had feared for Pertelot's life, and in that fear learned to spring locks from the cat called Cottonreel. How he had freed cats and bitten a dog. Sealink regarded him admiringly. He described his long trek: how the water froze on his face. How not to cross a river. Exhaustion and hunger. The Mau wept silently as he told the story of the fire, and the sixth kitten, beyond help in the linen cupboard. He related in such detail his encounter with the old lady and her marvelous food—melted butter and poached fish—that Sealink began to drool.

"Oh, it was hard to leave her, Pertelot; but I heard your voice in a dream. I cannot explain this. I heard our kittens call me, as if they were all the kittens in the world. I knew something then. Life was before me. Life had hold of me, and it drew me to the coast."

He told them how he had walked the cliff tops, his gaze inexorably drawn out to sea.

"Though I knew of course you could not be out there!"

Pertelot stared. "But, Rags, we were."

Sealink said, "Hey! We saw *you*!"

Suddenly they were all trying to talk at once.

"Up on the cliff tops, during the storm, we saw a huge cat—"

"Silhouetted against the sky—"

"Lit up by the lightning—"

"We were on a boat—"

Ragnar was delighted. He ran about in an excited circle. "I looked out to sea," he said, "but you must have been no bigger than an acorn!" He laughed. "I had just come off a highway. I was— This is so *interesting*. Don't you find this interesting?"

"And then when you came out of the highway like that, in front of us, out of the mist, we thought you were—"

"The Beast of the Moor."

Ragnar laughed. "Perhaps I am," he said. He considered this. "Perhaps we all are."

He sat down suddenly and resumed his grooming of the Queen. Under his scrupulous attentions she soon fell into a blissful, dreamless sleep.

After some time, Sealink, who had taken up position with her head resting on the King's flank, shifted luxuriously and said, "My, my, honey, you sure do generate some warmth!" She stretched, winced. "Cold gets in this damn leg," she said, looking down at it accusingly.

"You're hurt," observed the King.

"Dog bite, hon. Worst damn thing you can have. Still, he'd have got away with the rest of me without I had help."

And she told him about the trek across the ancient country— dwelling on bad weather, hard knocks, and, particularly, lack of decent food. When she came to the farmyard raid and its consequences—how she had woken up in Pertelot's mouth, being bumped up the side of a mountain in the dark—Ragnar said, "I would reply if asked, 'This is something quite hard to believe.' "

"You would, would you?" Sealink thought for a minute. "You keep an eye on her in the clinches, hon," she said, "that's my advice. She's small but she's real tough, the Queen."

She looked down at herself. "Whereas I am generous in many senses of that word."

She gave him a direct look.

"Much like yourself, I guess," she said.

What Ragnar made of this was unclear, since he had chosen that moment to examine her wounded leg. It was swollen and not a good color.

"Hm," he said.

He began to pass his tongue across the affected area in long, firm sweeps. Waves of pleasant heat swept up through Sealink's haunch and flank, swirled up into her stomach and neck, then her head, until even her thoughts felt warm. After a little time, the King sat back and observed her professionally. Her eyes were half-closed and she gave a strange double purr—deep muffled vibrations at the base of her throat counterpointed by a light trilling like distant birdsong. He nodded to himself. Sealink shook herself deliciously—she felt as limber as a kitten again!—and flexed the damaged leg, which extended itself in a single lithe movement. She stared at it in astonishment, then transferred her gaze to the King.

Ragnar Gustaffson Coeur de Lion regarded his handiwork thoughtfully.

"Well," he said. "That is good."

Sealink stared at him.

"Hon," she said, "it seems a waste that you don't share yourself around a bit more."

Ragnar looked abashed.

The Queen of Cats awoke with a start just then, her head coming up sharply from deep sleep, so that at one moment her face was blind and still, the next alive with anxiety. Then her gaze lit upon Ragnar's shaggy coat, and the nightmare passed.

"Oh, Rags!"

They contemplated each other with such passion that Sealink felt a sudden need to examine a clump of sedge some feet away. Once there, she relieved herself discreetly, covered the place with loose peat, and watched the pair with narrowed pupils and a contraction of the heart. The mist had dispersed, leaving behind it a swathe of desolate moor. Rags and Pertelot sat by the shining moonlit mirror of a lake fringed with icy reeds and bulrushes; their world had, for the moment at least, shrunk to an envelope of warm fur and hot breath. Sealink had a sudden, fleeting memory of a pair of mismatched eyes, and muscular haunches packing out a rough tortoiseshell coat.

She sat stock-still and sniffed.

"What?" she asked the air.

It was the broken highway from which Ragnar had emerged,

an apologetic twist of light shimmering and buzzing uncertainly in the damp air. Sealink put her nose to it.

"Tell me," she whispered, as if it were alive.

And then, "Mousebreath!"

She half expected to see his silhouette emerge, dwindling gradually from his wild form to the one she knew so well. A thrill of electricity shot the length of her spine; her tail rose to welcome him.

Nothing.

She inspected the highway curiously.

It was frayed and ruptured, spilling itself into the ground at her feet, pooling and evaporating like the spilt milk of a million years. But there was life in there, even now. They were still trying to travel. She could hear them, confused and hurt, a distant but discernible murmur.

She stepped in, and was caught at once in its flow. Ghostly shapes poured toward her, as if attracted by her presence; but none of them was Mousebreath. They were pale and attenuated and their eyes burned as pinpricks of light in the distant gloom. She felt their panic, cold and clear as a howl of warning: ghost cats of the ancient country, fleeing an unseen foe. They surged through her like a wave, icy and hot at the same time, and she felt the life of each one separately as they passed—an old farm cat and three of her partners; two ferals who'd lost their ninth lives on a distant road; a fine, scarred old tomcat brought down by septicemia; seven domestic cats who had traveled the highways together for a hundred years, their energies faint and fading; kittens by threes and fours—the lost, the discarded, and the dispossessed.

They were afraid for their souls. She could feel it.

As they went, dispersing onto the moor through the broken neck of the wild road to condense into the air of the world as damp gray mist, they left an image with her . . .

Something wrong. Something huge . . .

"Wait!" she cried. "Wait!"

But they were too afraid. Something had entered the wild roads.

Something dark and mad with greed.

She fled the broken highway straight toward the lake.

"Ragnar! Pertelot!" she cried. "The Alchemist is on the highways!"

The King and Queen of Cats sprang apart, fur on end.

"Run! Now!"

The pool, spreading like a sea of tinfoil, barred their way. Ghost cats spilled around them, cold and gray. All they could do was strike out blindly through this writhing fog with its cargo of decayed messages and ebbing memories, then in clear air head north and east.

Sealink ran out in front, her tail like a pennant. Pertelot followed some way behind, her great belly swinging with each desperate stride, her breath rasping. Ragnar pounded along behind Pertelot, water spraying up around him as he ran. Every so often he turned to stare back at the broken highway.

They ran until Pertelot fell down suddenly in a puddle of peaty water, and lay, oblivious of the cold, in a distressed heap, her flanks heaving with exertion.

"The kittens," she cried. Pain made her gaze unfocused and inturned. "I can feel them. They're coming!"

Ragnar nosed at her uncertainly. "We aren't safe here," he said.

"The Eye! Oh, help me, Rags, I can feel the Eye expand!"

"Hold fire, hon!" said Sealink. "This ain't the time or place, y'hear me? You clench those muscles and hold on real tight. We gotta be moving on from here even if Ragnar and me have to carry you."

And she pushed at the Queen's wet sorrel rump.

"Stop that at once," commanded Pertelot.

She lifted her head and braced her forelegs. A moment's struggle, and she was upright again. "I can hold on for a while, Ragnar," she said, with a kind of forlorn dignity. "But tell her to stop doing that. I hope we reach Tintagel soon."

She gave a last look back at the ruptured highway.

"Those poor cats," she said. "I don't believe they're any threat to us."

* * *

The landscape unfurled itself under their paws that night and for the days that followed. Swathes of fescue and bilberry, crisscrossed with meandering tracks, rolled past craggy outcrops and ruined cottages. Acres of dead bracken were giving way to the virid curls of new shoots. The cats avoided the highways, for fear of alerting the Alchemist to their presence, but there was no further sign of him. They made good progress despite Pertelot's condition. She rarely spoke but placed one paw in front of the other with a swaying determination, her face tight and set.

Around them the moors were strangely quiet, and food was hard to come by. The area seemed lifeless and suspended, a region of limbo. On the third day, Ragnar could stand the sight of Pertelot's haggard face no more, and called a halt. He disappeared for an hour, leaving the two females cloistered beneath a stand of hawthorns. Pertelot at once fell into a disturbed sleep. Her paws twitched; her mouth opened and closed as if in rage or fear; but when Ragnar woke her on his return she would not speak of her dreams. There was no need to speak anyway: he had brought with him the limp corpse of a rabbit. It was thin and stringy, hardened by a winter life, but they wolfed it down in silence and soon afterward continued their journey.

They came down off the moors at last, and there was a scent of spring in the air. The fields were touched with an elusive dappled light. The uncanny silence and lifelessness of the uplands gave way to birdsong. If they stopped walking, they heard the scurry of tiny feet. Sealink bounced down the sides of the hedgerows, pouncing on anything that moved, until at last, by sheer luck, she stunned a vole. This she ate. "Oops. Sorry, hon," she apologized to Pertelot, under Ragnar's owlish gaze; but Pertelot was oblivious. She slunk along, belly brushing the grass, in the lee of the hedges, starting at every sound.

For some days the Mau had been paying little attention to her traveling companions. She seemed to have retreated into some inner country, where, beset by invisible perils, she kept herself close. She spoke only to the unborn. She lagged behind or ranged distractedly ahead, growling at shadows in the hedge-row. When they stopped for a rest she would fall immediately into a heavy sleep, only to wake with a start a moment later, eyes wild, every sense alert.

"I am disconcerted by this," Ragnar told Sealink.

"You and me both, babe."

Hills fell away below them now, green with new grass and bright splashes of color undulating to the horizon, beyond which there was the sense of immanence: a vast, open space like the promise of the future. Salt sharpened the air, so that each breath felt distinct in the lungs. Soon, there were huge white gulls wheeling and boasting overhead.

The calico sniffed happily.

"The sea!" she announced. "I can smell it!"

She thought for a moment. "I shall see my old man again!" she said. "Wow! That ugly old bastard!" She frisked her tail in the air and increased her pace. "Tell you what," she said to Pertelot, "let's swap!"

But Pertelot would not be amused. All day long the fur had bristled along the ridge of her back and she had carried her tail and ears low. Now she scurried along in fits and starts from one piece of cover to the next, stopping every so often to howl softly and lick at her flank.

Eventually, they crested a hill from which they had a clear view of the ocean. Deep green and blue, sparkling in the early sunshine, it stretched as far as the eye could see beyond an expanse of turf dotted with pink cushions of thrift and red campions. On a round, peninsular headland, the stonework of an ancient fortification curled protectively around the cliff, lines softened by ruin and lichen, until it dropped out of sight on the seaward side. Elsewhere the dark, slaty rock outcropped at random, blocky and jagged. Turf fell away from the base of the rocks in little bumps and ridges to reveal scars of ruddy soil.

Dense stands of gorse curved landward, distorted over many generations by the sea wind. Into one of these dived the Queen. Once inside, she could be seen turning and turning like a kitten chasing its tail or washing herself in neurotic flurries of effort. Mewing sounds spilled without meaning from her mouth. She stared out distractedly. She hissed at Sealink. She hissed at her husband.

"Go away!" she told them. "Go away!"

Determined to help, Ragnar shouldered resolutely into the gorse. He was hindered by his great size and by his long coat, which snagged on the dry bracts and spines.

Reaching the Mau's curious nest, he nuzzled at her comfortingly until she reared up with an earsplitting yowl and bit him. He leapt backward.

"*Pertelot—!*" he began.

Then he stopped and stared.

Milk had started to leak down her fur.

Chapter Twenty-two
THE GOLDEN DAWN

I am the cat of cats. I am
The everlasting cat!
Cunning and old, and sleek as jam,
The everlasting cat!
— WILLIAM BRIGHTY RANDS

*A*fter they left the village, Tag and his companions walked three nights and part of a fourth.

It was a rocky coast, all raked inlets and thorny headlands. Landward, hill succeeded windy hill, each one crowned with its silent outcrop or ancient empty fort. In each deep hollow zawn the sea banged like a monstrous distant door. Moonlight made the lanes mysterious. Out to sea, silver glimmered on the oily violet swell.

Tag and Cy slept the first day wrapped in a sea fog and woke to find a million drops of water on the branches of the dense, wind-thickened headland vegetation. Each one held for a moment the deep red light of the ocean sunset, then quivered and fell.

"Time to go, I think," said the ginger cat, coming up suddenly out of nowhere.

As soon as they left the harbor, he had developed business of his own. He was always off here and there on sly errands or holding talks with local cats. He met them in all sorts of places—in barns or on the rocky tops of cliffs, once even between the feet of some cows in rough pasture below the coast road. The cows huffed and blew placidly, their breath a warm sweet envelope for this unlikely parliament. On their part, the cats sat facing one another and didn't seem to speak.

They were all black.

Tag watched a little anxiously, and later asked, "Who were they?" He meant perhaps, Who are you?

But the tom replied, "Oh, just cats."

426

"They looked a rough bunch to me."

Coppery eyes glimmered with amusement in the dark, and, "Just good friends," was all the answer Tag got to that.

Three nights on the road together—three nights, and part of a fourth. Yet Tag learned no more about their new companion than this: he was a likeable rogue. He was always as hungry as he had been that first morning in the litter bin. He was always as cheerful. He always had something to say about the weather. He played I see, I jump with Cy until she quite forgot her first impressions of him. He was good at drawing her out and at cheering her up when she got bored or lost the use of her back legs. He could always make her laugh. And where Tag caught bank voles, the ginger tom—a hunter who avoided the obvious game—offered her herring gull eggs just then in season, and a starfish from some salt-swept beach below the cliffs.

"Try some of these," he would encourage her. "They're good."

"They are!"

She loved his colored neckerchief.

"One day," he promised, "I'll tell you how I got it."

He was a gypsy, he said, and you would never tie *him* down. He needed room to roam. Despite that, he had a "friend" at every lonely home along the coast. He was a paradox.

Tag thought, I like him, this cat who wears a collar yet rejects a name. He thought, But who could trust him? And his doubts came into focus suddenly, at the end of the third afternoon, when he woke up to find the quarry they had been sleeping in full of tiny blue and scarlet birds.

Grim rock walls gleamed in a decaying western light. The little birds hovered and darted in the cold and damp of this unpromising arena, their wings trembling with color and life. There was a prolonged drowsy hum like a chord of music. At the center of it Cy and the ginger tom sat facing each other. Their eyes were shining in the eerie light. They were whispering.

"You do one of these."

"No, you do one of these!"

Birds spilled from their mouths and flew up into the gathering night.

"What's going on?" said Tag angrily. "What are you up to? Do you want him to *find* us?" Rearing up on his hind legs, he boxed Cy's ears.

"Stop it!" She hissed and ran off.

"Hey," said the ginger tom. "Why the fuss?"

Tag was so angry he could hardly speak. "I don't want this!" he said.

The tom said, "It's just a cat thing, Tag." Then he said, "Hey, let's all do it!"

"No," said Tag.

Cy crept up and tried to lick his ear. "It's just a cat thing," she said.

Tag turned his back on them.

All the rest of the journey he let them walk ahead and kept as far from them as he could. In that way he came at last to Tintagel, a peninsula at the end of the wildest of roads, many months after he had first dreamed of it, a silent and fearful cat.

It was the place he remembered. At the same time it wasn't.

The hours before midnight: under a new moon in a white sky the headland stretched away toward the cliff edge and the sea. There were gorse bushes, a sense of vast space, the sound of water crashing on the rocks below. This was all as it had been in the brief nightmares of a kitten who always woke happily in a dull and comforting house. It was the dreamer—with his memories of hard travel, bizarre events, and the deaths of friends he had barely come to know—who had changed. He was no longer just Tag, a cat. He was Mercurius Realtime DeNeuve, the apprentice Majicou, and he brought no answers to this site of an old dream, only questions.

What would happen to him now? What would happen to all of them?

Even as he watched and wondered, clouds rushed landward to obscure the moon. Within seconds, rain was boiling toward him in silver moiré patterns. The gorse bushes thrashed in the wind. Everything seemed to vanish under a weight of darkness and blowing vapor until their fur was plastered to shivering ribs.

"What now, then?" shouted the gypsy.

"Hush!" said Tag.

He narrowed his eyes and leaned forward into the driving rain. He had the feeling that some kind of motion had stopped just as he looked. Something out there. Something in the tossing gorse. Something that would prefer to go unseen if it could.

There! Furtive gleams of light slipping to and fro between the headland rocks!

"Who's down there?" he called. "Hello?"

"Hello!" echoed Cy from behind him. "Tango Terry callin'!"

"Shut up. Hello?"

No answer.

"I'm soaked to the skin," advised the ginger tom. For all that, he still seemed to be enjoying himself. His eyes were bright. He might have been stalking herring gulls across the tide-wracked strand. "Let's at least—" He stopped. Cocked his head to one side. "What's that? Listen!"

It was only the faint cry of a gull down by the rocks and the sea. But Tag leaned forward, sniffing the wind. Suddenly, he saw them there: two pairs of cats' eyes, huddled close. Suddenly, he knew.

"Ragnar?" he said. "Sealink?"

He rushed forward.

"Ragnar! Sealink!"

The eyes vanished suddenly.

Then, "Look," cried a familiar voice. "It is our old friend Tag!"

And another voice answered, "No one's my old friend, hon, till I see them up close and in good light."

"And so," said Ragnar Gustaffson Coeur de Lion, perhaps an hour later, "that is how I was changed by my experiences." He gave Tag a keen look in which was mixed amusement, intelligence, pride. "Though I have thought about it, I cannot say which of these events changed me most. I can only say, if you ask me: I am not the same cat I was."

"I can't stop looking at you!" Tag said. "Let me look at you!"

He couldn't stop looking at any of them. Their coats were full of burrs and dried salt. They were tired, careworn, and sore of paw. Their eyes had the haunted look of cats who had traveled farther in a month than most cats travel in a lifetime and who had encountered on the way things cats rarely encounter.

These are my old friends, he thought, made brand-new by the stories they have to tell. This is what happens when you part and meet again. Then he thought, But if I'd looked at them at Piper's Quay, would I have seen these other cats, tucked inside the ones I knew, already waiting their turn to be?

He didn't care. Here was Ragnar, full of journeys, exploits, hairsbreadth escapes; a rover of the Old Changing Way, a king, and a father of kittens! yet no less untidy about the ruff and with the same warm smell. Here was Sealink, saddened, thinner, hurt; but still that same great, generous, unrelenting heart. When the Mau came sniffing suspiciously at him from out of her nest of gorse, he saw that she had changed the least—and the most. Those lambent eyes raged with a sense of her own destiny. When the kittens moved within, you could almost see the years move with them, like patterns just beneath her taupe fur. The pregnancy had empowered her and taught her how to be in the world, and it had brought out the Ancient Cats like a procession of gods walking free in her gaze. She frightened you with a look, and then whispered, "Mercury, you have grown into the most attractive animal!"

Tag shivered. He was Mercury! Tintagel Court to Tintagel Head: two landscapes, one superimposed on the other less like a dream than a prophecy.

"Let me look at you," he said.

They made such a strange, half-sad half-glorious sight, the three of them, huddled less for shelter than security in a kind of tunnel between the gnarled trunks of some wind thickened gorse bushes. Cy and Pertelot lay curled up in a shallow, sandy depression at the seaward end, where the tunnel was kept dry by overhanging rocks. Every so often, Cy rested her head on the

Queen's belly and talked to the kittens. "How was your day? I made *birds*!"

"So. Now we are here," said Ragnar, looking happily from face to face.

Only two things had marred their meeting.

Among all the purring and scent marking and rolling about and face rubbing of old comrades, it would have been easy for a newcomer to feel left out. So Tag had stepped forward a little shyly and formally, saying, "This is my new friend," and turned to urge the ginger tom forward. Only to find he was gone.

"Guess he's shy, hon."

"Shy? I don't think so—"

But the clouds had rolled away from the moon. Behind Tag, only deserted ground stretched landward, steadily rising in the fish-skin light. Not even the shadow of a cat remained.

And then Sealink said, "Where's that old Mousebreath, babe? Can't wait to cuff his gnarly face."

Tag stared at her. He didn't know what to say.

Sealink stared back, and her eyes filmed slowly with puzzlement.

"He's not here, Sealink. He's dead."

She blinked. "But he's coming soon?"

"Oh, Sealink, Sealink. He's dead. Majicou's dead too. We're all that's left."

"Dead?"

Sealink looked away.

There was a long silence. Then, "Mousebreath!" she called out into the darkness. "Mousebreath, you bastard, answer me! How come you do that to me when I need you? Die?"

"Sealink," said Pertelot. "Sealink—"

"You *die* out there? How could you!"

"I'm so sorry."

Sealink rounded on her. "Don't you tell me nothing. He wasn't yours. You ain't lost no one here!"

"Please don't quarrel," said Tag.

He explained what had happened at the stream. He said, "We tried and tried to help him, but—"

The calico got to her feet, suddenly at a loss. "I ain't good at this," she said. "It ain't no one's fault." For a moment her eyes went empty and hard. "No one here," she said, "any rate."

Then she turned and walked off toward the edge of the cliff, her tail low, the tired, ponderous dignity of her gait only a skin over panic and loneliness.

"Sealink!" begged Tag.

"Leave her," whispered the Queen. And she detached herself gently from the sleeping tabby and took herself and her belly awkwardly to the cliff top in the wind.

What comfort she was able to give Sealink there, they never learned.

"So."

Ragnar Gustaffson Coeur de Lion curled his front paws beneath him and fixed Tag with eyes as green as sea-worn glass.

The joy of that first meeting had passed; but perhaps its sorrows had passed too.

"Cats," Ragnar maintained, "are most adaptable. If you ask me how I learned this, I must admit: from a blue-eyed white called Cottonreel, who also taught me how brave it is merely to live your own life. Oh, and to open a cage. Very useful, I can show you that."

"Rags, I don't have one about me just now."

Midnight was not far off. Sensing that her labor was near, the Queen had retreated to her den in the gorse, with Sealink couched on one side of her and Cy on the other. Ragnar had taken Tag out along the cliff top in the darkness and rushing wind, to look at the stars. Now they crouched, partly in the lee of the old fortification, listening to the wind rush around its broken stones while they considered their situation and spoke of strategy.

"So. As you say. We five are all that are left. This being so, we must decide how to act. If you look up, Tag, as Pertelot has encouraged me to do, you will see that the equinox is almost here. Tintagel waits, under a white wind, a trail of light. But for what? We have no idea. The Queen, the kittens, all of us are in danger while we stay here."

"Majicou meant us to come."

"It is a pity that we do not know why."

Tag was forced to agree. "Without Majicou, we can't face the Alchemist," he said. "We're only cats."

"Yet it is too late to move the Queen."

Tag looked out over the sea. "We'd better try," he said. "And soon."

In the teeth of the wind, he heard a voice at his side say quietly, " 'Only cats'? Would you give up so easily?"

There was a silence.

Then the voice said, "I am one who becomes two; I am two who become four; I am four who become eight; I am one more after that."

It was the voice of a cat. Or was it?

He turned.

It was the gypsy tom.

And behind him were gathered his "friends" from the cliff tops about Tintagel.

They looked no less intimidating than they had along the road—old bruisers and wiry females whose style was to be head-down into whatever the coastal weather brought them. They had fought the wind and rain—not to say dogs, foxes, and one another—all their lives. Some had scarred chops, missing ears, bald patches, and gaits stiffened by tendonitis. They had been waiting all their lives for a chance like this. Or, to put it another way: they had been waiting all their lives for this precise chance.

"Who are you?" demanded Ragnar Gustaffson Coeur de Lion of the ginger tom.

"Yes," said Tag. "Who are you?"

The coast cats closed around them, in a maneuver full of quiet menace.

Then the ginger tom gave a resounding laugh. As it echoed away out to sea, he began to shift and change. All his hard companions began to change too.

"Don't you know me, little cat?" he growled.

Tag had closed his eyes. "No," he whispered. "I don't."

But he did.

"I am one who becomes two; I am two who become four; I

am four who become eight; I am one more after that. Tag, I am the Majicou as you well know! And these are my long-time companions, who have guarded this coast so well while they waited for—" He laughed again. "Ah, for what?"

"Majicou!" said Tag. "*Majicou!* I didn't know it was you! I *didn't*! Oh, Majicou, you're back!"

"Now I have seen everything," said Ragnar, in a satisfied voice.

"But, Majicou . . ."

"Yes."

"How?"

"Ah, Tag: if I could tell you that."

"But—"

No sooner had they been introduced—"This is Amabraxas. Here you have Ogby, Fortran, and the Widow. This scruffy old demon is Mousebreath's uncle Tinner, and these are his grandchildren, Jack Fiddle, Mooncranker, and Fish Head Lil."—than the guardians of Tintagel had dispersed. Most of them had given a silent nod, although Jack Fiddle had told the King, "You're all right, squire." His grandfather had only sniffed. In minutes they had disposed themselves with quiet efficiency across the headland or among the ruins of the fortification. You could see them if you looked hard. They were like shadows. Some studied the sea, others the land.

"Tag, what do you know about death?"

"Nothing."

"Good. I died. I was sad, and then I was not. I was in bitter pain, and then I was not. Do you understand, Tag? I was smoke along the ghost roads. I was part of what it is to be a cat. And then—"

"What then?"

"I have been granted a tenth life, Tag—"

"So you're back! You're back!"

Majicou was silent. "Tag," he said eventually. "It's not a game. The highways found me a ginger tom, dying as I was dying. They poured my spirit into him and discharged their energies into me, just for a time. Tag, they have lent me just enough life that I may try to complete my task. No more."

"No!"

"To be loaned a life, even for a while—"

"No!"

"Tag—" But Majicou never finished.

Amabraxas stepped lightly out of the shadows and said, "Majicou. Some new devilry."

"Cy!" cried Tag. "No!"

Out on the headland, colored butterflies were drifting above the gorse bushes.

They found Cy sitting on a bare patch of earth a little way in front of Pertelot's refuge. Her neck was wrenched around so that she faced a point in the air about a foot above and to the left of her head. Her eyes were turned up into her skull. She was making a low crooning noise, and her spark plug was pulsing with white light.

"Stop!" Tag ordered her.

But Majicou was between them suddenly. "Tag, no!"

"She'll bring him down on us."

"I want him here, Tag. All along, I've wanted him here. For good or ill, this little cat must give herself to that. This is the time and place. This is where we meet, and everything ends—"

Cy toppled slowly over and curled up. "The lee shore!" she whimpered. "The lee shore! It's a bad world, Silver." She drew herself into a ball and covered her eyes with her paws. "Silver, it's a bad world. We're out here in it, raw blind like day-old kits. Calling all cars! Help!" She kicked out like a kitten in its sleep and was still.

"Wait, Cy! It *isn't* a bad world! Majicou, he's hurt her—"

Before Majicou could answer, there was a faint sound like expelled breath. It was as if someone had set fire to the gorse. And yet there were no flames: only orange embers whirled up against smoke by the wind. White sparks fountained into the air, to shower down among the assembled cats.

Cy lay supine at the source of this conflagration with her legs spread out and her head forced forward at an odd, broken-looking angle, as if she had been pinned to a board. Her eyes were open and she was rigid with fear. From the plug in her head a fierce invisible energy seemed to issue, filling the air about her so that she shimmered like a mirage on a summer day. "Silver," she said—and her voice, deep and wrenched, seemed to come from a long way down some white bare corridor—"I hurt." Sparks poured from her in gouts—not simply from her mouth, which was stretched open as if by some laboratory device, but from her nose and ears and her round, staring eyes. "Silver. Help me."

The Alchemist had no further use for its proxy. It was using her up, burning her up to increase its own power.

Tag raced forward. As he touched the edge of the conflagration, he was bowled over and shoved upright again in the same gesture.

Blue lightning lit up the ocean. Out to sea, a monstrous figure inflated itself briefly, as if the skin of some huge spotted jungle cat had been animated by nothing but air—as if the air were wearing it. It floated to and fro, propelled by the wind, its dangling rags of lower limbs weighted down by marrowbones. None of the cats saw it.

"Hobbe," it whispered to itself. "Hobbe."

It flapped lazily for a moment; then it was gone.

But there is always another moment. When the lightning flashed again, it was like writhing blue cords, a cat catcher's net that had been dropped over the entire headland. They were all trapped in it. The very world became entangled. Everything seemed to slow down. Tag saw Ragnar running toward Pertelot's refuge, and Majicou running after him; he saw the guardians of Tintagel, converging from every point of the compass; he saw Sealink emerge from the gorse: all slow, slow, slow. Their shouts came to him as if through glue.

Majicou, "Tag! Ragnar Gustaffson! Wait! This is not fire! No one is in danger—"

Ragnar, over and over again, "Pertelot!"

And Sealink, who, for a moment unaware of the confusion outside, announced, "It's begun."

As she spoke, the refuge went up in silent white flames, and she plunged out into the night, staring behind her in astonishment. "Now, how am I gonna get back in there?" she said disgustedly. The gorse crackled but was not consumed. The lightning crackled and failed. Things speeded up again.

"Tag!" cried Ragnar. "The Queen!"

They prepared to hurl themselves into the flames.

"Stop," ordered Majicou, "both of you." He rose menacingly up before them. *"This is not fire.* Look. Feel it. Is there any heat?"

They stared.

"Then what is it?" demanded the King.

"More than one force is at work here tonight. Your kittens are not yet born. But they're already alive, and among them is the Golden Cat. Perhaps they have made themselves safe while we act—"

"They ain't going to remain unborn for long, hon," advised the calico cat.

Majicou stared at her.

"And we better act now. Look!"

Whatever the Alchemist had turned itself into, it wasn't a cat.

Half-clothed in mist, it trudged painfully toward them from some lunar distance, supporting itself on a staff made from the leg of a panther.

At the same time, it was rushing at them from every quarter of the headland: a boiling, shifting mass constantly assembling and reassembling itself out of the night, the earth, the mackerel-skin light of the sky. Now it lunged toward them in a faint halo of cobalt light from a secret discontinuity among the stones of the old fort. Now it broke out of some small coastal highway, tortured and thrashing like a broken hose.

It was tiny. It was huge. It was everywhere at once. It was all those things and none of them. It spoke.

"Hobbe," it said. "Hobbe, Hobbe, Hobbe."

It said, "You devil, I knew I'd find you here!"

Its voice was thick and curdled. Since the fight among the sarsen stones, its road had been hard. Lost in a maze of ruptured highways—burning with rage and desire down every wrenched, coppery perspective; tottering through constant darkness toward every gleam of daylight; deluded by mirror images; led astray by the very mathematics that had allowed it to penetrate the Old

Changing Way; deceived, dazed, and disoriented—it had begun to disintegrate. Where cat and cat skin had once run seamlessly together, all was in rags. The alchemical fluids leaked. The machinery smoked. Vertigo roared unchecked through all its manufactured senses; while its lower limbs, yearning back toward the human, had cracked out of sheer mechanical stress, so that stillness was now beyond it, and it must dance less to dance than to keep upright.

Bent forward from the waist so that it could barely look up, it bawled, "Something wrong here, old Hobbe!"

Everything was wrong. Only the *Panthera*, the staff, remained. Only the staff and the dream; only the Eye of Horus opening upon the truth of the world like a flower.

An image of a golden cat flared strong and true in the Alchemist's dissolving visual field.

It would repossess the Mau.

It would—

"Come to me!"

Tag stared.

Ragnar stared.

Sealink stared. "Honey," she said to no one in particular, "that ain't natural."

"Quick now!" said Majicou. "Or we're lost!"

Rain blustered in suddenly from the sea. The illusory fires burned on. The Alchemist stamped over the headland, chanting and deteriorating and shaking a staff full of lightning. Awed and unnerved, the cats stalked to and fro, lashing their tails indecisively.

"Wait, Majicou!" they called.

But the ginger cat wouldn't listen. "No time!"

And he sped out in front of them, ten, twenty, fifty yards across the headland, growing larger as he approached his ancient enemy.

"Come on then!" cried Tag.

Suddenly they were bounding across the barren ground together, throwing up loose earth like tigers in a sand garden. Small birds woke up in the gorse bushes; seagulls took to the air left and right and wheeled above the cliffs in panic. Tag ran.

With him ran a Norwegian king and a New Orleans queen. Behind those three ran the guardians in a silent, flowing wedge like a shadow on the ground—Amabraxas, Mooncranker, Fortran and the Widow, Ogby, Tinner, Jack Fiddle, and Fish Head Lil. As they ran, they shed every memory of hearth or home they might have had and every hope they ever shared with a domestic cat. Their breath was hot in the night air. Cold and hunger meant nothing to them. They shed without thought the iron heat of their lives. On and on they seemed to run until the headland became a gray blur and only movement had meaning.

And then it was among them, bursting out of the earth at Majicou's feet.

"Hobbe!"

It seemed as surprised as the cats by the success of this ambush. Staggering back and away, it brought the black staff around in a wide, humming sweep. The Majicou leapt over it. As Tag, in his turn, passed beneath, the air shivered, and there was a dull loud *thuck*.

Amabraxas, caught in midair by the claws of the staff, made a soft sound somewhere between a mewl and a groan, and was cut nearly in two. The Alchemist turned to watch his fall.

"Ha! You see? Hobbe? You see?"

"I see your death," growled the Majicou, "which I have wanted for these hundreds of years."

For a time the Alchemist held them at bay with the *Panthera*, discharging from it long green bolts of light. Ogby, dashing in too close, fell to the first of these, with a howl and a reek of scorched fur. Mooncranker, trying to retrieve the rigid but still breathing body of his friend, fell to the next. After that, they were more careful; and soon they had their enemy ringed. This caused Sealink to admit, as she and Tag circled and dodged warily in the windy dark, light splashing up around them like neon in the rain, "I feel more like a dog than a cat, hon. Can that be right?"

"Pay attention!" Majicou ordered them. "Or you'll die too."

The Alchemist laughed. "How well you know me, Hobbe!"

Majicou had already been fatally distracted.

The crucified tabby, her limbs outlined in cold flame, heard them come, but there was nothing she could do except whisper, "Silver. It's— Silver, I hurt—"

Off in the dark, beyond the ruins of the old fortification, among the rocks at the very edge of the cliff top, in a dark dry corner sheltered from the wind, a breath of air moved faintly to and fro. Ashy motes drifted listlessly about in the cold. With a faint apologetic *pop*, the night unzipped itself and out they poured, already lifting their heads for a sniff of their prey . . .

Cats.

Black cats, white cats; cats gray, brown, and marmalade. Longhairs, shorthairs, and Sphinx cats with no hair at all. Cats large and small, old and young, male and female and somewhere in between. From Tintagel Court—the last good place they had known—to Tintagel Head, it was one nightmare to another.

On the way, they had lost all sense of themselves. Now, unassuaged, unhealed, silent as death, they flowed inland, and the first Tag knew of them was when they rolled him over like a kitten in the tide and he felt himself begin to drown.

Blunt claws, bad teeth, runny eyes. Bodies pressed up to his, forelegs clasping and pulling him down, odors wet and sour in the dark.

He came up spitting and yowling for help. But there was no help to be had. Fortran and the Widow had gone under the wave and would never rise again. Their old comrades had fallen back among the Tintagel stones and were trying to stem the flow, there in the windy dark. Majicou and the King found themselves islanded on a flat outcrop of shale, the Alchemist looming over them; while, outweighed and overborn, Tag and Sealink were pressed away landward.

They cut and jumped together for a while in the uncertain, iron-smelling dark. Then Tag remembered the fight in the warehouse. He laughed and said, "Things look bad for us, Sealink."

But the calico's eyes were impassive, and she only answered coldly, "I ain't here for no 'us,' hon."

"Sealink!"

"These cats are goin' to pay for Mousebreath," she said. "After that, who cares?"

"Oh, Sealink, Sealink—"

Shortly afterward she was swept away. He watched her until all he could see was a glint of teeth and claws. Then his own situation was brought home to him so suddenly that he was forced to attend. Throughout the rest of that desperate night, though, he tried to keep an eye open for the calico; and he worried less for her wounds than for her wounded heart.

The Queen's defenders fought. But they were driven and diminished. By the dying light of the tabby cat's crucifixion, a sea of cats tossed back and forth, silent, gleeful, slippery-eyed. The headland heaved with them. Apart from the standing wave, which in good light might be seen to be a calico cat, two centers of resistance remained.

Perhaps half an hour after he had parted with Sealink, Tag had found himself in the old fort.

There, from a ledge high up, Jack Fiddle and Fish Head Lil still held the ruins. He joined them because the alchemical cats gave him no choice, and in a lull in the fighting the three of them looked out across the headland. There was a sudden bright flare.

"Look there," said Fish Head Lil.

There was no answer from Jack Fiddle. His coat was matted. He crouched with his head low, as if he were concentrating very hard on some feat of balance; he hadn't moved for two or three minutes.

The vision had gone out of Tag's left eye again, and he thought the ear on that side had probably been torn right off. That was how it felt. Elsewhere, he had dull, deep pains. If he let himself think about them, he remembered Mousebreath's blood, streaming away into the cold, petrol-blue water, and he was afraid.

"Not long now," said Jack Fiddle suddenly.

No, thought Tag. Not long. We aren't much to reckon with here.

But he still had hope. The kittens were still alive. Pertelot Fitzwilliam's refuge was a column of pure white flame. In the light of it, made small by distance, he could see Ragnar Gustaffson and Majicou stand back to back to prepare their defense of the Queen. Alchemical cats hemmed them in. Just beyond the circle of light, an immense disintegrating figure trudged back and forth, roaring victoriously and shaking its staff. In response, the air seemed to quake. Lightning flared out to sea, and the blue glowing lattice of the cat catcher's net came down again over the headland.

Majicou reared up, one paw raised. His single eye flashed, all colors and none. Tag heard him cry, "Never!" He heard the roar of Ragnar Gustaffson Coeur de Lion. Everything began to slow down . . .

Above, in the night sky, something seemed to shift with minute precision. Mercury had slipped into Leo, and the Eye of Horus was celebrating its marriage to the King of the frozen North. As the equinox approached, the stars flared brightly; from the earth, a tenuous white fire flickered up so briefly to meet them that no one saw.

The first kitten had been born.

In that moment, something stirred to the east of Tintagel; and animals began to pour joyfully onto the headland from all the gentle landward slopes.

There were cats of course—city ferals with mangy coats, country cousins from cozy kitchens—and even some dogs, though they looked a little embarrassed. There were great stags like ships, radiating a kind of majestic heat into the night, their antlers gray iron. There were otters with gleaming black button eyes. There were bad-tempered minks who had escaped from cages, and a puzzled raccoon who had escaped from a zoo.

Badgers came snuffling and ambling down, all black-and-white livery and claws like earthmovers. There were shy, dangerous pine martens; and even a few wildcats, *Felis sylvestris* of the northern woods, savage-looking and proud, unable to stop themselves snarling at their allies in this unprecedented encounter.

But most of all, there were foxes.

Tongues lolling drolly, eyes as yellow as ancient amber, every kind and color of fox, with coats that ranged from brindle to bright red. Garden foxes, heath foxes, foxes from the woods. White socks, white bibs, white stars, long white grins as cunning as the old Reynard himself, they brought their energy and stink and liveliness, their wild and outré night language, to the service of the Queen. They had come for a celebration; they had come for a birth; they had come for what they could find. They had come with high expectations.

They had come to save the wild roads.

They had come for a fight.

Out in front of them all came Loves a Dustbin, and above *him* came the magpie they called One for Sorrow, and the air was full of birds.

The Alchemist raised his staff. The alchemical cats wheeled to meet them, but suddenly the headland was aflame. Heat blazed out from Majicou's angry eye. Pale fire poured up from the Queen's refuge. The cat catcher's net of lightning shriveled and withered like burning hair. Under the fierce white stars, the dustbin fox's strange army raged across Tintagel Head, paused for a moment to sweep up the beleaguered Sealink, and went on to cup the ancient fort like a hand.

Tag danced on his ledge. "Look!" he told Fish Head Lil. "Oh, look!"

A shadow filled the air above them.

"One for Sorrow!"

The magpie belled its wings and, with a rush and a clatter and a dusty smell of feathers, set down on the ledge at Tag's shoulder.

"Call yourself a cat?" he said.

"Yes! Yes, I do!"

"Raaark!"

It was a famous meeting. One for Sorrow strutted and preened; Mercurius Realtime DeNeuve stalked him up and down, making little playful darts toward him. A little later, disheveled and reeking, yelping with joy, Loves a Dustbin was among the old stones and all three of them were dancing for joy.

"I'm not seeing this, am I?" said Fish Head Lil to Jack Fiddle.

"Well, then," said the fox, looking down from the ledge at his assembled force. Their smells came up, rank and strong and wild. They were the smells of woods and fields and moors and mountains. "What do you think, Majicou's apprentice? It is not only cats that care." The breath of the stags heated the air. A badger bared its teeth, while foxes barked and milled around, and *Felis sylvestris* watched them all fiercely from its tawny eyes. "Have I fulfilled my task or not? I went the length and breadth of the land to collect this lot."

"You're late," said Tag happily.

The fox laughed. "That's because I met this useless creature on the road. A sad sight. He claimed that you had just tried to eat him again."

"Perhaps I had," said Tag. "I was hungry." He made a dash at the magpie. "Third time pays for all," he said.

"You say."

Then Sealink, standing a little apart from their celebration, still uncomfortable with her loss and anger, reminded them, "There's still work to do down there."

When he heard of how Mousebreath had died, a black look came into the fox's eyes. He led them down, and they chased the Alchemist's cats to and fro across the headland. Behind them, Jack Fiddle closed his eyes for the last time and let his chin rest on his paws.

It was a fight. Sealink and Fish Head Lil led a team of wild-cats to harry the outliers from the boulders and the gorse, cleaning out pockets of resistance. Meanwhile Tag and Loves a Dustbin drove the main body relentlessly back toward the cliff top to where the Alchemist itself roared furiously, waving its human arm angrily and trying to summon lightning from the unsympathetic sky. Above them roamed the magpie and Memory the raven at the head of a black skein of birds. And on the way, they were joined by Majicou and the King.

"Well met, Majicou!" cried the fox.

"Things are not finished yet," Majicou told him. But then he laughed and said, "Well met indeed, fox. Your death didn't await you, after all, along the wild road?"

Loves a Dustbin was embarrassed. "I feel fine now," he said.

"Look!" cried Ragnar.

The Alchemist had raised its staff, and with a broad, sweeping motion, pointed out to sea. At once, its cats began to throw themselves off the cliff and into the waves, cartwheeling away into the wind and spray, their limbs outstretched as if at the last minute they had tried to fly. "You see, Hobbe?" it cried. "I love cats. They would do anything for me!"

And suddenly it jumped backward off the cliff and was gone.

Tag shivered and approached the edge. Nothing could be seen but waves breaking on rocks. It was as if the Alchemist had never been.

Exhaustion and incomprehension swept over him and he sat down suddenly without meaning to.

Tintagel Court to Tintagel Head. Dream to nightmare, nightmare to reality: kitten to cat. Friends won and lost, the great task—accomplished? He was worn out, and his head hurt. A salt wind blew in off the sea and smarted in his wounds. He remembered Cy the tabby, and tried to get up. I must find her, he thought. In a minute I'll get up and find her.

He heard Sealink say, "Just deserts. They got their just deserts."

Ragnar Gustaffson Coeur de Lion, King among cats, replied, "I cannot find it in my heart to blame them for what the Alchemist made them—"

Then Majicou was ordering, "Listen! Nothing is finished. This—"

"Majicou," said the fox. "I think we'd better—"

Too late.

Lightning. A soft, apologetic cough in the air above the cliff, like a voice in a closed room. For a second, Tag could hear a thin and whining music of flutes and cymbals, cut off as if someone had closed a door at the end of an ancient corridor. A smell of incense and resin, abruptly extinguished. Then the familiar laugh, curdled and disintegrating.

"Hobbe! Ha-ha! Hobbe!"

Inland, the gorse blazed up and ran molten with light the color of Tag's fur, projecting long thin shadows across the headland. Shedding the whitened skulls of cats, jigging clumsily from foot to foot as its jaguar cape unraveled, fortified by the sacrifice of its army, the Alchemist tottered above Pertelot Fitzwilliam's refuge. It waved its staff and sang. As it sang, the protective fire dimmed and went out. The Alchemist reached down and, with its human arm, ripped the gorse bushes aside.

Tag was given a moment to see her there, a tiny indistinct figure exhausted by labor not yet over. He watched as the Alchemist bent over her, and she vanished from view. Then he was running. Behind him ran Ragnar and Majicou and Sealink. As they hurled themselves across the headland, their bodies blurred and lengthened, shedding strange, expanding rainbow rings into the shimmering sky.

Great Cats, cats of the highways, the rich, powerful scent of them filled the air.

Long muscles stretched and flexed, stretched and flexed. Huge paws thudded soft and rhythmic on the cold dusty ground. Light spilled off shiny fur, eyes like stones, teeth curved like sabers. Body heat poured away into the withering air, effort shed with a profligate contempt for pain, weariness, or the nearness of death.

Majicou, Ragnar, Sealink, and Mercury.

Their heat, their rage, their sheer energy, their ferocious denial of the emptiness of the world.

Great Cats.

But they were going to be too late . . .

Sixty yards. Forty. The Alchemist's human arm reached down.

"Here, kitty, kitty!"

Thirty yards.

"Majicou!"

"Run, Tag. Run!"

Twenty yards. Even their huge hearts weren't enough. Twenty yards was too soon to leap, and the clump of fingers had reached for Pertelot's scruff.

"Come to me."

Her eyes flashed emerald. Beneath the rose-gray fur, her body rippled and shifted with the anger of the inner cat.

Then a kitten mewed, and she was Pertelot again.

"Ragnar! Help!"

Too late . . .

* * *

Something had filled the air above the Alchemist's head like a cloud of smoke. Closer to, Tag saw that it was a wheeling, crying mass of wings.

Individual birds whirled and dipped like bits of newspaper on a windy day. They stooped and bobbed. They shrieked and spun. They were big birds, who had flown all night from roosts in churchyard, barn, and coppice—crows and owls, rooks and ravens. Gulls hovered and dipped and squealed. Kestrels planed above the melee or made sudden, precipitous descents. A single eagle hung above it all on wings like planks, awaiting its moment.

"Come to me. Come on then. Up you come."

Suddenly, birds were spurting through the air like a shower of broken glass. Through the shards, vague at first but gathering speed and mass as it came, appeared a mysterious violent shape: a bird of fire trailing fantails of sparks that plunged out of the mob and slammed into the back of the Alchemist's neck. Great wings battered at its head and shoulders. A pitted gray beak, old as the hills and hard as a stone, struck for its eyes. Detritus flew off.

"Raaaark!"

It was One for Sorrow: the bird behind the bird. Brought down by the force of his attack, the Alchemist struggled for a moment—bent forward, its weight shared between its forehead and its knees—in front of the Mau and her litter. Then it laughed and sprang upright again. Feathers flew. The magpie made a noise like an old football rattle and struck at its fingers.

"I'm One for Sorrow I am," he croaked. "You won't forget me in a hurry!" And he wrapped his wings like a feathered caul around the defaced head. The Alchemist staggered through the gorse, laughing and plucking at its face. The magpie clung tenaciously, and bit its fingers. Then it was over. There was a shriek and a snapping noise. The wings are the bird. When they go, the bird is gone. The Alchemist held up in triumph a writhing, cawing bunch of feathers. Its mouth opened wide.

"Ha-ha, Hobbe. Got your bird!"

One for Sorrow was thrown into the gorse, where he became still. Above him, his comrades wheeled puzzledly in the air.

"She's mine, Hobbe, and I'll have her back!"

It was as much a cry of madness and terror as of triumph. Around the Alchemist, the headland heaved and rattled with bad light. Cold stars looked down. Hundreds of years of thought had narrowed in the end to this. Disorientation, decomposition, an old meaningless music ringing in the ears—its own voice driving it on and on, however malformed, however disgusted, however tired. Hundreds of years of glory. A million experiments. All the wires and eyepieces. All the cats in their cages.

"Hundreds of years of first-class thought, Hobbe. The interventions of a god. I was a god."

Raw black winds tore in from the sea. Earth withered to black ash that coated the Alchemist's lungs as it tottered above Pertelot and her litter.

"I spared myself nothing for this! Hobbe? Do you hear? Do you think I spared myself anything?"

It stared down into Pertelot's refuge.

An expression of wonder transfigured its decaying face.

"But how beautiful," it whispered. "How beautiful."

And then, *"No. NO!"*

There was a single note of music. A delighted laugh. Tremulous as a dream, transparent as summer sunlight in a glass of water, slowly at first, then growing in strength and confidence, a fountain of golden light burst up out of the gorse.

It was light the tawny gold of cats. It was light substantial: solid light. Where it touched, it transformed, and nothing could ever be the same again.

In that light, the Alchemist was lost: all those endless years to possess something that cannot be possessed.

"Hobbe, I never knew—"

In that light, the Majicou struck: an eon-spanning leap across time. The sound he made was the sound of rocks in the tide.

They met, those two, embraced, tottered together in the backsplash of golden light. The great cat drove his claws deep between shoulder blade and tendon, pulling the Alchemist's head toward him. With a single pass of the carnassials, like a domestic cat at a bowl of meat, he cleaned one side of the face down to the bone. There was a grunt. A thick gurgle. Silence.

Then, "Oh, Hobbe. That hurt."

"You will hurt more."

"Walk like a *cat*, Hobbe."

The black staff swept out of nowhere in a flat lethal curve, and the Majicou was knocked back on all fours in a flash of electricity and a mist of his own blood. There he crouched for a moment, lashing his tail and shaking his head; then up he leapt. They met again, the one-eyed cat and his master: they met and they merged.

Tit for tat, blow for blow, faster and faster, until they were at each other in an exchange too dizzying to interpret. Around them, out of the night wind, out of their own stubbornness, they seemed to spin a concealing web. Faster and faster, like a dust devil in a windy corner, until Tag could no longer tell which was Majicou and which his opponent. Faster and faster, until, with a noise like the humming of power lines, a single new creature raged across Tintagel Head, ripping up rocks the size of houses and throwing them into the air.

All across the headland, birds and animals drew together for comfort. The sky was refulgent, bare, no longer a sky but a radiant inverted bowl the color of the inside of an eggshell. Up from Tintagel Head poured the golden light. Down to meet it crackled rainbows and lightning. The air was warm. The earth was purring with fear or readiness, a low, steady, rumbling noise as if the cliff were preparing to slip into the sea.

Tag took a pace back—and found his friends grouped close behind him.

"How can we help him?" he whispered.

It was the fox who answered. "We are required to do nothing more, Tag. Majicou foresaw this long ago. I warned him against it, but he meant to do it all along."

"Will he live?"

"Watch!"

As they watched, the new creature seemed to lose patience with the land. Rage drove it into the air above the cliff top, where it hung for a second, scattering birds to all corners of the compass, then shot out to sea along a flat, vicious arc, as fast as a cat's eye could follow. There it plunged into the water in an explosion of heat and vapor. Steam boiled into the air. When it had cleared, the surface of the ocean was as calm as a pond.

"Loves a Dustbin, I—"

"Wait, little cat! Wait!"

Silence stretched out.

The birds flew stealthily back, perched all over the Tintagel ruins, and began preening their feathers energetically.

"That's that then, I guess," said Sealink.

As she turned to walk away, Majicou and the Alchemist burst vertically out of the ocean and hurtled up into the radiant dome of the sky until they were nothing but a humming speck. Then, in a last despairing gesture, bound together like Kilkenny cats by the hatred of hundreds of years, they plunged back down to Tintagel Head, where—in an eruption of dirt and vegetation, a hot mist of vaporized rock—they drove themselves into the earth, and the earth sealed itself over them forever.

For a moment, there was a faint, rhythmic rumble, like a train going away into the distance. Then silence.

Silence that went on and on until the day broke, and all that golden light diminished to the pale warm sunshine of early spring, and all those birds began to greet a new dawn.

Pertelot Fitzwilliam of Hi-Fashion sprawled with her kittens in the sunshine, and they made themselves busy about her. She was still the most beautiful cat Tag had ever seen.

The fur lay along her slim curved bones like mottled rose-gray velvet watermarked with the faintest of brown stripes. Her face, as accurate as the head of an axe, the face of an ancient feline carved in stone, was turned in blind pleasure to the sun. All Egypt was in those eyes; but the scarab had been sponged from her weary forehead, and her Egyptian dreams no longer consumed her from the inside. Instead, lapped in the light and air of the cliff tops—wrapped in her love and her pride and her adventures, the sum of her life to that point—she was more rested than he had ever seen her.

Standing beside her, his sturdy legs almost hidden by his

thick black winter coat, looking robust and ready for the show bench, was a large, squarish cat as big as a fox with forthright eyes, flowing tail, and prominent whiskers. His nose was long and wide and in profile resembled the nose guard of a Norman helmet. Tintagel Court to Tintagel Head, nightmare to reality: the *Norsk Skogkatt*, Ragnar Gustaffson Coeur de Lion, almost as Tag had first caught sight of him, the very picture of a three-times grand champion!

When he saw Tag, his great mane bristled with pride, and he drew himself up with all the dignity of a King. Then he said anxiously, "So. What do you think?"

The kittens were red and sore-looking. They were blind. Tag thought he had never seen anything so strange or paradoxical in his life. He watched them mew and suckle, scraps of heat in a dangerous world. Nothing could be more vulnerable. At the same time they made him think of Ragnar's tale of the brave queen saving her young from the fire and of the story of Mouse-breath and Havana, and he knew that they were stronger than the headland itself.

Pertelot Fitzwilliam sensed a little of this, perhaps, in his silence. She raised her head. The Nile flashed out at him from her eyes.

"Well, Mercury?" she said.

"I think they're beautiful," he said. "Although not as beautiful as their mother."

After a moment he added, "But which one of them is the Golden Cat?"

The Mau laughed softly. "I've no idea," she said.

She said, "You choose."

"Perhaps we'll be able to tell when they get their fur," Tag said.

He was bone-weary. Now the excitement of the battle had worn off, his wounds hurt him again. But the kittens had made him think about Cy, so as soon as he could, he went to the place on the cliff top where he had last seen her. There, he sniffed sadly about, quartering the gorse and calling her name. But unless you counted a strangely blackened patch of earth, in which you might in some lights imagine the silhouette of a cat, there was no trace of the tabby. It seemed as if she had been used up, then allowed to blow away into the wind like a handful of ash.

Tag went and sat at the edge of the cliff. He knew he could never imagine the little cat's pain. Her whole life had been dominated by the Alchemist. But despite that, she had done her best to have a life.

"We mustn't let that go. None of us must waste that."

Later he thought, I miss her already.

For a long time he looked out over the shining sea. Then he heard the others calling him.

They had found the magpie, a little way away from the Queen's retreat. His wings were spread at an experimental angle, as if he had been trying to free himself from the earth in some new way. His beak was open on his strange, gray-purple tongue, in a formless silent cry of pain. They gathered around him, led by his old friend Loves a Dustbin. When he felt them near, he opened one eye and in a sad voice said, "Eat me, then."

"One for Sorrow," said the fox, "it's us. Don't be afraid. We won't eat you."

Silence greeted this.

Then the magpie said, "It was a good life. I don't want to leave. I particularly liked the gardens. I flew a few miles when it came to it—weather good and bad, sun and rain, windy days, thousand-foot air pockets and all. I was good at it. I was One for Sorrow, and I want you to eat me when I'm dead."

They stared at him.

"Do you see?" he said. "I did my bit—Majicou, the Alchemist, all that. I never much complained. It's not much to ask."

Tag was appalled. "You can't eat your friends," he said.

"Call yourself a cat?"

"Yes."

"Cats eat birds!" And then, more gently, "Tag, if you eat me, all of you, I'll never die. I'll always be part of you, the kittens, everyone. I'll be One for Sorrow, and you won't forget me in a hurry."

With that he closed his eyes.

A little later, he said, *"Raaark,"* and died.

The fox picked him up carefully, with velveted mouth, and carried him to the Mau's refuge, and there they ate him—Tag and Ragnar, Sealink and Pertelot and Loves a Dustbin. He made a mouthful for each of them. He made shining white bones. The wind lifted and distributed his tiny breast feathers, and as they danced away in the morning light, a highway was opened . . .

Though the animals were looking into it from outside, it seemed to stretch away in all directions at once. Cold winds blew down its long perspectives.

After some time, they became aware of a single black cat, distant at first, then closer, bounding along in a haze of its own heat. No hunger. No weariness. Only the flex and stretch of muscle moving over bone. The great cat's stride never varied. They knew who he was. They watched with a sense of dread as his huge head turned, and he stared out of the highway at them.

One eye.

They saw it.

Then he was off again, and they were bounding along inside the wild road with him. "Jump and eat!" he commanded them, in that huge and hollow voice.

"Jump and eat! Jump and eat forever!"

They ran on.

In the slowest of motion, in motion so slow that time seemed to fall into separate installments, a bird flew up in front of them. None but Tag had ever seen a bird like it, with its crest like a scarlet crown and feathers the colors of turquoise and brass. Its beak strained wide with a long and liquid song, the unrepeating song of the bird's life; and the notes of its song were gold.

"The highway is yours!" called the black cat, as he sped away into the darkness.

"Embrace your lives!"

By noon, animals were gathering all over the headland, preparing to return to their woods and fields, their railway banks and street corners. The wildcats had long ago left for the north, melting away with the great stags into the dawn. The eagle had planed amiably over the headland for an hour or two, but he was making everybody nervous, so he had drifted off up the coast to get some lunch. Loves a Dustbin saw off most of his army of foxes, and then, rather shyly, brought one of them over to introduce to his friends.

"This is Francine," he said.

Francine was his match in height, but perhaps a little lighter built. Her fur was thick cream below, the color of mahogany above. She had three black paws, and a diffuse black stain each side of a sharp muzzle. Her narrow yellow eyes followed everything that moved, and her nose was always lifted to the air. She had the look of a vixen who knew what she wanted.

"It's nice here," she said, gazing around in her sharp, nervous manner, "though I'll be glad to get back to town." She laughed. "You miss your familiar ways, don't you?" She caught a glimpse of the sea and stood close to Loves a Dustbin. "I'm sure I've never seen so many cats!" she said. "Did you say we'd be going soon?"

Loves a Dustbin stood by, looking at Tag and the others as if to say, Isn't she splendid? And indeed she did look quite splendid in the midday light.

"How will you go?" Tag asked Loves a Dustbin. He wanted to say, *Don't go.* He wanted to say, *Remember the day you gave me the chicken? Remember how we danced 'round the lamppost!* He wanted to say, *Stay a few minutes more.*

"The wild roads will heal themselves now," said the fox. "All we have to do is travel them." He hung out his tongue. "I plan to do that. I plan to travel, now it's over."

"Well I should think you've had enough of that," announced Francine to the company in general. "I know I would have."

Sealink stepped forward.

"Me and Fish Head Lil here, we was thinking of going back to the city with them," she said. "See a few sights, work out what to do next." She glinted at Francine. "I ain't never traveled with a *fox's mate* before, hon. You're a real cosmopolitan."

"Charmed, I'm sure," said Francine.

"Take care, little cat," said the fox to Tag. "We'll all meet again. I know we will."

"My name's Tag. Not 'little cat.' "

The fox laughed. "Watch out for mirrors," was all he said.

Before she left, Sealink suggested to Tag that they take a walk together.

"Take a turn around," she said, "and talk."

"Where can we go?" Tag said.

"You missed the point again, hon. Let's let the journey decide, huh? Before we waste half our lives choosing on a place to go!"

And so they ambled northward along the cliff tops for half an hour or so, until a steep path led them down to the beach below. A little bay curved away beneath the cliffs to a village with a pier. The sand was the color of Pertelot Fitzwilliam's coat, and the tidewrack smelled rank and full of promise. Out to sea, a white ship was moored beneath the cerulean sky, and around its stern a thousand herring gulls dipped and squawked.

"Look at this. Ships. And shells. And seafood! Oh, Tag, honey, I could die just thinking of some of the seafood I've et!" A huge purr broke from her, then faded slowly.

Tag breathed in the air.

Just to be with Sealink made him feel better. Her fur shone, and her voice was gold dissolved in honey. He felt that just to be with her was to be transported to some blissful yet bravura land.

"Your life still seems huge to me," he admitted. "It seems like a place in itself."

Sealink looked upon the ocean for a while. Her face was terribly sad. Then she said, "They call you Mercury now, babe. In a while they'll call you the Majicou. People look up to you. You got your own light to shine. Use it."

A bit chastened, he asked shyly, "What will you do now?"

"Travel, same as you. You take the knocks, you wait your turn, you walk the road."

"Where did it end?" Tag wanted to know.

Sealink laughed. "Ain't no ending, but it's a new beginning."

Tag laughed too. "Where would you begin again, if you could? Mother Russia?"

"I ain't so certain anymore," she said softly, and they walked on.

The village, nestling in the curve of the bay, welcomed them. They smelled the fish and chip shop. They heard the people. They saw the water, green and lucent as a cat's eye, washing around the stanchions of the pier. "You feel that, hon? That's the feel of iron, dissolving in the air!" They smelled the tidewrack, spread in a five- or ten-foot band above the waterline. The upper part of the beach was covered with perfectly smooth stones, a polished speckled pink. Birds were busy there among the hanks of weed, dipping and bobbing, choosing and casting aside. The stony wrack was packed with exotic objects washed ashore from boats—cans and bottles and lumps of tar and great tangled hanks of blue and orange rope, bits of graying wood with shapes you only ever saw in dreams.

"Hey, hon. Who's this?"

Ferreting about among it all with her bottom in the air was a small tabby cat.

"Oh, hi," she said. "You took your time. Are we living here now?"

Tag stared.

"But—" he said.

"Because they do good chips," she said.

Tag stared at her.

"I thought you were dead."

"Oh, I was dead, Jack. I was down there dead-dog naked in it. They had me, wires and all. I was, you know, 'Mayday! Mayday!' I was down the tubes. But I seen the New Black King, and now I'm brand-new too."

She said, "How can I explain? Oh, Silver, I was on some white-tiled highway. I seen— It was bad things all the way. That's where he found me, and he licked me clean. I seen *lights*. Such things!" She shrugged. She said, "I was there and then I was here. You lick me now," and offered the top of her head as a place to start.

The spark plug was gone.

"I don't wear that old thing anymore," she said. "That new King, he licked it right away. You know, there's a mouse under this piece of wood. It's a *tide mouse*. Do you want to help me kill it?"

Tag had never felt so happy in his life.

"Sealink, I don't understand this," he said.

No answer.

"Sealink?"

He turned, and she was twenty yards down the beach, stately haunches propelling her toward Tintagel even as he watched.

"Sealink? Sealink!"

The calico cat paused a moment. "Sometime, you ask Ragnar about that," she called. "He's got a hell of a tongue on him. But I'd bet she healed herself, you ask me. I told you she was the toughest thing you'd ever take on, honey!"

EPILOGUE

The kittens all turned out gold—not the gold of alchemical metal, but the tawny gold of cats—with deep, thick-piled fur that glowed in the evening sun. As spring moved to summer and they grew, this color deepened to a shade the King and Queen had never seen before, even on the lush Abyssinians and Somalis of the show bench.

They were called, respectively: Isis and Odin and Leonora Whitstand Merril—which Sealink had once claimed was her mother's name.

They lived out of the sight of human beings in the gorse of Tintagel Head. Their lives were filled with sun and rain, and the smell of the rock and the spicy scent of the yellow gorse flowers was like a message to them—be well, be strong, always love.

They watched the white gulls wheel overhead. They watched the violet sea.

"They're all Golden Kittens," said Pertelot with satisfaction.

"I think I would say this is true."

"You would, would you?"

"Although that one looks like me."

"Rags, you idiot."

Tag and Cy lived north along the coast, where Cy charmed the fishermen, and Tag charmed the tourists; and in the evening they stared out to sea together at the sunset on the water.

They visited Tintagel as often as they could.

There, the royal kittens crowded around, pushing and shoving and bowling one another over. They followed Tag proudly about. He claimed he couldn't understand why.

"We've heard about you."

458

"We've heard all about you."

"We've heard everything."

"Tell us about Loves a Dustbin and the Tandoori Magpie."

"Tell us about *bacon rinds*."

"Tell us about rats."

"Never eat a rat," said Tag. "You may regret it." And he began the story he always told them, the one he called "*The Wild Road,* or, *The Ninth Life of Cats*."

Odin listened quietly until Tag was near the end; then he jumped up and finished it himself.

"And that was how Majicou defeated the Alchemist!"

There was a quiet pause.

"Do you know," said Tag, "I don't think they'll ever defeat each other, those two. As much as the cat and the human, they're the body and mind: they're the wild and the tame, deep in each of us, never balanced except by their own struggle. Humans aren't bad—they're only human. Cats—well, not all cats are Great Cats."

He gave Odin a smart cuff.

"I tell the stories here," he said. "Actually, I was going to finish like this: And that is the strange tale of a cat called Tag. How he came to lose his first home. How he traveled the Great Highways with a magpie, a majicou, and a calico queen called Sealink. How he became the only cat of his generation to have a fox for a friend. How he came to take part in the most magical time of the world for cats—even counting their heyday in ancient Egypt. And how he met the most irritating tabby cat in the world."

"Your head in my mouth," said Cy comfortably.

"Wow," said the kittens to one another. "She bit him."

There was a silence, after which Leonora approached Tag gravely and said, "I'm a princess."

"So you are."

"Well then," she said, "I have to tell you this. Of course, you may have noticed."

"What?"

"They're still down there. Under the ground. Still fighting. I hear them at night."

"The waves!" Isis laughed. "You hear the waves against the cliff, that's all."

"I *hear* them," said Leonora Whitstand Merril.

And now turn the page for a special sneak preview
of Gabriel King's new novel

THE GOLDEN CAT

Available May 1999 in hardcover
from Del Rey® Books.

He set himself to face the east, and an abandoned pet shop in a place called Cutting Lane.

He stood uncertainly in the gloom, as he always did when he came here. A few feeble rays of light fell across the blackened wooden floors. There were faint smells of dust and mice, even fainter ones of straw and animal feed; and—there!—beneath it all, the smell of a human with a broom, long ago. If he listened, he could hear the broom scrape, scrape, scrape at the rats' nests of straw in the corners. He could smell a white sixteen-week kitten in a pen. The kitten was himself. Here he had taunted the rabbits and guinea pigs, eyed speculatively the captive finches. How they had chattered and sworn at him! He was always unsure what to feel about it all. Here his fortune had changed. Here the one-eyed black cat called Majicou had found him a home and changed his life forever. He still shivered to think of it.

"Majicou?" he whispered.

But he knew that the Majicou was long gone.

He sat down. He looked from corner to empty corner. He watched the motes dance in the rays of light. He thought hard. The color of his eyes changed slowly from jade to the lambent green of electricity.

"Something is wrong with the wild roads," he told himself, "but I don't know what it is."

His name was Tag and he was the guardian of those roads. At Cutting Lane, they stretched away from him in every direction like a vibrant, sticky web. He felt them near. He felt them call his name. He got to his feet, looked around a moment longer, and shook himself suddenly. He vanished, leaving only a slight disturbance of the dust and a trail of footprints that ended in mid-stride.

THE GOLDEN CAT
by Gabriel King

Published by Del Rey® Books.
Available in bookstores May 1999.

✎ FREE DRINKS ✎

Take the Del Rey® survey and get a free newsletter! Answer the questions below and we will send you complimentary copies of the DRINK (Del Rey® Ink) newsletter free for one year. Here's where you will find out all about upcoming books, read articles by top authors, artists, and editors, and get the inside scoop on your favorite books.

Age _____ Sex ❏ M ❏ F

Highest education level: ❏ high school ❏ college ❏ graduate degree

Annual income: ❏ $0-30,000 ❏ $30,001-60,000 ❏ over $60,000

Number of books you read per month: ❏ 0-2 ❏ 3-5 ❏ 6 or more

Preference: ❏ fantasy ❏ science fiction ❏ horror ❏ other fiction ❏ nonfiction

I buy books in hardcover: ❏ frequently ❏ sometimes ❏ rarely

I buy books at: ❏ superstores ❏ mall bookstores ❏ independent bookstores
  ❏ mail order

I read books by new authors: ❏ frequently ❏ sometimes ❏ rarely

I read comic books: ❏ frequently ❏ sometimes ❏ rarely

I watch the Sci-Fi cable TV channel: ❏ frequently ❏ sometimes ❏ rarely

I am interested in collector editions (signed by the author or illustrated):
  ❏ yes ❏ no ❏ maybe

I read Star Wars novels: ❏ frequently ❏ sometimes ❏ rarely

I read Star Trek novels: ❏ frequently ❏ sometimes ❏ rarely

I read the following newspapers and magazines:

❏ *Analog*	❏ *Locus*	❏ *Popular Science*
❏ *Asimov*	❏ *Wired*	❏ *USA Today*
❏ *SF Universe*	❏ *Realms of Fantasy*	❏ *The New York Times*

Check the box if you do not want your name and address shared with qualified vendors ❏

Name _____
Address _____
City/State/Zip _____
E-mail _____

king

PLEASE SEND TO: DEL REY®/The DRINK
201 EAST 50TH STREET NEW YORK NY 10022
OR FAX TO THE ATTENTION OF DEL REY PUBLICITY 212/572-2676

DEL REY® ONLINE!

The Del Rey Internet Newsletter...

A monthly electronic publication e-mailed to subscribers and posted on the rec.arts.sf.written Usenet newsgroup and on our Del Rey Books Web site (www.randomhouse.com/delrey/). It features hype-free descriptions of books that are new in the stores, a list of our upcoming books, special promotional programs and offers, announcements and news, a signing/reading/convention-attendance calendar for Del Rey authors and editors, "In Depth" essays in which professionals in the field (authors, artists, cover designers, salespeople, etc.) talk about their jobs in science fiction, a question-and-answer section, and more!

Subscribe to the DRIN: send a message reading "subscribe" in the subject or body to drin-dist@cruises.randomhouse.com

The Del Rey Books Web Site!

We make a lot of information available on our Web site at
www.randomhouse.com/delrey/

- all back issues and the current issue of the Del Rey Internet Newsletter
- sample chapters of almost every new book
- detailed interactive features of some of our books
- special features on various authors and SF/F worlds
- ordering information (and online ordering)
- reader reviews of upcoming books
- news and announcements
- our Works in Progress report, detailing the doings of our most popular authors
- bargain offers in our Del Rey Online Store
- manuscript transmission requirements
- and more!

If You're Not on the Web...

You can subscribe to the DRIN via e-mail (send a message reading "subscribe" in the subject or body to drin-dist@cruises.randomhouse.com), read it on the rec.arts.sf.written Usenet newsgroup the first few days of every month, or visit our gopher site (gopher.panix.com) for back issues of the DRIN and about a hundred sample chapters. We also have editors and other representatives who participate in America Online and CompuServe SF/F forums and rec.arts.sf.written, making contact and sharing information with SF/F readers.

Questions? E-mail us...

at delrey@randomhouse.com (though it sometimes takes us a little while to answer).